Fred Savage

Excerpt from Chapter Nine

Confused

He stood alone at the top of the hill. The November rain was beating down buffeted by blasts of wind that seemed determined to beat him into submission. In the pitch darkness, he turned his face towards the heavens.

He was screaming as unbridled emotions of rage and frustration poured out as if he were possessed by the devil himself.

"I hate you! I hate you! I hate this damn place!"

His fists clenched, his body shaking, he screamed at the forces of Mother Nature. His face was stinging from the pain of the wind driven rain. His temper was unchecked as he cursed and swore incessantly.

Finally, spent, exhausted, and drained to the point of having barely the strength to stand, he started walking back down the hill. He walked silently past the house not bothering to look at the glow of the light cast from the windows. He started walking down the paved road.

He still had some venting to do as he continued cursing and raving as he trudged through the darkness.

"No more! Damn it! No more! Enough! I'm damn near fourteen years old and I'm not taking it anymore!"

He continued walking in the darkness, not knowing or caring where he was headed.

In the back of his mind he heard a voice that he hadn't heard for years. It startled him.

It's about time you figured it out.

He started smiling.

Condensed from the original manuscript entitled 'Before Then' by Fred Savage.

Other works by Fred Savage
Throwaway Child

ISBN 0-7414-0750-7

Published by:

INFINITY
PUBLISHING.COM

Infinity Publishing.com
519 West Lancaster Avenue
Haverford, PA 19041-1413
Info@buybooksontheweb.com
www.buybooksontheweb.com
Toll-free (877) BUY BOOK
Local Phone (610) 520-2500
Fax (610) 519-0261

Printed in the United States of America

Printed on Recycled Paper

Published August, 2001

Fredman:

This should wrap it up. No more questions, Okay?
Brace yourself. We are all human.

This book is dedicated to Sharon

Table of Contents

Foreword Part Five

(Introduction to part five: First Knight.)

A Friend

No one liked Kevin. Not even me. He was such a loser. I always avoided him like everyone else. So why did he always smile and say hello to me?

It was so embarrassing. He always looked like something the cat dragged in. The jacket he wore looked like something he may have found along side of the road. He wore wrinkled shirts and high water pants. For the longest time he even wore two different kinds of shoes. He looked so ridiculous wearing a gum rubber boot on one foot and a black overshoe with inner tube patches on the other.

He was such an embarrassment.

My face turned red every time he would say "Hello Christine." He would say that to me every time he got on the bus. His stop was the next one after mine, about a mile from my house.

I always sat in the front seat with my best friend Vicky. I guess I'm just polite or something because I always smiled and said hello back. He always ignored Vicky as he continued towards the center of the bus to find a seat.

My mother says that I have a lovely smile. I have been one of the most popular kids in my class since I can remember. So has Vicky. We have been best friends since first grade. She hated Kevin from that first day he came to our school and has told me a hundred times that I shouldn't smile back at him.

Kevin started going to our school last year when we were in seventh grade. I didn't like him much then either. This year he started riding our school bus right after Christmas break. There was something very different about him. He was so easy to make fun of.

He was tall and thin and always went out of his way to avoid everyone. At recess time he would walk around the school grounds, just minding his own business and talking to himself. I probably never would have known he existed if he hadn't started saying hello to me.

Mrs. Almer says that he is 'such a dirty boy.' He never smiles unless he is in trouble, and he is always in trouble.

Mrs. Almer is our teacher. I overheard her talking about Kevin with Mr. Mathis at our Christmas party. He laughed and told her that he was also glad that Kevin hadn't shown up and wished her a merry Christmas.

Vicky and I are Mr. Mathis and Mrs. Almer's favorites. We always get straight A's.

"Hey look," Vicky whispered. Her desk was beside mine at the front of the classroom. She leaned across the aisle to watch as Kevin came into the room and walked down the aisle towards his desk in the back. "He forgot to comb his hair again."

I giggled and whispered back, "Maybe we should take up a collection and buy him a comb."

Kevin was nearly to his desk when Greg stuck out his foot to trip him. Kevin stumbled and fell headlong to the floor. His books went flying down the aisle.

Greg is a really cute boy and nearly as popular as Vicky and me. He has wavy hair and a smile that lets him get away with murder. He was thought of as one of the toughest boys around. I think he beat up Kevin once. At least that's what some of the others say. Mrs. Almer was his aunt and he was also our class president.

Everyone was laughing at Kevin. He got up and gathered his scattered books and papers. I noticed that his face was red.

Vicky leaned to whisper, "That's the second time this week. What a loser. You'd think he would learn."

Mrs. Almer got class started after yelling at Kevin for being so clumsy. I looked back over my shoulder and noticed that he was smiling. 'What a goof,' I thought. 'He doesn't even know that the entire class is laughing at him.'

At recess I looked at my hair in the bathroom mirror. It was a little out of place so I brushed it several times. Sarah held the door for me as I started back out into the hall. She was smiling as if trying hard not to laugh.

"I donated a nickel!" She said as she covered her mouth with her hand to hide her braces. "That was a great idea. Maybe if that loser has a comb he will use it."

Sarah was very tall for her age and thin. I craned my neck to look up at her as I asked, "What comb? What do you mean?"

"Vicky said that you wanted to start a collection to buy the geek a new comb. I told her that someone needed to tell him about his clothes too. He always dresses so dreadfully."

It was very cold outside with over a foot of new snow. The teachers had allowed us to stay inside for recess. Sarah and several others were boldly asking for donations for 'poor Kevin' when I happened to look out the window.

The school grounds were covered in a thick new blanket of snow. Kevin was standing alone near the front entrance. I caught myself feeling sorry for him.

The next morning Vicky was chattering about something she had watched on television last night when the bus stopped in front of Kevin's drive to pick him up. I tuned her out and watched as Kevin walked up to the road.

His house couldn't be seen from the road. There was only a narrow driveway that looked like an old camp road leading into the woods. I wondered how far off the road he lived.

Vicky poked my ribs and said, "Here comes your ratty friend."

I nudged her back with my elbow and tried to shrink inside my fur-lined parka as Kevin stepped onto the bus. I tried to act as if I didn't hear him as he said, "Hello Christine." In spite of my best efforts to the contrary, I smiled and said hello back.

On Friday Mrs. Almer was very excited as she introduced the man and woman who came to visit from the high school.

It was time to start thinking about what classes we should sign up for. We would all be in high school next year and they were explaining the difference between the general and college course options.

We were called to their conference area two at a time, alphabetically by last name. Kevin's name was next after mine and we were called together. I was flushed with embarrassment and tried to act as if I didn't know him as we sat at the table.

'Please don't say anything,' I thought. I knew he was going to speak. His pleasant "Hello Christine" sent shivers up and down my spine. Why couldn't he just take a hint? Not wanting to seem rude in front of the others, I kept a serious look on my face as I said hello back and looked away.

The two from the high school went over the information packets with us and then separated us to go over our choices. I overheard the man talking to Kevin.

"Kevin," he said, "Your grades at this school are barely passing." He was a thin man with a loud voice. I didn't mean to keep listening in but couldn't help myself as he continued. "Yet you have one of the highest scores, not just from this school, but out of all of those in this district, on all of the pretests for high school. Are you sure you want to take the general course?"

I had to strain to hear Kevin as he nearly whispered his answer. "Does any of it really matter? My social worker says I can quit school after this year, so it's not a big deal. I signed up for the general course just to satisfy him."

"Christine? Christine?" The lady across from me brought my attention back.

When I got off the bus I was feeling a bit down. Mother picked up on it the minute I walked through the door.

We live in a very nice house in the country about ten miles from town. She was always there when I got off the school bus and was always happy to see me. Today she had made soft molasses cookies for my after school snack.

"Mom?" I asked hesitantly, "Can I ask you something?"

"Sure sweetie," she replied. I noticed that she was wearing her blue jeans and remembered that as soon as dad got home we were all going to get a chance to ride on the new snowmobile that 'Santa' had brought us for Christmas.

We all knew that this new one was for dad. This was great, now I could have the old one all to myself.

"Why did dad say not to associate with that one kid? The Kevin that's in my class."

"Well dear, your dad has his reasons. That one's been in trouble since the day he was born. There's no future for him, that's certain." She placed her hand on my shoulder and asked, "Why? Has he been bothering you at school?"

"Not really," I answered. "It just bugs me that he always says hello to me when he gets on the bus. Today I overheard him say something about a social worker or something, and I was just curious."

I called Vicky to see if she could come over and ride the snowmobile with us. Their farm is just across the road from ours. Her mom said she could. We were already bundled up and waiting on the porch when dad got home.

I was surprised when dad asked me, "Has that Kevin kid been bothering you?" He looked first at mom then at Vicky. "And what's he doing riding your school bus? They live clear on the other side of town."

I told him that there was nothing to worry about and elbowed Vicky as she said, "I think he's got a crush on you."

We had great fun on the snowmobiles. Dad led the way with mom on back of his machine and Vicky and I followed on our old one.

The woods road behind our house circled for a long ways through the forest before coming out back onto the main road. Mom and dad had stopped where the road came out and were waiting for us.

The old woods road intersected the main one. Across we could see a large sign that said 'private property.'

"Hey Dad," I said, shouting to be heard over the sounds of both snow machines, "That's the road Kevin lives on. This is where he gets on the bus."

"I didn't know there were any houses down there." Dad answered. "It looks like a good road to snowmobile on, but it's private property."

Vicky and I followed them back the way we had come. I tried to keep up. I must admit, I was rather afraid of the darkness all around. The single headlight of the snowmobile caused the shadows to jump and move around in a real spooky way.

On Saturday Dad said it was okay for me to take the old snowmobile out by myself but not to go too far. I thought about calling Vicky to go with me, but my curiosity was up and I wanted to see where Kevin lived. I didn't plan on getting too close; I just wanted to see.

I bundled up in my new ski suit and started the snowmobile. The sun was out and the trees were all dripping as the temperature rose making it a most beautiful day.

When I got to where we had turned around last night, I was careful to look both ways as I drove across the main highway and started down the narrow old road. There were no tire tracks in the deep snow, only a path worn by someone walking in and out of wherever it was I was heading.

The road just kept going and going. 'I must have missed it.' I thought. 'No one lives down here.' The road wound and curved its way through the forest until finally I saw signs of life ahead. I steered the snowmobile around a clearing where I could get the best view.

The place was real small; I guess you would have to call it a shack. It had a lean-to roof on one side. Smoke was coming out of a rusty stovepipe protruding through the tin roof.

Parked up close, only a few feet from the shack, was a car covered with about a foot of snow. It was a station wagon with the hood up.

'Why would anyone have a car down here?' I thought. 'The road is plugged and it's probably going to be stuck here until spring.'

Then I saw Kevin come out of the tiny shack and look right at me. We were about a hundred feet apart. I hoped he wouldn't recognize me through my facemask and gunned the engine of my snowmobile and started tearing back up the trail.

On Monday, sure enough, Kevin greeted me with a cheerful "Hello Christine," as he got on the bus. I had meant to ignore him but I forgot myself and said hello back.

At recess we were all outside when Vicky ran up to me. "Look!" She exclaimed, "Greg is going to pound him again!"

Several boys were circled around Kevin. The language they were using was most terrible.

Greg had a grip on Kevin's coat front with both hands. He angrily shouted, "Pick it up! Now!"

"What's this all about?" I cried, "What's going on?"

Joan looked at me and said, "Where have you been?" Her freckled face was glowing with glee as she said, "Remember? It was your idea to take up a collection. When Greg tried to give him the money he threw it back at him."

It turned out to be a really bad day for Kevin. Mr. Mathis came out to break up the fight, but not before Kevin's coat sleeve was nearly torn off. He was sent to the principal's office.

Vicky leaned across the aisle to whisper to me as Kevin returned late to the classroom. "Do you think he might have learned anything?"

I watched as Kevin made his way back to his desk. I'm not sure what I was feeling as I noticed the hurt expression on his face and a look of sorrow in his eyes. This time he stepped over Greg's extended foot and took his seat.

I turned and stared at Vicky. "What on earth are we doing?" I whispered. Her unsympathetic look caused anger to start boiling inside me as I said; "He never did anything to anyone."

Vicky turned back in her seat as class began. It irritated me that she still had that same smug smile on her face.

I don't know why, but that was the day I started looking at Greg from a different point of view. If not for his terrible accident, about a week later, I may have decided that I didn't like him at all.

Greg says that he doesn't remember much about the accident, except that he was in the hospital for over a week. He wasn't sure if a car had hit him or not. He only remembered walking home in the dark and waking up in the hospital.

Mrs. Almer had us all work on a special get well card for him. Both she and Mr. Mathis got really mad at Kevin when he refused to sign it.

When Greg returned to class he was greeted as a returning hero. I think that was about a week or so after Valentines Day and about the same time as Kevin stopped riding my school bus.

In the eighth grade the days of exchanging Valentines cards were behind us. Only those boys and girls going steady did that. It was a couple days after, on a Friday, when Kevin surprised me with one. I didn't know what to say as he handed me the large red envelope.

"I'm leaving now," he said, "I wanted to give this to you."

I didn't know what he meant by 'I'm leaving' and didn't want to hurt his feelings. I told him thanks and walked away with my face flushed with embarrassment. I hoped that Vicky hadn't noticed.

I placed the envelope inside my history book. 'I'll pitch it later when he's not looking,' I thought to myself. I didn't open the card until Sunday. My curiosity got the best of me. I just couldn't help myself.

It was a very nice store bought card that said 'A Friend Is Forever.' Inside he had written a short note in scrawling handwriting. It said; 'Thanks for always saying hello back.'

On Monday I planned to thank him in front of the others. I don't know why, but it was something I was going to do. I decided that I didn't care much what Vicky or Sarah or any of the others would think.

Kevin was absent on Monday and Tuesday. On Wednesday, Sarah asked me if I had heard the news.

"Heard what?" I asked. Sarah was always gossiping and even though I am just as guilty, I thought her to be a much worse gossip than me. "Tell me the big news flash."

"Your lover boy is gone." She sighed and giggled at my startled expression. "You know, the brilliant one?"

"What are you talking about?" I exclaimed.

Joan was smiling smugly as she approached with Vicky. Her baggy dress made her look extremely overweight. "The state people took him away," she said. Then she paused and placed her hand over her heart as she breathlessly continued, "Your lover boy is gone, gone forever."

"Your sweet little valentine," Vicky said jokingly. For the first time since we have been friends, her mocking tone irritated me as she imitated Joan's breathless style and said, "He will be missed, surely he shall."

I don't know where Kevin finished out the eighth grade or even if he did. Sometimes, when I think of all the gossip, I get so confused I could just scream.

Sarah's uncle is a highway patrolman and she claims that the state people took him after discovering that he had been living off by himself since Thanksgiving.

She claims that someone's parents turned him in.

I don't know why I'm crying as I write these last few words but I can't help it. I think I've got something in my eye. I need to find a box of Kleenex.

No one liked Kevin. Not even me. He was such a loser.

WHITE KNIGHTS

(Throwaway Child - Book Two)

PART FIVE

FIRST KNIGHT

The Guardians

From places on high they watch.

Chapter One

The Deal

<u>State Courthouse, Bangor Maine, late May, 1961</u>

They sat waiting patiently in Judge Palmer's chambers talking quietly at the conference table.

Ruth Green was visiting quietly with Nadine Keller. There was no mistaking that they were sisters. They had the same shade of auburn hair and blue eyes. Even their smiles were the same. Although Nadine was a couple inches taller, if not for the three years that separated them, they easily could have passed for twins.

Ruth had given up her job as assistant regional director of children's services to stay at home and be a full time mother. Her new son now occupied her time and she enjoyed being a stay at home mom. When she was offered the job as social services director, it took very little will power to say no.

Her husband, Roy, provided a good living, and their lives were progressing nicely. Her daughter, Marilyn, was especially happy to have mom at home.

Detective Brett Miller and the newly appointed social services director, Mark Page, were quietly discussing other matters. Brett looked more like a lawyer than a detective as he sat there with a stack of file folders in front of him.

He was wearing a dark blue blazer and an expensive gold band watch. His taste was questionable when it came to selecting the proper necktie. Today he was wearing a loud tie with broad red and green stripes.

Nadine had laughed a little over it when she arrived with Ruth. She had jokingly commented that real soon all that was going to change.

They all stood as Judge Alfred Leroy Palmer entered the room. Even though he was entering a room to be among friends, he was unquestionably a man who commanded respect. He greeted them warmly.

"Mrs. Green!" He said with a bright smile. "It's so good to see you again!" He shook her hand and asked, "How is that new little boy of yours doing?"

"He's fine." She replied with a smile, "It's good to see you again too." She embraced him and gave him a kiss on the cheek.

The judge was obviously in a good mood as he continued. "Mr. Miller, it's good to see you." As he shook hands, a bright smile again crossed his face as he said, "Miss Keller, I've been hearing rumors about you two. What's that ring on your finger?"

Nadine smiled back and tried not to act embarrassed. She held up her left hand to show off her diamond engagement ring. "I guess the rumors are true." She said. "I hope you got your invitation." She smiled as she looked across the table at Brett.

The judge continued, "I did, and I was very pleased to have received it. I can tell you officially, I will be there!" He laughed with the others as he continued. "Mr. Page, it's good to see you again as well. Congratulations on your promotion."

Mr. Page was a thin man in his mid thirties with thinning hair. His thick glasses set in black frames made him appear to be years older. He exchanged pleasantries and soon they were ready to proceed with the business that had brought them all together.

Judge Palmer began. "This meeting is somewhat informal and off the record. I think we can all agree to that." He got right down to business as he turned his attention to the new social services director.

"Mr. Page, where is the boy now?" He asked.

"He was released from the hospital nearly two weeks ago and returned to the central children's home."

"How is he doing?" The Judge's voice had a trace of sadness. He seemed tired. His dark face took on a weary look, as if he already knew the answer.

"As well as could be expected," Mr. Page replied. His voice lowered as he looked at the judge over the tops of his thick glasses. "I'm afraid he's been through far more than any normal person, adult or juvenile, should ever have to endure."

He glanced around the room as he said, "Mrs. Butler and Mrs. Olson at the children's home both say that he's very quiet and keeps to himself."

Nadine added, "He doesn't remember anything about his ordeal, your Honor. The doctors say that he has blanked out nearly everything. Brett and I visited him several times in the hospital, and when we stopped in at the home to say hello, he didn't remember us from only two weeks ago."

She had tears in her eyes as she continued, "Henry and Joan Silva also stopped in to see him and he has no recollection of them either."

Judge Palmer shook his head. "How does all this affect the current situation?" He asked.

"Judge," Brett said softly, "I know for a fact that young Kevin is an eye witness to the murder of Jesse Bishop. He saw Raymond Satterfield do it. It looks like we'll get a conviction; even without his testimony. Satterfield's lawyer has already offered a plea bargain."

"Yes, I'm aware of that." Judge Palmer said.

"I'm sure we can all agree that if this case is overturned on appeal and he walks, the only thing standing between him and a real prison term will be the threat of that boy's testimony." Brett paused and exchanged glances with Ruth and Mr. Page. "If young Kevin is returned to his family, I fear that would place him in grave danger."

"Are you sure?" Judge Palmer asked.

"It was Joel Bellinger who confirmed it." Brett opened a file and took out a paper. "He squealed like a pig to save himself. That's why we dropped all charges against him and Nancy Mentor, and that's the real reason Satterfield changed his plea to guilty, involuntary manslaughter."

Brett paused for a moment as he passed several documents to the judge. "His strategy more than likely will be to ride this out and then fire his current attorney. No doubt he will claim he was unfairly represented. If his new attorney can get a retrial later, without the boy's testimony, he'll probably walk."

The judge repeated his question. "Are you sure?"

Once again Detective Miller referred to the file in front of him. "Mr. Bellinger claims that after Satterfield threw the late Mr. Bishop off the sentry walk, he looked over at a window and swears that he saw Kevin watching."

Brett paused to paraphrase from the document in his hand. "He said, and I quote, 'As our eyes met, the kid's eyes went wide in an expression of fear at having been seen, and he disappeared from view,' end quote."

"This does shed a new light on everything." The judge murmured softly. "Your solution seems quite far fetched. Explain it to me."

"We recommend that young Kevin remain in the custody of the State, your Honor." Brett paused again and passed the Judge another document. "We know for certain that both Satterfield and Stan Morgan have contacts, coconspirators if you will, within the social services department."

"I believe with certainty that there is no foster home we can place him in that we can be sure is safe. That's why we came up with this idea. As long as he is a ward of the state, the last place anyone would ever look for him will be with his natural family."

Mr. Page added, "As long as he is a ward of the state, Satterfield and his ilk will have to assume that he has been placed in foster care. Somewhere where his contacts have no knowledge. That's why only the four of us are here. The fewer people who know about this, the better."

Judge Palmer took a few minutes to read the documents. He peered over the top of his glasses and said, "I agree. It says here that his natural dad is remarried. That's good. Normally he would be sent back with them anyhow." He paused again and asked Ruth Green. "Are you sure you want to be the go between on this?"

"Yes, Your Honor." Ruth answered softly. "As far as I know, the Stone family is just that. A family. The dad went through some hard times, due mostly, in my opinion, to his first wife and some really difficult relatives."

She paused for a moment. "I think the dad is trying to put the pieces back together. Some things can't be undone. The youngest girl has been put up for adoption and the retarded boy is doing fine in a special home. The dad and his new wife have petitioned for custody. The oldest girl and the middle boy have already been sent home with them."

She exchanged glances with Brett and Nadine as she continued. "Since I no longer have any association with social services, it's doubtful that my name will come up with Satterfield's bunch. I'll do what I can in making the arrangements. I think this is our best chance at keeping the boy safe."

Judge Palmer sounded disgusted as he directed his question to Brett. "What do you think Satterfield's chances are of winning an appeal for a new trial?"

"I'm afraid they are pretty good." Brett answered, "For now, all they know is that we have the boy and that he did see everything. They don't know that he doesn't remember anything. We've convinced the defense that we are willing to cut a deal to spare the boy from having to testify. Once a little time has passed, they will have had plenty of time to cast doubt on Joel Bellinger's credibility. That's where the problem lies."

Judge Palmer sat quietly as Mr. Page added. "As it turns out, it won't take much for a good defense team to shed tons of doubt on both Mr. Bellinger's and Mrs. Mentor's credibility." He opened a folder that Brett had given him and continued, "It seems that both have prior arrest records. Matters that were never disclosed on their applications; things that Ray Satterfield obviously knew about."

Judge Palmer's dark face was expressionless as he asked, "Matters? What do you mean?"

Mark Page continued. "It would appear, Your Honor, that Mrs. Mentor, the *widow*, Mrs. Mentor, lost her husband under some extremely suspicious circumstances." He paused for a moment and motioned towards Brett as he continued.

"Detective Miller found out, only after they cut the deal with them, that Joel Bellinger and Nancy Mentor have worked as a team for a long time."

"This just doesn't get any easier, does it?" Judge Palmer asked. "You say you have a solution?"

"Yes we do, your Honor," Nadine said, "We have everything set up. If the situation should arise where the boy needs medical attention or any assistance from the state, they will only use his case number. We are hoping that if he does start remembering anything, our people will know first."

"I guess that exceptional situations call for exceptional solutions," Judge Palmer murmured. "I'm sure you all know that I visited with the boy at the hospital here in Bangor, and I must admit, it is difficult to look at this objectively. After all, 'we all know the same friends.'"

They all smiled at his remark. Mr. Page wasn't sure what the judge's comment meant as he said, "Sir, I'm the only one here who has never met the boy. As far as he or his family will know, I'm just another social worker assigned to his case."

"What if there is trouble?" The judge asked.

"Like what?" Brett asked in turn.

"Well." Judge Palmer said, "What happens if he ends up hitting someone in the head with a shovel?" They all laughed quietly at the way he poised the question. Mr. Page wasn't sure what that comment meant either, but smiled along with the others.

"We can never be absolutely sure. I guess we'll just have to wait and see." Brett said. "I am sure that trying to place him through the system would be a mistake." He paused and handed the Judge more documentation. They watched quietly as the Judge took a few minutes to read the papers. He raised his eyebrows in an expression of surprise.

Brett said, "At first we thought that this bunch had skimmed 'untold thousands' of dollars from the various budgets. Now it has been confirmed that it was well over two million dollars."

Mr. Page nearly choked on his glass of water. "What did you say?"

Brett said it again. "Well over two million dollars. It's a safe bet that Satterfield and Morgan are the only two who know where that money is."

"Damn." Judge Palmer whistled softly as he continued to read the documents. "That kind of money can buy a lot of trouble. Trouble we don't need. I know your main focus and cause for concern is Ray Satterfield. I think it good advice to caution you not to underestimate the former warden, Stan Morgan. Have you seen the report from the US Marshal's office?"

Brett and Mr. Page exchanged glances as they each nodded in affirmation.

They discussed several of the more heinous crimes that Morgan and several others had been charged with in relation to the boy's reform school. Brett explained that the biggest obstacle in getting a conviction was finding witnesses who would testify.

Brett said, "I hope there is no doubt as to the seriousness of what we are trying to do. We know they've got the money to hire the best legal defense. It also stands to reason that they've got the money to hire those who work outside of the legal system."

"I'm going to go along with your recommendation." Judge Palmer's expression was one of concern. His gaze made the new social services director uncomfortable as he added, "Mr. Page, I assume that if anything changes, I will be informed."

"Most certainly, your Honor." Mr. Page stated. "We all need to be aware that we may have to play somewhat of a shell game with this boy from time to time; at least on paper. We still may need to move him around on occasion, but I will keep you informed."

"Meaning what?" The judge asked.

"I've studied the boy's file. I get the distinct impression that despite our best laid plans and intentions, we may have to wing it from time to time."

Judge Palmer smiled along with the others. There was no question that Mr. Page had made a point.

Mr. Page paused for a moment and wiped his forehead with a napkin. Almost as an after thought he added, "And your Honor, I hope the five of us can agree that for this to work, we need to be absolutely certain that word of this arrangement doesn't leave this room."

Judge Palmer left the meeting with a feeling of apprehension. His instincts told him that despite their best efforts, something was bound to go wrong.

He had reluctantly gone along with the plan formulated by Mark Page. He knew as well as anyone that there just weren't a whole lot of options.

The boy had adjusted quite well living with the Silvas. He had been taken from them just before Christmas. He didn't know why it would come to mind now, but he thought it ironic that Kevin had been destined to spend two Christmas seasons in a row with strangers.

He knew that Kevin would be better off in a special home. Preferably it would be someplace with an environment to help the healing process. The boy's memory was totally erased. What he needed was professional care, hopefully before it was too late.

Unfortunately, that would put him right in the sights of two extremely dangerous characters. Now, after all that had happened, the boy was going to be released to more strangers. His own family.

As he sat at his desk, he realized that he was indeed too close to this situation. He knew Kevin. He liked him. It was with a feeling of helplessness that he quietly opened the Stone file.

As he slowly thumbed through the file, he felt as if the weight of the world was on his shoulders. He felt certain that luck had run out for young Kevin.

Kevin had cheated death more than once. Of this he was certain. He had been hospitalized for beatings and accidents more times than he could count.

He had been left for dead under the porch of a dilapidated shack. He had nearly died in the hospital in Stockton before the doctors discovered that a sliver of glass still remained in his throat.

The confinement at the reform school had been another near death experience. He shook his head as he tried to picture what that boy had gone through.

As he turned over another document, he wished that he could have met Gene Richard's friend, constable Hank Farr from Medway. It was Hank who had found the boy left for dead beneath the porch. Hank had been at the hospital with Gene when Kevin turned himself in, nearly a year ago, after running away from the Silvas.

He was grateful that Ruth Green and Gene Richards had led the fight to keep Kevin out of reform school. He knew them both to be terrific people and very competent social workers.

It was the state's loss that she had decided to quit and be a stay at home mom. He knew that Gene Richards would be coming back soon. He had been offered Ruth's old job. At least that was something good.

It came as no surprise to him, when Ruth had eagerly jumped back into the fray to help keep the boy safe now that everyone knew the gravity of the situation. She was a real trooper. He just hoped that Mark Page wouldn't do anything to change her involvement.

The state was going to be losing another excellent employee soon. He smiled as he thought of Nadine Keller and Brett Miller being engaged.

They were a good match. Brett had insisted that she be a stay at home housewife, and hopefully, soon, a stay at home mother. That was a wedding that he was definitely going to attend.

As he thumbed through the file, he thought that perhaps he should ask his friend, Judge Herrol, to take over this case. That thought only lasted for a moment. He shook his head as he solemnly placed the file in the top drawer of his desk.

August 1961

Joel Bellinger and Nancy Mentor were waiting in the car parked beneath the bridge on route one just south of Rockland. It was a hot afternoon and the windows were all rolled down. Joel reached for another cigarette and lit it from the one he was about to toss out the window.

"Quit acting so nervous." Nancy said calmly, "They will be here soon, and we can get all this straightened out."

"Damn! I hope you're right. I'm sure they'll understand. We didn't have any choice but to testify. Right?"

"That's right." Nancy's reassuring tone seemed to put Mr. Bellinger at ease. "We'll work this out. Trust me. They're convinced that you can find the boy."

Looking nervously around he commented, "This is one desolate place to be meeting anyone." He looked as uneasy as he felt. His shirt collar was open and he had loosened his tie due to the heat. His handkerchief was nearly soaked from wiping the sweat on his forehead.

He watched as Nancy got out her compact and focused her attention in the tiny mirror as she applied a fresh coat of lipstick. She was a very attractive woman and it was amazing to him that she would be the one who remained so cool over the whole deal.

This was a role reversal that only added to the seriousness of the situation. When they had worked for the State, he had been the one in charge. As regional director of children's services, he had called the shots. She had set up this meeting and assured him that she had taken care of everything. He was certain that she could be trusted.

Joel was nearly forty years old. His dark wavy hair and a somewhat thin face made him look years younger. Today, his age was showing in his eyes and in his tired expression.

He smiled as she commented; "It won't be long until you have enough money to buy yourself a small island somewhere."

Joel laughed, "I am glad you set up this meeting. If we can deliver the boy to them, our problems will all go away." He chuckled, "Their offer of fifty thousand dollars reward money won't hurt either."

They were both anxious to get this meeting over with. Joel had been a key witness for the prosecution against both Ray Satterfield and Stan Morgan. He had witnessed the murder of Jesse Bishop, and testified to that in court.

Although Nancy had never been called to testify, her statements had also been entered as evidence. The convictions should have been the end of it, but now it looked as if Satterfield and Morgan would each be granted an appeal. Ray Satterfield had a reputation for getting even. He had thrown Bishop to his death after learning that he was about to turn states evidence on them.

Ray Satterfield had recruited them as a team. Over the past few years they had worked well together. Joel was still frustrated that Nancy had broken off their intimate relationship shortly after the death of her husband.

Their professional arrangement had worked well ever since. He often wondered if it was the money or having the kind of absolute power over others that kept her involved. After witnessing her treatment of some of the children in their care, he believed her to have ice water in her veins.

Although they had both been involved in skimming thousands of dollars and falsifying expense vouchers, neither had any idea at the time just how much money was involved. Now they knew that it was in the millions. They both felt entitled to some of it, even as reward money for delivering the one credible witness against Satterfield.

Mr. Bellinger was confident that he could deliver the boy to them. It would be his pleasure. He still seethed with rage any time someone would ask how he got the burn marks on his neck. In his mind, this was a chance to get even with that rotten little delinquent who had belted him in the head with that red-hot cast iron frying pan.

Satterfield had been wrong in thinking that the kid hadn't made the connection between his office and central office in Bangor. The boy scratching both his parents name on the hood of his car should have told them that he knew about Dr. Coleman's involvement as well.

"That's hindsight." He murmured.

"What's hindsight?" Nancy asked.

Realizing that he had been thinking out loud, he said. "I was thinking about that time we had to stand there and watch that little monster mess up my car. Remember that?"

She nearly hissed her reply. "Who could forget?"

He glanced at the freshly painted hood. "I can still see where he did that. We should have killed that little bastard right then." He knew his voice sounded angry as he continued.

"If those spineless wimps, Garrett, and Coleman hadn't panicked the way they did, we could have kept a lid on it. I wonder if either of them turned states evidence." He chuckled. "Hell, if that were the case, we wouldn't be the only two trying to kiss up to Satterfield now."

"Yes," Nancy mused. "There's not much backbone with those two. It all came apart when they found out that the kid knew about Melinda."

"You never should have tossed that hot grease in her face." Joel almost sounded remorseful. "She was just having a temper fit."

"Temper fit or not," Nancy snarled, "I don't take that kind of crap. She had it coming."

"Hindsight." Joel said.

"Your biggest mistake was not checking out 'Detective' Brett Miller a little closer." Nancy said. "I knew there was something different about him. Damn those undercover cops."

They were silent for a few minutes. Joel was fuming when he broke the silence.

"I'll tell you one thing. It will be a real pleasure to deliver that little son of a bitch's head on a platter."

"You still should have checked deeper. It was Miller, not that damn kid, that brought us down."

"No doubt." He took a long drag on his cigarette and sighed. "He sure had us all fooled. It's still hard to picture him as anything but an incompetent accountant."

He flicked his cigarette out the window as a car with out-of-state plates approached slowly, driving carefully on the dirt road that ran under the bridge. The driver waved to them and pulled alongside. He rolled down his window.

"Hi there!" He said. "You must be Joel." He was a thin man with a lean, hardened face.

"Yes." Mr. Bellinger answered. His voice was cracking. It was obvious that he was afraid.

"I'm Mr. Morris," the man said with a smile. "My associate, Mr. Dean, needs to talk to you for a minute." His voice rose slightly as he looked past Mr. Bellinger. "Mrs. Mentor, would you kindly join me for a moment?"

While they were speaking, Mr. Dean got out and walked around to open the door for Nancy. Joel shuddered at the sight of him. Mr. Dean closed the door and stood leaning against the car with both elbows resting on the window ledge. He waited patiently as Mrs. Mentor got into the back seat of the other car.

"Ray Satterfield sends his regards." He said in a gruff sounding voice. "He said he's glad you listened to Nancy and decided to work this out."

"I just wanted you to know that we had no choice!" Mr. Bellinger's voice was still breaking, nearly sobbing as he tried to explain. "When the state offered us that deal, we had no choice. Ray knows that, right?"

"Sure he does."

"So we've got this worked out. Right?" Joel's voice was once again breaking. Mr. Dean was very intimidating. He was a large man with the build of a professional wrestler.

"Yeah, it's worked out with Ray. He even reached an agreement with Stan Morgan."

"What?"

Mr. Dean said, "Just a minute, let's give Mr. Morris time to back the car around." His grating voice and unwavering stare caused Mr. Bellinger to shudder.

Joel asked, "Shouldn't Nancy be listening in on this? She knows as much as I do."

Mr. Dean's laugh was hollow as he chuckled, "We're aware of that, but she's got, oh, I'd say at least five thousand reasons not to care."

Mr. Bellinger's eyes went wide in fear as he turned his head to watch the other car as it started backing up. He noticed that Mrs. Mentor was sitting in the back seat looking straight ahead.

He never heard the shot that splattered his brain matter all over the inside of the car.

No one spoke as they drove Nancy to where she had left her car at the vacant end of a large parking lot in Rockland. Mr. Dean got out and once again opened her door.

"Mr. Satterfield asked me to say thank you." He passed her an envelope. "Go ahead and count it if you like. Five thousand dollars, its all there."

"I'll call you if I find out anything," she said. From the tone of their voices one would have thought they were talking about something as trivial as the weather.

"We hope you do. Mr. Satterfield's offer of fifty thousand dollars still stands."

"Too bad about Joel." She said. "I guess those are the breaks." Her smile caused him to take a step back. He knew that at one time she and Bellinger had been close.

"Yeah." He murmured. "As long as word gets out that no one testifies." As he turned towards his car he said over his shoulder, "And lives."

He got back in the car with Mr. Morris. Mrs. Mentor smiled and waved goodbye to them.

Mr. Morris waved back in his mirror as he drove off. He thought that Mrs. Mentor looked quite attractive in her nice dress and matching hat.

He guided the car around the parking lot and pulled into a parking space where they could watch. Mr. Dean sat quietly, cleaning his wire rimmed glasses with a white handkerchief.

Mrs. Mentor was still standing beside her car counting the money in the envelope. He smiled as Mr. Dean adjusted his glasses and said jokingly, "This is where it gets interesting."

"Yeah," Mr. Morris replied, "I still say two would have been enough."

"Maybe." Mr. Dean said, "But you know Stan. He wants to be certain that everyone gets the message."

They watched as Mrs. Mentor unlocked her car and got behind the wheel. A truck passed in front of them temporarily blocking the view. They knew that she was reading the note that had been left on the front seat.

After counting the money, Nancy got in her car ready to drive away. She noticed a note that had been placed on the seat and opened it. It simply said, 'a deal is a deal.' She inserted the key into the ignition switch and turned it.

The explosion sent car parts flying through the air as a ball of fire engulfed the car. It violently rose a few feet off the ground and settled back down in roaring flames.

"Damn," Mr. Dean murmured, "I guess you were right! Two sticks would have been enough."

Mr. Morris offered no reply as he put the car in gear.

Chapter Two

Beginnings

Joey:

Jack and Dora Spence owned a nice cape style house on a quiet street only a few blocks from the elementary school in Bucksport. From their front porch they had an excellent view of the surrounding area and of Fort Knox, which sat majestically on the opposite side of the Penobscot River.

Jack worked shifts at one of the local mills and was due to retire in four or five years. They had lived in the same house since they had it built over thirty years ago.

Dora was two years older than Jack. She had one son, David. David had been nearly three years old when they had met and Jack was the only father he had ever known.

David had moved away several years ago to take a job in the small town where his wife had been raised. They had three children; the youngest was now eleven years old. Jack and Dora never got to see enough of their grand children.

It came as no surprise to those who knew them when they started taking in foster children. The constant heartbreak of having those children for only a short time, and then having to let them go as circumstance changed, prompted them to take in a little boy from up in the north country.

When they first went to meet him at a special home in Bangor, Jack had been apprehensive. Dora had explained that this boy was retarded. He wasn't sure how he would react. He had never been around retarded children before.

Dora had met the boy previously when she was doing volunteer work for a local children's home. She assured Jack that he would like him.

The first meeting went quite well. They were seated in a small waiting area in a large home in downtown Bangor. The sounds and commotion coming from the main part of the house caused Jack to be nervous.

Several children were fussing in the background, shouting and making an awful noise. Jack was having second thoughts. He didn't know what to do when a retarded child with her leg in a brace hobbled through the door. She stood staring at him.

"Don't worry, Dear." Dora said. "She's just curious."

"I'm afraid this isn't a very good idea." Jack said. "I don't think I'm cut out to deal with children with these types of problems."

"Don't be making up your mind too soon, Dear." Dora whispered, "You'll see, little Joey is different."

Jack had no idea what she meant by different and hoped that she knew what she was doing. He knew instinctively that he wasn't cut out to raise a child with severe mental problems.

The girl continued staring at him, causing him to feel uncomfortable. Her drooping eyelids and slack jawed expression really bothered him.

"I'm just not sure." He whispered to his wife.

"Patience, Dear." Dora whispered back. She smiled and added, "Mrs. Bradley and I have this all worked out. If she can handle a house full like this plus three of her own, we should have it quite easy."

Her comment did little to calm Jack's nerves. He tried to act pleased as the retarded girl squealed and burst out laughing.

Dora leaned close and whispered, "Here she comes."

Mrs. Bradley opened the door and took the young girl by the hand. She led her to another part of the house and returned a few moments later.

Jack looked up and smiled at a young boy who was walking close to Mrs. Bradley. He looked to be four or five years old. The boy smiled back and bashfully clung to the lady as he peeked around her at them.

The lady greeted them with a warm smile. "Hi Dora." She said. As Dora stood up, she looked at him and said, "I'm Emma Bradley. You must be Jack!"

He was surprised when she ignored his extended hand and gave him a hug. "Welcome to our home."

"Pleased to meet you." Jack murmured.

They followed the lady and her son inside to a small office area. Now Jack was really nervous. There were several children who appeared to be at least twelve or thirteen years old simply throwing fits in the living room area.

Mrs. Bradley ignored all the fussing and confusion. This obviously was everyday routine to her.

One of the younger boys was sitting on a hassock holding an empty box. He seemed to be calling out to them in a loud monotone. Jack tried to ignore all the commotion and did his best to suppress a shudder.

Mrs. Bradley sat across the table from them and opened a file that had been lying by itself on one end of the cluttered table. She was smiling broadly as she exchanged glances with Dora.

"This is young Joey's file." She smiled at them and added, "He's really doing much better. We've only had him here since November, and he is adjusting as well as we could expect."

The boy beside her looked up and smiled at Jack. Jack smiled back and said, "How are you?" He reached across the table to shake hands.

"Oh! I'm sorry!" Mrs. Bradley exclaimed. "I forgot to introduce you." She leaned over and picked the boy up and helped him onto her lap.

"Mr. Spence, I'd like you to meet young Joey Stone."
She paused for a moment to get Joey's attention. "Joey, say hi to Mr. Spence."

The boy smiled at him and said 'Hi' in a faltering tone. He looked nervously up at Mrs. Bradley and then smiled at Dora.

Jack could have been knocked over with a feather. He murmured, "I thought this was your son."

Mrs. Bradley explained that Joey didn't fall into the traditional category of mental retardation. He looked normal and for the most part, acted normal. Apparently he had suffered brain damage of some kind. The doctors had assured her that it was irreversible.

"When we first got him here," She said softly, "He still hadn't tried to walk." She paused for a moment as Joey slid down from her lap and stood with both hands resting on the edge of the table. He appeared to be fascinated with Jack.

She continued, "He still needs to hold onto someone's hand, or in our case," She paused as she placed her hand on the boy's shoulder. "In our case he likes to have a grip on my dress or his arm around me."

This changed everything for Jack. He had taken an instant liking to young Joey. They knew from the start that it wasn't going to be easy raising a mentally handicapped child. He and Dora were determined to give it their best.

They brought Joey home after the fourth or fifth visit with him at the group home. He also had taken an instant liking to Jack. His face lit up every time he saw him.

He still had poor coordination and needed close supervision. Soon he knew that 'Daddy Jack' would always be there to help him up each time he fell.

Dora was Mom, and he quickly made the adjustment of living with them.

<u>Jean:</u>

Reverend Lance Halstead had known Leroy and Kathy Harmon for many years. He and his wife Cora often visited with them when they were in the Auburn area. They had been members of the same church for several years prior to the Halsteads moving to Millinocket to pastor a small rural church.

Kathy was unable to bear children and they had decided that adoption would be best for them. Reverend Halstead had officiated at the christening of the Harmon's first child, Rachel. The Harmons had known the birth mother and adopted Rachel as an infant.

Although his church was in Millinocket, Reverend Halstead was up to date on any news concerning the Stone family in Medway. He and his wife would never forget their first experience with the Stone family that stormy summer night not so long ago. They had found six year old Kathleen along side of the road during one of the most frightening thunder and lightning storms they had ever experienced.

Lance often commented to Cora that there had to have been a guardian angel on his shoulder causing him to make that wrong turn and take that back road that night. If they hadn't happened onto the Stone girl in the darkness, he believed that she surely would have died.

On more than one occasion they had both shed tears as they heard one gut-wrenching story after the other concerning the Stone children. They routinely included the Stone family in their prayer requests.

They both thought it incredible that the oldest boy had survived his ordeal. At first, the stories were that young Kevin had been found dead beneath the front porch of his house. Upon hearing that a dog had kept the boy from freezing to death, they both believed that once again the guardian angels had been watching over that one.

Neither would admit it openly, but they both believed that Satan himself possessed young Kevin. The incident with a member church in Medway had convinced them of that. It was the only explanation that made any sense to them.

As young as he had been at the time, Kevin had been the only suspect. There was no way that a normal nine-year-old boy could have been so blasphemous. It just didn't add up.

For this reason, Kevin, in particular, was a constant prayer request for both of them. Now, this latest opportunity to make a difference for that family convinced them that God was listening.

Reverend Halstead's church was involved with several local charitable organizations and often worked closely with the state social services people. When he got word that the state had put the youngest girl up for adoption, he believed it to be a divine answer to their prayers. He was nearly in tears when he informed his wife.

"Cora." His voice was trembling as he told her the news. "Remember all these years we have been praying for an opportunity to make a difference for that family in Medway?"

Cora sensed that he had something important to announce. "Yes, Dear, I do." She replied.

"We thought all hope was lost after what happened last winter." His voice nearly broke as he continued. "The youngest daughter has been put up for adoption."

The look in her eyes caused him to pause and smile. Cora had an incredulous expression as she said, "We were just praying for them, today, at the women's fellowship." Her eyes went wide. "Do you think maybe Leroy and Kathy?"

They both kneeled to pray as he whispered, "The Lord truly does work in mysterious ways."

He immediately contacted the Harmons.

Leroy was at work and Kathy had just put Rachel down for a nap when the phone rang. It was Cora. She was as excited as Kathy had ever known her to be.

They both agreed that it would be the Lord's will if it were to happen that this child end up in their care. When Leroy got home, he was ecstatic at the news.

The state had insisted that the girl's birth name and any information concerning the circumstance of the adoption be kept confidential. Cora and Lance were the only two involved who knew Jean's last name. Leroy and Kathy accepted this and never asked questions that would break the rules of confidentiality.

When Leroy and Kathy met 'little Jean Doe' they instantly fell in love with her. Her auburn hair was naturally curly and she had the cutest smile.

It was several months before she would allow either to hold her close, especially her new father. She didn't come without problems. She was prone to temper tantrums and was extremely strong willed. They both believed that the good Lord had blessed them once again.

With patience and understanding that only parents are capable of, they were determined to raise their two daughters within the guidelines of the church. In their view it was the one true church.

<u>September 1961</u>

It could have been a scene right out of the redneck handbook as the small truck came into sight nearing the top of the small hill. It was a rusted out relic, probably ten or twelve years old. The rear view mirror on the drivers' side door was wobbling and dipping up and down with each bump in the road.

Anyone with common sense would have agreed that the two boys on the back of the pickup truck shouldn't have been there. They were soaked from the late summer rain that had started out as a light mist and then turned into a steady drizzle. Although they were smiling and enjoying the ride, one would have to ask, 'What's wrong in this picture?'

The small truck shook and rattled noisily as it laboriously made its way up the incline of the narrow paved road. Clouds of blue smoke trailed it as the nearly worn out engine strained to make the grade.

In the front, the driver had a firm grip on the wheel as the truck tried, almost as a living thing, to get away from him. He was a clean-shaven man with a bright smile. He was clothed in a dark blue work uniform, the kind one would expect to see a gas station attendant wearing.

Beside him, crowded together on the narrow bench seat, were two more adults. The taller thin man next to the door wore a loud tattered flannel shirt with bright red suspenders. His face was a mess from a stubble of whiskers along with several streaks of dirt and grease across his forehead.

One would have thought that the large man in the middle, with his tobacco stained teeth and constant drool at the corners of his mouth, should have been the one near the window. He more often than not missed the small can held between his knees each time he paused to spit. The soggy butt of his non-filter cigarette broke off as he paused to spit and take another drag.

The crowded cab was filled with smoke from three cigarettes, all going at the same time. The windows were rolled about halfway up now that it had started to rain.

The steady clinking of the empty beer bottles rolling around on the floor and under the seat could be heard over the sounds of the loud engine and the defroster fan that was on high speed to keep the windshield from fogging up.

All four tires, several of which were nearly bald and had canvas showing, appeared to be nearly flat under the heavy load. The truck's rear suspension was strained nearly to the breaking point under the weight of a cargo that was easily twice what the small truck had been designed for.

The hardwood slabs were heaped nearly two feet above the top of the cab. The boys sat perched on the top of the load, facing the front with their feet braced against a rusty tie down bar that was fastened to the truck's roof.

Kevin and Artie were enjoying another fun ride. They could hear laughter coming from inside the truck. Occasionally they would look at each other and laugh at some of the adult language they could overhear.

What made this ride special for them was that Kevin had snitched a couple beers from the five-gallon bucket that was tied haphazardly near the end of the load. He assured Artie that the adults were so drunk that they would never miss it. They were anxiously sipping and guzzling their ill gotten brews, feeling grownup and reveling in the excitement of getting away with it.

This was the third load that they had hauled today. Dad and two friends from work were getting an early start in stocking up with firewood. The first load had gone to Ben's place; the second to Tony's, and this one was for them.

Even though there was no way the adults could have heard them they talked in loud, excited, whispers as they proposed one toast after the other.

Artie was giggling as he whispered, "Here's a toast to that rock." He pointed and added, "That one right there!" Then he chugged from his bottle.

"You forgot to clink!" Kevin said. He was also laughing. "Here, you fool." He reached over and clinked bottles with his nine-year-old brother.

They soon forgot to whisper as they laughed and giggled incessantly. It wasn't long before they were both even more intoxicated than those role models in the front seat of the truck.

The truck was going slow when Artie dared Kevin to drink a toast standing up. It was tremendous fun as they laughed and attempted to keep their balance.

It was Kevin who said. "Here's a toast to that big tree coming up."

Artie giggled and pointed. This was such fun! His pint bottle of malt liquor was nearly empty, as was Kevin's. At first it didn't dawn on either of them what that tree leaning across the road ahead meant.

"Look." Artie giggled. "There's a bird!"

The bird perched on the limb of the tree ahead flew off as the truck approached.

"We're higher than the birds!" Artie exclaimed. "Can we fly yet, Kevin?"

Kevin had been watching the bird fly off. He lost his balance and sat down abruptly.

"Oops!" He said. "Get ready to be a monkey!"

Artie was laughing as the tree started sweeping over the cab. He pitched his bottle and gasped as the thick branches got closer. It was happening fast. His voice was terrified as he whispered. "We ain't monkeys, Kevin."

The tall thin maple tree leaned precariously over the roadway about ten feet above the pavement. The weight of ice and snow from a long forgotten winter storm had bent it to about a forty-five degree angle. The thick leaves, dripping from the new rain, appeared like a wall in front of the two boys who now stood staring, their eyes round in anticipation.

The truck was going about fifteen miles an hour. Ben was halfway through telling a joke. He stopped talking abruptly as he noticed the low hanging tree limbs coming up.

"Hey, Kevin!" He shouted, "Don't we still got two boys up on top?"

"Oh crap!" Kevin exclaimed. As the treetop swept over the cab, he jammed on the brakes.

It only took about thirty feet to stop the truck. Before it was stopped, Ben jumped out the passengers' door. He was laughing uncontrollable as Kevin and Tony also jumped out to see what had happened.

Young Kevin and Artie were both hanging on for dear life to the tree limbs. Their weight wasn't quite enough to cause the tree to touch the ground. They were each struggling to hang on. Their feet were only about two feet off the ground.

"Crap," Tony said. "Have you ever seen anything like this?" He was a big man, and was the first to reach the boys. His breath was putrid as he stood face to face with young Kevin. He pushed down on the tree branch and said, "Just let go boys."

Big Kevin and Ben were cracking up with laughter. Tony let go of the branch and the tree partially righted itself. This left the two boys standing somewhat shaken before them. Artie started crying and young Kevin stood silently with his eyes wide.

Ben rode on the back of the truck, with young Kevin, for the remainder of the drive. He laughed uproariously along with Tony as Kevin and Artie both threw up on the ride back. Young Kevin was puking from above precariously balanced on the load. Artie was blowing lunch at every dip in the road with his head out the passengers' side window.

Big Kevin swore that this had been too close a call, and that next time they would leave the boys at home.

<u>July 1962</u>

Henry Silva was as excited as Joan had ever seen him. The excitement of finalizing the adoptions papers for Adam showed in his face as their attorney handed them the final documentation.

"Congratulations, Henry." He said.

"This is so great!" Henry sounded almost giddy. "We've waited so long. I can't wait to tell Adam."

Henry was sitting in a chair in front of the attorney's desk. Joan was standing beside him with her arm around his shoulder. "I almost can't believe it." She said softly. She asked the attorney for the second or third time, "Are you sure it's final?"

"It's final Joan." He got up and slowly walked around his desk He smiled and shook Henry's hand. Then he embraced Joan. "Congratulations, Mom." He said. Then, addressing Henry, he said, "You've got a fine son there, Dad." As if an afterthought, he added, "And by the way, happy birthday!"

It had been a long struggle, but now it was over. What made it even more special was that today was Henry's birthday. He was sixty-three years old.

The state had insisted that they get a release signature from Adam's biological father who was serving out a life sentence in the state prison. Their attorney had insisted that they do it right. It had taken a long time and they were glad that it was finally over.

As they were leaving the office, Joan looked uncertainly back over her shoulder.

The attorney smiled and said in a loud whisper. "It's final! Quit worrying and get going. You don't want to be late picking your son up from school!"

After they left, he said to himself. "That's one lucky boy."

Adam was adapting well. It had been over a year since his mother had died. It had only taken a few months for him to get back in the routine of living with them.

Their new German Shepherd had become his best friend. He and Shep were inseparable. He was as excited as they were when he started writing his name as Adam Silva.

Things had changed dramatically for those students who were now bussed into the main elementary school in Exter. This was big city for most of them. This school had all the amenities and was only a few blocks from Henry's hardware store. Adam usually rode in with Henry in the mornings and walked back to the store for a ride home after school.

Adam talked about his adventures with Kevin all the time. He and Joan would often get out the scrapbook with the pictures they had taken.

They always laughed at the one they had taken in front of the chicken coop. In this picture, Adam's face was alive with a smile as big as the sky; Kevin's expression was serious. They were both wearing heavy winter coats and the snowdrift in the background was nearly as high as they were tall. They were both kneeling. Lying stretched out on the ground in front of them was a hypnotized chicken.

The eight by ten picture of the four of them continued to hold its place in the center of their fireplace mantle. Joan thought that Henry looked so handsome in that one. His silvery hair was slightly askew but his smile brought his face to life. Kevin and Adam were standing on either side of her, each with an arm around her shoulders.

Adam had developed an interest in music. Midway through fourth grade his uncle Andrew bought him a new coronet. Before he finished fifth grade, this talented young musician was playing with the junior high school band.

The years went by quickly. His aunt Beth and uncle Andrew made no secret of the fact that he was their favorite. When Andrew died of a heart attack on new years day the second year, Adam was devastated. Uncle Tommy took up where Andrew had left off and the family ties grew stronger with each holiday and special occasion.

Slowly, but surely, the memories of having Kevin with them faded. It wasn't long before his name was almost never mentioned. Joan and Henry had thought about trying to track him down just to know that he was okay, but after a while, they decided to just let it go.

Chapter Three

Kevin the Terrible

Fall 1961 - Sixth Grade

The pirate ship looked as though it had been recently outfitted with satin sailcloth and solid gold trim. As Kevin watched through the telescope, he tried to imagine the value of a single link in the solid gold chain that held the ship secure to the solid gold anchor that only moments before had been lowered over the side.

'I must be swift, I must be brave.' He thought as he watched the horrifying scene unfold in the powerful lens of the telescope. 'Wait, wait for just the right moment.'

He was watching silently from his position of concealment between two large rocks that protruded from the sea about a hundred feet from shore. He waited patiently as flocks of sea gulls ascended into the air and flew towards land. It was as if they too were aware of the danger presented by this ship of evil.

The pirate ship had sailed into the small harbor only minutes before. It's black flag with a scull and cross bones embroidered with golden thread was waving in the gentle breeze. They were after him, he was sure of it.

'Where is that evil slime ball?' He thought. He had crossed swords with the evil Captain Crap for Brains several times before. This would be the last time! He nearly gasped as he watched his nemesis stride boldly onto the deck, walking unsteadily on his diamond studded peg leg made of solid gold.

Captain Crap for Brains was wearing a brilliant blue robe adorned with gold and diamonds. Kevin shuddered as sunlight glittered off the evil captain's false eye, nearly blinding him through the powerful spyglass.

"Leave it to that butt nugget to get a fake eye!" He murmured to himself, "Instead of a glass eye, this jerk thinks he needs one made of solid gold! I wish now that I had scooped out both of his eyes with that spoon!"

Then Kevin caught his breath as Captain Crap for Brains shouted to be heard. The Captain stood gazing with his good eye across the expanse of water that separated them.

"I know ye are out there evil boy!" The captain's grating voice sounded horrible. It was so unpleasant that Kevin was thinking that maybe he shouldn't have stomped the evil jerk's throat with his spiked boots during their last fight.

He watched closely through the telescope as the captain continued ranting.

"I know ye are spying on us with me own telescope! That was me favorite telescope! Ye never should have stolen it ye little bastard! Ye have but one minute to give thyself up!"

The captain paused to wipe the slime off the side of his mouth. Since Kevin had cut his lower lip off in their last knife fight, he was constantly drooling.

The captain motioned to several of his pirates. "Bring the Lass on deck!" His laugh would have sounded evil if he could have completed all of it. Since Kevin had stabbed him in the throat prior to stomping it with his spiked boots in a past confrontation, the captain could only laugh in short, sickening sounds. It caused Kevin to shudder.

"Oh no!" Kevin exclaimed under his breath. He tried to control his apprehension as he watched the two evil henchmen bring out the princess.

She was dressed in a beautiful white ballroom gown. Her golden hair was blowing in the wind. She walked proudly with her head held high. She squinted her eyes briefly as sunlight reflecting off the evil captain's golden eye nearly blinded her.

One of the plug ugly pirates shoved her, knocking her down on the golden inlay of the ship's deck. She got up quickly.

"You'll not abuse me for long!" She cried, "Kevin the Terrible will save me!"

"Arrr, Lassie! That is where ye be wrong." The evil Captain snarled. "Yon gutless bastard lives in fear of crossing swords with me."

She turned and looked defiantly at the evil captain Crap for Brains. "He has bested you each time and still you have not figured it out! You truly live up to your name!"

"I'll not abide with ye insulting me family name!" The captain grated with an evil grin. His smile was toothless since his fight with Kevin only a short time ago.

"If yon little bastard won't come to me, he can watch as ye walk the plank!"

Kevin could hear every word that was spoken. He anxiously bided his time. His heart swelled with pride as the princess showed no sign of fear in the face of certain death at the hands of the evil Captain.

"You'll be so sorry!" She exclaimed. "My hero has already chopped off your leg and made you the most ugly pirate ever to live!"

Captain Crap for Brains scowled sourly at her.

She laughed and mockingly taunted him. "You truly do live up to your name!"

Captain Crap for Brains screamed his order, "Bind her, laddies!"

He forced an evil laugh as his pirates secured her hands behind her back with solid gold handcuffs. He stomped his peg leg in anger as he once again called to his archenemy.

"I know ye can hear me ye nasty boy! Thy wench has insulted me for the last time. Me mother was a Crap for Brains as was me father before me!"

"Arrr, it is a fine family name that goes back for centuries! I'll abide no more ridicule! Surrender now, or she walks!"

His good eye was filled with anger as he placed a heavy golden necklace around her neck and added, "Straight to the bottom with priceless ballast!"

The ugliest of the two pirate henchmen prodded her with his sword, herding her out onto the plank.

Kevin knew he could wait no longer. Without fear he stood up and shouted. "Here I am, butt wipe! Here I am!"

Captain Crap for Brains attempted to laugh again. "Ye sorry ass is mine, ye little bastard!" He turned to his crew of uglies. "Get ye in the boats and bring me his head!"

Kevin stood fearlessly on the rock as two boatloads of pirates started rowing towards him. He called to the princess. "Don't worry princess. I'm here. I've got a few tricks up my sleeve! I'll save you!"

"Oh my hero!" She cried. She stood fearlessly on the plank and watched with confidence as the pirates got closer and closer to Kevin.

"Hey! Crap for Brains!" Kevin yelled. "I meant to tell you that I hope it hurt when I cut your leg off. I want you to know that I used the dullest sword I own! And guess what? I've still got your missing eye in my pocket!"

His laugh caused the cowardly captain to shiver in fear as he continued, "In a few minutes you'll be able to bend over and see backwards after I shove it right up your butt!"

Captain Crap for Brains angrily yelled back. "In a few minutes it is I who will laugh when I have your head on me cabin wall! Ye will be sorry then; ye little bastard!"

"I'm already sorry!" Kevin yelled back, "Sorry that I didn't cut your throat all the way last time!" He paused as he noticed that the pirates had rowed their boats to within a few feet of his rock. They were closing the distance with swords raised in readiness.

He looked the meanest one in the eye and shouted, "I forgot to mention! I went to the future and brought back the coolest, most bitching machine gun you've ever seen!"

The pirate's eyes went wide in surprise as Kevin raised an enormous machine gun and opened up on them. They were mowed down and knocked overboard from the impact of thousands of bullets as Kevin fired mercilessly into their midst.

He laughed as their boats started sinking as he continued to shoot holes in them with his awesome weapon.

He stopped firing and called to captain Crap for Brains. "Now watch this you slime ball! Squint that good eye and pay attention. This gets really funny!"

His voice broke with laughter as a school of sharks surrounded the unfortunate pirates and started dragging those who had survived the onslaught of machine gun fire beneath the choppy surface.

He shouted, "Now it's just you and me!" He made a giant leap from the rock, easily jumping the three or four hundred feet that separated them. As he landed with a thud on the deck, he drew his sword and faced the evil captain.

Captain Crap for Brains was looking pale. His good eye was wide with terror as his archenemy fearlessly started walking towards him.

He was out of options. He would have attempted to run away if not for his peg leg. The drool running down the side of his chin needed wiped again as he gasped in terror.

Kevin was approaching, holding the captain's missing eye in front of him. Captain Crap for Brains realized that his only hope was to swim for it.

Having had that peg leg made out of gold had been a mistake. He was about to figure this out as he leaped overboard into the churning sea to escape the vengeance of Kevin the Terrible.

****

The bell rang. Kevin sat up straight and looked around. The evil Captain's features had faded back to those of Mr. Mathis who stood scowling at him from behind his desk.

The other students were getting up to leave. He picked up his books and followed them out of the classroom.

Chapter Four

Reality

For a while it seemed that Kevin was going to adjust to his new surroundings. When they picked him up at the central children's home he had almost no idea of what to expect.

He was told that even after he moved back with his family, he was still a ward of the State. It had something to do with some trouble he had been in. Dad and Irene didn't like that at all, but had no choice but to go along.

He was glad to meet his older sister, K'leen and his younger brother, Artie. Although he liked those who picked him up, for the longest time, he had no idea who they were. He had no recollection of any of them.

The state kept moving him around all through that next year. He found it harder and harder to get close to anyone. His nightmares grew more intense with each move. It wasn't long before his attitude was such that even those who professed to be trying to help him became the enemy.

He was moved to two different foster homes during his sixth grade school term. Some of the people were nice, some weren't. No matter where he was sent to live, there was always some kind of trouble.

<u>Pittsfield Maine January 1962</u>

The woman speaking was extremely obese. "This kid doesn't flinch!" Her eyes were ablaze with anger as she looked at Ruth Green. "Something's not right with him."

Her shrill voice caused Ruth to shudder as she continued. "He's slow to respond. Even nailing him along side the head has no affect. He still does things his way."

"What are you saying?" Ruth asked.

"We want him gone. Tell them in Bangor. As soon as we get our check for this one, he's out of here. He's scary."

"Has he ever caused trouble?"

"It's not that. My son helps us around here. He's sixteen. He says that Kevin is spooky."

"What?"

"Watch this." She called over her shoulder. "Bruce! Bring Kevin in here."

Ruth sat silently as an extremely large young man entered. He had his hand on Kevin's collar as he roughly escorted him into the room.

Kevin seemed to recognize her. She smiled back at him and said. "Hi Kevin, How are you doing?"

"Not worth a crap, Ma'am."

"See!" The lady said. "What did I tell you?"

"Watch your language around my Mother!" Bruce cuffed him, knocking him to the floor.

"What are you doing?" Ruth cried. She spun around to face the woman. "Stop this!"

The lady ignored her and said. "We can't abide his language or his behavior. Now watch this."

Ruth caught her breath as Bruce roughly stood Kevin up. Bruce said, "Take your medicine." He intentionally backhanded him again.

"See! He didn't flinch."

"Enough!" Ruth exclaimed. She quickly placed herself between Kevin and Bruce. "I'm reporting this! Pack his things. Right now!"

The obese lady met Ruth's glare with one of her own. "You may have a paper that grants you visitation, but don't think you can order me around! You can't take him anywhere. When we get our check, then he goes."

Ruth's voice was barely audible. "I'm reporting this."

The lady laughed. "Report all you want. Who else will take in these misfits? Say your goodbyes and get out."

Kevin stood with his head bowed. He was surprised that Mrs. Green was acting so upset.

She gently placed her hand on his shoulder.

"Kevin, you be as good as you can be while I try to straighten a few things out. Okay?"

For a moment the blank look in his eyes turned to one of awareness. He smiled at her and replied, "It's okay. I'm supposed to be punished."

"Not like this." She murmured.

"Maybe I'll see ya at the home." He whispered.

Ruth stormed off and got in her car. She stopped at the first phone booth she saw, and called Mark Page.

It was two days later when Mark Page showed up to take the boy to another home. The lady threw a fit, claiming that Mrs. Green must have taken the boy already. He handed her a paycheck and said he'd look into it.

When he arrived back in his office there was a note from the children's home. Kevin had already turned up there on his own.

Each time he ran away, he always found himself making his way back to the central children's home in Bangor. Somewhere in the back of his mind, he viewed that location as a safe haven. It was a place of rest and an escape from his bad dreams.

Each time he showed up the people there were nice enough, but they always shipped him out within a few days. When it finally dawned on him that they didn't want him either, he withdrew into his own world of make-believe and accepted the way things were. Soon, even these recent memories were blanked out along with the rest of his past.

His next move had been to a church run school for troubled boys. He had been housed in a large group home with several others. That stretch had only lasted a month. They were as glad to get rid of Kevin, as he had been to leave there. Once again, it was Ruth Green who came to his rescue.

He was alone in the sleeping area, sitting on his bed, when Mrs. Green and the head deacon entered.

"Hi, Kevin." Ruth said with a soft smile.

Kevin looked up. He knew he should know this lady, and pretended that he did. He thought that he was in some deep trouble and remembered to mind his manners.

"Hi, Ma'am. How are you?"

"Fine, Kevin." Ruth said. "The deacon tells me that you've gotten yourself in trouble. Again." She smiled and sat down beside him. "What happened this time?"

"What do you mean? Ma'am."

"Well, Kevin, they did call me. What's going on? These people are only trying to help you."

He could sense that this woman was genuinely concerned. It showed in her eyes as she brushed the back of her hand gently over the bruise on his cheek.

"Am I kicked out?"

"Yes."

Kevin looked at the deacon. His voice was serious as he said, "I guess you'll just have to call the Holy Spirit down on someone else."

The deacon took a quick step forward and raised his hand as if to strike Kevin. Ruth quickly got between them.

"We'll be leaving now." She said softly. "If that's okay with you."

The deacon glared at Kevin and said. "The sooner, the better. His belongings are all packed."

Kevin walked silently beside Mrs. Green as she led the way to her car. She helped him place the pillowcase containing his belongings in the back seat.

She said goodbye to the deacon and got behind the wheel. As they drove off, she asked Kevin. "Did they really try to call the Holy Spirit down on you?"

"They tried." He said. "Tied me up and everything."

Ruth's smile was grim as they drove past the still smoldering ruins of what had once been the churches parsonage.

"We won't even talk about that." She said softly.

Although the officials couldn't prove it, they believed Kevin to be the one responsible for burning the parsonage to the ground. They wanted him gone, that was certain. They said that they would rather be safe than sorry.

Her smile told him that everything was going to be okay. She glanced at Kevin and noticed that he was smiling too.

Ruth had a way of making Kevin feel comfortable. They enjoyed a quiet ride back to Bangor. The next day, another social worker drove him home to Brownville.

Each time he was returned to his family, he needed to be told who they were. He was quite comfortable around K'leen and Artie. Adjusting to life with the others was difficult.

To him, dad's name was Dad, Irene's name was Irene, and the old guy who lived with them was Gramps.

With his passion for vengeance, this young vigilante was soon a master of getting even.

East Brownville, Maine July 1962

Although K'leen and Artie still talked about their stay in the children's home, Kevin had no recollection of ever being there or of the people they talked about. It was a touchy subject at home anyway, and after only a short time, they had pretty much stopped talking about it.

K'leen still tried to be a good big sister to Kevin and the others. Although her past experiences had an enormous impact on her, she was still the one with the heart of gold. She still did anything she could to make life easier for everyone around her.

Gramps also lived with them. He was an inseparable part of the family. He moved back from Stockton after his brother died and dad had insisted that he move in with them. Over the years, he would remain one of the most respected people in their lives.

For a while, dad tried to spend extra time with Kevin and Artie. Sometimes he would take them with him in his old pickup truck to the mill where he worked to get loads of firewood.

As time went by, he had other kids to attend to. When Dad and Irene had their second child, Marie, little Matthew was just starting to walk.

Dad had taken a job at one of the sawmills in Dover. As before, he left early for work, and seldom got home while the kids were up. This routine worked as well as could be expected. As the years slowly went by, and they kept having one kid after the other, the small farmhouse got overcrowded in a hurry.

Uncle Richard and Aunt Teresa still lived in Milo and needed someone to help baby-sit for their three kids. K'leen moved in with them after that first school term to help out with the kids, and to be close to the high school.

They didn't see much of her after that, just occasional visits during the summer and sometimes during the holidays. She grew close to her surrogate family and adjusted rather quickly.

About a half mile down the road there was another farm where several kids Artie's age lived. He quickly became friends with them, and most of the time he was gone to their house to play. They had a television and Artie was always on their doorstep every Saturday morning.

Every Sunday, Irene would drop them off at Sunday school at the Evangelical Church in town. That first winter, K'leen and Artie had liked going there and they had lots of fun in their Sunday school class.

Although Kevin tried to fit in, it seemed that no matter what he did, he couldn't get anyone to like him. He was probably the most unpopular kid in regular school as well as in the house of God. He was always quiet and tried to be respectful around adults. He had no outside influences to gain experience from. Only school and church. He hated both.

The teachers at school would often join in with the students in ridiculing his clothes and his speech. Each year he hoped that something would change.

Mrs. Almer was a sixth through eighth grade teacher who could easily be referred to as mean and judgmental. There were those who would describe her as a bitter woman with a heart of stone. No one had been surprised, several years earlier, when her husband just up and left her after nearly ten years of marriage.

Although she was viewed to be an attractive woman, it was her spoiling for a fight attitude that was destined to keep her single. She was especially mean to Kevin and several others in the school that she took to be from white trash backgrounds.

She knew of his having been sent to reform school. She never questioned why. It made little difference to her. She believed that there was no hope for this one. Kevin was her new poster boy for everything that was wrong with the youth of today. She had taken an instant disliking to him and made no effort to hide the fact.

Until the Stone children came into the school system, she had focused on making life miserable for another poverty stricken family. She had grudgingly allowed the Smith boy to quit school, the year before, in lieu of facing assault charges. The school board was behind her all the way.

There had been no one to take up for him when she accused him of personal assault and wanton destruction of school property. He had nearly completed eighth grade, and his absence was viewed as no great loss. He had started high school the following fall and quit after only a couple months, confirming that she had been right about him all along.

Always on a do-good crusade to save the world, Mrs. Almer was also one of the local Sunday school teachers. She viewed both Artie and K'leen as worth saving. Young Artie was a very handsome boy with a bright smile and an energetic personality. K'leen was an attractive young girl who needed a mentor. The boy in the middle was beyond help. He was a lost soul. She was certain of that.

That first year she had made it her personal mission to save K'leen in the church. K'leen was too naive to know what was going on and welcomed the attention.

Kevin was wise to her from the start. She often treated him as though he was retarded, talking real slow to him during class and embarrassing him over anything and everything. The school's acting principal, Mr. Mathis, often did the same thing.

Mr. Mathis backed Mrs. Almer in every way. There were those in the gossip community who believed that they had something going on between the two of them. Something that was unrelated to education and in spite of the fact that he was a married man.

On this day, Mrs. Almer escorted Kevin outside the classroom. He had been sitting quietly at his desk with his thoughts somewhere far away. His lack of attention and perpetual ineptness irritated her to no end.

The class was learning how to talk properly on the telephone. Two old telephones were provided and each student was expected to call another and have a mock phone conversation. To date, Kevin had never spoken to anyone on a real telephone. He was undeniable nervous and incompetent when his turn came.

The class got a good laugh at his expense, as well as at one other student who also had never used a phone. He knew he should have been paying closer attention, and expected to get a scolding. The words Mrs. Almer used changed his entire attitude towards her and every authority figure he would ever encounter in the future.

Normally when a student was taken outside into the hall, they were led a considerable distance from the door, in order for the discipline to be private. This time, Mrs. Almer was standing in the hall, facing the open door and Kevin was told to stand right there. Everyone could hear.

"Kevin! This is the last time I'm going to tell you to pay attention." Her voice was nasty. Kevin's face took on a look of surprise as she continued.

"I know the others all think you are stupid! Do you know that?" Her eyes took on a fiery look of condescension. "Everyone; here and at Sunday school thinks that you're just plain stupid! We need to change that. Right now."

Kevin's face flushed with embarrassment. He wanted to bolt down the hall but she stood in front of him blocking the way.

"I don't think you're stupid." The tone of her voice changed to one of phony concern. "Do you think you are?"

Kevin stood silently looking down at his feet.

"Well, Kevin?" She asked. "Are you stupid? Is there any reason you can't change? Any fool can talk on a telephone! We are all behind you and just want to help."

His silence irritated her. "Answer me. Are you going to let those people be right?" She leaned forward and continued in a loud whisper. She could be heard inside the silent classroom as she added, "If you ever hope to amount to anything more than a cow pie in a pasture, you've got to let us help you."

Kevin remained standing silently, looking down at his feet. His hair was a mess; his clothes were way over sized and wrinkled. That was her next topic.

"How can you dress so good for Sunday school, and come to school looking like this?" Her voice turned nasty again. "You've got to change. Do you hear me?"

Kevin hadn't felt this low in recent memory. His mind was clouded with nothingness as he abruptly turned and started walking back down the aisle to his desk.

Mrs. Almer followed him back inside. "I'm not done with you yet. Come back here!"

He ignored her and returned to his desk. He opened a book and sat staring blankly at the pages.

The classroom was silent as Mrs. Almer went back to her desk to continue where she had left off. She had made her point.

Kevin noted that this was the first time that the other students weren't laughing at him. They sat in silence, not believing what they had just witnessed.

For a moment his thoughts cleared as her words replayed in his mind. 'Cow pie in a pasture.' He smiled and thought, 'What a rotten bitch.'

That first school year had gone by quickly. This was the third school he had been enrolled in since September.

This school was a two-story brick building and served through the eighth grade. Kevin's teachers were miserably generic. He had somehow gotten on the wrong side of them almost from the start. He seldom paid attention to them, and it was a long time before he bothered to take the time to remember their names. He would always remember Mr. Mathis and Mrs. Almer with bitterness and disgust.

Like so many schools, this one also had its share of bullies. It was a cycle that seemed to have no end. There were always those who took pleasure in tormenting those who appeared to be the most helpless.

This was something that Kevin never did understand. As time went by, he would often find himself in the middle of a scrap, on and off the school grounds, trying to protect those who were being picked on.

At Sunday school, some of the same kids from school were in his class. This shot down any hope of making a fresh impression with the others. His Sunday school teacher seemed to like him. At least he never gave him cause to feel unwelcome or left out.

He hated how Mrs. Almer acted so nice to K'leen and Artie. He instinctively knew what she was all about, and made no attempt to be respectful to her outside of school.

The disgusting incident at the church reaffirmed Mrs. Almer's commitment to make things miserable for Kevin. It happened late one Saturday night. Although no one could ever prove it, she would always know that he was the one responsible.

The rest of the church folks were about as hypercritical as any he had ever met. Somewhere in the back of his mind he knew this to be true. The only time he felt comfortable during church services was those rare occasions when the congregation sang 'In the Garden.'

Despite one incident after the other with Kevin, it was still a two-year break and a fresh start for K'leen and Artie. A much needed break from all the strife and worry that they had been through all of their lives. Artie adjusted quickly. He was turning out to be a very good student and was well liked in Sunday school.

K'leen didn't have a whole lot to do with them after she moved to live with Aunt Teresa. Whenever she did show up, she always asked for Kevin.

Aunt Teresa's house in town was a very nice one and K'leen hated having to do without running water and television when she visited them. She kept her visits brief.

She always tried to invite Kevin to come stay with her from time to time, but their aunt and uncle always had an excuse. Kevin didn't even know who they were, but he instinctively knew the score.

The reality was that all three of them should have had some kind of counseling. Their pasts were such that each of them, in their own way, was a ticking time bomb. It would be years later before the final repercussions of their early childhood experiences were felt. The tumultuous times were far from over.

Irene did what she could to help them adjust and fit in with their new surroundings. She treated them as if they were her own when they would allow it.

K'leen's escape was moving out to live with relatives. Artie was young enough not to know any different and it didn't take much for him to get adjusted. Kevin was the one caught in the middle.

There was no way he was ever going to trust an adult. He didn't realize it at the time, and never said anything about it, but that's the way it was. It didn't matter how nice or even how mean they were to him; he knew that he had been down that road before.

Occasionally he would have flashes of memory, usually at night when the nightmares turned real. It was as if he was always off balance. His mind was in a continual haze.

His grades in school were barely passing. No one noticed that anytime a teacher said something nice to him, however sincere, that he always got a nearly perfect score on that day's test.

He wasn't about to warm up or get close to anyone. Not even Artie or K'leen. Not even Gramps.

Chapter Five

The Best of the Worst

The second summer, Kevin started working in the woods with Rory Smith. Rory had bailed him out of trouble one afternoon when he was walking home from town.

The trouble was with a local bully named Greg, and his lackey, Jerry. The two bigger boys had been riding their bicycles and thought it would be fun to harass this white trash kid from school. Greg was related to Mrs. Almer, and shared an open hatred for Kevin.

When Rory arrived on the scene, they had Kevin down on the ground beside the road, pounding the snot out of him. The fight had started over Greg making fun of Kevin. He tried several times to run Kevin over with his bicycle. He and Jerry would peddle fast, and as they got close, try to slap him as they went by.

They did this several times without success. Greg cursed Kevin for being a chicken each time he ducked and jumped aside to get out of the way. He got real mad when Kevin called him some profane names and suggested that he should quit sleeping with his mother.

Kevin knew that he should bolt and run for the woods as the two boys abandoned their bikes and closed in on him. Knowing that he could never out run them, he determined to get in the first punch.

Greg was approaching fast, and as he was about to grab onto him, he fell backwards to the ground delivering a mean kick to Greg's crotch.

That would have ended it for Greg if not for Jerry also being there. Greg was screaming in pain. Jerry tackled Kevin and they rolled over and over in the center of the road, each trying to get an advantage over the other.

He probably would have wound up in the hospital if Rory hadn't been driving by. Rory had no idea who he was when he screeched his car to a stop and ran to help.

Greg had him down on the ground, wailing unmercifully on him when Kevin heard someone shouting at them. Greg's lackey was helping hold him down. Greg was livid, throwing punches at his face one after the other.

The sound of the car screeching to a stop momentarily distracted both bullies. A scruffy looking young man got out. He was wearing a pair of greasy suspenders over a filthy white tee shirt. He obviously needed a shave and looked like he could be a really rough customer.

Greg looked up with an expression of hatred as Rory shouted at them.

"Hey! That's enough!"

As Rory neared, Greg angrily muttered, "Get to hell out of here and mind your own damn business."

Jerry was easily intimidated by the look of anger on Rory's face and quickly jumped back.

Kevin looked up as Greg was lifted off him and violently thrown into the center of the road. He heard someone shouting, "Why don't you try that crap on me? You cowardly sons a bitches!"

Greg's stooge helped him up and they both walked off, cursing and swearing. Kevin could hear them threatening a lawsuit against the newcomer.

A fleeting grin crossed his face as he noted that Greg was walking his bicycle with his body bent forward, holding his hand to his crotch.

Kevin's eye was nearly swollen shut and his nose was bleeding. He squinted to see as Rory reached out a hand and helped him get up. A knight in shining armor couldn't have been a more welcome sight. He drove Kevin home and was invited to stay for supper.

Rory worked in the woods and needed to hire someone who could work with a horse and drag out the logs. The pay wasn't much; a dollar a day plus room and board. He asked Kevin if he would like the job.

Irene had known Rory and his family for years. She had heard the rumors concerning Rory being expelled from the school system, and only half believed them. She had seen Rory's mother in town shortly after his incident at the school. She had assured her that Rory had done nothing other than show open disrespect for Mrs. Almer.

Although Irene believed that Rory would never be mistaken for a good influence, she agreed with dad that Kevin could work in the woods with him.

Kevin had spent countless hours working around farm animals. This was the first time he had actually worked with a horse. He wasn't tall enough to see over the horses' back, and was dwarfed by the huge beast.

Rory was amazingly patient in teaching Kevin the dos and don'ts. "Never forget, Kevin." He said sternly, "You have to be in charge. Never let him forget that."

"Got it!" Kevin answered.

"I mean it." Rory insisted. "He's not a pet! This horse will kill you on accident and never know the difference." His voice rose to a near angry tone. "Don't you ever forget that!"

Kevin quickly came to the realization that Rory wasn't kidding and took his advice seriously. As he became accustomed to hauling out the long logs, one at a time, he realized the awesome power he was dealing with.

Trigger could easily haul out a log that Rory would cut up into many four foot long pieces. He knew he had to be careful. The horse could just as easily tear him apart if he were to get caught up on one of the logs.

At the start, Rory assisted him in hooking up the harness and pull rigging. In a matter of a few days, he needed only to stand back and supervise. Before the end of the second week, Kevin could handle it by himself.

Trigger was a spirited animal and Kevin caught on quickly how to handle him. Although he did heed Rory's advice, Trigger was like a pet to him, a very large pet.

No one had to remind him to feed or water his horse, or to rub him down or to check and adjust the enormous horseshoes. Rory was amazed that a small boy like Kevin could be in such complete control of an animal a dozen times his size. He was especially impressed each time Kevin dug fragments of rock or hardened mud from the horse's hoofs. Trigger would always stand calmly and raise each hoof as commanded.

The reports from Rory and his boss, Bill Riley, were all good. Kevin was an excellent worker and adapted quickly to the life of a woodsman. After only a short time, no one was ever really sure where Kevin was or what he was doing. When school started, he continued to spend as much time away from home as he could.

On Fridays, after school, he would ride the bus as far as the woods road that led down to the logging camp. He would catch it again on the way to school on Monday morning.

It was a routine that worked well for him. He hated school and he hated Sunday school. He decided after that first year that he hated it at home.

There was no denying that most of his problems he brought on himself. He instinctively knew this and never gave the subject much thought. He was withdrawn and bitter. Fair or unfair made little difference to him.

It wasn't long before he learned to lie without batting an eye, cheat to win, and steal without conscience. His role models were setting the example. He was listening and learning from the best of the worst.

He was smoking cigarettes and drinking beer habitually before he turned thirteen. He instinctively understood fair play, honesty, and pay back.

Those with whom he associated were truly a rough, scruffy, bunch. The loggers, woodsmen, and junkyard people he learned from had little tolerance for wimps and no use at all for the self-righteous.

When work was slow for Bill Riley and Rory, Kevin would take whatever work he could find from loggers and scrap yards in the area. Sometime he got paid, sometimes he didn't. More often than not, he did the work just to be away from home.

Those people worked hard and played rough. They were mostly a group of drunken Saturday night brawlers who knew no other way of life. Profane language was a part of everyday conversation, and there were very few rules to abide by. He soon fit right in.

****

It was late on a Saturday night, well into the early hours of Sunday morning when Kevin rode a borrowed bicycle from the logging camp all the way to town.

Rory and several others were already passed out back at the camp and he had the entire rest of the night to himself. His balance was questionable as he guided the bicycle in the darkness. His head was still buzzing from having had one too many beers.

He peddled as fast as he could under the light of a nearly full moon. Riding in the near darkness was somehow familiar to him. He couldn't recall just when, but he knew that he had been out at night on excursions like this before.

He got to the church, probably a little after one in the morning. He leaned his borrowed bicycle against a large maple tree and stood silently for a few minutes.

It was an impressive building with a tall steeple and arched stained glass windows. The wide front entry appeared inviting. On a beautiful moonlit night like this, it looked like a nice church. In his mind he could envision this church as being a friendly place where even he would be welcome.

Other than his Sunday school teacher, he couldn't think of a single adult member of that congregation who had ever been nice to him. He believed them to be nothing more than a bunch of self-righteous stuffed shirts.

It made no difference to him if his actions were right or wrong. His pulse was pounding with excitement at the thought of what Mrs. Almer would discover in the morning. This thought caused him to smile.

The pasture of a small farm bordered the church's cemetery. The barn was a considerable distance across the pasture, but it took him only a short time to get there and acquire the items that he needed.

It was downhill most of the way as he laboriously pushed the wheelbarrow towards his destination. He pulled the wheelbarrow backwards up the front church steps. It tipped over once, causing half of the contents to spill out onto the steps. He probably should have used a side door, but that was something that he had given little thought to.

He was prepared to smash the glass side panel to reach in and open the door when he thought to try the knob. The door was unlocked.

'The house of God is never closed' he thought to himself as he maneuvered the cumbersome wheelbarrow inside. He cautiously wheeled his cargo down the aisle to the front of the church. He was careful not to make a mess as he filled all the collection plates he could find with the fresh cow manure.

In the Sunday school area, he caught himself laughing out loud as he completely filled Mrs. Almer's top desk drawer. He took his time and carefully flatted some of the fresher manure on the top of the desk with a piece of cardboard from the desk drawer. He wrote the word 'pasture' in capital letters.

He carefully scooped the rest of his cargo into Mrs. Almer's chair. He took his time, being watchful not to make a mess on the hardwood floor.

The inside of the church was filled with a ghostly soft light shining in from the bright moon. It was light enough to make out the colors of the stained glass windows.

His expression was somber as he got behind the pulpit. Standing there, with both elbows resting on it, he lit a cigarette. He got out a warm beer that he had brought with him in his inside jacket pocket and opened it. The bottle overflowed and caused foam to spill onto the pulpit.

He wiped a little spillage away from the papers that had been placed there for tomorrow's sermon. A light reflecting off a shiny silver candlestick illuminated the words that the preacher had entitled the next day's sermon. 'The sweet love of Jesus knows no bounds.'

Somewhere in the back of his mind, he knew that he had been in a church under similar circumstances. His memory was clouded but he knew that this had happened before.

It had been late at night, like this. This wasn't the first time he wasn't supposed to be there. He knew this, but couldn't remember when or why.

For a moment, he could picture several people walking slowly down the center aisle. They were walking side by side, pushing a small-wheeled table between them. There was a small nicely carved box on the table. Their faces were out of focus.

In the front row, several children were sitting by themselves. A pretty young girl was sitting staring straight ahead. For a moment he thought he had made eye contact with her. He felt sad watching the tears slowly roll down her cheeks. He nearly called her name.

A vision of blood and gore flashed across his mind. People were standing in the pew with open hymnbooks. They were singing. A young boy was being dragged down the aisle towards the front door.

There was no sound. The boy was screaming in frustration. His temper was out of control as he attempted to escape the grip of two men in suits. The stench of dead flesh and a feeling of vulgarity caused his body to jerk. He came back to reality with a start.

The images were gone and once again his mind clouded over. The smell of his cigarette was unusually pungent in the still air. For a moment, he thought he was going to sneeze.

He sat down on the edge of the platform and slowly finished his cigarette and most of his beer. The sizzle sound when he dropped the butt into the bottle sounded exceptionally loud.

After placing the nearly empty bottle down beside him, he got up and slowly looked around. He was expecting to feel something. Perhaps guilt, perhaps regret, maybe even remorse. He felt nothing as he carefully exited through the same door he had entered.

He thoughtfully returned the borrowed wheelbarrow and shovel to the neighboring barn. He was nearly bursting with laughter on his ride back to camp as he recalled Mrs. Almer's words. 'Cow pie in a pasture.'

He knew he could never tell anyone about this night's adventure. Even the bunch he was in with would have thought it to be a bit much.

Someone was always breaking the rules. The rules about honesty and telling the truth meant nothing. The rules about keeping your word and brotherly love meant nothing.

Rules were meant to be broken. Over the years this had been proven to him time and time again.

Especially the one they called the 'Golden Rule.'

Chapter Six

The Woodsman

June 1963

Kevin paused for a moment to wipe the sweat from his forehead as he hooked on the logging chain. The horse was restless. Its tail was twitching wildly in an attempt to thwart the onset of flies buzzing angrily around him.

"Get up there!" Kevin shouted as he stepped back from the log that was now hooked to the harness rigging and ready to go. The horse arched its head around to look at him and snorted.

"Get up there!" The boy shouted again as he smacked the horses' withers with the palm of his hand.

The horse snorted and stood motionless, head high, ignoring the boy's command.

Kevin stepped closer to him and reached up to rub the horses' ears. "Hey boy, what's the matter? Are you tired?" He rubbed the sweaty neck with his glove. "How does that feel? Come on now, we've got to get these logs out."

His soothing tone seemed to placate the uneasy beast. He was standing on the left side of the workhorse, trying to shoo the flies away, when the horse stepped on his foot.

"Hey!" Kevin shouted frantically, "Get up there!" He slapped the horse hard on its side. He tried to pull away but the weight on his boot was too much. The ground was soft and his foot was now driven into the soil under the tremendous pressure.

He shouted desperately, "Get up there!" The horse stood calmly, frozen in place, it's tail twitching back and forth. The pain was intense and Kevin was panicked as he frantically shouted, "Hey Rory! Rory! Help!"

He could hear Rory's chainsaw in the distance and knew that his plea for help hadn't been heard.

The horse shifted his weight and pressed him against the trunk of a tree with its shoulder. He couldn't breathe under the tremendous pressure. For a moment he thought he was going to pass out. The horse was slowly crushing him to death.

He saw a beautiful German Shepherd and a mongrel looking Collie dog playfully chasing each other in a field. They dashed back and forth in front of the horse causing him to nervously shift his weight away from Kevin.

The scene faded as he gasped for breath and shouted again. "Get up there, damn it!" No matter how he shouted, the horse wouldn't move. He remained standing calmly, pinning Kevin's foot to the ground.

Frantically, he reached into his shirt pocket and pulled out his cigarette lighter. He reached towards the back end of the horse and held it underneath its belly and lit it.

He could smell the hair burning before the horse seemed to notice. When the flame hit the most tender of spots, the horse suddenly came to life.

It was an explosion of motion as Kevin threw himself backwards to avoid being crushed by the long log. At an instant dead run, the large workhorse bolted up the twitch path oblivious to the heavy load chained behind it.

Despite the pain in his foot and ribs, Kevin was laughing aloud as he painfully limped along the rough trail. He knew that it had been a close call as he slowly made his way back to the clearing where Rory was cutting up the long logs.

Rory had just finished a cut and shut off his chainsaw when he heard the workhorse charging up the trail. He turned to look. His eyes went wide in surprise as he dropped his saw and tried to scramble out of the way. The horse struck him with its right shoulder sending him flying across the woodpile.

The horse came to a stop when the log chained behind it caught up on a stump. He stood there snorting and treading his feet up and down.

Rory got up shouting.

"You son of a bitch!" He yelled. Then, looking back down the trail he shouted, "Kevin! Damn it! Kevin! What to hell is going on here?"

As Kevin came into sight, limping on his way to the clearing, Rory started smiling.

"I guess he got away from you, eh?" He shouted.

Kevin shouted to be heard as he limped along closing the distance. "The son of a bitch stood right on my foot! Then the son of a bitch tried to squash me against a tree. I thought I was going to die! I yelled for you but your saw was running!"

Rory yelled back. "Well, the son of a bitch just ran me down! He was definitely on his way to other places! What to hell gave him all that energy?"

"Hell, Rory," Kevin was now close enough to talk in a normal speaking tone. "The son of a bitch wouldn't move so I had to light his dick hairs on fire to get his attention."

For a moment, Kevin wasn't sure if Rory was mad or not. Despite the pain from having been knocked over the woodpile, Rory started laughing. "Hell, I guess we've had enough for one day. Let's unhook him and send him back to the camp. I need to sharpen my chain anyhow. We can start here tomorrow."

They unhooked the horse's harness and gave him a slap on the rump. As he disappeared from sight on his way back to the hovel Rory started laughing again.

"Did you really light his dick?" He was shaking with laughter as he said, "Poor Trigger, poor, poor, Trigger."

The logging camp and horse hovel were about a quarter mile from where they had been hauling out the logs. They walked back slowly, sweating in the hot humid afternoon. Rory carried the chainsaw over his shoulder. Kevin walked beside him carrying the nearly empty gas can and the ax. They were still laughing at Kevin's close call.

"I really hated to have to do that," Kevin said as he lit a cigarette, "Trigger is one damn good horse! But man, I thought he was going to break my foot! I'll bet the son of a bitch thinks twice before he tries that again!"

"Hell, Kevin, the son of a bitch did it to me once. I had to nail him up side the head to get him to move!"

They continued their walk. It had been a long day and both were anxious to get back to the camp. Their workday had started at dawn to take advantage of the cooler temperatures.

The camp was a small shack built on a set of skids. When the time came to move it, a logging truck could hook a chain on either end and tow it to the next location. It wasn't much, barely eight by twelve feet, but it was adequate.

Inside was a small wood burning cook stove that served as heat in the winter and was their only source for cooking. Now that it was hot weather, they slept outside on two old bench seats that Rory had taken out of some old cars.

They had rigged up a temporary lean-to with a shed roof off the front of the camp. The sides were enclosed with old screen windows and a makeshift screen door. This helped in keeping the bugs and insects out.

While Rory was sharpening the chain on his saw, Kevin tended to Trigger.

"Hey boy," he said softly, "How are you doing?" He crooned at the horse for a while as he rubbed him down with a damp rag. "Come on inside and I'll get you some grain."

The horse knew what to expect and obediently entered the hovel. Inside, the tormenting from the swarming insects was far less than outside. He waited patiently as Kevin cut open a bale of hay and scooped grain into his feed rack.

Rory noticed how Kevin was talking to the horse and smiled. He knew that Kevin was really good at hauling out logs. At thirteen years old he was as dependable as anyone.

Today was about the only time that Trigger had given Kevin any trouble that he knew of. Although it had been a close call for Kevin, he laughed aloud again at the thought of Kevin having to use his cigarette lighter on poor old Trigger.

He started a fire in the stove. While it was catching on, he walked the short distance to the spring and dug up what was left of their deer meat.

The spring bubbled icy cold water year round and a submerged five-gallon bucket with a lid served as their refrigerator. He grabbed a couple bottles of beer and returned to the camp.

The sun was going down as they ate on the small table inside the screened in area. They enjoyed a quiet time smoking cigarettes and playing a card game. As twilight descended Rory asked, "Well, do you think it's time? Those deer should be coming out about now and we're out of meat."

"Okay," Kevin replied, "But this time let me shoot it. That last son of a bitch ran for over a mile after you shot it in the guts like that. The way my foot feels, I don't want to be dragging one like that again!"

"That's fine with me," Rory laughed, "But your turn will come!" He reached inside the door of the camp and brought out the shotgun. It was a bolt-action twelve gauge 'goose gun.' It was about the biggest shotgun Kevin had ever seen. "If you miss one," Rory said, "I promise you'll never hear the end of it!"

They quietly made their way to the clearing where the deer generally came out just before dark. Rory waited long enough for Kevin to get where he needed to be and then started walking in a wide circle around the clearing.

As they had hoped, he spooked the deer right past Kevin. The shotgun blast sounded like a cannon in the stillness of the early evening.

That was pretty much their routine. They worked for Bill Riley, a logging contractor. The camp and workhorse belonged to him. In a good week they could cut and pile nine or ten cords of wood for sale to the pulp mill. There wasn't much money in it but it beat loafing.

This was the second summer Kevin had worked with Rory. Rory was a friend of the family and no one missed Kevin being gone for the summers. It was getting too crowded at home for him and Rory was about the only adult he half way trusted or got along with.

Rory had just turned eighteen. He was more like an older brother to Kevin than a boss. He had worked in the woods since quitting high school three years ago. His deep voice and the constant stubble of whiskers on his face made him appear to be much older. He easily passed for twenty-one and no one ever questioned his age when it was time to buy beer.

They both smoked the same brand of store boughts when they could afford them; otherwise they resorted to a backup can of tobacco and rolled their own.

Their camp was over a mile off the main road and neither worried much about getting caught shooting deer or anything else they saw that sounded good for dinner. The menu was usually Kevin's biscuits and fried deer meat.

Rory came from a poor family as Kevin did. He always drove rusted out old clunkers and was teaching Kevin to be a pretty good mechanic. Keeping the old cars running was a constant challenge. His latest, a fifty-two Chevy, was parked next to the camp with the hood up. As soon as Bill came with the pulp truck on Friday he would have a new battery and then they would have wheels again.

Until he could start his car, Rory had no way of charging up the old battery that they used to power the radio he had hooked up in the camp. For now, they were stranded unless either wanted to walk.

They had quartered the deer and dug out enough sand from the spring to bury it for later. It was still hotter than blazes, even in the open screened in area. They sat outside in the light of the kerosene lamp and were enjoying another beer. Rory tinkered with his chainsaw as they talked.

"I hope you can be quieter than you were last night!" Rory said. "You were really hollering for a while. What kind of nightmare was it this time?"

"Oh hell Rory, just more of the same." Kevin sounded as though he was trying to make light of the subject. "I keep getting memories back, you know, weird crap like we talked about."

"Hell, if I had been through what you've been through I'd probably have nightmares too." Rory said.

"I guess," Kevin replied, "But at least you remember what it was that you've been through." He paused and asked, "Is it really true? Did that old guy, you know, Gramps, is he the one that taught me to hunt and fish?"

"That's what they all say." Rory answered, "I never met him until Irene married your dad. I think it's really nice that they let him live with them." Then he added in a distasteful tone, "I still think you should be nicer to him."

His scolding didn't bother Kevin at all. "I don't mean to be rude to anyone, Rory. It's just that those people all expect me to believe whatever they tell me." He paused, "Rory, if I was in all that trouble, how come I ain't now? I've lived with those folks for damn near two years now and there ain't been no trouble. Even after Greg and that other jerk beat the daylights out of me. Remember that?"

Rory smiled as he recalled how they had met. "Yeah, I guess you're right about that." He grinned as he put the chain guard back on his saw. "If I hadn't pulled that little punk off you he probably would have blacked both your eyes."

"Next year I'll be old enough to quit school." Kevin said proudly. "At least that's what that social worker told me. I'll be fourteen and we should be able to make a good living right here. I've got near enough money saved to buy my own chainsaw."

"I wish to hell you had it now!" Rory said as he lifted his saw off the table and put it on the ground, "This old piece of junk won't last much longer."

"Hell, Rory," Kevin said with a grin, "If you'd just quit spending all your money on Katie you'd be able to afford two saws!" Then he added, "And don't think about bringing her out here this weekend! I'm staying right here with old Trigger."

"I thought you were supposed to meet with the state people again this weekend. Isn't it time?"

"Screw them dickheads," Kevin said, "I'm sick to death of that crap. If anyone wants to see me, they can just come on out here!"

"Oh well," Rory said, "Can't say as I blame you. I say screw 'em all. That's it. Screw 'em all."

On Friday, Bill showed up with the truck around four in the afternoon. It had been a good week and this time they had a full load. The logs had been cut into pieces four feet long, and were piled high in a clearing where the truck could pull up along side to load them.

It was hard work loading the truck by hand. Kevin wasn't big or strong enough to lift the larger pieces from the ground to the truck. Bill and Rory piled them on the flat bed and Kevin used a picaroon to pull them across the truck bed and then a wood hook to pile them up.

Bill knew that Rory needed a car battery and had brought one with him. As Bill drove off with his truck loaded to the top of the stakes, Kevin helped put it in the car. Once the car was started, Rory hooked up the jumper cables to charge up the spare battery that they used to power the camp radio.

Rory was in a hurry to get to town and was ready to leave about the time the old battery was charged. "See ya Sunday night." Rory said. He waved as he put the car in gear.

"I'll be here!" Kevin yelled to be heard over the sounds of the beat up old car, "Say hi to your mom for me and don't forget; more twelve gauge shells and I'm about out of smokes."

Rory stayed at his mother's place in town when he wasn't working. Having Kevin stay at the camp on weekends saved him from having to drive out on his days off to feed and water Trigger.

Kevin enjoyed his time alone at the camp. He idled away the hours listening to the radio and reading from the pile of old books and magazines that were scattered about the inside of the small living area.

As darkness descended he could hear a storm in the distance. He knew that thunder and lightning bothered Trigger and made sure the gate to the hovel was closed tight.

He napped inside the camp as the storm approached. The heavy rain beating down on the tin roof awakened him. He sat up straight and watched in awe as bolts of lightning lit up the outside.

He lit the kerosene lamp and sat at the table waiting for the storm to pass. As he leaned back in his chair he could hear Trigger stomping and whinnying.

A bolt of lightning lit up the outside in a continuous bright flash. He looked out the window in time to see that same German Shepherd that he had seen earlier running towards him with that same mongrel Collie close behind.

Something wasn't right. The sky was clear and blue; the green colors of the pasture seemed too brilliant.

He knew he was smiling as he reached out to pat the dog. Another clap of thunder shook the camp and once again he awoke with a start.

Chapter Seven

Bits and Pieces

<u>Second week in July, 1963</u>

Carlos Williams could best be described as one brutal son of a bitch. The local lawmen knew him well. It hadn't been that long ago when three sheriff's deputies had wound up in the hospital after trying in vain to subdue him.

They had tried to get him sent to prison for his drunken assault. The most a judge would allow was that he serve thirty days in jail and go through an alcohol dry out program at the VA hospital in Orono.

Carl was a decorated war veteran. Right or wrong, he was allowed more tolerance than most drunken brawlers. He was a big man, nearly three hundred pounds and tough as shoe leather. There had actually been four lawmen trying to subdue him, the town constable being the fourth. There had been no stopping him. He had charged into them like a madman, unstoppable and without conscience.

He worked in the woods, and owned a shack just across the line in Sebec Township. It was due to his drunken rages that his wife Lois and their daughter, Sally, were regulars at the clinic in Milo.

The town constable, Ralph Hollis, had tried countless times to get Lois to press charges. It sickened him every time he saw either of them with bruises. It was all too common to see this mother and daughter with black eyes or an arm in a sling. He knew that something needed to be done, and soon. Lois always insisted that whatever the injury, it had been an accident.

The last time, Lois had been to the clinic with a broken nose. She had finally admitted that it was Carl who was responsible. Ralph had taken a written statement, but at the last minute, she had refused to sign it.

Ralph's wife, Esther, was a nurse at the clinic. Both Lois

and Sally seemed to like her. Sally was thirteen years old, and pregnant. Lois had brought her in several months ago with a broken wrist. The doctor who examined her was surprised to discover that she was going to have a baby.

When Esther asked personal questions as to the father of Sally's baby, Lois had denied knowing. It came as no surprise to Esther when Sally tearfully detailed some very disturbing stories.

Lois Williams was walking quickly on the gravel road. The intersection to the paved road was only a quarter of a mile away. She could see it as she topped the rise. She knew Carl would be coming after her and needed to get to the pavement soon. She was certain that she could flag someone down and get a ride into town.

Lois was a frail, uneducated woman. Until now, she had not known any better than to put up with whatever Carl wanted. Now her Sally was pregnant. She was only thirteen years old. This time she had walked in on them, now she was certain. Sally was her baby, and Carl's. This time she was going to tell someone. She was going to talk to Mrs. Hollis.

She heard a horse whinnying off to the side of the road. A woods road opened up onto the gravel road and she could see Kevin Stone leading his workhorse towards her. She recognized him from the times she had seen him with Rory Smith.

As she waved her hand to Kevin she heard a vehicle coming up fast behind her. She half turned to look over her shoulder as he waved back. Her scream startled Kevin as Carl drove the pickup truck right over her.

"Oh damn!" Kevin exclaimed. He let go of Trigger and started running towards the road.

The truck had gone completely over Mrs. Williams and swerved off into the ditch. He could hear Mr. Williams spinning the wheels in reverse as he tried to back up in the loose soil.

Mrs. Williams slowly raised her head as he approached. She tried to get up. A moment later, the truck had traction and was rapidly approaching as if to run her over again.

"Hey!" Kevin yelled hysterically. His heart was racing as he grabbed onto Mrs. Williams. He pulled her out of the way as the pickup spun and chattered back over where she had been. "Stop!" He screamed, "Stop it! Just quit it!"

Now he was aware that Carl had seen him. He stood up waving his arms and yelled again, "She's hurt bad! What to hell are you trying to do?"

Carl got out shouting. "My damn brakes failed!" Kevin could tell that he was drunk. Carl was still shouting as he said, "I'll load her on the back and head to the doctors office in town." He bent over his wife and roughly slapped her face from side to side. "Hell!" He shouted, "She's just knocked out."

Making no effort to be gentle, he picked his wife up and nearly tossed her onto the bed of the truck. Kevin was about to yell again when he saw Rory approaching from the paved road in his old car. His heart was racing. His mind went blank as he ran out to flag him down.

Rory quickly surveyed the scene and shouted to Carl, "I'll follow you guys and then go on ahead to let the clinic know you're coming."

"That's fine." Carl mumbled. He got behind the wheel and waited for Rory to back his car around.

Kevin rode in the back of the truck. Thoughts and visions, which could only be described as dismay, flashed through his mind as he looked at Lois.

He glanced over his shoulder through the back window of the truck at Mr. Williams. He reminded him of someone else, but he couldn't remember who. A feeling of terror settled in the pit of his stomach. For a moment, he knew he was about to put a name to the person. Time stood still as a haze once again settled in his mind, clouding out those awful memories. He tried to control his breathing as he realized that he had been through this before.

He was brought back to reality as Carl spun his tires as he raced towards the main road, causing the truck to bounce and chatter as the rear wheels sought traction. Rory followed close behind, wondering just what to hell had happened.

Lois was awake with her head in Kevin's lap. He knew that she was hurt badly, and asked her what happened.

Her answer could barely be understood over the sounds of the truck as she told him, "He tried to kill me!" She sobbed as if in disbelief. Her thin face was bruised and covered with blood. For a moment her eyes took on a fiery look. "He's insane!" She cried. Her words were strained with pain and filled with anger. "He knocked up Sally, and wants to keep me from telling anyone."

"It's going to be fine, Mrs. Williams," Kevin said, "This

time you've got a witness! I saw the whole thing."

As Lois smiled at him, her body relaxed and her eyes closed. Kevin feared that she was dead long before they got to the clinic. When they were about a mile from town, Rory passed them in a cloud of blue smoke to hurry on ahead to alert the doctor.

Rory and Kevin waited outside the doctor's office at the clinic. The doctor was getting Lois ready for the ambulance ride to the hospital in Dover.

Carl had gone outside and was sitting in his truck. They could see him through the window of the waiting area. His door was open and he appeared to be talking to himself.

When Kevin told Rory and Mrs. Hollis what Lois had said and what he had seen, Rory shook his head in disbelief. He told Kevin, "You had better report this to constable Hollis, and I mean right now!"

Following Esther's advice, they hurried out the back door of the clinic and quickly walked the five or six blocks to the constable's office.

Ralph Hollis listened to what Kevin had to say. His wife had just called him from the clinic to let him know that they were on their way over. It was obvious that he was upset over this.

"Carl is still at the clinic." He said. "Does he still have that rifle in his back window?"

"As far as we know." Rory answered.

Ralph picked up the phone. He said, "I'm calling for help with this one."

They listened as he made his phone call. The courthouse and sheriffs office was only a block away. Within minutes a deputy pulled up out front.

"You guys wait right here." Ralph said.

Waiting there suited both of them just fine. They both knew Carl and neither was ashamed to admit that they were scared crapless of him.

Ralph hurried out the door and got in the car. The deputy turned on his overhead and siren as they sped off in the direction of the clinic.

They had gone no more than two blocks when they met Carl's pickup going the other way. The deputy made a fast u turn and started after him. In the few minutes it took to catch up, the truck was already stopped in front of the constable's office and

Carl was inside.

They were sitting in Constable Hollis's office when Carl stormed in. Without a word, he grabbed Kevin by his shirtfront and in an effortless motion picked him off the floor and slammed him into a wall.

He glared eye-to-eye and whispered, "You didn't see a damn thing!" He flexed his arm, slamming Kevin into the wall again. "Not a damn thing!"

"Quit it!" Rory shouted. As he tried to grab onto Carl's arm he was backhanded across the face. It was a violent blow that knocked him backwards over the railing that divided the entry to the Constable's office.

Kevin couldn't breathe. His head was swimming; he was seeing bright lights and dots. He knew he was going to pass out. Carl relaxed his grip a little, allowing him to breathe as he repeated his message, "You didn't see a damn thing!"

Over Carl's shoulder, sitting as if posing for a picture, were two dogs. Once again it was that same German Shepherd and mongrel looking Collie. Kevin thought he heard himself calling to them, and then the room went dark.

The dogs licking his face awoke him. He smiled as he reached up and playfully scratched the collie's ears. In looking around, he realized that he wasn't in Constable Hollis's office.

He felt as if he should try to get up. He suppressed a shiver as he noticed that a silver haired man was looking at him with a bright smile. Beside him were two smiling boys. Sitting in front of them was a pretty woman with silver hair. She was smiling too. Then, he noticed that these people were all standing frozen inside a golden frame. It made no sense to him. He shuddered as the frame slowly melted as flames appeared all around it.

A woman's face could be seen through a dense fog. She was a pretty woman with her hair a mess, leaning towards him. The fog cleared and the image came into focus. He could smell whiskey on her breath. His heart was racing. She was screaming something at him through the silence. He tried to call out but no one could hear him.

The ceiling of the room started turning slowly in a circular motion above him. As he stared straight up, the ceiling exploded in a vision of burning sparks and flame. It took sheer willpower to move his head. First he looked to the left, then to the right. There was nothing there, only an empty void with no floor, no ceiling, no walls, and no end.

A feeling of helplessness overcame him as he wondered where Rory was. He tried to call to the dogs as he spiraled downward and drifted back to sleep.

Kevin had been taken to the community hospital in Dover in the back seat of Constable Hollis's patrol car. Rory had again followed and spent the night in the waiting area. He had been assured that Kevin was going to be all right, and waited the night to take him home upon his release.

This was a time that Kevin was glad that he was still a ward of the state. The last thing he needed was for Dad and Irene to find out about all this mess and make him stop working with Rory. He was hoping that it could all be kept a secret as he walked to the waiting area.

Seeing Rory asleep in a chair, with his mouth wide open, caused him to smile.

Ralph Hollis and the deputy sheriff had arrived back in his office just in time to witness Carl slamming the boy up against the wall. Two revolvers aimed at his head convinced Carl to let the boy go and walk quietly to a jail cell.

The next morning, even before Kevin was released from the hospital, Carl posted his bail and went home. Ralph had watched in anger as Carl crumpled up the restraining order and court documents in his fist.

As he exited the building, Carl paused to open the door to the men's room and tossed them onto the floor.

****

Three days later, Carl showed up at their camp. Rory knew the seriousness of the situation and was trying to figure a way out.

"Listen Carl," he said in a nervous tone, "I'll talk to the boy, maybe he will change his story!"

With a mumbled curse, Carl backhanded Rory, knocking him off his feet. He towered over Rory. "No damn maybes about it!" He reached down and grabbed Rory's shirtfront and yanked him up. He slapped him several times across the face, and threw him to the ground again.

"That little prick had damn well better change his story!" Carl's anger was out of control. He was easily twice Rory's size and used to getting his way.

Rory scrambled up, but before he took two steps, Carl knocked him down again. He kicked him a couple times, herding him towards the horse hovel. Trigger whinnied and began stomping his feet up and down. The lanyard attached to his halter was tied to the outside wall of the hovel. He stood fretfully in place as the men approached.

"You tell that little prick that this is what his damn story gets him!" Carl picked up a pickeroon and with one violent swing, sunk the point right between the horse's eyes. Trigger went down instantly.

Rory attempted to get away again. Carl grabbed a length of harness and whipped him once across his back. Rory thought surely that Carl was going to kill him.

He was scrambling backwards on the ground in an attempt to get away. "Carl! No! No damn it! Leave me alone!"

Then they heard a cry, an agonized moan from back at the horse hovel. Rory could see past Carl that Kevin had arrived on the scene.

Carl had raised the harness strap to whip Rory again. The sound of Kevin's moan caused him to pause. His eyes went round in surprise as the sound caused shivers to go all the way up and down his spine.

Rory was curled up on the ground attempting to protect his head with his arms. Carl slowly turned halfway around to face Kevin. His timing was off as he swung his arm to deflect the blow as Kevin walked up and nailed him squarely on top of his head with an ax handle.

The next day, Rory was talking angrily to sheriff Bradley. "You should have seen the son of a bitch! I saw it and I still don't believe it!

He continued, "That big jerk about knocked the crap out of me! Then, when he grabbed that harness strap, I knew he was going to whip me to death. That's when Kevin walked up and got his attention."

"What do you mean?" the sheriff asked. "Did he shout or something?"

"Hell no!" Rory's voice was still loud with excitement as he recalled the incident. "He saw the horse laying there dead and sort of moaned real loud, I guess that's what it was, it sounded so awful! Trigger was laying there, his hind leg still twitching."

"That sound! I swear that boy couldn't have sounded more broken hearted! Then he just walked up to Carl and nailed him once with the ax handle and jumped back. Carl was in a rage to go after him, but that ax handle nailed him again. Met him right between the eyes at about a hundred miles an hour! I've never seen anything like it!"

"Did that put him down?"

"Hell no! It only pissed him off! He tore after Kevin like a damn bull."

"How did the boy avoid him?"

"I just don't know how to describe what happened. But Kevin nailed him in the knee and dodged out of the way! I... I've just never seen anything like it!"

"Then what? Damn it Rory! Carl is in intensive care! He's got more broken bones than they can count! Two broken knees, a fractured skull, and a broken jaw. The son of a bitch was dragged nearly to death. As if that's not enough, one of his hands is missing!" The sheriff sounded really angry. "I need to know just what to hell happened!"

"Well, he kept trying to get him, and Kevin just kept dodging and cutting him down to size. First one knee, then he nailed his wrist with the ax handle." Rory paused and shuddered, "He broke the poleax handle and picked up the crowbar. I could only lay there and watch."

"Damn. This is bizarre!" The sheriff exclaimed.

Rory continued, "Carl slipped and fell, then the boy broke Carl's leg with the crowbar. It was about then that Carl started screaming. He rolled over and over on the ground trying to get back to his truck."

Rory's voice broke as he continued, "All Kevin ever said was, 'Tell me you're sorry.' I think he broke Carl's jaw before he could do that. I scrambled inside the camp after the shotgun, but I must have passed out. The next thing I remember is waking up in the emergency room." Rory looked imploringly at the sheriff. "Did you really have to lock him up?"

"It wasn't our idea. Constable Hollis got a phone call and thought it would be best if he were kept out of sight until we get this mess figured out."

"I guess you have a point." Rory murmured, "Especially with all this other crap! I feel real bad for poor Lois! I hear she's still in intensive care."

Sheriff Bradley put his hand on Rory's shoulder. "I thought you knew. Lois died last night."

"Damn. I'm sorry to hear that."

"I need you to come with me and show me where it happened." The sheriff sounded discouraged, "I need to try to find his hand."

They didn't talk much on their way to the camp. Rory led him down the path to the horse hovel. Trigger was still lying there dead. He softly said, "I'll bet Carl regrets killing that horse a lot more than his wife."

Kevin had been in the process of making a beer run down to the spring when he heard a vehicle approaching the camp. He thought that perhaps it was Bill Riley with his pulp truck. He smiled and thought to bring an extra beer for him. As he neared the camp he heard Rory cry out in fear.

'Oh crap.' He thought. 'That's gotta be that damn Williams prick!'

He slowly made his way back, keeping the horse hovel between him and the camp. He caught his breath as he saw Trigger lying on his side.

His world changed to slow motion as he took several unsteady steps forward and dropped to his knees. Sound and color both took on a new dimension. His eyes took in the scene. He slowly raised both hands to the sides of his face.

The pointed end of the picaroon had been driven into the horse's forehead. The brilliant color of the blood and the glazed look in the horse's eyes spun together causing him to feel like he was going to lose his balance. Trigger's hind leg was twitching in slow motion.

His mind went totally blank. Emotions of dread and disbelief swept over him. He heard a moan that sounded as if it originated out of the pits of hell.

Time stood still.

His next recollection was half carrying a dazed and injured Rory to Carl's pickup truck. He was gasping for air as he pushed and prodded Rory into a slumped position in the passenger's side of the cab.

Carl had crawled to the pickup and was lying on his side under the back bumper. His right hand was outstretched and his body was twitching wildly.

A short length of quarter inch cable was dangling under the rear bumper, nearly touching the ground. He looped it around Carl's wrist and got behind the wheel.

The next thing he remembered was stopping at the paved road and getting out to check on Carl. It had occurred to him that he should try to load him on the back before starting out onto the paved road.

He remembered smiling as he noted that the cable was still dangling under the rear bumper. He looked back down the woods road and thought he could see Carl lying crumpled up in the center of the road between the wheel ruts.

He got back behind the wheel and drove his friend to the hospital.

****

"When I was in the children's home, a couple soldiers from the Air Force checked a couple of us out for the day and took us to a movie.

"What for?"

"I don't know for sure. I think they were sucking up to their Lieutenant or Captain or something. "

"What movie did you see?"

I can't remember the names; they were both war movies. It was a double feature. One was about paratroopers, the other about a submarine.

"So it was a good day?"

"I guess. I did learn that when you fight, when it's time for a reckoning, you fight to win."

"What do you mean by that?"

"Fair or unfair makes no difference. Not when it's kill or be killed."

Kevin was fidgeting nervously in his chair. The man opposite seemed equally nervous as he asked one question after another. Kevin was unaware of the profanity he was using. To him, it was just everyday speech.

"Did the man from the air force tell you that?"

"Hell, no. I've known it for years. Just didn't know how to put it into words until then." Kevin answered.

The man smiled at his choice of words. "I guess you just naturally curse and swear a lot, is that about right"

"I never thought much about it. What's the way I talk got to do with anything? You're just trying to find out the best way to screw me over. Right?" Kevin's serious tone seemed to impress the man across the desk. "I can see right through all those jerks that pretend to be nice. All they want is for their jobs to be easier. Right?"

With a wry grin, the man answered, "I guess you're onto me."

"What's going to happen next?" Kevin asked.

"Well, more than likely you'll be sent back to reform school. It's doubtful that Mr. Williams will be pressing the issue, but this is very serious."

"The son of a bitch kills his wife and you pious sons of bitches want to nail me?"

"I don't make up the rules."

"Can I go back to work while trial is being set?"

"Probably. So far, no one in authority has had anything negative to say about you. I guess that's why all this is so hard to believe. Can I ask one more question? Tell me no and I won't."

"Sure."

"Did you do it?" The man asked bluntly. "Keep in mind, there is no way I can ever repeat what you may tell me. Remember? I'm your court appointed attorney. I just want to know."

Kevin looked him right in the eye. "I ain't telling anyone anything. Do you really think I would trust a friggin lawyer?"

John Bartlett shrugged his shoulders. After having been a court appointed defense attorney for nearly twenty years, he was pretty thick skinned. The comment just rolled off. He could sense that Kevin understood that.

"Anything else?" He asked.

Kevin hesitatingly asked, "Who else will be there? At court I mean. Will I be allowed there this time? Will my relatives be there?"

"Chances are, you'll simply be notified." Mr. Barrett raised his eyebrows at the boy's reaction to his comment. "You're still a ward of the state. It's hard to say what they are going to do since you have a prior history, you know, reform school."

He paused for a moment as he noted a confused expression in Kevin's face. He wondered if Kevin was even paying attention to him.

"Even though you are technically living back home, the state is still in control. They don't legally have to inform your relatives, no matter what."

"Oh well."

The social services people had met with Kevin at the county court house. Like so many other facilities, there were no special accommodations for minors.

Sheriff Bradley had gone out of his way to accommodate his young guest. After returning from the camp with Rory, he had allowed Rory to share the same cell with Kevin. His explanation to the state people was simple. Even though Carl Williams was in the hospital in intensive care, they were both in protective custody.

Sheriff Bradley and Constable Hollis had a long meeting with the social services representative and a state appointed attorney. Both left the meeting with a renewed determination to keep a lid on things. Sheriff Bradley agreed to drive to Brownville and have a talk with Kevin's parents.

The third day after the incident at the camp, Kevin's dad showed up about an hour before they were to be released. The man from social services told him that he was waiting in the visiting area with Irene to take him home.

Rory and Kevin went out to see dad and Irene together. Rory's arm was in a sling and he said thanks to Kevin for holding the door for him. If not for Rory saying their names, Kevin wouldn't have recognized either of them.

"Hey Son! How are you doing?" Dad asked. He embraced Kevin and said, "We really need to get you back home. All this mess is too much to believe." He looked at Rory. "How are you doing?"

"About as well as I look." Rory said.

They laughed along with him as he added; "I won't be doing any pushups for a few days."

Irene took her turn at giving Kevin a hug. She was nearly

in tears as she held him at arms length and asked as dad had, if he was all right.

"I'm fine." Kevin's voice was nearly a whisper. Their reception was causing him to feel emotions that were new to him. "Me and Rory still have a few logs to cut up, and we need to take care of Trigger. Can't we finish that first?"

"Bill Riley already took care of that poor horse." Dad said. "We saw him this morning at Lois's funeral."

Irene had a bright smile as she added. "He sure speaks highly of you, Son." Kevin winced once again as she gave him another hug.

"I still need to help Rory finish up." Kevin murmured. "He got his arm hurt bad."

"It's not broken," Rory said, "It just got tore nearly off my body." He smiled as he added, "It hurts like hell."

They visited for a while, and both Dad and Irene agreed that Kevin could stay with Rory for a few more days.

Dad knew how important it was to Kevin as he said, "Son, I know this will all work out. You and Rory make a great team, and we hope everything will work out for you guys to keep on partnering up."

"Thanks, Dad." Kevin said. He was talking in a loud whisper, looking down at his feet, as he added, "I really don't know exactly what happened." He wiped a tear from his cheek and directed his next remark to Sheriff Bradley. "I just know that Mr. Williams would have killed Rory too."

Sheriff Bradley assured them that there would be no more trouble from Carlos Williams.

Dad treated them to lunch at a diner, and they parted company around two in the afternoon. As Irene embraced him to say goodbye, the image of the silver haired woman in the photograph flashed across his mind.

"Are you all right?" Irene asked.

"I'm fine."

"Well, you just have Rory bring you home sooner if need be. Okay?"

"I'm fine."

Kevin watched them get into the old pickup truck. He shivered involuntarily remembering the nightmare he had experienced after Carl had put him in the hospital. He waited at the diner while Rory walked the short distance to get his car.

Kevin's mind was spinning as he watched Rory pull up out front. His car was moving in slow motion. Kevin's entire body went rigid as if he had been shocked. It dawned on him that he had remembered the children's home in his conversation with the social services representative.

In his mind he could see the tall brick columns. He was approaching them fast, as if flying though the air. The doors opened; he paused to look into an office. A woman was sitting at her desk. She was talking seriously with a young boy. He thought he heard the boy say, 'Yes, Ma'am.' He smiled at how she was looking over the tops of her wire-rimmed glasses.

He was slumped against the front door of the diner with his head against the doorjamb when Rory got out of his car to see what was wrong.

He placed his hand on Kevin's shoulder as he asked. "Are you okay? Are you ready to go?"

"It is a real place." Kevin whispered.

"What?"

"Rory. It's real. It all happened."

"What do you mean?"

"All that crap, Rory. All that crap."

"Kevin? Stand up. Are you okay?"

Rory's voice was hard to understand. The sound of his voice had slowed to being barely understandable.

Kevin looked up at him. His eyes were out of focus. He knew he was whispering when he said, "Please, take me to hell out of here. We need to get back to the camp."

Chapter Eight

Breaking Point

First week in August 1963

Judge Palmer had been known to lose his temper before, but never on a magnitude such as this. He was seething as he unloaded on Mark Page.

"The deal is off?" He was fuming that Mr. Page had so readily agreed with the others present that they leave the situation concerning the Stone boy out in the open.

"I want that kid rounded up and placed in protective state care." His voice elevated as he nearly growled, "Is there any part of what I'm saying that you don't understand?"

"I understand perfectly, your honor." Mr. Page answered. He glanced across the table at the state appointed attorney. "If it were up to me, I'd drive up there and pick him up this afternoon."

"This has gotten totally out of hand!" Again the judge's temper flared. "Who authorized someone other than the original five of us to be informed about this?"

"Detective Miller has been promoted your honor. He's located out of the Portland office now. Detective Smiley here has been assigned to this case. Those in my office and in the Attorney Generals office have full confidence in him, including Brett Miller."

Judge Palmer had met Detective Smiley at Brett Miller's wedding and had no doubts as to his being competent. He directed his next remark to him.

"I was supposed to be kept informed anytime there was a change relative to this case."

The judge paused and eyed the four individuals seated at the table. "It seems that now there are no secrets. Is there anyone who doesn't know where the boy is?"

"I know you're upset, your honor, but considering the circumstance, we feel that that there is no need to keep this out of the records." Detective Smiley stated.

"What?" Judge Palmer sounded incredulous.

"You've got all the proper paperwork before you." Detective Smiley said. "I'm sorry to have to say that it doesn't make much difference anymore what you think."

Judge Palmer gave him a look that caused him to shudder. His voice lowered as he made eye contact with everyone present. He emphasized his points on his fingers as he continued. "One! This boy is still a potential witness for the state. Two! Ray Satterfield is out of prison on appeal. Three! Stan Morgan is out of prison on appeal. Do you need me to draw you a picture?"

"I'm sorry your honor." The state's attorney said softly, "But we just don't share your concern. Word's out and everybody knows that the boy doesn't remember anything. The state has no plans on calling him as a witness."

Mr. Page added, "In this case, the state feels that you overstepped your authority to begin with. His parents have petitioned for custody, and we intend to grant it."

"Why don't you just get a gun?" The judge's voice was ice cold. He looked Mark Page in the eye. "Just get a damn gun and go shoot the boy yourself!"

"What are you insinuating, Judge?"

Those present exchanged looks and silently rose as Judge Alfred Leroy Palmer stormed out of the room.

****

Bill Riley didn't think much about it when the two social workers stopped by his house around one in the afternoon to ask questions about young Kevin Stone.

He was fuming as he related what he knew about last week's incident at the camp. It was his horse that had been killed and he was still upset over that.

He told them that to his knowledge, Kevin was a good worker and had never been in trouble that he knew of. He said that due to all this mess, he wouldn't be able to log that section until he could afford to buy another horse.

Kevin and Rory were about finished there. As soon as Rory's shoulder was better, he and Kevin would finish cutting and piling the few long logs that remained. They would more than likely be finished by the end of the week. Then the camp would be boarded up, probably until next summer.

He cheerfully gave them directions to the camp. Yes, Kevin was sure to be there. The constable and sheriff had both thought it okay for him to go back to work. Bill explained that the magistrate had also talked to him, and he had agreed with the local lawmen.

The two men thanked him for his time and left.

He noticed, but paid no mind to the Massachusetts license plates on their car.

Rory stopped by the clinic to get some stitches removed from behind his ear before heading down to the camp. He was still recovering from the unmerciful whipping he had received from Carl Williams. His face was still bruised and his arm was in a sling. Esther greeted him warmly, and asked him to have a seat in the waiting area. He was nervously waiting his turn when Bill Riley walked in.

They were shooting the breeze when it came Rory's turn to see the doctor. Bill accompanied him, and was grinning from ear to ear as Rory yelped and gritted his teeth as the doctor removed several stitches.

He told Rory that the social services people had stopped by to talk to him, and he had sent them down to the camp. "You might want to be ready to give them a tow." He chuckled. "Those slicks will probably get stuck about halfway in."

"Was it that same skinny little jerk that Kevin tells about?" Rory asked. "He wears thick glasses?"

"One of them was wearing glasses, but it wasn't the thin one." Bill said. "They were driving a car with out of state plates. I think this is the first time they've been in these parts. The big one has a Boston accent."

"Well, I hope Kevin will remember to watch his language around them." Rory said.

Bill chuckled and said that he hoped so too.

****

It was a rough ride as the car bounced and dipped on the narrow logging road around three in the afternoon. The driver cursed each time the car bottomed out in the narrow wheel ruts or tree branches scraped the sides.

The man beside him didn't seem to mind. His window was down, and occasionally he would lean towards the driver when a tree limb would brush against his side of the car.

"It's got to be here somewhere!" The driver said. "We've gone nearly a mile already."

"Well," his passenger replied, "It isn't like we can turn around. I just hope we don't end up getting stuck. It looks like it rained hard here last night."

The forest opened up to a small clearing. They could see smoke rising above the roof of a small logging camp. The driver pulled over to the side of the road and stopped about fifty feet from the small shack. He sounded the horn as they got out.

Kevin was inside the camp and had heard the car coming. He was half hoping that it would be his Dad coming to get him. This past week had been a rough one. For the first several days he hadn't been able to stop crying. It was so unlike him. He really felt bad about Trigger.

He was angry that he had cried when he mentioned Trigger in front of those stuffed shirts from town. They had thought that he was crying because of what had happened with Mr. Williams. He figured, screw 'em; let them think what ever they wanted. Seeing the car, his first thoughts were that it was someone coming to take him back to jail or something.

He opened the door and walked out to see who it was. Two men were approaching, walking gingerly in the soft mud as if trying to keep their shoes from getting dirty.

The driver was a large burly man. He wore wire-rimmed glasses and was wearing a blue blazer. Kevin smiled as the two city slickers approached.

"Hi there! Are you Kevin?" The man who shouted the question was wearing a sport coat over a white shirt. His necktie was skewed to one side from the bumpy ride.

That same German Shepherd that Kevin had been seeing was standing off to the side of the car. His posture was ominous. The hair on his back was standing up; it looked as if he were going to charge at the two men.

Kevin gasped; the men were walking in slow motion. He knew the dog was growling, but there was no sound. He felt a release of static energy pulsating back and forth in his head as the men approached. The dog seemed to just fade away as it disappeared. He looked anxiously around wondering where it could have gone.

"Hey there, are you Kevin?" The man asked again.

"Yes, Sir, I am." Kevin answered as he let himself out through the makeshift door of the screened in lean-to. His eyes nervously swept the clearing as he added, "What can I do for you?"

The man offered his hand and said, "I'm Mr. Morris. Social Services asked me to check on you. This is my associate, Mr. Dean."

Kevin's expression was one of confusion as he shook hands with each. He said, "I guess if you drove all this way just to check on me, it must be important."

He opened the screen door and invited them to sit in the shade. "It's got to be past quitting time somewhere, can I offer you gentlemen a beer?"

They laughed and politely said no to his offer.

"Kevin," Mr. Morris said, "I'll get right to the point." He exchanged looks with Mr. Dean. "We both work for the Attorney General's office. Your friend, Mr. Miller, asked us to look you up to see if you would answer a couple questions for us."

"Mr. Miller? Who's that?" Kevin asked.

"You really don't know?" He exchanged glances with his partner. "He told us that you probably wouldn't remember, but it's real important, that's why I'm here." Mr. Morris said.

Kevin thought his tone was rather patronizing. There was something familiar about the man in the blue blazer. He realized that they wanted something. He could scarcely control the cold shiver that went up and down his spine.

"Mr. Dean cut in, "Will you help us kid?" He had a gruff sounding voice.

"Sure, if I can."

"Kevin, it concerns something that our office thinks you may have witnessed a couple years back. Do remember when you were in the detention facility in Brewer?"

A confused expression crossed Kevin's face again as he answered. "No." His tone changed to one of frustration. "Everyone keeps telling me that I was there, but I really got no damned idea what they're all talking about."

"Kevin, what do you remember? What happened before you came to live with your parents?" Mr. Morris asked.

"I don't know."

"You sure?" Mr. Dean asked.

"I'm sure I don't know, if that's what you mean."

There was something about Mr. Dean's tone of voice and mannerism that was starting to bother Kevin. His gaze focused for a moment on Mr. Morris who was sitting with his coat open. Kevin noticed that he wore a shoulder holster.

Mr. Dean had a large bulge under the left armpit of his blazer. For a moment, he could picture him wearing a uniform.

He glanced behind them at the car parked some distance away. He felt another release of static energy in the back of his head. Then he figured it out.

****

Rory was about a mile from the turnoff to the logging road when he met a car driving erratically, at a high rate of speed. He had to swerve over to his shoulder of the road to avoid a head on collision.

As they met, he flipped them the bird and yelled out his window. "Get your damn out of state ass off the road!"

Their car was covered in mud. He wondered for a moment if it may have been the social workers that Bill had been talking about.

He got to the camp about an hour before dark. He honked the horn as he approached. He was a little curious that Kevin hadn't appeared. Kevin had to know that he had brought groceries and a fresh supply of beer.

"Kevin!" Rory shouted, "Where the hell you at? I've got smokes and beer!"

There was no answer. He assumed that Kevin wasn't far away. He had talked about getting another deer, and he figured that was what he was doing.

He went inside the lean to with his first load. The shotgun was lying on the ground. The area by the table was stained with fresh blood. He looked back out the door and saw a fresh trail of blood leading towards the clearing. He smiled, thinking that Kevin had bagged another deer.

He picked up the shotgun and ejected a spent shell casing. He figured on giving Kevin an ass chewing for leaving it in the dirt like that. After he got everything put away, he carried the beer and perishables to the spring. He was half expecting to find Kevin there burying the deer meat in the cold sand.

Finding no sign of him, he made his way back to the camp and spread a couple shovels of sawdust over the blood soaked area. He lit the lamp, opened a beer, and sat listening to the radio.

Rory was surprised to see headlights through the trees around eleven o'clock. He had just settled in on the bench seat with a blanket and was about to drift off to sleep.

He could see a red light blinking and knew it was someone from the law. 'Oh crap!' He thought, figuring that it was probably the game warden.

It was a sheriff's vehicle, a four-wheel drive truck that skidded to a stop in front of the camp.

A deputy sheriff and a man dressed in a suit got out. The headlights were left on and the overhead light was still blinking as Rory opened the screen door. He recognized the deputy, but the man in the suit was a stranger to him.

"Hey there!" the man in the suit called. "Are you Rory Smith?"

"Yeah," Rory answered, "What do you guys want?"

"We're looking for Kevin Stone." The man's voice elevated as he added, "Is he here?"

Rory explained that he had arrived a few hours earlier and that there was no sign of Kevin.

The man asked, "Has anyone else been here that you know of?"

"I'm not sure." Rory was still nervous. Not knowing what to expect he said, "There was a fresh set of tire tracks since I was here last. Could be his folks stopped in and picked him up, I know they were talking about it."

"We just came from there." The man said, "And we talked to Bill Riley, they all think he's out here with you. "

A call came over the truck's radio. It was dispatch, needing to talk to them.

The voice was crackling over the speaker.

"Is Mr. Smiley with you?"

The deputy answered, "Yes."

"Tell him we just got a call. The state police pulled over a car with Massachusetts's plates. He needs to call in."

"Anything else?"

The static from the radio drowned out the reply.

"Dispatch, say again."

"The only information we have is that they found a body."

"What?"

"That's all we've got. Highway patrol pulled over a car with Massachusetts plates and made an arrest."

Detective Smiley took the microphone from the deputy and shouted, "This is Smiley. What to hell do you mean, 'a body?'"

"That's all we know sir. HP found a dead body in the car and made the arrest."

"We're on our way in."

Rory was anxious to find out what was going on. He had listened in on the conversation over the radio.

"What's happened?" He asked.

The man in the suit offered no reply as he got in the passengers door.

"Let's move!" He shouted.

Rory's voice was frantic. "Tell me! Did something happen to Kevin?"

"We don't know." The deputy replied.

He had nothing else to say to Rory as he hurriedly got behind the wheel.

****

Kevin instinctively knew that something was terribly wrong. Mr. Dean looked familiar. He knew he was on the verge of remembering something.

"Just a minute!" He exclaimed, "I've got to close up the wood stove!" He quickly scrambled up the steps into the camp. The men heard the sounds of the stove lid clanging into place.

Mr. Morris looked at Mr. Dean as his eyes went wide in surprise. Kevin was standing in the doorway with the biggest shotgun they had ever seen leveled right at him.

"I think it best if you both get to hell out of here." Kevin said. His smile was out of place.

"Kevin," Mr. Morris said in a smooth tone, "What's going on?" He smiled and turned sideways a little to look at Mr. Dean. "Put that gun away, we still need to talk."

"Kevin!" Mr. Dean's voice was filled with anger. "Put that gun down now!"

"To hell with you, Boss!" Kevin's voice rose slightly as his smile vanished.

"Listen to me, Kevin!"

"I've already listened long enough."

"You're already in a world of trouble." Mr. Dean said. Trying to sound calm, he added, "We just want to talk to you, that's all. If you don't put that damn gun down, you're in some deep crap."

"Maybe so; but not from you jerks." Kevin's voice had a trace of hysteria. "If you're from the Attorney general's office why in the hell are you driving a car with damned Massachusetts plates?"

His voice rose again, "I know you think I'm just a kid, but this is a real damn shotgun with a real damn finger on the damn trigger." His voice broke as he added, "And I really know how to use it." He thrust the shotgun forward towards Mr. Dean as he moved ever so slightly.

"Kevin! This is the last time I'm going to tell you!" Mr. Morris said. He seemed to be stepping back, and before Kevin knew what was happening, he closed the distance and grappled the shotgun away.

"You little prick!" He snarled as he tore the gun from Kevin's grasp. "No one threatens me!" He threw the shotgun to the ground as he slammed Kevin against the door opening.

When the shotgun hit the ground, it went off.

Mr. Dean's scream, combined with the sound of the shotgun blast caused Mr. Morris to distract his attention from Kevin for a brief second. The shotgun blast had struck Mr. Dean squarely in the thigh.

Kevin squirmed out of his grasp and bolted inside the camp and out through the back window. The sounds of the glass breaking as the hinged window smashed against the side of the camp were blanked out by the sounds of agonized screaming coming from Mr. Dean.

Kevin hit the ground running. His heart was racing, his mind blank, as he bolted through the forest.

The car was once again bottoming out at every bump in the woods road as Mr. Morris kept the engine racing. "That little son of a bitch!" He yelled, "I'll be damned! I'll be damned! We got aced by a damn child!"

He glanced at Mr. Dean. "Just hang on!" He exclaimed. "There's a clinic back there in that one horse town, we'll be there in a few minutes."

Mr. Dean's voice was trembling as he cursed his luck. His grating voice was weak as he said, "I told you! Just cap the son of a bitch. Who gives a crap what he remembers?"

His leg had been nearly severed by the shotgun blast. He was trying to stay conscious. He had lost a lot of blood. He was still bleeding badly despite the tourniquet that Mr. Morris had placed on his leg.

They made the turn onto the paved road. "I think the little jerk recognized you!" Mr. Morris exclaimed. His voice was intense with panic. "The bastard called you Boss!"

Mr. Dean was slumped against his door and offered no response. Before they got to the town limits, he realized that he had been talking to a dead man.

It was around midnight when Irene heard sounds coming from down stairs. She heard voices coming from the living room. She could hear Gramps talking to someone in a low tone, asking what was going on.

She got big Kevin up and they went down stairs together. Gramps was in the living room, standing by the couch. Young Kevin was curled up in the corner behind it. He was sitting with his back to the corner, hugging his knees and shaking uncontrollably.

Chapter Nine

Confused

Kevin resigned himself to living at home again. The state people had relinquished custody to his dad and Irene. He seldom gave the subject much thought. Home was just another roof over his head. His mood swings continued to go back and forth.

He had no conscious memory of the incident with Carl Williams or the visit from those men at the camp. Whenever Irene or dad or Gramps would mention it, he listened to their version, taking in the information as though he was hearing a new story for the first time.

It was the old guy, Gramps, who tried to make each day special. He often sat with Kevin and Artie for hours, teaching them to recite several poems that he knew by heart. He was especially patient with Kevin.

They were sitting on large blocks of wood in the woodshed that was attached to the back of the house. Artie had just recited one of Gramps' poems word for word. He sat there proudly, feeling special as Gramps and Kevin applauded him.

"Your turn Kevie." Artie said. "Don't you remember? You knew this one a long time ago. Huh Gramps?"

Gramps smiled at his excitement. "You sure did, Kevie! You used to have this one nailed!"

Kevin was feeling good. These few times that he and Artie and Gramps could be alone together were special. He surprised himself, and them, as he recited every poem that Gramps had ever tried to teach him.

"Good job Kevie!" Gramps exclaimed.

"I told that last one, about the flag, to Mrs. Green once." Kevin said proudly. "I can't remember for certain, but I think she liked it."

"Mrs. Green?" Gramps asked, "Who's that?"

He wasn't surprised when Kevin abruptly got up and stormed off. He exchanged glances with young Artie. He sighed and slowly went back outside. Kevin was walking out of sight over the hill behind the house.

He shook his head. When he got inside, he cautioned Irene that tonight Kevie was sure to be having nightmares.

School started the day after Labor Day. It was predictably no different than before. It all made very little difference to Kevin.

Mr. Mathis was constantly on him about something. He occasionally forgot to watch his language at school, as did many of the others. Mr. Mathis and Mrs. Almer missed no opportunity to punish him.

Their favorite students, like Greg and Jerry, could get away with anything. There was just something about Kevin that rubbed these two the wrong way.

He was always on the lookout for more trouble from Greg and a couple other bullies. They were always making fun of him over something. For the most part, he kept to himself and tried to stay out of trouble.

Each year there was a two-week break from school at the end of September for potato harvest. It was a long-standing tradition. This gave the locals a chance to earn some money picking potatoes in the fields. Kevin and Artie used the money they earned to buy school clothes.

Kevin welcomed any break from school and enjoyed the hard work. He would have preferred to be working in the woods with Rory, but even picking potatoes was better than going to school.

Irene and several friends had worked the harvest every year since they could remember. Kevin and Artie got to work along side of her. For the duration of the harvest season, they all got along well.

The sun was just starting to rise over the treetops. It was a cold, frosty morning. The pickers were lined up along the rows awaiting the first pass of the tractor that towed the large potato digger behind. They could hear it coming about a quarter mile away at the end of the field.

"I hope everyone's ready!" Irene exclaimed. She smiled and looked at Kevin who was a short distance away at his section.

"Kevin, are you ready?"

"Ready!" Kevin called back.

"Artie, are you ready?"

"Ready, Mom!" Artie exclaimed.

Irene tried to make it fun for them. Her cheerful disposition was often contagious and Kevin often caught himself nearly calling her mom.

The sound of the tractor was very loud as it approached. They knew they would have a lot of potatoes to pick up and place in the wooden barrels. They needed to be finished by the time it made its turn and got back to them digging up more rows.

They picked the potatoes up off the ground and placed them in large woven baskets. When they were full, they would carefully dump them into the barrels that had been dropped off the back of a flat bed truck earlier. As the barrels got full, the same truck would return and load them onto the back with the help of an electric winch.

It was still early; the frost was just starting to melt off the ground when the trouble started.

The truck was making its way slowly across the field, picking up the full barrels. Kevin looked up and saw that it was Jerry who was working the winch.

He was turned facing away from the truck, filling up his basket, when an empty barrel was tossed from the truck. It bounced once and rolled. Kevin had no idea that it was coming as he was bowled over and fell face down in the freshly dug soil.

He rolled over, his mind blank as to what had happened. Jerry was laughing and joking with the other kid that was working on the back of the truck.

Jerry's first mistake was telling Kevin to watch out for the next time.

Irene had witnessed the incident. She stormed over to the truck and told the driver to stop.

"I saw that young man!" She said. When Irene was mad, her voice could be very nasty. "Get down right now and apologize to him."

Apparently, Jerry forgot his manners as he made his second mistake. He muttered, "Go to hell."

Irene placed a foot on the rear frame of the truck, allowing her to reach up and grab onto Jerry's shirtfront. He was standing with his back to some full barrels and had no place to go.

Irene yanked him frontward and off the truck. A moment later, Jerry was picking himself up off the ground and wondering what to hell had happened. Irene was right in his face.

"You will apologize! Right now!" Irene was an average size woman with a temper. She grabbed a handful of his hair and marched him over to Kevin.

"Now, do you want to say you're sorry?" Her voice was filled with anger as she continued. "Or am I going to slap the living crap out of you?"

Jerry was now a believer. He knew she meant it. Kevin just stood there with an amazed expression on his face as Jerry nearly begged his forgiveness.

The field foreman showed up about then in his pickup truck to see what the trouble was all about. By the time Irene got through blessing him, he was one humble straw boss. He fired Jerry on the spot and quickly drove him off the field.

That event was the talk of the community for the longest time. Those who knew Irene weren't surprised. She was known to be a fiery one from time to time and this time someone had messed with her kid.

It wasn't until a week later that Kevin got up the nerve to thank Irene for standing up for him. It would be several years before he started calling her Mom.

The weeks continued to drag on. The routine of school set in and once again Kevin's attitude took a sharp downward trend.

He still got along well with Artie and Gramps. His attitude towards everyone else in the family was still in sad need of improvement.

In addition to little Matthew, they now had another baby, Marie. She was as cute as a button. She was just starting to talk, and Irene was pregnant again.

November 1963

It was on a Saturday morning that Kevin started getting an uneasy feeling. He felt a premonition that something was wrong. He felt a sensation like the release of static energy in the back of his head.

He was splitting firewood when he sensed that he was being watched. He looked up and gasped! They were sitting a few feet away at the end of the woodpile.

The German Shepherd was watching him with a curious look, the Collie sat calmly beside him.

"Do you see them?" He excitedly asked Artie. "Look! Over there."

Artie had just returned from dumping a wheelbarrow load of wood in front of the shed. He looked in the direction that Kevin was pointing.

"See who?" He asked.

"Right there!" Kevin exclaimed. "Can't you see them? Just look! Are you blind?"

"Kevie, it's just us out here." Artie shrugged his shoulders and started stacking wood into the wheelbarrow.

He wasn't surprised when Kevin angrily stormed off, muttering to himself.

That afternoon they got another visit from the social services people. Two men that they hadn't met before stopped by just before dark. They informed Dad and Irene that Kevin had been placed back in state custody. They explained that it was in his best interest until all the legal mess was worked out.

They acted disappointed when Dad explained that Kevin had stormed off earlier, upset over something. He told them that it wasn't unusual for him to act that way, and that he usually got back home before dark. He was surprised when they got back in their car and drove off.

When they told Kevin about the social worker's visit, he didn't seem to care.

He stood alone at the top of the hill behind the farmhouse. The November rain was beating down, buffeted by blasts of wind that seemed determined to beat him into submission. In the pitch darkness, he turned his face towards the heavens.

He was screaming as unbridled emotions of rage and frustration poured out as if he were possessed by the devil himself.

"I hate you! I hate you! I hate this damn place!"

His fists clenched, his body shaking, he screamed at the forces of Mother Nature. His face was stinging from the pain of the wind driven rain hitting him. His temper was unchecked as he cursed and swore incessantly.

Finally, spent, exhausted, and drained to the point of having barely the strength to stand, he started walking back down the hill. He walked silently past the house not bothering to look at the glow of the light cast from the windows and started walking down the paved road.

He still had some venting to do as he continued cursing and raving as he trudged through the darkness.

"No more! Damn it! No more! Enough! I'm damn near fourteen years old and I'm not taking it anymore!"

He continued walking in the darkness, not knowing or caring where he was headed.

In the back of his mind he heard a voice that he hadn't heard for years. It startled him.

It's about time you figured it out.

He started smiling.

The Guardians

They had been watching him, as he stood alone on the hill behind the small farmhouse cursing and raving like one gone mad. The scene was all too familiar. The forces of the storm surrounding him seemed to be putting out an extra effort to beat him into submission.

The place they watched from was peaceful. The background was like that of a dense fog with the glow of a golden light showing softly all around.

"Why are we here?" Marla asked, "Why this one. Why him? Why is it so difficult?"

"It's not for us to know." Angel's voice was soft. She could sense that Marla was troubled. "I only hope we can make a difference. This one needs us."

"What's the use, if all that happens is bad?" Marla asked. "We need to stop him! Can't you see that?"

"We can't stop him." Angel said. "We must always be watchful, we must always be ready, but we can never stop him."

"Should I possess him again?"

"No! Possession is a last resort. You did a marvelous job before, but it will kill him."

"I hope this is over soon." Marla looked imploringly at Angel. "When can I cross over?"

"Soon honey, soon."

"We have so many to watch over. Will it ever end? Will we ever win?"

Angel's voice was still soft as she exclaimed, "I have one to watch over... right now!"

Marla watched in awe as she learned yet another lesson.

The driver didn't see the child until it was too late. The windshield wipers had smeared and streaked the windshield in the steady drizzle of rain. As she saw the child's terrified expression in her headlights, she gasped and jammed on the brakes.

For a moment, time stood still. Then everything went forward in slow motion.

All four tires locked up, causing them to screech loudly. The child turned her head. As her eyes opened wide in fear, a dog darted across the road and ran in front of the car at the same time it was making contact.

As she was knocked out of the way, the dog was run over and yelped once as the front tire crushed its body. The back tire rolled over it with a sickening crunch. A moment later, time returned to normal as the car skidded to a stop.

The driver got out and ran shrieking towards her. The girl started crying as she rolled in the gravel on the shoulder of the road to get up. A woman was running towards the scene from the driveway of a house only a few yards away.

"Julie!" The mother cried as she ran to her daughter. "Julie! Oh my God!" She picked up the little girl and held her close.

"Are you all right?" The driver exclaimed in a panicked voice. She was shaking uncontrollably, her nerves shot, as she surveyed the scene.

The mother looked up, and with tears in her eyes said, "She's been told a million times not to play near the road! She was throwing the ball for Rex." Then she paused as she saw Rex lying crumpled up beside the road. "Oh no!"

Her husband arrived on the scene. He had been on the back porch when he heard the screeching of the car's tires. Both he and his wife were in tears as they realized what a close call it had been for their daughter.

They told the driver that there was nothing she could have done differently, and thanked her for her concern. She got back in her car and drove off.

None of them heard the conversation that was going on around them.

Angel watched the dog with a sad smile. The light faded from his eyes as death took him away.

Marla said, "That was very close. If you hadn't possessed the dog, the girl would have died!"

"I know dear." Angel said, "But look at what happened to him."

A soft light once again surrounded them as Marla asked. "Please tell me, is there anything we can do to help the boy?"

"No dear." Angel embraced her. "Just be patient. We need to be very careful when we possess. You never know what else is in there."

"What do you mean?"

"Us guardian angels come in many shapes and forms," Angel replied softly. "Never forget, so do demons."

They looked once again at the boy who was now walking down a different road in the darkness. He was cursing incessantly and muttering angrily to himself.

Kevin spent the night in a car that had been abandoned near the road. He shivered in the cold, trying only to endure until morning. He knew he was in the wrong, but that didn't bother him. He had had enough. It was time to be on his own.

This last dispute at home was over something trivial. It really wasn't a fight at all. He had overheard Irene and a neighbor talking. Both agreed that they should go to the funeral in support of young Sally.

Apparently Carl Williams had been released from the hospital a few days earlier. He had been taken home in an ambulance. He had posted bail and was still awaiting trial. His daughter Sally had been living at their home alone.

Sally was packed to leave when he showed up. She had already made plans to ride out with the ambulance attendants to find somewhere else to live.

Carl had committed suicide before the ambulance had backed out of the driveway.

"They say that Sally got the gun out along with some shells and made sure it was standing beside his bed before she left." Irene said. "Then she screamed at him for being cowardly and walked out the door."

Irene added, "That's when he put the shotgun under his chin, that's what they say, and pulled the trigger! The ambulance people went back inside after they heard the shot. Then they just drove off and sent the Sheriff and the coroner back to the house."

"Poor Sally." The neighbor said. "I hear she's going to live with some relatives now and finish school after she has the baby."

"Yes, that's what I've heard too."

Kevin felt cheated as he heard the story. The frustration within had reached a boiling point. He was seething as he tried to convince himself that it didn't make much difference. He knew he needed to get away from there. He needed to be alone.

The next morning he started thumbing to Bangor. His first ride took him as far as Lagrange. The rest of the day was more walking and thumbing. He was dropped off in Old Town just as it was getting dark.

He didn't have any money with him, and figured he'd have to borrow some groceries. He stopped in at a corner grocery store and asked the man if he had any work. The man said no, but to maybe check back later.

Kevin smiled and told him thanks just the same. He walked another half mile or so, and once again took advantage of an abandoned vehicle to sit in and eat the sub sandwich and drink the coke he had borrowed when the man hadn't been looking.

He started walking again, not knowing or caring where he was going. His plan was simply not to go home again.

He knew that Rory was cutting wood for someone over in Greenbush, and figured he would look him up and work full time. *Maybe he's got another horse like old Trigger.*

As he continued walking, and the rain started again, he realized the futility of his plan.

Just go back.

What do you mean?

You can use the old camp.

Yeah. No one will know.

No one will care.

He was soaking wet when he came to the Shell station near the railroad tracks on route two in Old Town. He stopped for a minute to be out of the rain under the canopy that covered the gas pumps.

A lady driving a brand new Ford station wagon pulled up at the pumps.

"Fill it up!" She said as she got out. She was a very unpleasant woman.

"Check the oil, and I want to see the stick before you go putting any in!"

Kevin's eyes were wide in surprise that she would talk to him like that. "Yes Ma'am." He said.

"Is there a restroom inside?" Her loud voice and rude manner reminded him of someone else.

Kevin met her look with a bright smile. "Yes Ma'am! It's around the side. Just ask inside for the key."

The lady went inside. Kevin suppressed a shudder as he overheard her rudely asking the man for the key.

What a bitch!

He noticed that she had left the keys in the switch.

Kevin quickly filled the car's gas tank. The lady was still inside the restroom when he finished and screwed the gas cap back in place. He glanced over his shoulder at the restroom doors as he placed the nozzle back in its holder.

He got behind the wheel. He started laughing as he eased the car onto route two. He was thinking that maybe he could keep it parked in Trigger's old hovel.

His mind was spinning as he recalled what had happened with Carl Williams.

You should have killed that bastard.
I know.

Chapter Ten

The Way Down

Late November 1963

Kevin really liked driving the new station wagon. It had an automatic transmission and a powerful engine. The steering was tight and it cornered really well. Best of all, it had an AM - FM radio.

It took him about four hours to make the drive back to Milo. He knew that in order to get away with this latest caper, he needed to get back as quickly as possible and get the car out of sight at the camp. His mind was spinning with possible plans as he drove on through the steady drizzle of rain. He hoped that the rain wouldn't turn into a snowstorm.

You've turned into a real son of a bitch.

Your point?

He got to the turnoff for the camp around midnight. The road was slick and muddy. He proudly tooled on down the narrow woods road. He smiled when his headlights illuminated the darkened shack.

Home sweet home.

Why don't you just shut to hell up?

Shut up yourself.

Who are you?

He left the car running with the lights on so he could see to get inside and light the kerosene lamp. Someone had placed a lock on the door. He stumbled around in the darkness and finally found the crowbar under the camp. He used it to pry open the padlock hasp.

Soon the place was filled with the light cast from the lamp. In looking around he noted that Bill or Rory must have stashed all the extra gear inside. It took him about a half hour just to clear out the empty gas cans, old horse harness and miscellaneous tools. For now he piled everything high on one of the bench seats in the lean-to.

When he went back outside to shut the car off, he got a nice surprise. Apparently the lady from whom he borrowed the car had just made a stop at the grocery store. He was ecstatic as he made four or five trips into the camp with enough groceries to feed an army.

Now don't you feel bad for calling her a bitch?

Hell no.

The next day was Sunday. He spent the time getting settled in and taking stock of his situation. He decided that it was pointless for him to just hide out. He figured that he would be better off if he got back in his old routine.

He found Rory's old windup alarm clock and set it. His plan was simple. With nothing better to do, he figured on attending school like always.

He reasoned that he could always park the car a couple blocks away and no one would ever know the difference. He selected a quiet location between a small park and the high school. Each day he arrived early and finished his last cigarette and cup of coffee in the car before walking the remaining distance to school.

The school routine was no different than before. The first glitch in his plan came the second day. Mr. Mathis mentioned something to him about hearing that he wasn't going to be going to that school anymore. Kevin smiled at his disappointed look as he assured him that he was, now that he had a place to stay.

That same day, Artie ran up to him wanting to know where he was staying. He made him promise not to tell anyone at home and told him the same story as he had Mr. Mathis. He told them that Bill Riley had offered for him to live at his house and that he was working part time for room and board.

"Will you be coming over to see us?" Artie asked.

"I doubt it. I work a lot."

"Is that why you don't want mom and dad to know?"

"Yes."

"Okay, Kevie. Can I tell Gramps?"

"No. Don't tell anyone. If you do the state people will just move me again. Remember how they are?"

"Mean." Artie said.

"Right." Kevin said. "Mr. Riley isn't mean. I'll be okay living there. Let's keep it a secret. For sure?"

"For sure." Artie said. He gave Kevin a hug and went back to his area of the playground.

Kevin seldom saw his brother after that. The recess times and the grade differences assured that they would almost never be seeing each other.

For the next few weeks, Kevin drove his borrowed car back and forth to school. He was really enjoying his freedom. For a short time, all of his grades went up.

He still got free hot lunch at the school. As his groceries at the camp started to get low he would go shopping with his 'midnight credit card' and 'IOU checkbook.'

There were a lot of cabins and summer homes on the south side of Sebec Lake. The second weekend he drove there and went from camp to camp, collecting whatever he wanted.

The camps were all left empty for the winter, but most had some supplies of dried or packaged food. He helped himself and was sure to leave an IOU at each location listing what it was he had borrowed. He often smiled and laughed aloud as he signed each note with a scrawling X.

He had a midnight credit card for gas. It was a length of siphoning hose he found at the camp that he and Rory had often used. When his tank started getting low, he would simply get it out from the back seat along with a five-gallon can and help himself.

He knew where both Mr. Mathis and Mrs. Almer lived. On more than one occasion he had caught himself laughing aloud and wondering if either of those fools ever noticed what awful gas mileage their cars got.

School dragged on. He kept his distance from the other kids, knowing that any one of them could cause more trouble for him than he needed. That same jerk, Greg, and his stooge Jerry were constantly taunting him. He ignored them when he could and avoided them whenever possible.

He knew his clothes were disgraceful, but short of raiding a clothing store, he had no choice but to make do with what he had. He had acquired several items of usable clothing on one of his camp raids. As soon as he could get his hands on some cash money, he planned on getting a haircut.

Christmas break came and the routine had remained unchanged. He still had plenty of firewood that had already been split and piled on the decks of several of the camps where he used his midnight credit.

He had folded the rear seat of the borrowed station wagon down and made several trips. The car held nearly a half cord of wood at a time.

The major glitch in his plan came during Christmas break when a severe snowstorm blew in. He had just returned from a shopping mission. He had a full tank of gas and boxes of groceries, cigarettes, and beer. This time he had shopped at the big supermarket in town.

It had started snowing shortly after midnight and no one was around. He knew he was getting overly bold when he smashed the glass in the rear door and let himself in. He had figured on really stocking up this time, and he did.

He took his time and made three or four trips back and forth to his car. He had left it parked with the engine running close to the back door. He was in no hurry as he stocked up on canned food and anything else that looked good to him.

By the time he got back to the camp road, it was snowing hard. Even though most of the road wound down hill, it was still a miracle that he didn't get stuck about half way in.

When he awoke the next morning there was over a foot of new snow. He realized that he wasn't going to be driving anywhere, at least not for a while. The car was stranded, probably until spring. It made little difference. To him, this was the good life. No hassles, no worries, and no regrets.

It wasn't until Christmas Eve that the nightmares came back to haunt him.

About the third day of being stranded at the camp, Kevin decided to walk out and poke around town a bit. It was hard going in the deep snow, but after about a half hour, he made it to the main road.

He thumbed a ride and was dropped off in Milo in front of the hardware store. He spent most of the afternoon going from store to store just for something to do. He smiled each time he overheard someone wishing someone else a merry Christmas.

In the towns' only department store, a line of children stood anxiously waiting for a chance to talk to Santa. This Santa looked to be as real as they got. His beard was real, and he had a twinkle in his eye that was undeniable.

Kevin stood watching silently beside a display of Christmas ornaments. He held no resentment towards the old guy, but knew that under that red suit was just another man. A fat man in a red suit who was trying to be nice to all the rich kids.

In his mind it was all a scam. Those who had money got Christmas. It was no more complicated than that. These were a bunch of spoiled, sniveling little brats who had done nothing more than be born to the right family.

Still, he smiled each time a small boy or girl climbed onto Santa's lap. Their expressions of awe were so cute. He thought the whole thing to be quite humorous as he watched the moms and dads as they stood uneasily in line hoping their kids wouldn't embarrass them.

The people at church had taught that Christmas wasn't about presents. It was supposed to be much more than that. He had a hard time believing that as he noticed several congregation members waiting in line with their kids. It was no surprise to him that they ignored him and acted as if he wasn't standing only a few feet away.

They don't speak to the likes of you.

Be nice.

It's a crock.

You knew that all along.

He was a bit surprised when a short, heavyset man wearing a gray sport coat placed his hand on his shoulder. The man was wearing a nametag that looked like a miniature Christmas wreath. He had extremely bad breath as he leaned close to Kevin and said in a low tone.

"You need to move along. We can't have people just standing around in the store."

"What?"

The man's voice took on a more serious tone. "Move along, now."

Kevin's temper flared. "Screw you!" He hadn't meant to be disrespectful, but it just turned out that way. He added, "I'm not hurting anything."

The store proprietor gripped his shoulder and roughly escorted him to the sidewalk.

"Unless you're with an adult, just keep out." His voice had risen, "And watch your language."

"My damn language is fine!" Kevin shook free of his grip and took a step back, ready to bolt if need be. He was nearly as tall as his antagonist.

He looked him in the eye and said. "If this is how you mean to act, you and that fat guy can eat reindeer crap and die!"

The man turned and walked back inside his store. He was muttering something under his breath. Kevin remained on the sidewalk, looking in through the window. His smile was out of place as he noted the expression of disgust on the proprietor's face.

He was looking at a new pair of boots at the shoe store when the storeowner asked if there was something he could help him find. He was really nice. He had a pleasant smile and was wearing a Santa hat.

Kevin said no thanks and turned to leave. He really didn't want any more attention. Someone else had overheard.

"Hey, Kevin. How are you doing?" It was Mrs. Hollis. Kevin remembered her from his times at the clinic with Rory.

"I'm fine Mrs. Hollis, how about yourself?"

"I haven't seen you in a long time!" She exclaimed. He could tell that her smile was sincere. "We heard that you left the country or something."

"I guess I just sort of come and go a lot."

She smiled and said, "Well, it's good to see you."

"Thanks."

Kevin was nervous. What he didn't need was for Constable Hollis to see him and start asking questions. He was hoping that she was alone.

She smiled as he said; "I'm hoping that I don't see you for a long time. Every time I do, I need stitches or something."

They enjoyed a quiet laugh. Kevin wished her a merry Christmas and left the store. As he walked outside it dawned on him that Mrs. Hollis was the first person to say something nice to him in a long time.

It's because you're such a low life.

Who are you to talk?

It's true.

Just who in the hell are you?

Christmas Eve, 1963

Kevin was sitting at the small table reading one of the magazines he had borrowed from the supermarket that night when he had stocked up on groceries. The small room had plenty of light from the extra kerosene lamps he had borrowed on one of his midnight shopping sprees.

The radio was turned down low. The sweet sounds of Christmas music filled the small room. It was some kind of preaching show with two men telling stories in between the music selections.

Outside, the temperature had been dropping since late afternoon. He had just finished putting wood in the small cook stove and had already filled up the wood box with enough firewood to last through the night.

He put the magazine down, and put on a pan of water to cook up some spaghetti noodles. The wind had picked up and the trees all around were groaning and creaking as they swayed back and forth.

Kevin was startled as a bright light lit up the outside in an intense glow. He watched out the window with a smile as two familiar figures dashed about, playfully chasing each other to and fro in the fresh snow.

He heard himself calling to them. The German Shepherd turned to face him with his ears standing straight up as if listening. The Collie also paused and looked at him. Both were panting and appeared to be having a good time.

A feeling of dread swept over him as he realized that anytime he saw them, something really bad happened shortly thereafter. *At least there's a fresh snow. Tomorrow I should be able to track them.*

He called to them again.

Someone on the radio was talking about something that had happened last Christmas. He was telling a story about how his sister had stopped in unexpectedly to visit on Christmas Eve. The man on the radio said, "When I saw Jean standing there, I was so overcome with joy that I almost forgot to invite her in!"

He was enjoying a good laugh with whomever it was he was telling the story to when Kevin gasped for breath.

Jean!

Who the hell is Jean?

The light from outside went out. Kevin sat up again and noticed that the pan on the stove had nearly boiled dry. He tried to drive the feelings of dread from his mind as he cooked his dinner.

How did I get to be here?

What to hell happened anyway?

That prick in the blue blazer. Who was he?

What prick?

Quit keeping it from me. And while you're at it, I want to know who she is.

You'd better quit with the questions.

The lady, who is she?

If you keep this up it will take more than those damn dogs to help you.

They're dead, aren't they?

You should know. It's your fault.

Sometime during the night it all came back. He sat alone in a rat hole cabin built on skids. He was as out in the middle of nowhere as anyone could get. It was Christmas Eve. All at once he remembered everything.

All at once.

Everything.

Chapter Eleven

Long Nights

Kevin was anxious for his birthday to come around. He knew that school started a few days after. He figured on walking out each day to the end of the road and catch the bus from there. He had taken it before, on Fridays after school and again on Monday mornings when he had worked out here with Rory.

It was New Years Eve. It had been a really rough few days since Christmas. He had been curled up in the camp for days, scared nearly out of his mind. If not for the bitter cold causing him to get up and bring in more firewood, he probably wouldn't have been able to cope.

Day after day he woke up crying. After that first day when he had tried to escape, he experienced uncontrolled episodes of temper. He sobbed and shook from daylight till dark. At night he cried himself to sleep. He felt no shame for this. He was just glad that no one had been around to witness his behavior.

On Christmas day he had been so upset that he had tried to get out of there and go home. A feeling of sheer terror engulfed him as he tore out of the camp and started running.

He was running, out of breath, making a beeline through the forest back to the main road. He was sweating, despite the bitter cold, when he tripped over some brush.

He fell headlong in the snow. His breath was coming in short gasps. He felt a presence. Something had followed him. He was panicked. He couldn't get away.

It's already here.

It was with him. He desperately fought his way through a pile of limbs and brush as he tried to stand up again. He lost one of his gum rubber boots. He pulled out of it somewhere in the brush pile as he frantically tried to free his foot from the entanglement that seemed determined to keep him there.

He scrambled across the forest floor like one fleeing for his life. He didn't know why he was running. He fell down again. He got back up. Panic! He was filled with panic as he clawed his way through the thick underbrush.

His energy was nearly spent when he tripped and fell partway into a spring that despite the bitter temperature was still bubbling icy cold water. He waded through water that was knee deep as he scrambled to escape.

He stopped running and fell to his knees as he realized where he was. He had run in a complete circle and was back at the camp. He raised his hands to his face as he realized that he was at the same spot where he had discovered Trigger lying dead only a few short months before.

He made his way back inside the camp and stoked up the fire in the stove as he got out of his wet clothes. He was dizzy. He felt nauseous as he remembered it all.

His foot was bleeding from running with only his wool sock on his foot after he had lost his boot. He had stepped on something during his awful flight. He tore up an old pillowcase to use as a bandage.

He reached up under the wall cabinet, between the wall studs, and took out the fifth of whiskey that Rory kept stashed there. He was thinking that Rory must have suffered brain damage when Carl Williams beat the snot out of him. That was the only explanation for him forgetting to take his whiskey with him.

After sponging out his wound with the rag soaked in whiskey, he sniffed the bottle.

Hell, this ain't so bad.

Try it.

Screw you, beer's good enough for me.

Lightweight.

For the next few days he was torn between awful temper fits and bouts of crying. It was a confusing time for him. When he finally calmed down around the third day, his mood became somber. He sat listening to the radio in the background while he slowly recalled everything. His memory was clear. His mind was working perfectly.

I said go away.

What?

I don't need you any more.
What do you mean?
Go away.
You had better think twice about this.
I don't even need those damned dogs anymore.
I'm sorry. It really wasn't your fault.
Just go to hell away.

Kevin was slowly developing a new attitude. He was sure that he could get by on his own, but the solitude and loneliness was getting to him. As the days and weeks wore on, he wished that the snow would melt so he could drive his car. The walk in and out of the camp was a long one.

The car was parked close to the camp with its hood up. Each day he started it and let it run for a few minutes. He kept the jumper cables hooked up to charge the battery that he used to power the camp's radio.

There was a girl in his class that seemed to be different from the others. His first day riding the school bus, he tried something different. He said hello to her in a bright cheery tone. He hoped his face didn't show his surprise when she smiled and said hello back.

Every day after that it was the same. He always smiled and said hello to her. She always smiled and said hello back. It helped to get each day off to a good start. Even when the teachers, or Greg, or some other jerk would hassle him, he knew that every morning would start anew with a cheerful greeting when he got on the bus.

The first week back from Christmas break; the eighth grade students took the pre tests for high school. Kevin was in a good mood that day. He concentrated, and did his best to get a high score. He didn't particularly like the people who came to the school to talk to them about the test scores, but he did like going to the counseling meeting with the girl from the school bus.

Greg was forever harassing him. His stooge, Jerry, was starting to feel like he was some kind of a tough guy. Kevin kept avoiding them as best he could. Sometimes, when his mind was on something else, Greg would trip him in the classroom or Jerry would walk by his desk and knock his books onto the floor.

He finally had enough. It was sometime around mid February when Greg and Jerry cornered him in the schoolyard.

Kevin hadn't expected them to be so bold. Greg had tried to shame him about his clothes earlier during class. At recess he outdid himself with his insults.

Several boys had gathered around him on the playground. He had been walking around, minding his own business when they flocked around him. Most were grinning and thinking that it was fun. Greg wasn't.

He told Kevin that he was sick of how he dressed and that he needed to buy a new comb. At first Kevin smiled, trying to make light of the whole thing. He held out his hand as Greg passed him a hand full of change.

Kevin stood for a moment, looking down at the coins in the palm of his hand. The sheer meanness of what Greg was doing sank in. His face turned red as anger started boiling inside him. Without a word he threw the money at Greg and turned to walk away. Greg wasn't about to let it go, and grabbed his shoulder and spun him around.

It was the same old cycle, all over again. Greg was a lot bigger than him, and grabbed onto his coat front. He was yelling something. Kevin's head was spinning in disbelief. He attempted to get away. In raising his hands to squirm out of Greg's grip, he hit him under his chin.

Greg was furious. Kevin shrugged himself out of his coat while Greg was holding it and nailed Jerry in the mouth with the palm of his hand.

His mind was in a spin. He couldn't think what to do. For a moment the haze nearly cleared. Before he could get his thoughts straight and before he could turn, Greg was on his back and he was face down on the ground.

Mr. Mathis arrived on the scene and broke up the fight. He roughly escorted Kevin into the office and gave him a real chewing out.

He was feeling pretty wounded when he made his way back to the classroom.

This isn't right.

I don't have to take it anymore.

I thought you wanted me to go away.

I wasn't talking to you.

As he made his way to the back of the classroom, Greg extended his foot to trip him. He smiled as he stepped over it on his way back to his desk.

You'll get yours.
You son of a bitch.

There was no way Kevin could win a fair fight with Greg. He knew this to be a fact. He was seething on the inside for days. Why had Mr. Mathis punished him?

His thoughts became mixed as he tried to recall just how he had come out on top in the past. He smiled as he realized that most of the time he had come out on the short end of the stick.

What to hell, there's no such thing as a fair fight.

All you need is an equalizer.

He found himself smiling as he recalled beating the crap out of the Champion boys. He could see Joan's face clear as day as she whispered, "Did you really do that?"

That was one hell of a day.

For a moment he thought he was going to be gripped in fear again as he recalled the incident with Lois Williams. He really felt bad for that poor woman.

It didn't bother him that he couldn't remember the details of kicking the crap out of Carl Williams. Rory had told him what details he knew, and Kevin had no cause to doubt his account.

Nail the bastard with a big stick.

That'll soften him up.

He was trying to focus on what to do about the current situation when he started crying. He started thinking about Henry and Joan again. His emotions went back and forth as he remembered some really good times.

His mind wandered back to the day when Henry had taken both he and Adam hunting that first time. He heard himself laughing as he recalled how excited Adam had been when they treed that porcupine.

He burst into tears again as he recalled the day that he and Henry had found Shep and Collie shot to death. He knew now that they were the dogs he had been seeing. They had saved his life more than once. He hoped that Henry and Joan had gotten another German Shepherd. That was Joan's favorite breed.

He remembered Joan, asleep in the overstuffed chair when he kissed her goodbye. He smiled again as he recalled her startled expression that morning when she had rushed around the corner to the kitchen as he was taking a large pan of biscuits out of the oven.

Was that really three years ago?

Yeah. Remember?

It was the same time you fried those inbred sons a bitches.

May they burn in hell.

The scene at the stained glass window of the church was as clear as a picture. Jean's cute smile and the sound of her laughter played over and over in his mind.

He did a lot of reminiscing as he recounted some of his more daring adventures. As he recounted his greatest feat, slashing all those tires and scratching his parent's name on Mr. Bellinger's car, he became aware that he was laughing. Putting the dead cat in Mrs. Mentor's file cabinet took the cake. He was laughing uncontrollably. As he came back to reality, he sighed and wiped another tear.

How did I ever get away with that crap!

Now he knew why all those people had been out to get him. Ray Satterfield, Dr. Coleman and that jerk at the reform school. Some things he just couldn't remember, but he believed that to be no different from what anyone else would recall.

That jerk killed Mr. Bishop!

He remembered it clearly. Mr. Bishop had worked at the detention facility in Brewer. He was about the only one there that had been half decent to him.

He remembered a joke that he had overheard Mr. Bishop tell to someone. He knew that it had been funny, but couldn't remember the punch line.

He had been sitting by the door that separated his quarters from the jailors station. He had been listening in on the conversation on the other side. He remembered the time like it was yesterday.

"There was this drunk who goes into the bar, see." Mr. Bishop had a loud voice; Kevin smiled remembering how he had told his joke.

"The bartender had a one hundred dollar bill in a small frame behind the bar. The drunk asked him what it was there for. The bartender says 'it's a bet.'"

"What kind of bet?" The drunk asked. Kevin smiled at how Mr. Bishop really sounded like a real drunk in telling the drunk's part.

"Well," the bartender said, "If you want to win it you've got to do three things."

"What?" the drunk asked. "I could sure use a hundred dollars."

"First, you've got to beat the crap out of the toughest guy in here. Then you've got to go upstairs and please Betty. She's the old whore that works upstairs. I mean you've got to really please her. Screw her till she can't take any more!"

"What's the third thing?" the drunk asked. He was so inebriated that the bartender doubted if he was really getting all this.

"There's a rabid dog down stairs with an abscessed tooth. He's the meanest damn dog you'll ever see. You've got to go down there and pull his tooth."

Kevin laughed aloud remembering how Mr. Bishop had nearly cracked up telling the next part.

"The drunk looked around and saw the biggest, meanest son of a bitch you could imagine sitting at the end of the bar. He staggered down there and POW! He knocked him off his stool and proceeded to stomp the living crap out of him."

"Then he staggered down stairs." The way he paused caused those on the other side of the door to crack up laughing. Kevin remembered having to hold his sides as well. He didn't want them to know he was listening.

"You should have heard it! The bar was silent as everyone listened to the horrible sounds of that rabid dog. He was growling and howling. Soon all you could hear was that dog whimpering and whining. After a few minutes the drunk staggered back up the stairs."

Kevin wished he could remember the punch line. The drunk had staggered up the stairs and said something.

That had been the same day he had borrowed those letters from Mrs. Green. He knew that he shouldn't have been reading someone else's mail, but his being a snoop didn't bother him. He grinned as he remembered reading the letter from Nadine. He hoped that Mrs. Green had somehow gotten her letters back.

For a moment he felt sad again as he recalled Ray Satterfield grabbing onto Mr. Bishop's shirt collar from behind and throwing him to his death. Dr. Coleman and Mr. Bellinger had been there too.

What a bunch of pricks.

Damn, that was rude.

He was up most of the night, remembering things that should have bothered him. He stared for a moment at the flame of his match as he lit a cigarette. He recalled tossing the match into uncle Rick's trailer.

I was hoping the son of a bitch would yell and scream.

Maybe should have used gasoline.

Yeah. Maybe.

I hope the son of a bitch knew it was me.

He did.

His mom's face, leaning towards him as she cursed him out terribly, was once again as clear as a picture. He could still smell the whiskey on her breath. This time it didn't bother him as he sat all alone at the table.

Alone, in a camp out in the middle of nowhere, he cried for the last time.

Just like a damn baby.

Quit it.

You've got to stop this.

I said for you to go to hell away.

You need me.

Like hell I do.

****

The boy scouts met at a clubhouse about a mile from the school, on the edge of town. Greg and Jerry were both boy scouts. Greg was working towards his eagle badge and took the whole thing a little more seriously than Jerry.

The scout meetings were held on Wednesday nights. Greg lived a few blocks from the clubhouse and usually walked to the meetings. They always started their meeting with a short prayer and a salute to the flag.

No one noticed that someone was peering in through a window with predator eyes. They all stood with their hands over their hearts, reciting the pledge of allegiance.

When the meeting was over, Greg started walking the few blocks to his house. He was walking quickly as he got to the area in between streetlights. He never would have admitted it, but he was a little afraid of the dark.

He thought he saw a movement out of the corner of his eye. He felt a severe pain in his head as his mind exploded in a brilliant flash of vivid lights and stars. Then there was only darkness. It was a good thing. Had he been awake, that hardwood club nailing him time and again would have really hurt.

Mid February marked the arrival of the Chinook winds. The temperature rose and there were several days of warm rain. This melted the snow enough for Kevin to drive his borrowed car, slipping and sliding, up the winding woods road and out to the main road.

His first trip out he made a few stops, and using his midnight credit, stocked up on various supplies. The ground froze in the early hours of the morning making it relatively easy to drive back and forth on the muddy camp road.

The weather report on the radio was calling for more snow and he knew he had to park the car somewhere other than at the camp. When he figured he was stocked up enough on groceries and essentials, he decided to leave the car parked in town.

He drove it to town on a Sunday morning and left it parked behind the high school about three or four blocks from his school. He figured on leaving it there in case there was more snow. He hitched a ride back to the camp road.

As it turned out, his timing couldn't have been better. It did snow some more. He had already taken care of the most worrisome aspect of not having it parked close.

He didn't have to worry about the battery for the camp's radio anymore. He had picked up a really nice transistor radio and nearly a whole box of batteries on one of his shopping sprees.

It was a good thing that there was nothing to tie him to the car when the constable found it. Although it was essentially undamaged, the lady from whom it had been borrowed was extremely upset when she came to pick it up. She threw a fit over the empty beer bottles and trash that had accumulated behind the front seat.

He was glad he had taken it out of the woods when he did. He knew he would have been in even more trouble, had the car still been there, when Bill Riley and a deputy Sheriff drove down to get him.

END PART FIVE

Foreword Part Six

(Introduction to part six: Damned And Destined For Hell.)

The first time I saw Kevin, he was smiling. It was his first day at the reform school. He was the only kid I've ever known to get out of the big hearse and smile.

I was sent to the boy's reform school when I was fifteen. They were strong on discipline, sometimes downright cruel. If you stayed out of trouble and did as you were told, things weren't that bad. I guess I thought I'd had a rough life or something. At the time everyone said I had a real bad attitude.

My parents couldn't handle me. They were a couple of crap heads anyway. It was obvious that they favored my older brother and sister. The unwritten rule at home was 'blame Brian.'

The local law finally got tired of me always being in trouble. When they made their recommendation to send me here, my parents didn't protest at all. They all thought that it would straighten me right out.

Maybe they didn't take up for me because I had just put Grandpa in the hospital. Hell, I don't know. I still think the old prick deserved it. He was always ordering me around. It was always, 'Brian do this or Brian don't do that.'

The old bastard finally pissed me off to the point where I grabbed his bible away from him. I used it like a brick up against the side of his head. I tapped him good and knocked him across the room with it. Mother and Grandma were there and got real excited over the whole deal. They called the cops that time.

I think it was because I nailed Grandpa with his own bible that causes me to remember Kevin so well. He's the only other guy in the world that I know of that got caught right in the middle of a crap storm due to a bible.

Being caught and charged with grand theft auto may have also had something to do with my being sent here, but what to hell. I still think that if I hadn't nailed that old fart with his bible, things might have been different.

No, I'm not saying that I wouldn't have wound up here anyway. I really liked that car. Nonetheless, when your life sucks like mine does, any excuse will do.

I met Kevin the first day he arrived. He was an average looking guy for his age. I'd guess that he was probably around five foot two or three, and maybe weighed a hundred pounds.

He wasn't any tougher or meaner than any of the others. I think it was his not giving a damn about anything that earned my respect. I'll never forget his last day when 'old warden Bastar really blew a fuse. I mean really.

I've never heard of anyone, who claimed to be a man of the cloth, getting so upset. We all called him 'Reverend Bastard' behind his back. I think that this was his first and last job as a warden. I heard that he had replaced another warden about a year or so before I got here.

I can't say as I've ever seen or heard of anyone losing it like he did. Not before or since Kevin. He just had a way of bringing out the worst in authority figures.

The fresh meat usually arrived on the first Friday of each month. We always looked forward to their arrival. Sometimes it would only be one new kid, sometimes two or three. A couple of months had gone by without any new arrivals at all.

The new guys were always brought in from the processing center in an old school bus that was painted a light blue color. It was a small bus, maybe a twenty passenger, with wire mesh fastened on the inside to cover the windows.

The windows were painted black from the outside and the front was caged with a dark canvas that prevented the occupants from seeing where they were going. I think it was so that if someone tried to run away, they wouldn't know how to get back to town, or something like that.

Anyhow, we called it the big hearse. When it stopped at the warden's office several of us were outside. We stopped what we were doing to see who was going to get out.

I'll never forget that first minute. Kevin stepped off and stood quietly, at attention, as the driver waited for one of the screws to sign for him. He looked in our direction. I met his gaze and was rather surprised to see him smile.

I knew there was something different about this new guy when Casey McGinn turned as white as a sheet. He was standing right beside me. Maybe one of Reverend Bastard's sermons had gotten to him. He gasped and chokingly said something about Satan and turned and ran in a panic to the dorm area.

That first day, I knew that the new kid was receiving his orientation from the officials who worked for Warden Bastar. We had a bet going about whether or not he would cry that first night in the dorm.

Hell, we'd all be surprised if he didn't, everyone did. I can remember when it was my turn. As tough as I was, even at fifteen, I think I cried for two or three nights in a row. Everyone is always extra rotten and rude to the 'fresh meat.'

For dinner on Fridays, we were always served some kind of fish. We always looked forward to it considering the slop we were fed the rest of the week.

One of the 'screws bitches' started hassling him at evening chow. A screws bitch was probably what you would call a trustee in the big house. Around here, they were the lowest life form and despised by everyone. This one's name was Jerome. He was a real suck up. He got to share a private room with Casey McGinn. They were both rats. They were both bullies, even here.

Warden Bastar had assumed his Reverend Bastard role and was saying grace before we could eat. He did this two or three times a week. I guess it made him feel special to be eating with us. We all knew that his table was never served the same slop as us.

Sometimes he droned on until the food was really cold. Kevin sat there looking straight ahead. Jerome was walking slowly up and down the rows of tables making sure that everyone bowed their heads and closed their eyes during the prayer.

Kevin was sitting quietly, staring straight ahead when Jerome nailed him hard in the back of his head with the open palm of his hand. "Bow your head, now!" He said.

Kevin lowered his head and tried to ignore him. I was sitting across from Kevin and could hear Jerome as he leaned close to whisper. "Casey is scared crapless of you. We'll see about that. We'll just see."

"Who in the hell is Casey?" Kevin whispered back.

Smack! Jerome nailed him along side the head. He looked up at the warden and raised his voice.

"Sorry to interrupt Reverend Bastar. But we've got a blasphemer sitting right here!"

The day turned to crap for Kevin. We all had to wait as he was roughly escorted from the dining area by a screw and several bitches. Reverend Bastard used this as an excuse to do some more preaching and allowed that we could thank the new kid for having another cold meal.

Our dorm area was a large open room with two rows of metal-framed bunk beds. I don't know where they kept Kevin the first night, but just before lights out the second day, a screw's bitch led him down the center aisle and showed him to a bunk across from mine.

After lights out the taunting began. I joined in with the others; after all, it was a tradition. There never was a response from Kevin. Come to think of it, he probably got a better night's sleep than the rest of us.

As the days wore on, the hazing from the bitches never let up. They were always slapping him; shoving him down and making him do extra chores. It didn't slow down until about the middle of the second or third week.

The only bitch that left him alone was Casey McGinn. He always stayed as far away from Kevin as he could. We never did find out why. It was unusual for a bitch like him to go easy on anyone. I think it was on a Thursday, right after noon chow, that it all came to an abrupt end.

The area to the kitchen was enclosed with a wall of wire mesh right behind the serving counter. Kevin was assigned to kitchen duty with several others and me. Jerome was in charge. Three or four screws were sitting at one end of the dining area just shooting the breeze and not paying much attention.

I was at the counter outside with two of the others. That left Kevin alone behind the mesh. He called to Jerome.

"Hey, Jerome!" He pronounced the name in a long drawn out sound, really mocking him. I thought, 'oh crap! He's really asking for it.'

Jerome had a short fuse anyway. He kicked the heavy mesh door open and charged in. I think what happened next is still talked about to this day among those who are currently guests at that facility.

Jerome charged inside the kitchen area and immediately fell headlong to the floor. I don't know what he tripped on, but even as he was hitting the floor, Kevin nailed him good with a heavy metal stool.

The sounds and instant commotion caused the screws to leave their coffee and come running.

Before they got there, Kevin had blocked the door with an overturned wheeled cart and placed some kind of wedge beneath the door. It all happened so quickly. The screws had no way of getting in. Jerome hadn't realized it yet, but he had no way of getting out.

I've seen some severe beatings in my stay here, as well as in my prior days of hell raising on the outside. I've never seen such a beating as was administered to Jerome.

He stood up about the same time as Kevin finished blocking the door. Losing his temper was the worst thing that could have happened. He had no concept as to the gravity of the situation as he charged at Kevin. In his past fights and rumbles, charging like a bull had always been sufficient to get the job done. It was different this time.

The three of us inmates stood off to one side as the screws tried in vain to open the heavy door. When they saw that wasn't going to work, one stayed while the others ran out the front and around to enter through the side door. The three of us stood and watched through the wire mesh.

By the time they got there, Kevin was sitting calmly on a rolling cart, waiting patiently for them. For a moment, while the screws were breaking down the side door, I wondered if Kevin even realized how much trouble he was in. I'll never forget the smile on his face as he turned his head and looked at us.

The screw at the mesh door was still shouting. The others entered in a rush through the side door and one of them quickly grabbed Kevin. He twisted his arm behind his back to keep him restrained. The others took one look at Jerome and one of them ran to call the ambulance.

That event was the buzz of the day, week, and month. Hell, for the longest time, no one talked about anything else. The topic didn't change until the crap really hit the fan when Kevin was released from solitary about two weeks later.

I think it was Harold who was in the warden's office when it happened. He told us that after they got Kevin cleaned up, he was stood before warden Bastar.

The warden, at one time or other had insisted that each of us read to him from his big family bible that sat on a coffee table in his office. He was really proud of that bible.

Kevin had already been forced to read from it prior to being sent to solitary confinement. Reverend Bastard had insisted that it would give him something to think about over those next two weeks.

This time, as he stood there, Kevin looked him right in the eye. This was not a good thing to do. We were all forbidden to ever make eye contact with the warden.

Warden Bastar asked Kevin if he thought two weeks had been enough time to get close to the Lord. Harold says he remembers what happened nearly word for word.

"I appreciated this chance to get close to Jesus." Kevin's voice was a loud grating whisper. "Really I did."

Harold always laughs when he tells this next part.

"Just check and see." Kevin said. "Last time I was here I borrowed a few pages for later. I knew there wouldn't be any toilet paper in solitary. Know what? I wiped my ass all the way through the second half of first John."

Warden Bastar had never been known to personally strike an inmate before this. His temper flared. The screw had grabbed onto Kevin and it was easy for Reverend Bastard to backhand him across the face.

Harold say's that Bastar's face turned as white as a sheet when he opened his precious bible and turned to first John. Then his face turned beet red when he noticed that a bunch of pages had been ripped out.

Harold says the beating that Jerome was still getting over was nothing compared to what they did to Kevin. I guess Harold just backed himself as out of sight as he could in a corner, and just watched.

It all happened about the same time as those state police cars and a couple of outside pricks showed up. It's a good thing they did. Harold says that old Bastard would really have beaten Kevin to death.

The head screw had finally rushed in after hearing the commotion. I think he nearly lost his job over that deal. He was with those outside pricks that stormed the place. I guess it was him that pulled old Reverend Bastard off from Kevin. His temper got out of control too, when he was ordered to throw that unholy boy back into solitary.

I don't know exactly what happened next. Instead of doing as he was ordered, the head screw helped some other jerk put Reverend Bastard in handcuffs. Some one said that this prick actually worked for the feds or some such place as that. I only know that he did take charge. Harold says those screws were 'yes sir' this, and 'yes sir' that. Then he called for an ambulance.

We never heard whether Kevin died from that awful beating or not. Rumor says he did. They say he died in the hospital, in the next bed right beside Jerome. I shudder to think. The thought of that being true really sucks.

I like to think that he got over it and went on to some kind of normal life. I really can't think what a normal life for him would have been. Guys like us are damned and destined for hell. There's no doubt about it.

Someone said that a Judge from Bangor got Warden Bastar fired and locked up in a county jail somewhere. Hell, we'll never know for sure. The warden that replaced him was just another jerk. This one had a baldhead and we all referred to him as a talking prick with ears.

Harold says that he was watching as the ambulance attendants loaded Kevin onto a gurney there in the office. He was awake and the blood had been wiped off his face.

He swears that Kevin smiled at him.

PART SIX

Damned And Destined For Hell

Chapter Twelve

Hard Times

March 1964

Judge Palmer had raised more stink than anyone would have thought possible over the incidents that led up to Kevin Stone's disappearance. Detective Howard Smiley wound up right in the middle of it.

The Stone kid had disappeared the third week of November. Detective Smiley now agreed with Judge Palmer that he should have revoked the parents' custody sooner.

Although foul play was suspected, the parents were never informed. They were never told that he was missing. They thought that Kevin was once again living in foster care.

Palmer had made a few phones calls. The attorney general came down on him in person. He was all over Howard Smiley, like white on rice, even though he had followed procedures and done everything by the book.

He suppressed a smile as he thought that perhaps he should have reworded his comment. It had been a bad idea for him to suggest that what the Judge thought didn't make any difference.

He understood that Judge Palmer was acting in the boy's best interest. He grinned as he thought that had he been the Judge, he would have done no differently.

His first priority was to find that kid. He was anxious to meet him. Brett Miller seldom took such a personal interest in anyone involved in his casework. Howard knew Brett well and believed that there had to be something special about this one.

He wondered if Brett's opinion would change if he knew about Kevin's involvement in that heinous incident where a man had been beaten half to death and dragged for nearly a mile on a muddy woods road behind a pick up truck.

The local lawmen wouldn't say much about it, at least not to him. He could read between the lines. He was, after all, a detective.

Brett had never been able to get the kid to admit to seeing anything concerning the death of Jesse Bishop, but believed that the boy had witnessed the whole thing. Howard smiled, wondering if he would have any better luck.

Although the boy's testimony was still important, it made little difference now. Satterfield and Morgan were going down. There was no doubt about that.

The informant had been found. He would have expected Mark Page to be a little more careful in making that bank deposit. Fifty thousand dollars was a lot of money.

The damn fool had deposited it into his account, in person, all at once. The domino effect of that one act of stupidity had resulted in a three year long case being wrapped up in a matter of a few short weeks.

Mark Page had spilled his guts during his interrogation. Even with his lawyer present, he had been scared half to death. He had no doubt that what happened to Joel Bellinger and Nancy Mentor could also happen to him.

Satterfield, Morgan, and the ever-slippery Dr. Coleman had all been rounded up and were now facing new charges in an airtight case. It had been over three years since Brett Miller led the charge. Three years and this case was still pending.

The evidence was clear. It had been Dr. Coleman using his practice as a front that laundered most of the money from their operations. This deceitful bunch had cashed in on the misery of nearly every child that had been through his office.

Stan Morgan hadn't given up peacefully. The arresting officers had been forced to draw their weapons and put the cuffs on two of his trusted aids. Following their arrest, they had been taken to separate facilities.

It was the two henchmen who were singing like songbirds to the prosecution. They were gladly giving up Morgan in exchange for the promise of lighter sentences.

Perhaps the most surprising event had been John Morris trying to cut a deal. He was an unusual one. It turned out that he was a contract killer from Boston. He had come all unnerved after his arrest.

When the patrolman pulled Mr. Morris over, he had sat quietly in the front seat, holding the body of his dead partner. As it turned out, the late Mr. Dean was his half brother and a former guard who had worked closely with Stan Morgan at the boys' reform school.

He had been talking to the dead man, crying and shaking uncontrollably. When all was said and done, like Mark Page, he sang like a canary.

Detective Smiley and the local deputy had returned to the sheriff's office after getting the call over the radio. He had immediately called for more detail. It was his phone call to Brett Miller in Portland that led to Ray Satterfield's arrest.

Within the hour Brett Miller was in front of Ray Satterfield's house in downtown Portland. He had plenty of backup and an arrest warrant.

Satterfield had nearly eluded the authorities. Somehow he had received word of the highway patrol stop and arrest of John Morris within hours of it happening.

Detective Smiley tried to suppress a grin as he recalled his phone conversation with Brett. They had both laughed over the phone when Brett explained that if he had arrived only a few minutes later, Satterfield would most certainly be a Brazilian, or perhaps a Mexican by now.

His car had been running in the driveway, warming up, when they surrounded the place. He had a suitcase packed and a large gym bag stuffed full of cash when they made the arrest.

****

The state had decided to prosecute Stan Morgan and Ray Satterfield together. Two of the charges against them were capitol murder and conspiracy to commit murder.

Both were facing consecutive life sentences if convicted. The trial was set to begin the first week in March. They had hired one of the best defense teams in the country.

Despite the overwhelming amount of evidence against them, they were sure that they would beat most of the charges. Their lawyers were building a strong defense case.

It would be their word against Mark Page and John Morris. Their defense assured them that most of the testimony against them would be dismissed as hearsay evidence. On the first day they were ready for the trial to begin.

Morgan and Satterfield were confident that there would be no credible witness against them. They still had many contacts and all the friends that money could buy within the system.

They had already taken care of young Kevin Stone.

****

Kevin was a little surprised when he heard the sounds of the four-wheel drive truck approaching the camp. His first thought was to cut and run when he saw that it was a sheriff's vehicle. That thought quickly passed.

He figured that enough was enough. He hadn't seen anyone near the camp since shortly after Christmas break when someone had driven a snowmobile once around the clearing and skyrocketed out of there.

He knew it was time to face the music.

Maybe they'll send me back home.

Listen to me.

Damn! I just thought of something.

You're not listening.

What if old Bill is pissed?

Kevin walked outside and waited nervously as the deputy and Bill Riley got out. Bill was smiling broadly as he approached. Kevin remembered the deputy from that time he and Rory had been allowed to share the same jail cell.

He smiled, as they got close.

"Hey Bill, I was just getting ready to cook up a batch of biscuits. Your timing couldn't have been any better!"

Bill smiled and extended his hand, "It's good to see you Kevin. I'm glad you've been taking good care of the place."

"Come on in."

Deputy Stan Hawkins was in no hurry. He was a thin man with a wide toothy smile. He could stand to gain a little weight. The idea of fresh biscuits sounded good to him.

They talked and visited about lots of things as Kevin quickly made up his biscuit recipe. He put on a pot of water to boil. When it was ready, he made up some instant coffee. They were on their second cup when the biscuits were done.

"This is Gramp's secret recipe!" Kevin boasted. "I hope you like 'em."

"I've met old Gramps." Bill said. "In fact, we were out to your place earlier. He sure seems like a nice man."

They visited for a few minutes about Gramps as Kevin bragged on what a great woodsman he was. He was smiling the entire time. He hadn't thought much about it, but this was the first time in years that he had been able to remember all these good stories. He really liked Bill Riley and felt more at ease than he could remember.

"I know you guys have to take me back," he said. "It's okay, I've had enough of being on my own."

Stan smiled and asked, "Have you been down here the entire time? We've had a bulletin out on you since December."

"Yeah," Kevin answered, "Just here and school."

"What?" Bill cut in.

"Do you mean to tell us that you've been going to school all this time?" Stan asked.

"Haven't missed a day!" Kevin said proudly.

"Talk about hiding in plain sight!" Bill added.

"I'll be damned." Stan whistled softly. "Wait till Mrs. Hollis hears this." He laughed and looked at Kevin. "Me and Ralph have her half convinced that she has you mixed up with someone else! I'll be damned."

They took the time to straighten up a few things before leaving. Bill assured him not to worry. He was welcome there anytime. He jokingly said. "After all, you're living at my house and working for room and board." They laughed at his comment.

"One thing I do want you to know, Kevin," Bill continued, "If you get all this mess straightened out and need a place to stay, I will let you move in and help out. I know Ruth won't mind either."

The drive to town was a pleasant one. Bill insisted that they be dropped off at the shoe store. He told Stan, "We'll walk up to the courthouse in a few minutes."

Kevin didn't know what to say when Bill bought him a new pair of shoes and a complete change of new clothes. He carried everything in a sack to the courthouse. They both agreed that he needed to get a bath before putting them on.

It was decided over the phone that the state people would pick him up the next day around noon. Bill made arrangements with the magistrate for Kevin to stay the night at his house.

The rest of the day went by quickly. Bill's wife, Ruth, was a real nice lady. Kevin had met her several times before and liked her a lot. She cooked a nice dinner and they all enjoyed a pleasant evening.

The next morning Bill stopped by the barbershop with Kevin on their way to the courthouse. When he arrived dressed in new clothes and a very nice coat that Bill had given him, the magistrate smiled and said that he nearly hadn't recognized him.

Kevin said goodbye to Bill and whiled away the next hour or so in the sheriff's office. He was surprised when sheriff Bradley told him in a low tone, "Kevin, there is something you need to know."

"Yes Sir."

"The state people who are coming to pick you up aren't from Mayberry. Not like we try to be here."

"What do you mean?"

"These people go by a different set of rules than we do around here. I want you to keep that in mind, and try to keep your nose clean."

"Yes Sir."

Sheriff Bradley was still nervous over this whole deal. He remembered how the state attorneys had handled the situation dealing with Kevin's involvement in the Carl Williams case.

In his mind, those people were cannibals. He was still fuming over the fact that they had seriously considered prosecuting Kevin over that mess. Everyone knew Carl to be an animal, after what he did to his wife and daughter.

He had been in law enforcement for many years and believed in doing things with a more common sense approach. Sheriff Bradley wasn't the only one that thought Kevin should have been rewarded.

Ralph Hollis had also made it clear, as had the magistrate that there would be no charges against Kevin. He hoped those sharks from the state department would leave well enough alone.

The rules changed the day Kevin was picked up at the courthouse. The two men from Portland didn't say much as they started the drive back. Kevin made a point of trying to talk to them hoping that they would turn out to be more friendly than first impressions implied.

The driver was an older man with a gray moustache and an easy smile. He introduced himself as Mr. Noel. His partner was much younger and said his name was Mr. Smith.

Mr. Noel and Mr. Smith shook hands with Sheriff Bradley and assured him that the boy was going to be okay. They explained that they were in somewhat of a hurry. It was a long drive to Portland.

They waited until they crossed the county line before Mr. Noel pulled over and stopped the car. Mr. Smith got out and opened the rear door. He roughly placed Kevin in handcuffs and told him to shut to hell up.

Kevin's mind was spinning from the rough treatment when he came to a conclusion.

Those Judas sons a bitches!

You should have listened to me.

"Yeah, those Judas sons a bitches." He murmured.

"Who are you calling a son of bitch?" The man called Smith turned in his seat and raised his arm as if to strike Kevin. "You just sit there and keep your damn mouth shut!"

Kevin met his glare with a forlorn look. "They sold me out, didn't they?"

Smack! He was backhanded across the face.

The very essence of time and reality took on a new form. He was caught up in a turbulent system of black clouds and unbalancing forces. The static energy in the back of his mind started. This time it didn't stop.

The man in the front seat laughed and told the driver to take a quick look at the expression on Kevin's face. His voice sounded like he was talking through a long tube. Kevin slumped back in his seat.

The crap storm had just begun.

Those Judas sons a bitches.

Sorry.

After a few miles, his thoughts started to clear. He found out from listening that they weren't going to Portland after all. They were headed for the detention center in Brewer.

Kevin sat silently in the back seat, trying as best he could to get comfortable with his hands cuffed behind his back. The handcuffs were tight and cut into his wrists.

He was slowly getting a grip on his emotions. His cheek was bruised and his jaw hurt. He tried to think up a plan of escape as the miles went by.

The two in the front talked quietly at first. As the drive wore on, and Kevin remained silent, they soon acted as if he wasn't there.

Kevin had thought at first that the older man behind the wheel was the one in charge. As the miles went by, and they talked more openly, it became obvious that the younger man, Mr. Smith, was calling the shots.

The driver was worried over something to do with the paperwork. Kevin took advantage of their not paying attention to him and wriggled around in the back seat. In only a few seconds, he was sitting, slumped as before against the door, this time with his hands cuffed in the front. Neither man in the front seat seemed to notice.

Now that his hands were in front of him, Kevin waited his opportunity to say goodbye to these jerks. They were engrossed in their conversation when the car came to a stop at a yield sign. A car was approaching on the main road. That's when Kevin opened his door and bailed out.

He couldn't help himself as he shouted over his shoulder. "See you assholes later!"

"You son of a bitch!" Mr. Smith exclaimed as he tore out of the car after Kevin. "Stop! Right now!"

Their car was stopped at a rural intersection where the road across from them came out from under an old railroad trestle. The driver of the approaching car that they had stopped for sounded his horn and jammed on his brakes as Kevin darted across the road.

Mr. Noel remained in the car. He raised his eyebrows in an expression of surprise and Kevin reached the railroad trestle across the road and started climbing in his attempt to get away.

His worried expression turned into a smile as Mr. Smith caught up with the boy. He pulled him back to the ground after he had climbed only a few feet.

Kevin was roughly escorted back to the car. Mr. Smith had his hands full as Kevin twisted and squirmed to get away. He was cursing in anger as his hands were once again cuffed behind his back. This time Mr. Smith put a second set of cuffs around his ankles. As he had done before, he backhanded Kevin and told him to shut to hell up.

By the end of the third day Kevin was starting to figure things out. He was once again a guest at the detention facility in Brewer. He was in some kind of trouble all the time. His attitude towards those in charge was less than cooperative.

The staff psychiatrist labeled him as an escape risk, after reviewing his file. When Kevin yelled at him, referring to him as an asshole just like Dr. Coleman, he was labeled potentially violent. He fast tracked Kevin's commitment papers to the reform school in Thomaston.

Those in charge took everything very seriously; they had no sense of humor at all. He knew he had to get out of there. It wasn't at all like the last time. He was a young adult and they weren't taking any chances with him.

He was still locked up in a separate ward, but this time he had no freedoms at all. He was busted; there was no doubt about that. He never did find out what for, or even why. He wasn't allowed to ask questions. Anytime he tried, he just got himself deeper in trouble. He was advised to keep his mouth shut and do as he was told.

He had no idea at the time that someone had manipulated the paperwork. It was another colossal screw up that would eventually be traced back to the source and straightened out.

These people were simply going by the book and doing their jobs. The paperwork they had was proper. It was all in the paperwork. He had no say in the deal. He had no rights. He was a ward of the state.

The processing center for the boy's reform school was located at the county jail facility in Rockland. Kevin arrived there late in the afternoon. He was issued a change of clothes. His new attire consisted of a faded gray jacket, gray pants and a gray shirt. He was also fitted with a heavy pair of work boots.

Around seven the next morning they herded him onto an old school bus that had been painted blue. He had a sinking feeling in the pit of his stomach as the driver closed the heavy door that separated the passengers' compartment.

These recent events had happened so quickly that Kevin hadn't had a chance to make any kind of adjustment. He was off balance, still reeling since that first day when those two jerks had stopped the car and put the cuffs on him.

He was thinking that if those handcuffs hadn't been so tight he would have made it over that railroad trestle to freedom. He smiled thinking that had he succeeded those sorry bastards would still be looking for him.

The ride to the reform school lasted for about fifteen dismal minutes. Inside the bus it was nearly dark due to the painted windows and a heavy dark canvas that covered the wire mesh at the front.

When he stepped off the bus he had no idea where he was or what to expect. He stood looking calmly in the direction of several boys who were standing near a gate watching him. For some reason, it was at that moment that he remembered the punch line to Mr. Bishop's joke.

Where's that whore with the abscessed tooth?

He smiled ear to ear as he tried not to laugh.

It was part of the warden Bastar's policy to personally meet and address each new arrival. He believed that he had the insight to tell the difference between those who were worth saving and those who were not.

He had allowed most of the corrections staff to retain their rank and positions since he took over the daily operations. He believed the corrections Captains and those with decision-making power were all closely aligned with his philosophy. Most went along with his administration style and claimed to share his beliefs in harsh punishment.

Kevin knew from the start that warden Bastar was a real psycho. He obviously had a few screws loose. Kevin was taken into his office after his initial orientation.

The guards had explained the rules, especially the one about cursing, in no uncertain manner. He listened to their advice. He was adjusting. Slowly but surely, he was starting to take it all in stride.

Hell, this isn't so bad.

Compared to what?

It was warden Bastar that had him worried. He was wearing a white collar and a black shirt when they met. He had the appearance of some kind of priest.

Warden Bastar proudly explained that he was an ordained minister. The first thing he did was make Kevin put his hand on a large family bible that sat on a coffee table in front of his desk. He placed his hand over Kevin's and prayed for him.

Son of a bitch.

He really thinks he talks to God.

When the warden was finished praying, he noticed that Kevin had a smirk on his face. He instructed one to the guards to remove it. He did.

Kevin had been slapped around before, and took it quite well. He picked himself up off the floor and stood at attention as ordered, head bowed, staring at the floor.

I know girls that hit harder than that.

Amen.

The corrections officer who led him to the dorm area was a giant of a man. His nametag identified him as Manning. They were making their way up the stairs of the main dorm building for campus B.

"You remember the basic rules and we'll get along fine." He was escorting him with a firm grip on Kevin's shoulder.

"Yes, Sir." Kevin said. He sensed a tone of kindness in the guards' voice.

He was immediately picked up and slammed against a wall. The guard had a grip on his shirtfront. He easily held Kevin against the wall with one hand. Kevin was scared crapless as the guard snarled.

"I ain't a damned Sir!"

Kevin's heart was racing with fear. This prick reminded him of Carl Williams. His unshaven face and dark hair made him appear ominous as he added. "You will address me as Boss Manny. You got that!"

"Yes, Boss Manny." Kevin gasped.

"You new pricks are always the ones that cause us the most trouble." He let go of Kevin's shirtfront and stepped back. "Are you getting all this?"

"Yes Boss."

"Captain Stevens and the Warden expect me and Boss Sorenson to teach you how things are run around here." Boss Manny angrily grabbed onto his shirtfront and picked him up again, slamming him into the wall.

"Do you understand me? Maggot!?"

"Yes, Boss."

The guard relaxed his grip a little and then slammed Kevin against the wall again. "Don't you even think about embarrassing me! Have I made my point?"

"Yes, Boss." Kevin rasped.

Boss Manny released his grip. He jerked Kevin around and herded him towards the stairs. He followed close behind and showed Kevin to his bunk.

"Just follow these guys to the mess hall." He said.

"Yes, Boss."

Boss Manny snarled at several of the other boys who were standing at attention at the end of their bunks, hoping that he wouldn't notice them.

"I'll leave it up to you little pricks to explain the rules to this maggot. Now hurry to hell up. You don't want to be late. Tonight they're feeding you undeserving maggots fish. The warden won't abide any late comers."

Kevin's head was spinning as he followed the others to his first experience in the mess hall.

What a prick.

So much for kindness.

Hell, maybe he just likes slamming people against walls.

Don't laugh, asshole. That hurt.

Chapter Thirteen

Time Out

Kevin was thrown in to the general population at the end of the second day. His first night had been really rough. He had made the mistake of talking at the dinner table while Warden Bastar was saying grace.

He figured things out quickly. The guards were to be addressed as boss. They were referred to as screws behind their backs, and the young trustees were 'screws bitches.' The prick that got him in trouble was a 'bitch' named Jerome.

He had been roughly escorted from the dining area and placed in a cage that had been built on a cement slab a short distance from a small building. At one time it had been used as an incinerator to burn trash.

Now they used this charred, wire link enclosure to cool off the troublemakers. He was forced to strip. Then one of the screws roughly herded him inside the cage.

Jerome was smiling as he approached dragging a length of fire hose that had been neatly coiled on the wall inside the small building.

"Hey tough guy." He said in a nasty tone. "Want some soap?" Jerome turned the hose on and kept it turned all the way on as he knocked Kevin off his feet with the powerful blast.

Kevin's temper flared. *Don't let it show.* He tried to get a grip on his emotions.

Hell this isn't so bad.

Don't you need a bath anyhow?

Crap! This water is cold.

No colder than taking a bath in the spring at camp.

Kevin's smile made him appear to be on the edge of insanity as he got up and held onto the wire mesh of the cage. He raised first one arm then the other as he turned around slowly.

"Hey bitch!" He yelled, "This is so cool! Be sure to get under this arm." He was laughing, almost hysterically. The screw also started laughing as he watched.

"Be sure to get my ass!" Kevin yelled between fits of laughter, "I want it nice and clean for when you kiss it."

He thought Jerome was going to blow a fuse when the screw turned off the water.

"Enough for now," the screw said. He opened the door and instructed Kevin to get dressed. Jerome was sent back inside. He stormed off muttering to himself.

The screw led Kevin to an isolation cell and locked him in. It was a caged area in one corner of another small building. There was no cot, only a ragged wool blanket to wrap up in.

Kevin decided that he should take Jerome very seriously. He was one cruel bitch. He reminded him of 'poor Greg' from back home. He knew that Jerome was going to make life a living hell for him if he could.

He sat wrapped in the blanket with his back against the wall. His thoughts were of escape. He knew that he had to get out of here. After what seemed like forever, he drifted off to sleep.

The next morning Kevin was still sitting against the wall, wrapped in the blanket, when Jerome and another bitch stopped by to taunt him.

Now he knew to whom Jerome had referred when he had whispered at the dinner table that Casey was scared crapless of him. Kevin looked up and smiled as he recognized Casey McGinn.

His mind flooded with memories as they approached. He felt a moment of panic as he recalled the incident, long ago, when Casey had kicked him squarely in the face while his cousins had been holding him.

Those cruel bastards had nearly beaten him to death that time and they had gotten away with it.

The feeling of panic was instantly replaced with one of triumph as he recalled kicking the crap out of Casey when he had evened the score.

He smiled as he remembered how Casey had begged and pleaded for mercy when he had set things right. He nearly burst out laughing as he pictured Casey covered in blood and manure. He could still hear him, clear as day, saying; 'I'm sorry.'

It's a small world.

Who would have thought that jerk would be here?

Remember? The bigger those jerks are.

The harder they fall.

He wasn't afraid as Jerome neared the cage. Casey stayed behind Jerome as he asked how he liked his first night.

"It wasn't that bad!" Kevin said with a smile. He looked past Jerome and said. "Hey Casey, you still got that snake bite on your ass?"

Jerome's face took on a look of confusion as Casey nearly choked as he replied, "I'm sorry!" He turned and nearly ran outside.

Jerome put his face up to the wire mesh and told Kevin in a hateful tone, "You'll get yours, you little prick."

Kevin's grating whisper caused a cold shiver to go up and down his spine.

"You and that other bitch may work for the warden, and the warden may work for God." Kevin approached to within inches of the cage.

"Did you know that, Jerome? The warden really works for the Lord Jesus. Just ask him."

He looked Jerome in the eye. "Ask Casey who he thinks I work for."

Jerome took several steps back. He couldn't match Kevin's fanatical stare.

"You're one crazy bastard!" He murmured.

"They say that Christ returned. Bitch. Ask Casey what he thinks of my return."

Jerome quickly turned and walked outside to regain his composure.

By the time Kevin was led back to the dorm area at the end of the second day, he was exhausted. The day had started with his confrontation with those two bitches, followed by another daylong indoctrination by the head screw.

These bastards are mean.

Kind of like Carl?

Crap.

This ain't nothing.

He was asleep within minutes of climbing onto the mattress on the top bunk. He was oblivious to the taunting that was going on around him. It was actually a comfortable mattress. He went right to sleep.

The Guardians

He could hear the taunting going on around him, even after he went to sleep. The voices were all mingled with each other and nothing made sense. He smiled as he lay on his side and drifted further into the land of dreams.

He felt a gentle touch, as though someone was stroking his temples and forehead. The peaceful feeling was one he hadn't felt in a long time.

He opened his eyes with a feeling of anticipation. He was alone in a beautiful green field. The color of the grass was brilliant, almost as if it were glowing. It felt cool and soothing beneath his bare feet.

In looking around, he wondered where he was. He thought he was awake, but knew that this place wasn't real. His mind was working, he was thinking clearly. The sensation of being somewhere between awake and asleep was a welcome one.

The rolling fields went on forever, ablaze with flowers and all sorts of brilliant colors. The scent of the nice spring day caused him to smile. He walked slowly, occasionally reaching down to pull a handful of grass. He slowly released his grip and watched the blades of grass blow away gently in the warm breeze.

As he neared the top of a small knoll, he sensed that he wasn't alone. He stopped and watched in awe as two familiar figures once again appeared. This time he knew they heard him as he called their names.

Shep nearly bowled him over as he excitedly brushed against him. Collie was a bit more reserved, and sat patiently as Kevin playfully wrestled on the ground with Shep. When her turn came, she too was full of fun and play.

The dogs playfully chased each other and him as he ran laughing through the meadow. He could hear his own laughter as he fell and rolled in the lush grass.

The afternoon sun was warm as he lay contentedly with his head on Shep, scratching Collie's ears. Shep was his pillow and lay stretched out with his paws crossed, panting. Kevin playfully pushed Collie away and Shep barked each time she would playfully rush onto both he and his boy.

It was a good dream. Kevin was relaxed, happy and secure in the moment. He sensed that they weren't alone. He was resting with his head on Shep; Collie had her head in his lap. A shadow crossed his face. He opened his eyes a little not knowing what to expect. His peaceful mood and feeling of tranquility caused him to welcome the sight of two strangers.

A woman wearing a beautiful white dress was standing before him. She was the most beautiful woman he had ever seen. His eyes opened wide as she stood smiling at him. The sunlight was behind her, causing her hair to appear as if it were made of pure light.

He stood up slowly. Shep shifted his position to sit by his side. Collie took her station on the opposite side. Kevin smiled at the newcomer. Then he smiled at her companion, another very pretty young woman who was standing at her side. She was also garbed in a beautiful dress. The afternoon sun appeared to be alive in the glow of her face and hair. Her smile was stunning.

The woman in the white dress spoke first.

"Hi Kevin." Her voice was soft. She had the softest, sweetest voice he had ever heard. She smiled. "I hope you're not afraid of us."

Kevin didn't dare speak. He knew his heart was racing, but it wasn't from fear. He instinctively knew who they were. He had seen glimpses of them in several dreams and nightmares. He didn't answer. He was afraid that to do so would cause him to wake up.

The second lady spoke. She looked first at the dogs, then at him. She said, "They wanted to say goodbye."

He knew that if he spoke he would awake. He slowly stepped forward, and stood between them. He hugged them gently and whispered. "Thank you."

For a while there was only serene darkness. The kind that can only be found in peaceful sleep. The feeling was interrupted as he felt a backwards momentum. He looked up and watched them walk out of sight over a small rise in the field. The dogs were playfully dashing back and forth between them.

From over his shoulder he heard a voice say, "We are with you, always." It was a beautiful voice.

He turned to face the sound. This time he did gasp in fear. Uncle Rick was standing before him, not ten feet away. He was standing with his hands on his hips. His face was grotesque.

Behind him were hordes of similar figures. All dressed in dark garb, all reeking of pure evil.

His heart was racing as he spun around to warn the two guardians. Once again he gasped! His heart was racing. The green field was gone, replaced with an expanse of wasteland as far as he could see. Wisps of smoke were everywhere. The stench was nauseating.

He felt a hand firmly grip his shoulder. The words were repeated. "We are with you, always." This time they sounded as if they were spoken from the depths of hell.

He spun back around in time to see Uncle Rick's image fade away in a wave of dismal color. Like a reflection driven from a clear pool of water by the splash of a stone, it vanished. As the ripples stopped, he could see his own reflection. Once again, he caught himself gasping for breath.

One side of his face glowed softly with an amber radiance. When he turned his head the other side of his face was gnarled and twisted, blackened by pure evil and contorted in an expression of hatred.

He awoke with a start.

He sat up in bed and looked around. In the dim light that came in through the windows from the security light outside, he remembered where he was. He shrugged his shoulders and went back to sleep.

It wasn't long until one of the screws bitches was walking down the center aisle, banging on the bed frames and shouting for everyone to get to hell up.

Chapter Fourteen

Stone Chapel

The dense fog rolled in off the ocean sometime just before sunrise. It was one of those early morning fogs that cloaked their world in a damp blanket of gloom and despair. Visibility was limited. From the central formation area, the buildings on the west side appeared as ghostly shadows.

Kevin stood at attention along with the rest. They all stood silently, eyes straight ahead, as the screw paced back and forth. He called out each name as he paced from one end of the front line of boys to the other.

The scene was similar to that of a military boot camp. They were all dressed the same in their uniforms of faded gray shirts and pants. They all wore the same heavy work boots and gray work jackets. It could have been a scene from an old confederate war movie.

The screw with the clipboard screamed each name, hoping that someone would fail to answer loud and clear. That's when the harassment would begin.

There were several dozen of them. They were standing in a formation three rows deep. After roll call there would be about a half hour of physical exercise, then the line for the mess hall and breakfast.

Kevin had learned from the start to play by the rules. If he was told to do pushups, he did pushups. If he was ordered to low crawl across the parade ground, he low crawled. It wasn't long before he was just another face in an ever-growing population of wayward souls.

The bitches in charge of the morning's exercises usually made only a halfhearted attempt. Unless there was someone to single out for humiliation, it was just a matter of enduring until it was time for chow.

Before turning them over to the bitches, the screw asked for volunteers. He explained that a work crew from the main prison was renovating the old maximum-security facility. Extra help was needed in cleaning up the debris. When that was finished, they would be required to report as usual for their work assignment in the shoe shop.

Kevin understood the basic rule of never volunteering to these people for anything. The thought of working somewhere other than the shoe shop appealed to him. He knew better than to speak up, but he also knew how to be picked. He made eye contact with the screw. That was generally all it took to get these crap assignments.

He was singled out along with three others. He knew Brian and another boy, Raymond. The fourth one was a really big young man named Alex. He was seventeen and stood over six feet tall. He was a good-natured type and didn't mind being picked. To their surprise, they were allowed to skip exercise and go straight to the chow line.

After chow, they were lined up and marched in single file behind a work crew leader from the main prison. A screw accompanied them, leading the way through a maze of locked gates and high fences.

In the dense fog, the gray stone structure appeared to be a living, breathing thing. Gaping holes in the roof and broken out windows on the upper floors gave it an ominous appearance. Pigeons were flying in and out of the openings, almost daring them to come closer.

As they neared the old building, Kevin was nearly overcome with panic. As they filed in silence through heavy oak doors, he remembered that he had been there before.

The head trustee from the men's prison turned out to be a real decent type. He was a tall heavyset man, determined to make parole soon. As leader of the honor work crew, he wanted to get the job done right.

They were lined up with their backs to the main cellblock wall when he started speaking.

"Names make little difference here." He said. "As long as you show respect, you can call me Big Jim."

He eyed each of the boys as he said, "This job should last for about a week." His no nonsense approach was impressive as he explained the job.

"We need to have this main cell block cleaned up spic and span by the end of the week. I can't get it done without you." He was the first taskmaster in a long time that wasn't shouting and intimidating them. His smile told them that this was going to be good work duty.

"Keep your act together." He cautioned, "Never forget; I'm an inmate, just like you. Show respect for the bosses and we'll all get along fine."

He looked at Kevin. "I need a high speed equipment operator and someone who can drive a truck." He smiled again. For the first time in what seemed liked ages, Kevin smiled back at someone. He stood silently at attention in acknowledgment that he had been picked.

Kevin was the youngest one there. The other boys were all seventeen and eighteen years old. He was awarded the position of high-speed equipment operator. He was given a large push broom and assigned to sweeping out the cells in the main cellblock.

Brian was the truck driver. His job was to drive the wheelbarrow down the cellblock aisle and up the ramp to a dump truck that had been backed up to the main entry steps.

The cleanup job was to last for a week. They were marched back to the main compound each day around noon. They were still required to meet their quotas at the shoe shop, and sometimes the nights were really short.

Still, it was a welcome relief for all of them. There were no screaming bitches on their backs, nothing to worry about other than impressing their new boss.

The second day, Kevin was on his hands and knees, scooping debris out from under the metal cot frames attached to the concrete walls of the cells. He heard Brian comment. "Hey, look what I found."

He was still on his hands and knees when he stuck his head outside the door to see what had Brian's attention.

He was showing Alex a small leather bound diary.

"It was stuck up under the springs." Brian said.

As he passed it to Alex, he heard Kevin exclaim, "That's mine!" His eyes went round in surprise as Kevin nearly flew across the wide aisle as he tackled Alex.

Big Jim rushed down the corridor at the sounds of the disturbance. Brian had backed up against the wall and stood watching. Alex had Kevin pinned to the floor with his weight. Kevin was cursing incessantly.

He didn't raise his voice. He was hoping that the screw hadn't heard. "Knock it off!" He exclaimed as he grabbed onto Alex. He roughly got the bigger boy off from the smaller one. Alex immediately stood with his back against the wall. His nose was bleeding and he had a confused look on his face.

"What to hell happened?" Jim asked in an intense whisper. "Do you fools want to get us all in trouble?"

Alex sounded incredulous as he asked, "What to hell got into you, Kevin?" He looked at Big Jim. "I wasn't doing nothing and he just lit into me."

Kevin's voice was panicked as he said, "It's mine. Damn it. I want it back." His stream of cursing and profanity caused these hardened individuals to involuntarily take another step back.

"What's yours?" Jim asked.

"He thinks that book is his." Brian said. "I found it under a bed spring." He sensed that Kevin was about to go completely off the deep end. Trying to defuse the situation, he added, "I'm glad I gave it to Alex when I did."

His comment caused Alex to grin.

"What do you mean yours?" Jim asked as he picked up the small book. "How could anything found over here belong to you?"

"I used to live here." Kevin's voice was still breaking as he sat with his back to the wall, hugging his knees. "I don't want anyone else to read it. I need to throw it away."

"We'll just see." Big Jim opened the book and read aloud the writing on the first page. "'To our new friend Kevin. Welcome to our home.'"

He paused and gazed at Kevin. He was remembering a story he had heard about a boy who had supposedly died over here nearly four years ago. He asked. "What do you mean, you used to live here?"

Kevin offered no reply. He sat staring blankly at the opposite wall.

"Well?"

Kevin's voice was a whisper. "I lived right there, in that room." His baleful look caused Big Jim to shudder as he added, "Until my mom came right here and got me."

"Your Mom?"

"She came right here and got me."

"I'll be damned!" Big Jim murmured. His eyes narrowed as he read Kevin's name in the front of the book.

He stood thumbing through it for a few minutes while Brian and Alex watched in silence. The stub of a pencil was still in its holder. The book was completely filled with the same paragraph, written over and over again. He gasped when he thumbed his way to the last page.

"My God." He murmured. "It is you." He closed the book. "I thought it was all a story."

Alex and Brian stood silently. Neither had any idea of what was going on.

Kevin slowly stood up as Big Jim passed the book back to him. "Here kid. This really is yours."

His expression was somber. As Kevin took the book from him he added, "Do whatever you want with it."

Brian and Alex watched in amazement. Whatever Big Jim had read on those pages had affected him. His face was as white as a sheet.

"I'm sorry Kevin." Alex said. "I didn't mean for you to be mad at me."

"Me neither." Brian said.

Kevin's mood changed instantly. It was almost frightening as he smiled and answered. "No problem."

They went back to work, careful not to disturb the boy who tore each sheet, one by one, into small pieces and crumpled them into the wheelbarrow.

It wasn't your mom.

I know that now.

The rest of the week went by quickly. Shortly after the incident with Kevin, Brian noticed Big Jim talking to the screw in charge. After that, they were all treated with a new kind of respect. He never did figure out why.

****

As the weeks dragged on, detective Howard Smiley became more determined than ever to find the Stone boy. He had checked out every possible avenue of investigation, to no avail.

He knew that the trail started at Sheriff Bradley's office. They were the last ones who had seen young Kevin. He doubted that they were keeping anything from him.

It was surprising that there was no state report or documentation to substantiate the local sheriff's story. No paperwork at all. There was nothing that could be verified from social services.

Kevin had been released to two men who had identified themselves as being from the central office in Portland. They had left no paperwork behind, only a handshake and sincere thank you to the sheriff.

Howard was starting to suspect that perhaps it was another shell game. He was hoping that it would turn out to be effort on behalf of those in the upper chain of command to keep the boy hidden. It was with this angle of investigation in mind that he set up an appointment with Judge Palmer in Bangor.

He realized that he needed to walk on eggshells around Palmer. He had inadvertently crossed him only a short time ago, and now he needed his assistance.

The meeting went about as good as he had expected. The Judge was still upset with him and offered little help. Smiley came away knowing that there was no way that the Judge had arranged for Kevin to be out of sight.

It was nearly two months after his disappearance that Detective Smiley received an anonymous phone call. Within hours, he found the paper trail.

****

Warden Ellis Bastar was a fire and brimstone preacher with a college degree in psychology. He had started his career in another state as a guidance counselor in a big city youth correctional facility.

He had served the same facility as assistant warden for nearly ten years. He was as qualified as they came when he sent out his resume for this position.

Control of the boys' reform school had recently been shifted to the department of corrections. The social services people had failed miserably in running things. The shakeup had opened the door to try new ideas.

His methods of converting those lost souls to Christianity had failed miserably in the past. He knew it was all due to the fact that he had never been the one in charge.

Now, with the Lord on his side, he was determined to rehabilitate these young dregs of society. He was a true believer in harsh discipline. There was no room for failure, not in his book.

He had many expected obstacles to overcome. The first and foremost one had been in the quality of the hired help. For the most part, the guards and office staff personnel didn't share his zealous approach.

Within a week of taking on this new job, he had fired several employees and disciplined several others. This set the example for those who remained.

His first rule was that there was to be no cursing or taking of the Lord's name in vain at his facility. Most everyone went along with that and he enforced this rule with a vengeance.

He presided over evening mess two or three times a week. It was the only time he came into contact with the inmate population. His table was screened off from the main part of the dining area by a heavy wire mesh. The long table, with room for the guards, sat on a narrow raised platform. He insisted on saying the blessing at each meal.

His table was served with a higher quality of food than that fed to the inmates. The guards dined with him while the young trustees maintained a vigil over the other inmates in the dining area.

He gave credit and thanks to his God for nearly everything. He believed that the awesome profit from the shoe shop was indeed a blessing. His bank account was growing more impressive each month. This helped to offset his somewhat pathetic salary.

With the board's approval, he had allowed his brother in law to set up the shoe production area as a means of rehabilitating those inmates who had few job skills. The fields of training included production, maintenance, and quality control.

When the board approved the initial setup, it had been with the understanding that all profits were to be spent on inmate rehabilitation. The money was to be used to buy books and supplies for the school. Each worker was to be paid a token wage as an incentive.

This arrangement worked flawlessly. After deducting for operating expenses, there was always a profit to show to the board. They were impressed and often cited his operation as a model example of prisoner rehabilitation.

They knew that the wardens' brother in law also took care of the paperwork. What the board didn't know was that he maintained two sets of books.

Warden Bastar's office also maintained a close relationship with the local military recruiters. The war in Vietnam was in full swing, and often his young wards were offered early release incentives for enlisting. It was another area of praise and accomplishment on behalf of the new program.

The warden's boys were already well disciplined by the time they got to military boot camp. It was another arrangement that worked really well.

****

Warden Bastar wasn't too concerned the day he received a conference call from Judge Palmer in Bangor and a detective from the Attorney Generals office.

They informed him that there had been a mistake made in sending the Stone inmate to his facility.

He brought them up to date on the latest happenings concerning the boy in question. He assured them that paperwork or not, this one deserved to be there.

Despite all that he told them, he was asked to have the boy ready for pick up around five the next day. The judge assured him that he had taken care of the legal work.

He smiled into the phone as he assured those on the other end that young Kevin would be standing tall and proud when they showed up to get him.

He angrily instructed his assistant warden to leave the boy in solitary until the next morning. There would be plenty of time to get him cleaned up and ready then.

Chapter Fifteen

Salvation

The education administered to the inmates was at best, a real joke. The first three days of the week, the younger inmates were required to sit in a classroom while the teachers droned on.

Most everyone looked forward to Sundays. That was generally thought of as a day off. The choices were few. If an inmate wanted, he was allowed to attend services that started at nine in the morning and lasted until noon chow.

There were several chaplains in the prisons' cadre of religious counselors. This meant that they got to listen to something other than the fire and brimstone raving of the esteemed Reverend Bastard.

Kevin told them that he was Catholic. Those services were much easier for him to stomach. Unless he was under fire for something, he never missed a Sunday.

The state had minimum rules and requirements for rehabilitation and education that were reluctantly met. The state made only a token effort in assuring even a basic education for these youthful dregs of society. The general philosophy was that these boys were there to be punished, nothing else.

Warden Bastar delivered a raging sermon to them each Wednesday afternoon. Kevin often marveled at how 'Reverend Bastard' really acted as though he thought that he was some kind of messenger of the Lord.

The second three days of each week were what could only be described as slave labor. Although the officials insisted that it was a combination of rehabilitation and on the job training, there was no denying the sheer meanness of those in charge.

There was a new warehouse building on the north end of the reform school compound. It was a shoe shop with all of the equipment necessary to make quality shoes.

They were required to work three ten-hour days each week. Each inmate trainee was expected to make his quota or there was hell to pay. The equipment often ran twenty-four hours a day.

The schedules were usually staggered for the younger inmates. Half of them worked the first three days of the week, and attended school the next three, while the others were rotated to the work area.

It was an awesome profit center for warden Bastar and his cronies. Some of the older inmates were required to work twelve to sixteen hour days, six days a week.

Kevin had only worked there a few days before he decided that he hated every minute of it. His thoughts were always of escape. He refused to give up. There had to be a way out.

It was about his fifth or sixth week that he did get out. Not really the way he had hoped, but out just the same.

The routine was one that he adjusted to quickly. There were a lot of inmates and he quickly became just another number. He kept his head down and did as he was told.

Boss Manny and Boss Sorenson were easy enough to get along with once he figured them out. Sorenson was kind of quiet and let the bitches do most of the screaming and yelling. Boss Manny was always in someone's face.

Kevin kept in mind the treatment he had received from Boss Manny his first day. They were a tough pair and Kevin soon learned the ropes on how to avoid being noticed. He shied away from Boss Sorenson as much as he could.

Kevin had made a point of not getting close to anyone. He was determined to mind his own business. He believed that eventually someone would tell him why he was there and when he could expect to be released. Until he could find a way to escape, he planned on enduring as best he could.

He never did exchange words with Casey McGinn after that first morning. Casey stayed away from him. Rumors had started and most of the older kids left him alone as well. The only problem was that prick, Jerome.

An eighteen-year-old named Brian had befriended him that first week. Brian was quietly serving out his three-year sentence and was hoping to be released soon. He had recently turned down an offer of early release in exchange for joining the military.

Brian also hated Jerome, as well as most of the screws and their bitches. He maintained a low profile, not wanting anything to happen to screw up his chances for release. This scrawny new comer took his advice seriously and adapted quickly.

Although Kevin considered Brian and a couple others to be friends, he didn't count on any of them watching his back. After the incident at the stone chapel several of those inmates who had harassed him in the past, started cutting him a little more slack.

Apparently, Brian viewed himself as some kind of mentor. He was always giving Kevin advice. A few days after the extra duty at the stone chapel was over, he had a quiet talk with Kevin.

"One thing to remember." He said. "You've got to take what ever they dish out."

"I guess." Kevin murmured.

"If they say jump, don't even ask how high. Just jump."

Kevin smiled at him. "Out of all the pricks in here, you seem to be the nicest one. What's your angle?"

"I don't want nothing from you, if that's what you mean." Brian answered. He was starting to feel uncomfortable.

"Then what? You'd be better off giving me crap like the others. It would put you on the good side of Jerome."

Brian's answer made the hair on the back of Kevin's neck stand up as he said.

"Remember? I was there at the chapel with you. I don't want to end up getting my throat cut while I'm sleeping." His voice was a trembling whisper as he added, "Big Jim told me what was written on those pages."

Kevin's face was ashen as he walked away.

Don't you remember?

I don't want to.

It wasn't you anyway.

Meaning what?

It was me. I wrote everything.

His main cause for concern was still Jerome. His pride had been severely injured by Kevin and he wasn't about to let it go. Whenever their paths crossed, he went out of his way to provoke and harass Kevin.

Sometimes he would nail him in the back of his head with an open palm. He was always assigning him to the dirtiest of chores. Brian marveled at how this new kid just shrugged everything off and carried on.

Jerome seldom bothered Kevin face to face. Even though he was much bigger than Kevin, he was about as cowardly as they came. Casey wouldn't tell him why he was so terrified of Kevin, and after awhile, he forgot about being careful around him. It was in the laundry room that he made his first big mistake.

Kevin and several others had been assigned to laundry. It was a chore that generally lasted until well after midnight. They were required to stay until the last of the work was done before being allowed back to the dorm.

There was another fourteen year old who was in the same dorm as Kevin. The bitches had targeted him from the start. This kid was trouble. He had a genuine mean streak. Rumor had it that the warden had ordered extra harsh treatment for him. He just couldn't keep his mouth shut.

The kid's name was Martin. Jerome made a point out of harassing him. He was easily riled and anytime he lost his temper, the screws would drag him away. He spent more cycles in two day solitary than anyone else.

This night, Martin was running the laundry presses. Jerome and another cruel bitch named Oliver were hassling him. They were taunting him when he predictably lost his temper. Realizing that he was about to be awarded with another stretch in solitary, he begged pitifully to Jerome.

"Please! I won't do it again. I'm sorry!"

The screw in charge came over to see what all the fuss was about. Kevin could see from where he was standing. A feeling of anger came over him as he realized that Martin had reached his breaking point.

Martin's biggest mistake was grabbing onto the screw and begging for mercy. Kevin watched silently as they slapped the snot out of young Martin.

Serves the little jerk right.

Maybe.

Jerome noticed that he had stopped working to watch.

"Hey boss, look over there. Is it okay if we take a few minutes and adjust his attitude?"

The screw looked down at Martin who was curled up on the floor, sobbing and begging. He grabbed him by his collar and started dragging him down the aisle towards the front door. He grinned and called over his shoulder. "I don't see a thing boys."

It didn't go exactly as Jerome and Oliver had hoped. Kevin had disappeared behind the soaking tubs. They split up and rushed to the rear of the room. Neither saw Kevin as he ducked under the counters and dashed towards the door.

The guard had just reached the door on the other end of the building. He was in the process of dragging Martin through it, when Kevin dashed around the presses.

"I'll help you boss!" He said loudly.

The screw that was standing outside held the door as Kevin grabbed onto Martin's feet. He laughed at Kevin's willingness to help carry Martin outside.

Behind them, Jerome and Oliver were cursing. Both screws laughed at them and ordered Kevin back to work.

Heat and hot water for the reform school was provided by an outdated, coal fired boiler. It was located in one of the older brick buildings in the basement below the laundry facilities.

One end of the basement was walled off with cement blocks. A thick metal door opened to the area that was home to the solitary confinement suites.

At the other end of the area, a set of concrete stairs led to another metal door that provided outside access to the cellblock area. The short corridor was usually damp from water draining from the boiler room. It was an area to which little time was allocated to cleanliness.

The small cells had seen an enormous increase in use since Warden Bastar took over. His harsh methods of discipline included what he referred to as time out for the boys to get close to the Lord.

Each inmate was given two meals a day and a new slop bucket. Often, in the confined space, the slop bucket would overturn and as a result, the stench in that small area was nearly overwhelming.

The maximum stretch allowed by state law was forty-eight hours per confinement. Each incident was to be reported, each inmate incarcerated there was to receive a medical examination upon release.

These rules created a lot of record keeping. The officials at the school kept each stay to just under the forty-eight hour time limit. It kept the paperwork simple.

Young Martin was returned to the dorm area after his two-day stretch in solitary. He walked resignedly towards his bunk. He had been hosed down in the incinerator cage, and looked as if he had just stepped out of the shower.

No one had any noticeable sympathy for him as he slowly walked down the corridor between the rows of bunk beds. He was carrying his blankets as he quietly made his way to his bunk.

Kevin couldn't help but feel pity for Martin. Even here, in this crap hole, there was a certain sense of camaraderie amongst the inmates. There were times when they had to stick together, especially in alliance against the screws and bitches.

He was lying stretched out on his stomach on his top bunk with his chin resting on his forearms. He watched quietly for a moment as Martin started making up his bed.

"I saw what happened Martin." Kevin said in a quiet tone. "That damn Jerome and his faggot buddy set you up."

Martin looked at him with an expression of surprise. This was the first time he could recall that someone had taken his side.

"They'll get theirs." He muttered.

"You've just got to learn to play the game." Kevin insisted. "Every time they want to mess with you, they just get you to lose your temper."

"What to hell do you know about it? Besides, I've seen them knock you around too." Martin's temper had flared, making Kevin's point. He was rude. Even towards someone who was trying to be decent to him.

Another boy cut in.

"We all get knocked around. You just need to learn to keep your damn mouth shut."

Martin turned towards him in anger. As he was about to reply heatedly he noticed Kevin smiling and holding a finger in front of his lips.

"Shush." Kevin whispered. "This is what we mean."

A couple others joined in the conversation. One said, "Martin, my boy. You make yourself an easy target." He grinned and craned his neck to see around the corner of the bunk to check if any screws or bitches could over hear.

Seeing that the coast was clear, he added, "Those kiss ass pricks will never let up on you until you learn to do what this new guy does." He nodded towards Kevin. "You've got to take their crap and carry on."

Kevin interrupted with a remark that caused several of them to burst out laughing.

"Gramps taught me that lesson a long time ago. Sometimes you've got no choice when people dish it out." His serious tone held their interest. His gaze shifted from Martin to several of the others. "He says that 'you've got to learn to eat a ton of crap just to get through life.'" His voice lowered as he added, "But then he told me, 'Don't you ever learn to like the taste of it!'"

Martin sat down on the edge of the lower bunk. He had no reaction to the humor of Kevin's remark. The same look was on his face that Kevin had witnessed in the laundry. It was that hopeless look of despair.

"Are you just trying to get sent to the psyche ward?" Kevin asked. "Or do you really like getting slapped around? It makes little difference to the people around here."

Another boy added, "Old Reverend Bastard's idea of psyche treatment is more of his preaching. No way can you want more of that!"

Another boy exclaimed, "Jesus saves!"

"Psyche ward is better than the cell block."

"Never forget that."

"You unsaved son of a bitch!"

Everyone laughed at the remarks. Even Martin smirked as he retorted, "Someone needs to save old Bastard, that's for sure."

Kevin was prone on his top bunk. He smiled as he noticed that nearly half of the dorm residents were now gathered around Martin's bunk. Most of them were smiling and offering like words of encouragement. Everyone was talking at once.

"You do kind of suck, kid. But what to hell, you deserve to be here."

"You all deserve to be here, 'cept me!"

"Like hell we do."

"Speak for yourself."

"The rest of us are just innocent little delinquents sent here by mistake."

"I'm innocent!"

"Me too! Just ask my momma."

"The great reverend Bastard says that the good Lord will keep and bless pricks like you."

"Takes 'em right to his bosom, he does."

The joking and good mood had spread to nearly everyone in the dorm area. Martin still didn't get it.

"What do you sick pricks care anyway?" He snarled. "You're nothing but a bunch of low life jerks."

The big kid on the bunk across from him made a motion as if to strangle him. He was shaking with laughter as he sat there with both arms extended towards Martin. "This is exactly what we mean! Just shake it off. Laugh a little."

"Hey," another boy cut it. "Even in this crap hole there's plenty to laugh about."

"Who does the good Lord take to his bosoms?"

"Hell, if you'd a listened to the reverend you'd know."

"Wish I had a smoke."

"Hell yes. What was the question?"

"Who's got bosoms?"

Kevin noticed that Martin was smiling as the comments and conversations went on around him.

"Crap, don't get caught with smokes."

"I still say I'm innocent!"

"No crap."

"Still wish I had a smoke."

The laughter and comments became even more mixed as everyone cut in. Kevin remained quietly listening. It was almost comforting to know that they were all in the same boat.

Amidst the confusion of everyone talking at once, he had to strain to listen in on Alex and another boy.

"We can get a real laugh at the bitches."

"Take poor Jerome for instance." The boy who was talking was another who was constantly being set upon by Jerome. "The only reason that brownnoser is a bitch is cause none of us will put up with him."

"He is a rat."

He laughed and told Alex, "Sooner or later, one of you big guys will stomp the living crap out of him!"

"I volunteer!" Alex was one who could do it too. He stood towering over the others as he added, "If there was some way to get away with it!"

"You'll have to wait your turn."

They were all talking at once.

"Don't laugh. He's a psycho."

"How about the food in that crap hall they call mess? It is a mess. That's the real joke!"

"No crap. Well, lot's of crap served there."

"Picture this! Jerome and Casey McGinn in the cage and this time one of us holding the fire hose!"

"I'd love to see that."

"Hey, Martin, which one hosed you down this time?"

"Jerome."

"Hell," someone cut in. "I'd never hose either of those bitches down."

"Kiss ass."

"Screw you."

"Yeah, what would you do?"

"I'd put more trash in and burn the assholes."

The conversation went from one subject to the other as the boys enjoyed a rare occasion of amity.

"Piss on 'em all." Kevin murmured.

A boy who was close enough to overhear said. "That's a hell of an idea. How about if we put some cheese inside the incinerator cage and let those rat sons a bitches go in after it. We could all stand around and just piss on them."

"I wouldn't piss on those pricks if they were on fire."

"Hell, they all eat crap anyways."

"Yeah, but not crap sandwiches!"

"Damn straight. None of 'em like bread!"

The laughter coming from the dorm didn't go unnoticed by the screw on duty. Someone on the outer edge of the group noticed Boss Sorenson standing silently just inside the door. He had been listening in on them.

The place got deathly quiet. The screw didn't say a word as the boys quickly dispersed and went back to their bunks. When he announced lights out his tone was unlike they had heard before.

He made sure the door was secure. No one heard him as he said under his breath, "Goodnight boys."

He smiled grimly as he made his rounds to the other dorm areas. He was thinking that he was becoming more hardened with each passing day. He was a family man with kids of his own. Maybe it was time to start thinking about a career move.

Hearing the boys laughing and joking had put him in a somber mood. 'Something's got to change around here,' he thought. 'Warden Bastar is sending all these boys straight to hell in a hand basket.'

He paused as he turned out the lights in the downstairs dorm area. His voice could be heard clearly as he said, "Good night boys."

No one said goodnight back. The silence was deafening. He smiled sadly and continued his rounds.

Kevin was sleeping soundly when he felt someone shaking his shoulder.

"Wake up." A voice whispered.

In the dim light from the outside security lights, he could make out Martin standing by his bunk.

"What?"

"I couldn't sleep. I needed to say thanks." Martin's voice was trembling as he passed a folded piece of paper to Kevin. "I don't need this now."

Kevin nearly gasped as he unwrapped the paper.

"Will you get rid of it for me?"

Kevin sat up and swung his legs over the side of the bed. He could tell that Martin had been crying.

"Sure." He answered.

He whispered good night back as Martin returned to his bunk.

In the dim light he carefully rewrapped the rusty double-edged razor blade.

The son of a bitch was going to slash his wrists.

Don't get caught with that.

I'll be damned.

You already are.

Think he would have done it?

Not a doubt in my mind.

Chapter Sixteen

Shackles

Shackles of Conscience

The Monday morning shift change for the guards started with a brief meeting in the main orientation room. It was a large room two doors down from the warden's office. The room was crowded with wooden desks facing a podium and chalkboard.

The two uniformed men had arrived a few minutes early and were having a whispered conversation in the back row. The smaller of the two appeared to be in his late twenties. He was a well-groomed man, smartly dressed in his uniform. His tie was straight and he sat at a desk with his hat resting on a file folder.

"Wyatt, you had better keep quiet about this." Manny said. "It will cost you your job for sure."

"I've had enough." Wyatt said. "He always asks; today I'm going to tell him."

"Don't do it." Manny pleaded. "We put up with enough crap already."

"Do you want to get caught up in another crap storm?" Wyatt whispered. "That's where this all is headed if we don't do something now."

"I still say Big Jim was pulling your leg." Manny said. "He's got that Stone kid mixed up with someone else. You'd better leave well enough alone."

Manny was a huge man. He looked ridiculous crammed into a desk that was designed for high school kids. The collar of his uniform dress shirt wasn't nearly large enough to be buttoned around his thick neck.

He looked as if he had slept in his clothes. His tie was askew and he was one of the few who could get away with wearing an open collar. The new warden was serious about enforcing their dress code. He was sure to catch hell for his two-day stubble of whiskers.

"You ain't gonna bring up the Stone kid. Are you?"

"Maybe."

"I just slapped the snot out of him a few days ago."

"What for?"

"He got mouthy." Manny sounded dejected. "The little prick needs to learn to mind his own business."

"What happened?"

"He yelled at Oliver to lay off one of the others."

"Can't be having that."

"No. Then, when I slammed him against the wall, he told me I had bad breath." Manny grinned.

"Then what did you do?"

"What could I do? I already slapped the snot out of him."

"Did that end it?" Wyatt asked.

"Should have, but the dumb son of a bitch laughed at me."

"He did?"

"Yeah. Right in my face."

"Then what did you do?"

"What could I do? I already slapped the snot out of him."

"Hell."

"I just laughed along with him and told him to get his act to hell together." Manny said.

"I still ain't seen no paperwork on him."

Wyatt paused to look his friend in the eye.

"You can back me or not. We were both looking for jobs when we found this one." He grinned. "Right?"

"Damn you Wyatt Sorenson. Don't do it."

"Where's your sense of humor?"

"Don't tell me your conscience is starting to bother you."

"Would it matter?"

"Captain Stevens will have your ass!"

Wyatt turned to face the front of the room as the assistant warden, Mr. James entered. He was wearing his usual sport coat over a white shirt and tie. The shift supervisor, Captain Stevens walked in along with several guards.

Captain Stevens was wearing his dress uniform. He stood behind the podium with Mr. James, scowling as several others entered and sat at the desks. When it looked like everyone was there, the assistant warden began.

"Warden Bastar will be joining us shortly, gentlemen." He said. "We've got a few things that we need to go over, then you can get to your posts."

He went over a short list in a monotone voice. Several of the guards weren't paying attention and were talking back and forth as Mr. James droned on. Wyatt thought that was quite disrespectful.

Warden Bastar appeared at the door and stood glaring. The room went silent except for Mr. James who finished going over his list and asked, "Any questions?"

The room remained silent.

"None. Okay." He looked towards the door as warden Bastar made his entrance.

"Good morning, Sir. Anything you need to add?"

The warden went through his usual motions of trying to endear himself to them. He stood smiling as he asked if anyone needed to discuss anything.

Manny leaned towards Wyatt and whispered. "Silence."

Wyatt called from the back row.

"Warden Bastar. There is a matter we need to discuss."

"What's that? Officer Sorenson."

All eyes were on Wyatt as he opened a folder. Although the warden always asked, it was an unwritten rule that they weren't to bring up anything without first clearing it with Captain Stevens.

"Sir, I'm aware of the proper chain of command, and I assure you I have discussed this with the Captain." Wyatt paused. He shrugged off the hateful glare coming from Captain Stevens. He directed his remarks to the warden. "I assure you that I'm bringing this up for all the right reasons."

He passed a sheet of paper to the man in front of him. As it was passed to the front he continued. "We've got a couple underage inmates in B Campus. They don't belong there."

"What?"

Wyatt continued to look around the room as he said. "No one under fifteen years old is supposed to be over there. Ever." He looked at the warden. "Your rules, Sir."

Warden Bastar stood holding the sheet of paper. Wyatt said, "Sometimes the treatment these boys receive is unquestionably cruel and unusual, Sir."

"Are you trying to tell me how to run my prison?" It was obvious that the warden was upset with Wyatt for bringing up that subject in the presence of others.

"No, Sir."

"Then make your point."

"We all know who young Martin is. Sir." Wyatt said. "He was thirteen when he got sent here. The rules clearly say that he can be isolated in regular lock down, not in the solitary unit."

"What are you getting at? Are you suggesting we offer rewards for his kind of behavior?"

Predictably, the others laughed at his statement.

"No, Sir." Wyatt was starting to wish he hadn't spoken up. "Except, Sir, if word got back to the corrections board officials, we could all be in a world of trouble."

"Are you threatening me?" The warden gazed around the room, "Are you threatening all of us?"

"No, Sir."

Manny rose to address the warden. "He's just trying to head off trouble, Sir."

"Are you another do gooder?" The warden asked.

"No, Sir." Manny winced as he received a glare from Captain Stevens. "Sir, I've escorted young Martin in and out of solitary more times than I can count." His face was red as he added, "It's against your rules." He quickly sat down.

"Are you trying to cause trouble with all this? We've got nearly two hundred inmates here. Are you suggesting that we should start rewarding bad behavior?" His attempt to belittle Wyatt had no affect.

"No, Sir." Wyatt answered.

"Then what?"

"The second name, Sir."

"What?" The warden read the name aloud. "Kevin Stone."

"Yes, Sir."

"So?"

"He was here before, Sir. Three years ago."

"And?"

"He's fourteen now, Sir. He's been back for over a month and I've still seen no paperwork on him."

Wyatt's comment had struck a chord. He paused as the warden's face turned red.

"Sir, it was due to underage kids like him doing hard time that brought the whole thing down on Warden Morgan and the rest of us." He looked around the room again. "That's all I'm trying to say, Sir. I don't want to go through that again."

The warden exchanged looks with Captain Stevens. "I'll look into this." He murmured.

The warden stood behind the podium, making eye contact with each of his guards. They knew what to expect and bowed their heads as he closed his part of the meeting with a short prayer.

Mr. James asked Wyatt and Manny to stay as the others were leaving. Manny nearly cringed as Captain Stevens ordered them to stand at parade rest.

For a few minutes, they had the room to themselves. They could hear a hushed conversation outside the open door.

"You just had to open your big mouth!" Manny whispered.

"What's the worst that can happen?" Wyatt whispered back. "Are they going to fire us? I don't think so. And for what? No, these jerks are more scared than we are. They are the ones with something to lose."

"I should have kept my mouth shut too." Manny said.

Captain Stevens waited until warden Bastar was back in his office before entering the room. He was a tall man, but only half Manny's size. He got right in his face.

"This time I am going to write you up." He sounded angry as he paced slowly around them, eyeing their appearance. "You're a damn disgrace to the squad."

Mr. James walked back through the door. He stood with his hands on his hips and added. "The warden says the next time he sees you, he expects you to be clean-shaven."

Wyatt knew that there was more, and remained silent. Stevens leaned close to whisper in his ear, "Don't you ever challenge the warden in front of anyone again."

"I didn't mean for it to be a challenge, Sir." Wyatt replied.

"Ever!"

"Yes, Sir."

"It sure as hell sounded like a blackmail attempt to me." His voice raised; he could be heard several rooms away. "Next time, discuss it with me first."

"I did, Sir."

Stevens ignored his remark and continued. "If I had my way, both your sorry ass's would be run to hell out of my squad!"

He continued to rag on them while Mr. James wrote up a disciplinary notice and handed it to Manny.

"If you'll excuse us for a minute, Captain. I would like to have a word alone with these two officers."

Stevens turned abruptly and stormed out of the room.

"It is his squad." Mr. James said.

"Yes, Sir." They replied in unison.

The assistant warden's voice was soft as he looked at Manny and said, "Try to dress a little better. Okay?" He tried to suppress a smile. "Now get to work," he added.

The reform school was divided into two distinct groups of boys. The 'A' group were those model inmates; the ones that the outside world got to see. The warden had a select group who always got off easy in the work details and whose parents often came to visit.

Theirs was a separate dorm area, located in one of the newer, more modern buildings. The warden had labeled that area as Campus A. An inmate could expect to be transferred there after thirty days if he kept his act together.

Campus B was where the new arrivals and those who were considered to be flight risks were housed. These were a bunch of young thugs. Some were convicted rapists, murderers and thieves transferred from the main cellblock.

Their environment was similar to a never-ending cycle of military boot camp. The harsh treatment administered to them was the exact opposite of what the reverend Bastar was preaching.

It was this group who made up the majority of the work force. This was the group of youthful dregs that got the crap duties and constant harassment.

When an inmate turned eighteen he was either allowed to serve out the remainder of his sentence there, or in some cases, depending on the conviction, transferred to the main prison.

The third area was solitary. A small area shrouded in misery and despair. Solitary was touted as a last resort. It was actually a revolving door that placed each inmate at the mercy of the head screws and their bitches.

The hard time area was supposed to be the main cellblock. The inmates there were housed two to a cell, just like at the big house. Since they were all under twenty-one years old, the state pulled regular inspections of that area. Those locked down in the main cellblock were treated according to the rules.

Wyatt knew that the new system wasn't working. Morale was at an all time low. It had declined every day since warden Bastar had moved in like a hurricane with his new philosophies.

He had thought about quitting back during the turmoil of the power shift several years ago. He was wishing now that he had. Maybe Manny was right. Maybe he was getting soft. Something needed to change.

Wyatt and Manny were just a couple badge numbers among the dozens of guards who came to work each day. They had both hired on under the old administration. Both had hoped that warden Bastar would have changed things for the better.

Being assigned to B Campus was considered crap duty. The day after they spoke up at the meeting, it didn't bother either of them when they were permanently reassigned to Campus A.

"I guess Captain Stevens meant it when he said he didn't want us in his squad." Manny said.

Wyatt smiled, acknowledging his comment, and continued writing something in a tablet.

It was another Monday morning. Once again, they were the first to arrive in the orientation room. As usual, Manny's huge frame was crammed into the small desk. He looked like something the cat dragged in.

Wyatt finished what he was doing and said. "We've still got our jobs."

"Yeah," Manny replied. "Can you believe it? Permanent day shift. Someone else can handle all that crap over in B."

"Thanks for sticking up for me." Wyatt said.

"No problem."

"I mean it. Thanks."

"No more night work."

"Yeah."

"At least now I don't have to listen to you saying goodnight to those little pricks. They don't need to be tucked in."

"Hell, what was the harm?" Wyatt asked.

"They ain't your kids."

"So?"

"I think you've gone soft."

"Really?"

"Makes no difference. Most of those little pricks will end up next door anyhow."

"So? What was the harm?" Wyatt asked again.

Manny offered no reply as the room filled up with those scheduled for the Monday morning meeting. It was more of the same only this time with a different Captain.

Although Manny tried to act it, he really wasn't surprised when Wyatt announced that this was his resignation letter and handed a sheet of paper to the shift Captain.

As the others filed out, he asked Wyatt if he would stay a minute and help him write his.

"You don't have to do this you know." Wyatt said.

"What to hell. It'll feel good to be free."

"Yeah."

"I still can't figure why you started saying goodnight to those little pricks."

<u>Shackles of Right and Wrong</u>

Kevin was awake before first call every morning. It was an instinct that he had developed from the first day. He lay there waiting for it all to begin.

He enjoyed this quiet time. It was like that of the calm before a storm. Each day he knew there would be a proverbial crap storm. Some days the storms were minor, sometimes the entire day was one continual reign of crap.

These few minutes permitted him a quiet time to think, a time to be alone in the temporary solace of his thoughts. His thoughts were always of escape. He was in survival mode.

This morning, he was thinking that he might as well have a little control over today's storm. He smiled as he waited. He was clutching a large sock filled with small rocks. He had crammed it full and tied the open end in a knot. It was a lethal weapon. It was heavy. He thought of it as a sleeping pill.

He heard footsteps approaching up the stairs. He lay quietly, staring into the darkness of the ceiling. The door at the end of the dorm room slammed open. The lights came on. He squinted his eyes and waited expectantly as the shouting began.

The obnoxious young man that strode down the aisle shouting for them to get to hell up was referred to as the wakeup bitch. He always clanged something against the metal frames of the bunk beds as he cursed and yelled at them to get to hell up.

He heard someone on the other end of the dorm mutter.

"Asshole."

Kevin knew that the wakeup bitch would be followed closely by whichever screw was on duty that day. By the time he got there they were expected to be standing at attention at the end of the rows of bunks awaiting head count.

Kevin remained still as the bitch passed. He was confident that no one would be watching. He was wishing that it would be Jerome, but what to hell, Oliver would do. He grinned and swung his legs over the edge of the bunk.

This is vengeful.

That's what the good Reverend says.

This prick deserves it.

Agreed.

Don't miss.

The wakeup bitch was two bunks past Kevin's. He drew back and threw his sleeping pill with all his might. The projectile nailed him squarely in the back of the head.

If not for the explosion of bright lights and brief flash of pain, he might have heard Kevin's soft whisper as he said,

"Goodnight, bitch."

The young trustee dropped to the floor like a sack of potatoes as the lights went out.

The screw arrived a minute or so after Kevin put Oliver down for a nap. Word had spread almost instantly. Those who were having trouble waking up were now transformed into a group of scared, wide-awake young men.

"Oh crap!"

"Who did this?"

"Anyone see?"

Kevin said. "We're in a world of crap now."

Several of the boys gathered around the unconscious trustee. They heard the screw coming up the stairs. One of the boys was shaking the wakeup bitch.

"Wakeup, damn it."

He groaned.

"He's starting to come around!"

"Screw alert!"

"Back off."
"Quick, get to hell in line."
"Who in hell did this?"

They stood in silence at attention in their proper places. The screw entered carrying his clipboard. His eyes went wide in surprise as he noticed that they were all standing tall and silent.

He walked down the center aisle thinking that something was different.

"What to hell!" He shouted. He hurried over to kneel at the side of the young trustee. "Hey!" He shook him a few times. Oliver started to come out of it. The screw helped him sit up. He glared over his shoulder. "You bastards stay right there. Don't move a muscle."

He sent the boy nearest the door downstairs to summon another guard. Within minutes the place was swarming with uniformed guards and several young trustees.

Kevin remained standing at attention along with the others. All this commotion was causing him to have second thoughts over the whole deal. He had expected a crap storm, but this was a hurricane.

Oh crap! Oh dear!

You can say that again.

Oh crap! Oh dear!

The wakeup bitch definitely had a headache, but was nearly recovered. He and several screws were tearing back and forth, up and down the aisle. The boys were slammed into their bunks and jerked around violently as those in charge determined to find out who was responsible.

The parade ground was shrouded with the usual early morning fog. The screws were especially riled up this morning. They were determined to find out who had assaulted their young trustee. Oliver was the center of attention as he insanely yelled and cursed at them.

The screws showed no signs of compassion as he walked with his heavy boots on the backs of the boys. They were forced to low crawl back and forth across the parade ground. They were still in their underwear. They hadn't been allowed to get dressed despite the bitter cold.

It got quite ugly. It was certain that if anyone had known, they surely would have given up the guilty one.

As those thirty or so young residents of the third floor dorm in B campus endured a double dose of harassment, Kevin was glad that no one had seen him. Before the warmth of the sun drove away the fog, he was nearly ready to turn himself in.

Still, he smiled inwardly each time he caught a glimpse of the blood stained collar of their primary tormenter.

Kevin didn't mind working late into the night at the shoe shop or the extra duty in the laundry area. He had been assigned to handle Martin's duties in the laundry room. This helped make the time go by more quickly.

A couple screws and the assistant warden had taken Martin away. They had shown up on the parade ground during morning formation and singled him out.

He had no idea of what he might have done as he was dragged kicking and squirming through the locked gate that separated the two campuses. Kevin never did find out why they dragged him off like that.

Rumor had it that Martin had been reassigned to campus A. They all doubted that one. Campus A was for the goody two shoes bunch. Martin definitely wasn't one of them. They believed that he had once again been thrown into solitary.

Idle time was something that weighed heavy on Kevin's mind. As long as he was nearly exhausted when he went to sleep, the nightmares stayed somewhere in the background.

The last thing he had to worry about was idle time. Since the assault on the wakeup bitch, the third floor dorm residents were all assigned to double duty.

Their day started with the usual melodious wake up call. Now there were two of them to listen to each morning. The grind wore on and seldom did a workday end before midnight.

It wasn't until a week after the incident in the dorm that things started to calm down. Sickbay rapidly filled up with those who were suffering from bouts of pneumonia, severe colds and exhaustion.

The assistant warden had personally interviewed each boy. Although there were several prime suspects, no one was ever ratted out with any degree of certainty.

Kevin's turn came shortly after morning formation the second day. The assistant warden, Mr. James, had arranged for them to be escorted in small groups to the main office building. They stood silently with their backs to the wall in the hallway.

Kevin waited his turn quietly. They were forbidden to talk and he knew to go by the rules. He had to suppress a smile as two boys were roughly escorted outside after they were caught whispering. He could hear them as they called out the number of pushups to the screw.

Mr. James seemed like a nice enough man. He had a pleasant smile. Kevin thought it to be almost sincere.

"Mr. Stone," he said as he extended his hand. "I'm pleased to meet you."

Kevin's surprised look caused him to say. "You can relax a little. This is an informal meeting. I'm pleased to meet you." He remained standing, reaching across his desk to shake hands.

He's sucking up for something.

What's his angle?

He needs a rat.

Just keep your mouth shut.

Kevin met his look and shook hands. This was unusual. They were forbidden to make eye contact with any of the supervising guards or the warden.

"Kevin, I've talked to nearly all the boys in your dorm. No one knows anything about the incident involving the young trustee. Do you?"

"No, Sir."

He stood with his head lowered as the assistant warden opened a thin file. Mr. James said,

"Someone has to have seen something."

"Yes, Sir." Kevin's voice was barely audible.

The screw that had escorted him inside spoke up harshly. He was standing directly behind Kevin.

"Talk clearly, Boy!" He said.

Mr. James sat staring silently at the screw. After a few seconds he said, "Mr. Hawks, would you excuse us please? Would you mind waiting outside?"

"Sir?"

"We need to get answers. I'm afraid your presence is causing this one to be intimidated."

"Yes, Sir."

The screw quickly walked to the door and took up his station just outside.

Mr. James once again addressed Kevin.

"Why are you here, Son?"

"I ain't your damned son!" Kevin's voice rose.

Oh damn.

You've done it now.

The screw stormed back into the room. Kevin braced himself for the beating that was sure to follow.

To his surprise, the assistant warden raised his voice to the screw. "Hold it!" He held his hand palm first in the guard's direction. "It's okay. Just wait outside. I'll handle this."

The guard scowled at him. He turned and once again left the room.

Mr. James asked again in a soft voice.

"Why are you here?"

"I guess because someone assaulted one of your trustees." Kevin answered.

"No, Son." Mr. James caught himself as he added, "I mean, Kevin. That's not what I mean."

Kevin remained silent.

"Look at me."

Kevin made eye contact with him.

"Why are you here? In my school?"

"You really don't know, Sir?"

"This is all the file I have on you." Mr. James held up the thin folder. Kevin sensed that Mr. James was talking in a low voice so that no one else could overhear. It seemed as if the assistant warden was trying to find out the answer to the same question as Kevin.

His mind was in a spin as he blurted. "You'll have to call the sheriff's office back home. It was them two faced sons of bitches that sent me here."

It dawned on him that he wasn't supposed to use profanity around the officials. He hoped the guard hadn't overheard. He expected him to come storming back into the room.

His body tensed as he heard someone enter the room and silently approach from behind.

Mr. James abruptly changed the subject as he asked, "If you can think of that kid's last name, I can check him out."

Kevin instinctively knew to play along. He got the distinct feeling that Mr. James was intimidated as warden Bastar spoke softly.

The warden was wearing his usual phony smile. He asked Kevin if he was learning to walk with Jesus.

"I'm still working on that, Sir." Kevin answered. He remembered to keep his head lowered.

"Did this one have anything to offer?" The warden directed his question to Mr. James.

Mr. James appeared to have lost his quiet composure. "Nothing yet, Sir." He answered.

Warden Bastar suspected nothing when Kevin said to Mr. James.

"Milo, Sir. I think that was his name. Milo."

"I'll add it to my list."

The warden escorted Kevin back to the row of boys standing in the hall. Kevin looked back over his shoulder and noticed that Mr. James was wiping his forehead with a white handkerchief. For some reason his heart started racing with hope.

Don't forget the rules.

I won't.

Never trust these bastards.

Never.

Don't get your hopes up.

I won't.

He sat quietly as the remaining two boys were paraded into the assistant warden's office. It was still early when they were marched back through the gate into campus B.

It came as no surprise to any of them when they were ordered to low crawl the rest of the way. The ground was covered with about two inches of wet heavy snow. The meeting had put them behind schedule. They were ordered to their feet and double-timed to the production area.

This was one of those rare days that no one minded working inside in the warmth of the shoe shop.

Chapter Seventeen

A Time of Reckoning

It hit the fan a week or so later shortly after lunch. Kevin was assigned to kitchen duty. The dining area was nearly empty. Brian and a couple others were working at the front counter. Kevin double-checked the setup.

Are you sure?

We wouldn't want him to think Casey a liar.

I guess not.

Brace yourself.

Brian and the others were out of the way, right where he wanted them to be. The screws had gone to the other end of the dining area.

His voice was mocking as he called to Jerome.

"Hey Jerome." He pronounced Jerome's name as a long drawn out word.

"Oh, Jerome, Dear. You really need to see this."

Predictably, Jerome's temper instantly took over and he came charging into the room.

Kevin had arranged the entrance to allow only one-way straight in. As Jerome charged in, he tripped on the length of hand-braided rope that Kevin had stretched across the narrow aisle.

The grease spread out on the floor insured that gravity was on Kevin's side. Jerome hit the floor with both hands outstretched to break his fall. This momentarily left him in a vulnerable position. Kevin nailed him once, as hard as he could, with a heavy metal stool.

Jerome's face hit the floor with a sickening thud. Kevin jumped squarely between his shoulder blades as he leaped over him to block the door.

He slammed the door shut and kicked a wooden wedge under it. He heard the screws yelling as he upended a heavy wheeled cart and braced it against the door with a folding chair.

Jerome was getting up. Kevin slopped a bucket of dirty dishwater on him and nailed him along side the head with the empty bucket. He couldn't help but laugh at the enraged expression on Jerome's face as he slipped and cursed as he scrambled to his feet.

Jerome looked like a drowned rat. Blood was flowing from his nose as he charged at Kevin in a rage. He screamed, "You son of a bitch!"

Kevin used Jerome's forward momentum against him as he quickly sidestepped and once again tripped him to the floor. He jumped again and landed with both feet squarely on Jerome's back.

Jerome was lying there with the breath knocked out of him when Kevin first started beating him with the heavy metal tray. He knew that Jerome's wrist and several fingers were broken as he raised his hands in a failed attempt to defend himself.

He realized that he needed to stop before he killed him. The guards were yelling excitedly outside the door, still trying to force their way in.

He scooped another bucket of dirty dishwater out of the large double sink and once again soaked Jerome. Jerome tried to sit up. Kevin knelt beside him.

"Hey Jerome. How are you doing?" He slapped Jerome's face back and forth with his hand. "Jerome, I want to know how you are doing. Are you having a good day?"

"Please! Oh God!" Jerome cried, "You're crazy, you're crazy, for God's sake, stop!"

"Oh Jerome." Kevin said in a soothing tone, "We've already talked about God. Remember?"

He whirled around and picked up the heavy metal stool. He nailed Jerome repeatedly with it. He heard a leg break. Jerome started screaming. He was powerless to get away.

Kevin put the stool down and leaned close to whisper in Jerome's ear. "I want you to remember this." He slapped Jerome's face. "Stay awake now!" He was still talking in a soothing tone. "I want you to see it coming."

He let go of Jerome and climbed onto the thick hardwood counter. "Hello Bitch!" He shouted mockingly as he jumped and landed with both feet on Jerome's stomach. Jerome puked for a few seconds and went limp.

The guards had stopped their attempt to get in through the wire mesh door at the front. They were outside, beating down the wooden door to the side entrance.

Kevin picked up a handful of green beans that were a part of the mess on the floor. He sat quietly on a low rolling cart and munched on them as the guards finished breaking their way in.

What can these pricks do that uncle Rick didn't?

Not much.

The screws weren't nearly as rough as Kevin had thought they were going to be. One twisted his arm behind his back to restrain him. Another gasped as he stooped to examine his injured bitch. They agreed that the reform school's infirmary wouldn't do. Not this time. One ran to call an ambulance.

Kevin was standing in chains before warden Bastar. He remembered to keep his head bowed and not to make eye contact. He hoped that 'Reverend Bastard' wouldn't resort to preaching. He should have known better.

He was directly in front of the warden's desk. He was told to kneel and read from the bible while the warden made a call to the hospital to see how badly Jerome was hurt. The warden remained surprisingly calm over the whole deal.

When he wasn't looking, Kevin carefully borrowed several pages from the large bible for later. He tried to tear them out cleanly, in full sheets. With his hands in cuffs, it was awkward.

There was something different in the way the screws treated him after that. He was roughly escorted to solitary, but still something was different.

As the days wore on, it became apparent that someone was bending the rules. Twice a day food was placed in front of the door, as was the rule. He couldn't see outside due to the opening for food and water being on the bottom of the door. What was different was that it was good food. The water was fresh. Something was going on.

He knew that both he and anyone caught talking to him would be severely punished if caught. He kept quiet each time he heard footsteps coming down the corridor.

The floor area was ample for him to lay curled up on his side to sleep. Each morning, at first call, a screw unlocked his door and exchanged slop buckets. The screw didn't speak. Those were the rules. Kevin doubted that it was the screw that brought the food and water.

Sometimes he would lose his temper. There was no way to move around freely. There was barely room to stand up in that confined space. He whiled away the hours doing push offs against the wall and running in place. There was no way to tell what time it was, or even for sure if it was night or day. He looked forward to the screw exchanging slop buckets.

Doesn't it just suck?

What?

Looking forward to a new crap pail.

Where's that whore with the abscessed tooth?

Those who listened from time to time on the outside thought that he had lost his mind each time they heard his laughter echoing in the corridor.

By the end of the second week, he was really no worse for wear. Being alone was nothing new to him. The screw spoke for the first time and informed him that this was his last day in solitary. He should be okay if he could keep his act together. He exchanged slop buckets and left.

This time, when the food was left outside, he heard a loud whisper. "Kevin. I really am sorry."

He smiled as he heard Casey McGinn's footsteps fade down the corridor.

The screws that took him from the cell made no effort to be gentle as they herded him outside into the old incinerator. As he had been that first night, he was hosed down with the high-pressure fire hose.

He gritted his teeth and made no response as the screw threw a fresh bundle of clothing at him and told him to get dressed.

He was allowed to eat in the dining room after everyone else had left. He tried not to smile as he noted that the kitchen area had been cleaned up and looked neater than it ever had.

He remained sitting in the dining area for several hours. When the time was right, the screws herded him across the yard to the warden's office. He was smiling as he stood outside the warden's door.

No.

No what?

Forget it!

Forget what?

Don't do it!

Warden Bastar watched with a solemn smile as Kevin was escorted inside with his head bowed. He really thought that this one might have learned his lesson. He had stood silently in the corridor and had heard the boy's insane laughter coming from solitary. He was certain that the lesson had sunk in.

He checked his watch; it was a quarter to five. The officials from the Attorney General's office were waiting outside in the main entry.

"Mr. Stone." The warden's voice was soft. "I hope you've learned from this experience."

Steady.

"Yes Sir." Kevin whispered, staring at the floor.

"I am hoping that these past two weeks gave you ample time to get close to the Lord."

"I appreciated this chance to get close to Jesus." Kevin said in a loud grating whisper. He slowly raised his head and looked warden Bastar in the eye. "Really I did." His smile was out of place.

"Lower your eyes, Boy!" The screw cut in.

Kevin ignored him as he continued. "Check and see for yourself. The last time I was here I borrowed a few pages from your precious bible. I knew there wouldn't be any toilet paper in solitary."

Kevin paused for a moment and grinned at the look on the warden's face. "Know what?" He added, "I wiped my ass all the way through the second half of first John."

The screw gasped and grabbed onto his shoulders from behind. He didn't know what to say or do.

Warden Bastar stormed around his desk and frantically opened his bible. He looked like he had seen a ghost as he turned to first John. He started shaking with rage as his face turned red.

"Blasphemer!" He screamed as he tore into Kevin.

The ranting and raving and all the shouting that accompanied what happened next made it seem a lot worse than it was. The screw held Kevin until warden Bastar wrenched him from his grasp and started throwing him around the room.

Everything was cleared off the warden's desk as Kevin was thrown across it. He reached up and tipped over the tall bookcase as warden Bastar continued his insane temper tantrum. He was shouting something about 'Satan be gone,' or something like that, when the room went dark.

Kevin was only out for a few minutes. He remembered hearing someone arguing with warden Bastar. Something went wrong for the warden. His vision was blurred as he watched someone in a suit knock the warden to the floor and place him in handcuffs. Kevin thought his voice sounded familiar.

He kept his eyes shut. The voices faded and he was overcome with silence.

By the time the ambulance attendants had him loaded on the gurney he was awake again. His mind was nearly clear. He didn't think he was hurt badly at all, but wasn't going to let them know that. The worse they thought he was hurt, the easier it would be for him.

He tried not to, but couldn't help but smile as they were wheeling him out of the room. An inmate had picked up the wardens bible and passed it to a screw. The screw calmly tossed it into the wastebasket.

He went back to sleep.

Kevin kept drifting in and out of consciousness. He was held overnight in a special observation room at the medical center in Rockland. It was a special secure area with a keyed door. The hospital routinely treated inmates from the prison and the boy's reform school.

His injuries were all minor. He was somewhat bruised and battered, but it was nothing compared to what he had been through in the past.

He knew he needed a plan. He thought up one fast when he was sent to x-ray around noontime. The hospital's security person accompanied him. He remained still on the gurney as he was wheeled into the waiting area.

The guard was surprised to turn around and find the gurney empty, and Kevin gone.

He ran out into the corridor. "Hey," he shouted. "Has anybody seen a kid?"

A nurse hurried over.

"How could he have gotten away?" She opened the door and looked at the empty gurney. "I thought you were supposed to stay with him!"

They issued an alert for the rest of the hospital and proceeded to monitor the doors. The guard hustled out the front door, looking desperately for his ward.

It was a good thing that Kevin had developed strength in his upper arms. He clung to the underside of the gurney, hoping that they wouldn't hear his breathing.

After they scurried off, he peeked out the door and boldly walked two doors down and entered an empty room. As security personnel flocked to the area, he got in the bed and turned facing away from the door. He tried not to laugh when someone quietly entered and actually searched the room and under his bed.

After only a few minutes the commotion in the halls started to settle down. He could hear them saying that they thought he had already gone out the front door.

He doubted he would get far if he did try to exit the hospital. His plan changed minute by minute.

There was a hospital walker in one corner of the room. He checked the closet. He needed clothes before he could go anywhere. The only thing he could find was a blue bathrobe. He put it on and walked unsteadily down the hall with the walker. An elevator door opened. He smiled at the lady who held the door from closing as he slowly entered.

When the door closed he pushed the button for the top floor. The elevator stopped twice on its way up. He overheard someone saying that they were going to the cafeteria, and got out on the same floor.

No one paid him any mind as he slowly made his way down the hall. His clothing problem was solved when he made a brief stop at the maintenance closet. An oversized set of coveralls, a faded jacket, and a pair of rubber boots completed his new wardrobe. He adjusted the ragged baseball cap on his head and boldly walked to the emergency room waiting area.

He went into the bathroom and carefully removed the bandage from his forehead. He was surprised to notice several stitches. He used the paper towels to wash away the iodine stains.

He took a seat next to an older couple who were waiting their turn to see the doctor. He said hello and sat quietly thumbing through a magazine.

Hide in plain sight.

Good advice.

Think where we would be if I had listened to you.

We're not out of the woods yet.

Kevin made his exit from the hospital about a half hour after the afternoon visiting hours started. No one paid him any mind as he walked beside a man who was helping his wife slowly walk outside.

From the hospital windows he had been able to determine which direction to go to get to the main highway. He knew that wandering the streets would get him picked up as quickly as trying to hitch a ride.

His first stop was the rear parking lot of the county courthouse.

Now what do we do.

Watch this.

A fifty-two Chevy was parked in the shade between a large truck and a dumpster. It was the same model as the old piece of crap that Rory drove, except this one had a standard transmission and was still in good shape.

He shimmied the wing window open with a flat piece of metal that had been lying on the ground next to the dumpster. In less than a minute he had it started. He put the car in gear and drove off.

Chapter Eighteen

Kindness

<u>First week in May, 1964</u>

"We didn't take into account the boys resilience." Howard Smiley sighed and passed a folder across the desk to Brett Miller. "I'm afraid there's no way to undo this."

Brett skimmed through the pages as the others sat silently around the conference table.

"It's frustrating." He said. He looked at Howard. "I was right there, right beside the boy, all the way to the hospital." He rolled his eyes as he added, "Who would have thought."

"I wish I had gone along with you on this one."

"Me too."

"What are you going to tell Palmer?" Howard asked.

"I'm winging it." Brett said.

"That's about all you can do."

"When Judge Alfred Leroy Palmer does see this," Brett paused and smiled as he said, "It's certain that he's going to blow another fuse."

Howard looked at his watch. "More than likely. I'd say in about five minutes."

Judge Palmer left his meeting with the attorney general with a positive feeling. It was unlike him to go this far out on a limb for anyone. The rules were set. Now that the boy had been found, there would be no charges against him.

As soon as all this mess was cleared up, he would be remanded to his parent's custody. They agreed that the state would remain liable for any future medical bills.

He smiled as he realized that the only problem was going to be keeping the boy out of trouble. Jerome Harris was going to be okay. The doctors had removed his spleen and set several broken bones. His attorney had decided to press charges only against the reform school.

He felt partially responsible for all this mess. Hindsight didn't account for much. If he had been able to get the parent's custody rights revoked sooner, most of this could have been prevented. If Kevin had been back in foster care, none of this would have happened.

Brett Miller was in town for the duration of the trial. He was a close friend to Howard Smiley. Howard had been best man at his wedding. Judge Palmer smiled as he realized that he should have gone a little easier on Detective Smiley.

It was Smiley who had finally located the boy. He claimed that a little bird had told him where to look. The paper trail had been a hard one to follow and Judge Palmer was impressed at Smiley's tenacity.

The state had authorized him to personally make the phone call to the boys' reform school. He was confident that everything would work out. The warden had personally assured him that Kevin would be standing tall and proud by the time Brett Miller was scheduled to arrive under escort of the state police.

The circumstance surrounding young Kevin ending up in the hospital was still a bit unclear. Brett had told him what details he knew, and of his arrest of warden Bastar. Judge Palmer was hopeful that Kevin's injuries were minor.

It appeared as if the same old cycle was about to start all over again concerning the boy's reform school. The assistant warden and two former guards had come forward with new allegations of inmate abuse.

The story was already in several newspapers. A reporter from the states' largest paper was having no trouble finding one credible witness after the other to interview.

The attorney general's office was once again investigating charges of corruption and the misuse of state funds. This news came as no surprise to him. He had thought all along that too much had been swept under the rug by the corrections department.

He walked into the conference room right on schedule. Miller and Smiley were sitting across from each other. Several attorneys sat on either side of them. He smiled when they all rose as he entered the room.

His expression turned to incredulous as he was told the news. He tried to shrug it off as he looked at Detective Smiley and said, "A day late and a dollar short."

His grin told them that he understood fully. That boy was an elusive one and he had done it again.

****

Kevin was starting to get a grasp on just how much trouble he was in. As he drove north on highway one he remembered something Rory had said. "There's not a car made that can outrun those police two way radios." He knew he had to get off the road soon.

He was thinking that he needed to find Rory. There was no one else he could count on. Those Judas sons of bitches back home had sold him out. He believed that to be a fact. Sheriff Bradley had tried to warn him. He was certain now. The sheriff's comments had proved it.

He couldn't understand why Bill Riley had been so nice prior to throwing him to the dogs. It made no sense. He grated his teeth as he realized that Rory had worked for Bill.

Better leave him out of this.

Chances are Rory would be no different. He was overcome with paranoia as he tried to think of a safe haven.

Who can you trust?

Think.

You can't go home.

Who?

No. Not them.

Think about it.

Don't drag them into this.

Think about it.

Don't drag them into this.

Are you sure?

They were just being nice.

He had only gone a few miles when he turned onto a side road off highway one. Camden was only a few miles ahead. There were bound to be a lot of cops there.

A storm system was moving in. The ominous clouds made it seem later than it was. It would be dark soon, and he wanted to be holed up somewhere.

He had only driven a few miles when he saw a bunch of abandoned vehicles scattered randomly in a field. He could see a barn roof through the trees. The spring rains had softened the ground and he nearly had to floor it to get the car in position between an old truck and a car that was rolled over on its side.

He got out and raised the hood. Next, he opened the trunk and propped it open with the spare tire. There was a heavy winter coat in the trunk. He tossed it into the back seat. He carefully placed a rusty metal basket that had been lying on the ground over the front windshield for effect.

Hide in plain sight.

You're learning.

There was an unopened pack of camel's lying on the floorboard. Inside the glove box he found several books of matches and an open package of peanut butter crackers. On the back seat he found a thermos full of black coffee and an opened bag of potato chips.

He wolfed down the crackers. The coffee in the thermos was still warm. He sat quietly, listening to the radio as snow started to accumulate on the windshield. He knew he would have to start the car several times during the night to keep warm. He looked at himself in the rearview mirror.

You look like you were shot at and missed.

Yeah, crapped at and hit.

He grinned wryly at his reflection. His entire body hurt. He felt as if he had been run over with a steamroller. It was going to be a few days before he got over this last beating.

He knew he should be feeling remorseful about something as he tried to take stock of the situation.

He was an escaped convict.

Convicted of what?

He was driving another stolen car.

Oops.

He didn't know if Jerome was dead or alive.

So?

Warden Bastar was sure to be more than pissed over the whole deal.

Praise the lord.

Where's that whore with the abscessed tooth?

He was laughing, silently to himself, as he figured what to hell. He would come up with a plan in the morning. He enjoyed another smoke and a second cup of coffee.

The late spring snowstorm caught the local farmers quite unprepared. Donald Rowe owned a dairy farm in West Rockport. He owned three hundred and twenty acres, three barns and over a hundred milking cows. He also owned part interest in the dairy processing plant in Rockland.

His main interest and occupation was running the farm. He had three sons and one daughter. His oldest son worked with him on the farm. The other two had moved away and he seldom saw them except for holidays. His daughter was married and taught school in Camden.

They had prospered over the years. His business provided steady work for two full time hands. He looked forward each weekend to the visits from his grandchildren.

His son had cautioned him against using the calving shed on the south end. When he woke to a foot of new snow, he was wishing that he had listened to him.

He bundled up in his heavy winter garb and started up the old Farm All. One of the hands helped him load the flat bed trailer with bales of hay. He put the tractor in gear and started out, hoping he wouldn't get stuck.

Kevin realized that he could never drive the car in the fresh snow. He had used up nearly all of the gas in the car's tank just trying to keep warm during the night. He didn't want to risk running out if he were to get stuck in the mud.

He knew that there was a large barn just over the rise behind this small junkyard area. He reasoned that his best bet would be to hide out there until things cooled down.

At first light he started out through the deep snow. He hurried as fast as he could. The rubber shoes he had borrowed from the hospital's maintenance closet were cold. They were way too large and he had no socks.

There was an old trailer house parked behind the barn. It sat forlornly on concrete blocks and appeared to be abandoned. The glass of the storm door was broken and the inside front door was slightly ajar. It was still snowing when he walked up to the trailer and opened the door.

Apparently the place hadn't been used in some time. There was no furniture, and collections of junk and piles of old clothes and miscellaneous household items were heaped everywhere. He poked around in the bedrooms and found a very used pair of leather boots and several pairs of socks.

He also found a pair of wool pants that fit him quite well. He borrowed a couple flannel shirts from a pile near a doorway, and put both of them on.

He was nearly warmed up by the time he stashed his old clothes and shoes under the kitchen sink cabinet. He placed them all the way to the back behind a rusty dish rack.

Cover your tracks.

There was a small wood stove sitting in the middle of what once had been a proper living room. The stovepipe looked to be in good condition.

Scattered amongst a collection of junk on the counter, he found an old note and several envelopes addressed to someone named Rowe.

He stood for a few minutes looking out the window at the old barn. It was obvious that it also was abandoned. He had been hoping that there would have been a chicken coop where he could borrow some eggs. He was figuring on a few lean days when he heard the sounds of a tractor.

A tractor was slowly approaching. Kevin stepped back from the window and watched. As it started up out of a small valley in the narrow wheel ruts that served as a road, he noticed that the rear tires were constantly spinning.

The driver guided the tractor around the other side of the barn and disappeared momentarily as he opened the throttle to get a run for the next dip in the road.

The tractor was nearly to the top of the small rise when it became obvious that it couldn't make it up the incline in the soft soil. Both large rear wheels were throwing mud high in the air as they spun in the deep snow.

Kevin was smiling as he watched. His smile vanished as the tractor suddenly slewed to one side and a rear wheel came all the way off the ground. The tractor paused momentarily at its center of gravity. The driver was hanging on for dear life when it tipped over on its side.

This crap can't be happening!

No way. Not to us.

What are the chances?

Just stay back. No, wait. There is a reason.

Huh?

It's them; they're clearing the way for something.

Again?

I'd bet money on it.

I hope you know what you are doing.

Trust me.

Kevin followed his first instinct and bolted out the door at a dead run as the tractor rolled over the driver. The engine was still running full throttle when he scrambled around the trailer. He was nearly panicked as he made his way to the uphill side of the tractor and tried to think what to do. The driver was shouting. His desperate voice only added to Kevin's excitement.

The rear wheel that was on its side on the ground was still spinning and fighting for traction. The other was spinning slowly. There was no way to get near the throttle or the kill switch with the wheels turning. He scrambled across the front end. His excitement nearly got the best of him as he reached into the open engine compartment and pulled the ignition wire.

He turned his attention to the farmer who appeared to be pinned beneath. The tractor had jackknifed and the man was inches from being crushed against the tongue of the flatbed trailer.

The old man's face was ashen as he quickly pushed himself away. Kevin helped to steady him as he scurried backwards on the ground to get a safe distance from the rig.

The old man tried to mask his anxiety. "Damn! That was close!" He looked at Kevin and laughed.

"Hey boy, I'm sure glad you showed up when you did, but hell, I don't see any real damage." He paused as Kevin raised his eyebrows in surprise. Then he asked, "Do you?"

Kevin smiled back at him and said, "I guess not. I really thought you were in a world of crap for a few minutes."

"Might a been, might a been." The man said. He was obviously making light of the situation. He continued wiping snow and mud from the front of his clothes as he said, "I hope you're going to tell me that you're out here looking for work! This snow really has us behind schedule and I could use a good hand for a few days."

"Looking for work? You bet!" Kevin laughed and said, "Just point it out."

"You got a name?"

"Yes Sir. Kevin. Kevin Stone." Kevin hoped the man hadn't noticed him catching his breath. He hadn't meant to give his real name.

"I'm Donald Rowe." The man took off his leather mitten and shook hands. "I took you for a farm boy. The way you scrambled over like that and pulled those wires."

"What ever you need done." Kevin said with a smile. "I'm your man."

Don liked to talk and Kevin enjoyed the walk back to the main farm. Mr. Rowe was limping a little by the time they got to the main farmhouse. He invited Kevin inside and introduced him to his wife.

"Eva, this young man is Kevin Stone. He's going to be working for us for a few days."

Kevin exchanged pleasantries with her and wondered for a moment why neither had asked any questions as to where he was from.

"As soon as Don gets changed, I'll find some dry clothes for you too." She said with a smile. She was tall and thin. Her sparkling blue eyes made her seem much younger than she was.

Eva fixed him a nice breakfast while he waited for Don to change into a dry set of clothes. Kevin could tell that she was a real nice lady. He determined that silence was golden and decided to wait until asked before making up a story to fit the situation.

Don ushered him into a bedroom and waited while Kevin changed. Eva had laid out several pairs of pants and several shirts on the bed.

As Kevin was changing his shirt, Don watched with a solemn expression. He could see the large black and blue marks on the sides of his ribs and on his back. Don had already commented that he probably should have a bandage on his forehead until those stitches came out.

Despite everything that was happening, Eva and Don never did ask Kevin a single question. Not even later on that evening when Eva gently removed the three stitches from the gash on Kevin's forehead.

As it turned out, he never did have to come up with any fabrications. They put him up in an extra bedroom in the old bunkhouse. It was a small house that had been built mainly for farm hands. He was told that he could take his baths and meals in the main house, and it was up to him to cooperate with the other hands in keeping the heater stove going in the bunkhouse.

Eva rounded up a pair of coveralls and a pair of winter boots that fit him quite well. She was always fussing over him, and after a few days, he started to be more relaxed around her.

The two or three day's work turned into nearly two weeks. Each day, he wondered when, and after awhile, if, they were ever going to ask where he was from.

Kevin sensed that Don knew all about him, but decided to stick it out for a while to see what would happen. After lunch on the second Friday he found out why.

Arnold Shaw was surprised to get a phone call from upstairs in the sheriff's office three days after his car had been stolen. The timing couldn't have been better. He was about to have to finance another one from a local car lot.

He worked in the maintenance department of the jail facility, and had been as surprised as anyone to find that his car had been stolen right out of the parking lot. It wasn't much, but at the time it was all he could afford.

The car had been found abandoned along side the road, about two miles from town. He was very surprised that his thermos was still on the back seat. He was very pleased to find that the car had a full tank of gas and he found a twenty-dollar bill in the glove box.

The two farm hands were friendly and easy to get along with. Rudy and Jake had both worked for the Rowe's for several years. They were a couple of hillbilly types who liked their work. Kevin warmed up to them immediately.

Don had introduced him as Kevin 'Sloan.' Kevin nearly blurted out a correction when he did, but knew that it had been no mistake on Don's part. The pay was ten dollars a day and payday was every Friday.

The days were long; the work never ending. Kevin adapted to it from the start. He really enjoyed working around animals. The milk cows were all Holsteins, his favorite. It was on the second Friday that Don and Eva asked him to stay for a minute as the others left the kitchen after lunch.

Don did most of the talking. He passed Kevin an envelope with his pay in it.

"Kevin, I'm driving into Augusta this afternoon, and I'd like for you to come along, if you want to."

He smiled at Kevin's puzzled expression.

"You've earned enough money to get you by for a few days, and you can get out anyplace you want." His voice was filled with genuine concern as he added, "The authorities know that you are here. We told them."

Kevin's heart started racing. He was about to bolt for the door when Eva cut in.

"Kevin." She said his name softly. "We're not turning you in." She looked at her husband. "After what you did for Donald, we owe you more than you can ever know. We really are thinking of your best interest."

"How long have you known?" Kevin asked her.

She smiled and answered, "Since you told us your name. Anytime someone escapes or walks away from either of the prisons, we always get a call. It's just standard procedure for anyone who lives this close."

"You can turn yourself in at the state administration building in Augusta." Don said. "There's a Detective Smiley there that really wants to talk to you." Then he quickly added, "If you decide to."

"No one knows that Don is driving over there today." Eva said. "But they are headed this way to pick you up sometime this afternoon."

"I made a few calls after you got here." Don placed his hand on Kevin's shoulder. "There's a judge in Bangor that guarantees you won't be sent back to that hell hole."

"I won't hold it against you if don't trust those people," Don said, "But there's really not a whole lot of options. That's why it's up to you if you want to go along with my idea."

Kevin's face had turned ashen. He looked at Don and forced a smile. His voice was a whisper as he said, "I guess I'll ride with you. At least for a ways."

He walked over and embraced Eva. "Thank you." He whispered. "I really mean it. Thank you."

Don liked to talk, and went on and on to Kevin about how he thought the whole thing would work out.

Kevin laughed along with him as he said, "The strangest thing happened! I found an old car parked on my property. I think the spark plugs must have gotten soft or something. One of the boys hooked onto the front bumper and it started right up."

He looked at Kevin with a broad grin as he exclaimed, "Without any keys!"

Kevin laughed and said that it was nice that Don had test driven it back to town.

That uneasy feeling began as they approached the outskirts of Augusta. The static energy started in the back of his head and he couldn't get it to stop.

Don pulled the truck over and pointed off to the right at the capitol building. "The new administration office is just on the other side of that building, the one with the shiny dome." He pointed to the left. "The bus stop is a couple blocks that way."

Kevin knew it was time to tell which way for Mr. Rowe to turn the truck. Instead of answering, he opened his door and got out. He walked straight across the street and never looked back.

When Detective Smiley arrived at the Rowe's farm around three in the afternoon he was once again overcome with frustration. Just like before, he was a few hours late.

Mrs. Rowe told him that she hadn't seen Kevin since lunch. Mr. Rowe had driven somewhere on business and she would be sure to ask him to call when he got back.

Chapter Nineteen

Surrender

After walking across the street, Kevin picked up his pace and was nearly running. A feeling of panic swept over him as he realized that there really was no place he could go.

He calmed down a little as he walked quickly down a street leading to the capitol building. He took his time and walked slowly to the new administration building.

There was a park type bench on either side of the walkway leading up to the main entrance. He sat quietly for a few minutes considering his options.

Don had mentioned a judge in Bangor who had told him that there would be no charges against him. His face lit up as he remembered Judge Palmer. He hoped that was to whom Don had been referring. He had never heard of Detective Smiley, and hoped that he would be a fair man. Lately his experiences with police officers and judges had been anything but pleasant.

The secretary at the front desk greeted him cheerfully. Her desk was nearly covered with bouquets of fresh flowers. He told her that the flowers were pretty and asked if she knew where Mr. Smiley's office was. She told him second floor and pointed down the hall to the elevators.

The doors opened to a maze of cubicles. The secretary for that area wasn't at her desk, so he walked on by. Detective Smiley's office was the first one. He took a seat in a chair and quietly waited.

Are you sure?

No.

Is there any other way?

Listen.

There was a stack of newspapers on the floor beside a magazine rack. Kevin started thumbing through them. After a few minutes, he walked around the desk and thumbed through several file folders that were stacked on one side.

His curious streak had the best of him as he boldly sat at the desk and thumbed through Detective Smiley's appointment book. He smiled wondering how long it would take Detective Smiley to make it back from the Rowe farm.

It was late in the afternoon, around four thirty, when a lady peeked in through the open doorway and asked him if he was waiting for someone. He was standing at the window watching the people walking by on the sidewalk below.

"Yes Ma'am." He answered with a smile. "I thought I had an appointment with Detective Smiley."

"I think he's gone for the day." She said. The lady had a nice smile and Kevin felt quite at ease. "Maybe you should check out front to see what his schedule is."

"I'll do that Ma'am." Kevin said.

The lady continued on her way, thinking that those farm boys were so polite.

Third week in May, 1964

The trial was entering its final phase. The prosecution team for the state had expected it to last no more than two weeks, three at the most. It was now well into the sixth week. They were still certain that they would get a conviction.

The trial was held in the state courthouse. The first couple of weeks the courtroom had been nearly packed. As the case dragged on, public interest predictably faded.

Court was declared in session on Monday morning the third week in May, with the honorable Judge Herrol presiding. They all rose as he entered the courtroom. It was predictably boring as the defense team called yet another expert witness.

Boring to some, but not to the young farm boy who sat in the back row. He sat hunched down to where he could barely see over the top of the bench seat in front of him.

I can't see them like this.

You do look like a hayseed.

What do you think? Miller?

Yeah, dark blue.

A yellow tie?

You can't be that desperate.

He quietly got up and left the courtroom.

Judge Palmer waited for Detectives Miller and Smiley at the bottom of the wide stairs that led into the courthouse. They were returning from lunch break, and hurried to join him.

Judge Palmer was a material witness in this case and had been subpoenaed to testify again. Smiley was on one side of him, and Miller on the other, as they started slowly up the steps.

Brett noticed a young man standing at the top of the stairs, holding a sheet of paper in his hand. He was wearing a nice blazer with matching pants. It was dark blue, like his. The boy's white shirt and loud yellow necktie completed the picture.

Howard noticed at the same time and quietly commented to Judge Palmer to take a look at Brett's twin. They were smiling as they got to the top of the steps. Brett smiled and told the boy that he liked his suit. The boy smiled back and entered the courtroom behind them.

They all four walked down to the bench behind the prosecution table. As they took their seats, Judge Palmer turned to look at the boy who was standing quietly behind them.

"Do you need something son?" He asked.

The boy smiled. Judge Palmer stood up as if he had sat on a tack. The look of recognition on his face was priceless.

Brett stood up as Kevin passed him a sheet of paper. His face also took on a look of surprise.

"I never would have known you!" He said. He reached out to shake hands. "All dressed up like this."

Judge Palmer did likewise.

Howard had also stood up, but still had no idea what was going on. He thought perhaps the boy was simply another acquaintance or perhaps a court page.

Later he would say that he nearly had a heart attack when Judge Alfred Leroy Palmer proudly introduced him to his young friend, Kevin Stone.

The dynamics of the trial changed that same day. Kevin had written in scrawling handwriting what he had seen. The next two days were long and drawn out. He was asked the same questions over and over by different people.

He knew that he needed to be extra cooperative and told them what details he could remember. He especially liked his meetings with Mr. Miller.

Brett asked him how he could have known that he was a policeman the first day they had met over three years ago.

Kevin smiled, remembering that day. He still recalled how nice Nadine had looked, and what a wonderful smile she had.

Brett told him that he and Nadine were married and that they had just had a son. It didn't surprise him at all. He thought that they were a good match.

He explained, "That first time when I was in the detention facility, I got to poke around about anywhere I wanted." He hoped that his being a snoop wouldn't be held against him. "There was a file in one of the cabinets. You had applied for a job there right after you graduated college. It had your picture and everything."

Brett nearly laughed. "I'll be!" He exclaimed. "Now I remember. I was sending resumes out everywhere." He smiled and added, "I'm glad it was just you who saw it."

He was still curious as he asked, "How did you know that Nadine and Ruth Green were sisters?"

"They look like twins." Kevin said. He hoped that answer would suffice. He didn't want Mr. Miller to know that he had read Mrs. Green's mail.

Brett asked, "Have you stayed in contact with the Silva's? It's been what, three or four years now. Did you know that they adopted young Adam after his mother died?"

Kevin said he was sorry to hear about Adam's mother dying, but was glad to hear that it had worked out for the best. He said he didn't remember much about those people.

He never was called to testify. He was glad for that. He was allowed in the courtroom when the jury returned with their verdict of guilty, all accounts. He cheered along with the others when the verdict was read.

He had expected to be sent back to the detention center in Brewer. He didn't mind it at all when he was placed in a group home. There were several others there in his age group and he got along well with all of them. He was saddened to learn that the children's home where he had once stayed had been shut down.

In mid July he was surprised to find out that he was going to be returned home to live with his own family. He tried to act pleased at this information and hoped that it would all work out.

He was anxious to see K'leen and Artie again, and felt as though he needed to make amends with Gramps. He hoped he would be able to adjust.

He was given the state placement tests. This was the second time he had taken them and it was decided that he could start high school in the fall. This was good news to him. To him, this meant a fresh start, a new beginning and chance to make amends for his past.

He had been subjected to countless hours of counseling and therapy. He looked forward to meeting with those people and enjoyed each session.

All the reports were good. He had fooled them all.

The group home had a really nice television. It was a black and white set and the picture was very clear. As long as all their chores were done, they were allowed to watch it almost anytime.

The nightly news was dominated by stories of civil unrest in the Deep South. He watched in amazement as news broadcasters showed footage of people being chased by police dogs and knocked off their feet by streams of water from powerful fire hoses.

Just like those pricks in Thomaston.

This isn't right.

The other news story that wouldn't go away was coverage of a war that was starting to become very unpopular with just about everyone. The adults were talking about it every day.

Vietnam?

Why not?

Hopefully. In a couple of years.

Cling to that.

END PART SIX

Foreword Part Seven

(Introduction to part seven: Rumors of War.)

We never did understand why Jason joined the Marines. He had everything going for him. He was an honor student, and a credit to our high school.

I remember the day that Jason came back to visit our school about six months after he graduated. It was somewhere around the first of December.

He looked so mature and proud wearing his military dress uniform. I remember how proud I was of him as he went from one classroom to the other. He was welcomed by all as he said hello, shaking hands with his former teachers and classmates.

Jason graduated in '68. He was at the top of his class, with a full scholarship to the University in Orono. His joining the service was a real shock. I was more surprised than anyone to find out that he had enlisted.

He left for Vietnam a few days after he visited the school. The next time we saw him, he was also wearing his dress uniform. This time it was almost a year to the day after he graduated, and it was at his funeral.

I can still remember his first day at high school. He was enjoying making a big deal over finding his homeroom teacher. He was dressed in bib overalls and looked like some kind of hick trying to find his way back to the farm.

"Are you Mr. Chad?" He asked in a booming voice. "If you are, then I'm in the right place."

I laughed and assured him that I was. "Just find a seat," I said. "You're a little early." I smiled at his attire and asked him if his mom knew that he had taken up farming.

That was the only time I remember him dressed like a hayseed. He really was a nice kid. He was always helping others, always the one with a word of encouragement. I was especially looking forward to having him in my science and biology classes.

The way our school was set up, the students had the same homeroom from their freshman year until they graduated. It was a system that worked quite well. It allowed us, as teachers, to really get to know our students.

There was another young man in my homeroom that I remember well. This one was the total opposite of Jason. He came with a chip on his shoulder and a look in his eye that dared anyone to try to knock it off. His name was Kevin Stone. I think he set some kind of record for times in detention his first two years.

Young Kevin, at first impression, appeared to be somewhat slow witted. As his homeroom teacher, I got to review the transcripts and notes from his elementary school. This boy was surprising. In a margin on an eighth grade evaluation, someone had written 'will quit soon.'

His pretest scores for high school were very impressive; in fact, his scores were higher than Jason's. I think that's why I tried to cut him a little extra slack. According to the placement tests, he was already academically past his sophomore year. This included math, English and general science.

I made a mental note to discuss this with Mr. Jules. He was our assistant principal and the one who had administered the tests. I doubted if there had been any way that Kevin could have cheated on those exams. It made no sense that his prior grades were all barely passing.

I think it was the way that Kevin and Jason got along so well that causes me to smile anytime I think of Kevin. Jason was unquestionably a mentor to him. There were times, after I had come down on Kevin for something or other, that Jason would talk quietly with him. I believe that Kevin never would have made it through the system if not for Jason's encouragement.

There was that one time, after I lowered the hammer on Kevin that he nearly did throw in the towel. We all thought for sure that his high school days were over.

For several days he showed up late and skipped detention. He was only a few days from being expelled when I noticed that he and Jason were sitting outside on the school steps. They were talking and laughing about something. Whatever Jason told him turned everything around. He served his detention and made up his homework assignments.

Whatever it was that he said always brought Kevin back. I can't count all the times Jason told me that Kevin wasn't a bad guy; just give him a chance. Over time, I sensed that the defiant look in his eyes wasn't always a bad thing. Some kids are just that way.

I seriously doubt that they had much to do with each other outside the classroom. Jason was athletic, and even his freshman year, he was first string on both the basketball and baseball teams.

As the years slowly went by, it was obvious that Jason was going to be the one graduating at the top of his class. It was so predictable. This kid was just smart.

It is also quite easy to predict which students will be graduating dead last. Yes, we teachers are human too, and often have our own little side bets on these types of things.

For the first few years, the Stone kid was somewhere at the bottom of the list. His contemptuous attitude was such that it was hard to care a whole lot about him.

He had a rough background, and a few of us had been cautioned about this one. He was known to be an overall bad influence. Even as a freshman, he always had a pack of cigarettes in his shirt pocket.

As time went by and he started driving cars, his lot in life became obvious. One could always expect to see countless empty beer bottles behind the seat. We thought for sure that it was the law that was going to do him in.

We teachers were all aware of the rumors and the bits and pieces of gossip that circulated about this one. I tried to confirm the one about him living in his car that winter of '67, but could never pin him down.

For a while he stayed with the Cross and the Nelson families and from time to time at his own home. I knew his stepmother and often asked her to keep me informed. There was something about Kevin that caused me to do what I could to insure that he didn't quit school.

His closest friend was a kid named Mitch Nelson. Until the time they started hanging out together, Mitch had been destined to be a dropout. There was something that changed in him after he and Kevin became friends. I think Kevin was to Mitch, what Jason was to Kevin.

One of the teachers told me that Kevin had been in more schoolyards fights than anyone they had ever heard of. He had been picked on nearly all of his life. Once he got some size to him, he would light into anyone who was picking on smaller kids.

Mitch's reputation from grade school was that of a bully. I guess he was always picking on someone. His reckoning was long over due when he crossed paths with Kevin.

Maybe that's another reason I smile when I think of that oldest Stone boy. Although he had never been blamed for starting trouble, he was always in some kind of a scrape.

They say he taught Mitch a lesson, a bloody one, out at Sebec Lake. I guess Mitch's dad still brags about that. He claims that they nearly beat each other to death, and that was just what Mitch needed.

Jason went out of his way to assist Kevin in the few classes they shared together. I must admit; I was stunned when Kevin made the honor roll, twice, his junior year. That was about the same time he started working in the school workfare program and driving his own car.

Kevin was always quiet and respectful in my classes and in homeroom. Any trouble he may have been in, always happened off the school grounds.

Maybe that's why it was so hard for me to believe all the reports and ignore the accusations from the local law and game enforcement officials. I know that if they could have, they would have hung him out to dry.

Like most high schools at the time, we were all torn up over a far off war that just wouldn't end. At the beginning, I was supportive like most folks. As it dragged on, the sheer horror of the whole thing sank in.

In '66 we lost a young man who had joined the Army after graduating. We all saw him in his dress uniform when he stopped by to visit the school around Thanksgiving. The next time we saw him, he was in his uniform, and as it was destined to be with Jason, it was at his funeral.

I remember seeing Kevin and Jason sitting together at the funeral services. Neither had much to say. It was that look in Kevin's eyes that caused me to start treating him with a little more respect after that.

I'd like to say I stopped counting, but who could forget such waste? All told, from '66 to '72 we attended the funerals of five young men who had gone through our school. Two of them were closed casket services.

I clearly remember two more who were wounded in that awful war. One was severely crippled for the rest of his life. At least a half dozen others who had gone through our school system came back unscathed, including Kevin.

Kevin's guidance counselor, Mr. Washman was also his industrial arts teacher. For a while, Kevin did very well in his classes. It was at the start of his senior year that Mr. Washman unloaded on him in the hallway. This turned Kevin's attitude back to one of disrespect and contempt. I was in the teachers lounge and overheard the whole thing through the open door.

Kevin had been excited and smiling all that day. Jason had been trying to talk him into going on to trade school after graduation, and Kevin was finally starting to listen to him. He had done quite well his junior year, and the start of the senior term was also looking promising.

It was Jason's enthusiasm that caused Kevin to ask Mr. Washman if he could try to get him into the college courses.

I'll never forget the open contempt Mr. Washman had for him. I like to think that if I had been Kevin standing there in the hall being humiliated like that, that I would have knocked that ornery old man right in the teeth.

Over the next several months, Mr. Washman was plagued with car trouble. Someone was always messing with his car or his truck, causing all kinds of mechanical problems. I soon came to realize that Kevin was behind it.

I had a confidential talk with him one morning, and we laughed over the whole thing. He never admitted anything, but we had a good laugh, and the pranks and personal vandalism against Mr. Washman stopped.

Their senior year wasn't much different than the year before. I remember several times when the police, and once, a game warden came to the school to talk to him. He never offered any explanations, but I got the scoop in the teacher's lounge anytime something happened.

When graduation day rolled around, Kevin was as proud as I had ever seen him. He had a girlfriend. They were about as unlikely a match as one could find.

Sarah Carter was a really nice girl from a good home. How Kevin ever hooked up with her is beyond me. I am sure that she was the reason that almost overnight; he turned into a surprisingly good student. In fact, as I recall, there were never any police visits or complaints after the two of them started dating.

I didn't see much of Kevin after he graduated. Not until nearly a year later. He had taken a job at one of the local mills and appeared to be doing fine. He married Sarah Carter and they were expecting a child. Those few times I did see him, he was always happy and enthusiastic.

I remember that winter as being a terribly long one. It was one of the longest I have ever endured. It seemed like spring would never come.

Jason wasn't one for keeping in close touch. This surprised me as much as than anyone. I had expected him to be a lot better about writing.

I saw Kevin at Jason's funeral. It was one of those rare occasions when he wore a sport coat and tie. I didn't see any tears, but could tell that he was as shaken up as anyone.

I can't help but think that it should have been the other way around.

It should have been Kevin. He's the one who should have joined the Marines. He was more the type. It should have been Jason sitting quietly at his funeral.

I know that makes me sound bitter. I can't help it. I guess it was just one of life's little twists that we have to accept. We never did understand why Jason joined the Marines. I still miss him so much.

He was my son.

Teacher: *The evil that men do is immeasurable. History is documented with acts of unspeakable cruelty that man has inflicted upon his fellow man.*

Student: *So are deeds of kindness.*

Teacher: *This is true.*

Student: *Why is it that we speak often of acts of war and not of kindness?*

Teacher: *Both can be found in times of war.*

Student: *Why then, must we have war?*

Teacher: *Without war there can be no peace.*

Student: *Beam me up.*

PART SEVEN

Rumors of War

Chapter Twenty

Mixed Signals

Bangor Maine, July 1964

"Mail call!" Percy had a loud voice. He really wasn't shouting, but it sure seemed that way to everyone else. He was standing in the foyer outside his office door with several letters in his hand. He ran the group home and everyone liked him. "Come on everyone! Let's see who's got mail."

Percy did his best to make mail call an event. There were several young adults at that location that never got mail of any kind. He had a knack of making them feel a part of the family by making it a tradition for all to share in the excitement. Most of the residents, including Kevin, sometimes read their letters aloud. It was different, but it drew them together as a group.

He called out several names, including Kevin's. Kevin laughed at how Percy was always excited over handing out the mail and thanked him for the letter.

"Is it another one from your mother?" Percy asked.

"My step-mom." Kevin replied.

"That's nice." Percy said. "I hope you appreciate what she's trying to do for you."

Kevin smiled. He liked how Percy was always so positive about everything.

"I'm trying to. Runt."

"Your folks are due down today. Aren't they?"

"Yeah."

"Well, if Irene brings more cookies, you'd better share!" They enjoyed a laugh and joked about Irene's cookies.

"You can have 'em all if they're as hard as last time."

"Hey. I've got milk. Bring 'em on!"

Percy was a short man in his mid forties. Everyone referred to him, as 'runt' and he didn't mind. On the door to his small office he had hung a sign that said, 'Keep your act together lest ye suffer the wrath of the Runt.' It wasn't a fancy sign, just something he had scrawled on a piece of paper, but the residents took his message seriously.

Kevin made a mental note to write a letter for Percy to read to the others when he got home. He knew Percy would like that. He was one of the kindest men he had ever met.

It was another letter from Irene. She had written to him every week since they had found out where he was. He figured on sharing it with the others later. He went outside and sat on the top step of the porch to read it.

Irene always mentioned something in her letters about each of his brothers and sisters. In this letter she told him that Artie was excited about him coming home soon, and K'leen had been by several times. She had given K'leen his address and she had promised to write.

Matthew was doing well and said to say that he missed him. Marie had developed a very good vocabulary and was jabbering a mile a minute. The new baby had been born a month ago. He now had another brother, little Jeremy.

Wow, another brother.
Quit being sarcastic.
Why? They're just being nice.
Let's give them a chance.
If you say so.
You really need to go away.

Kevin had reacted a lot differently than he had thought he would towards Dad and Irene. They had driven down to Bangor to visit him at the group home about two weeks ago.

They had been brought up to date on the past events and were anxious to see him. They had met with Judge Palmer and a representative from social services prior to coming to visit. They thought they had everything pretty much figured out.

The state people believed that Kevin had been in his family's care up until the time of his incarceration. Dad and Irene thought that he had been in state care since November.

They never did find out the identities of the two men that had stopped by back in November and told them that Kevin had been placed back in state custody. It was strange that they had arrived to pick him up, and then left in a hurry when they found out that he wasn't home.

None of it mattered now. Kevin was due to come home soon, and they were both anxious to get all this mess behind them.

They knew that Kevin was expecting them as they parked in front of the home. Irene looked up as she got out and smiled brightly as she saw Kevin standing on the front porch. He was smiling as he vaulted over the porch railing.

She was very surprised when he ran towards them. She was the first one he embraced, and this was the first time she had known him to be happy to see her. He was smiling ear to ear as Dad came around the car.

"Hey Dad, did they tell you?" Kevin said excitedly. "I passed all the tests for high school."

"That's great, Kevin!" Dad exclaimed. "We were told that you had to take some more tests and it's good that you passed!"

"Come on in." Kevin said. "I want you to say hello to Percy. Remember him? He's the little runt who runs this place." As if an afterthought he asked, "Did you bring more cookies? Percy doesn't have many teeth left after that last batch, but he's a real sucker for punishment."

"No cookies today, Son." Irene said.

"I guess my lucks not all bad." Kevin replied.

He had fun teasing Irene. She didn't mind. Kevin was as relaxed as she had ever seen him. Whatever influence Percy and the others at the home had on him was good.

They enjoyed a good visit with Percy and several of the others who lived there. Percy said that he felt as if he had known them for years because of what Kevin had been telling him and after hearing several of Irene's letters.

They all enjoyed another quiet laugh and Irene tried not to blush as he made her promise to make up another batch of her famous hard rock cookies.

Irene asked Kevin if he would like to go with them to visit with his Aunt Stella and his cousins. Kevin thought that to be a great idea.

Aunt Stella still lived in the same apartment, and Kevin was overjoyed to find that it was only about a half mile from the group home. As long as he kept out of trouble, he would be allowed to walk over and visit with them almost anytime. His cousin, Michael, was also allowed to visit him at the group home.

When they dropped him off, they were once again surprised at how he was acting. Neither had expected him to be this well behaved and pleasant.

Kevin was feeling good as he waved goodbye. He stood on the porch and watched the car drive out of sight.

Don't get your hopes up.
Will you just go away?
Nothing's changed.
Leave me alone.
You'll see.
Just go away.
When you get home. You'll see.

Kevin was officially released from state care the last week in July. It was a boring ride back to Brownville. He didn't think much of the social services worker who drove him home and was glad when he was dropped off.

He was determined to make amends for his past behavior and to stay out of trouble. The memories of the reform school were still fresh in his mind. He knew that with his past record, it wouldn't take much to get him sent back there.

****

His determination for a fresh start may have worked if not for the voice in the back of his mind. He took it to be his conscience. He couldn't get it to stop.

It was when the nightmares returned to haunt him that he withdrew back into his own little world. It wasn't long until his mind once again clouded over, and as before, he lived day to day.

****

Bill Riley was excited to hear that Kevin had been reunited with his family and that it looked like everything was going to work out.

His wife thought it a good idea to ask if Kevin would like to mow their lawn and do some cleanup work around their place. They both knew that Kevin would prefer to work in the woods, but there was no work near enough for him to get back and forth.

They both expected that Rory would be back working for them once he finished a job in Greenbush. They hoped to be able to once again pair the two of them up.

Bill was in for a rude awakening when he discovered that Kevin had no interest in working for him. It really bothered him when Kevin's misplaced hatred and contempt for him came to the surface. It took him by surprise when Kevin unloaded on him when they met in the parking lot of a grocery store in town.

It was on a Monday that Kevin hitched a ride to town and went from one business to the next asking if anyone had work. He had received some sound advice from Percy at the group home in how to get a job. He knew it was going to be tough. After all, he was only fourteen.

His first stop was at the car lot on the edge of town behind the police station. He was a pretty good mechanic, and told the man that he was willing to do anything. The man seemed rushed and made no effort to be polite. He mumbled that he had all the help he needed. Kevin walked away feeling a bit put down.

Maybe we'll see that jerk later.

Yeah. Maybe.

He renewed his determination to find work when he made another stop at the large grocery store. It was the same one he had raided last winter. He was smiling ear to ear as he entered and asked the lady at the front if he could speak to the manager.

He had a brief visit with the storeowner and figured out from the first minute that he hadn't a prayer of a chance at getting hired. The man told him it was due to him being so young. He could tell that the man knew about his past and wouldn't have hired him if he were the last person on earth in search of a job.

He went outside, determined to have better luck at the next location when he saw Sheriff Bradley's patrol car in the parking lot. He looked up and caught his breath as he saw Bill Riley leaning against the car, having a conversation with the Sheriff. He quickly turned and started walking in another direction, but not before Bill spotted him.

"Hey! Kevin!" Bill called. He was smiling in anticipation of seeing Kevin.

Kevin felt the hairs on the back of his neck stand up.

It's them!

Those two-timing bastards.

Get out of here!

Now!

He froze in mid stride as Sheriff Bradley called to him.

"Kevin, hold up there." The sheriff got out of his car and smiled at him. "We haven't seen you in a long time. Come on over and chat for a bit."

Bill noticed that Kevin was standing there trembling. His face was ashen as he slowly turned and stared at them. The look in his eyes was unlike they had ever seen.

"Well, what's up?" Bill was joking as he exclaimed. "Did you get all stuck up or something?" The look on Kevin's face caused him to stop smiling.

Kevin's face went from ashen to bright red. A feeling of dread swept over him and settled in the pit of his stomach. A release of static energy started in the back of his head as his mind went blank.

His voice was breaking as he shook uncontrollably. He started cursing and raving at the both of them.

Sheriff Bradley stood in amazement, as did Bill, as Kevin unloaded on them. His profanity reached a new level as he called them a couple of 'Judas sons of bitches' in between fits of cursing. They had never heard such language from one so young.

Sheriff Bradley's face took on a stern expression as he took a step towards Kevin, saying, "Kevin! My God son, what's gotten into you?"

"You sold me out! You Judas son of a bitch!" Kevin's voice was hysterical. "You assholes stay to hell away from me!"

Sheriff Bradley had taken only a couple steps in Kevin's direction when Kevin turned and bolted across the road. He was filled with rage. He didn't think to check for cars as he fled in a blind panic.

There were several patrons of the store standing beside their cars listening and watching in amazement as they witnessed the scene.

An elderly lady shrieked in terror as Kevin ran in front of a car. They all caught their breath as the car's brakes locked up causing the tires to screech loudly.

Somehow Kevin dodged around the front of the car. He lost his balance and rolled once on his shoulder and scrambled up again. He continued running away from them.

Sheriff Bradley stood silently beside Bill as Kevin disappeared from sight. He was running through a grove of hardwood trees.

They exchanged amazed glances. It was Bill who broke the silence.

"My God." Bill's voice was barely audible. "What to hell just happened?"

"I don't know." Sheriff Bradley exhaled as though he had been holding his breath. "I sure as hell don't know."

Kevin was running in a blind panic. He was gasping for breath when he took cover in an alley behind one of the local stores. He remained concealed behind a dumpster as he tried to get control of his emotions.

Damn that was close.

Those Judas sons of bitches.

Never trust them.

Never!

When Kevin got home just before dark Irene was waiting to talk to him. Sheriff Bradley had already stopped by and told her what had happened.

"It's going to be okay, Kevin." She assured him. "Sheriff Bradley and Bill got to talking it over. They both know that they were the last two people you saw before those state people took you away."

She tried to embrace him and was a bit startled when he violently pulled away. "Kevin. They didn't sell you out. Judge Palmer already told your father and me that it was a mix up in the paper work."

Kevin seemed to be ignoring her.

She raised her voice slightly and added, "That's all it was. Just an awful mix up."

Irene was really surprised as Kevin said with a broad smile. "Guess what? I got a job!"

The comment and the cheerful smile simply didn't fit the circumstance. Irene shuddered involuntarily and said, "You did! That's great. Where?"

"For the Sloan farm." Kevin answered. He was making it up as he went along. "They need someone to help with the haying and farm chores. I know you don't like them, but the pay's good and I do need to buy school clothes."

"Yes, I suppose so." Irene murmured.

"I don't need to be there until second milking and should be home before dark every day!"

Irene was still at a loss over his abrupt change of attitude. She wondered for a moment if he even heard what she had said.

The rest of the summer went by quickly. Kevin knew without a doubt that neither dad nor Irene would ever check with the Sloan's to see if he was really working there. They had been feuding with each other since he could remember.

His former days of midnight raids and stolen cars were merely a preview of what was to come. Those gut wrenching nightmares and endless nights of cold sweats and silent screams were far from over.

When high school started it wasn't that bad. Kevin adapted quite well. He didn't much care what anyone thought or said about him. He quickly became just another student.

Neither Irene nor dad ever questioned him about his job on the Sloan farm. He appeared to be doing fine and occasionally showed up with new clothes for school.

When the schools were shut down for the potato-picking season, Kevin once again joined them in working in the fields.

Chapter Twenty-One

The Vigilantes

Medway Maine, August 1964

The young porcupine was simply attempting to cross the road. The night was nearly pitch black due to a low cloud cover and a light mist of rain that was falling. As he scurried on his way across the damp pavement, he stopped to view the bright lights that were approaching fast.

He froze in place as he heard the thunderous sounds of the powerful automobile engines. The four bright lights, side by side, were suddenly upon him.

The prickly little guy just didn't know any better. This was the last thing he saw, as he became just another road kill on a winding back road in northern Maine.

The two cars were obviously drag racing as they sped side by side down the highway. It was a race between a new Dodge and a fifty-six Chevy, both driven by teenage boys who were determined to win.

The Chevy was way out in front coming off the line when the driver missed a gear. The Dodge screamed on past it as they approached the top of a small hill.

John Decotos was driving his fathers brand new Dodge. It had an automatic gearshift and a slant six engine. His girlfriend sat in the middle and his younger brother, Billy, was riding shotgun.

The kid they were racing had rebuilt the Chevy's engine and installed a new four-speed transmission. The two eighty-three Chevy should have easily outdistanced the Dodge. It probably would have had the driver been sober.

"Watch out!" Billy yelled. "That pimply faced son of a bitch is coming around us!"

"Not tonight, he's not!" John's voice was loud and excited as he shouted to be heard over the sounds of the two cars. He kept the gas pedal floored as the car topped the small hill.

"Crap! Crap! Did you see that porcupine?" Billy shouted hysterically. "I heard its guts splat!"

John paid no mind that the Chevy was now along side of them as he laughed uproariously. The six-cylinder engine was screaming as John once again veered across the centerline to prevent it from passing.

The girls in the back seat of the Chevy were shouting with glee and excitement. The one with both elbows on the seat back was shouting, "Faster! Faster!" The boy who was riding in the front was clinging to the dash with a white knuckled grip, trying not to be sick.

They came sliding around a sharp corner at the bottom of the steep hill. The two cars sideswiped. The collision and the shower of sparks that followed caused both drivers to panic and jam on the brakes.

"Oh crap! Oh crap! Dad's going to kill us!" Billy's panicked voice was drowned out by like cursing from his older brother and a scream of terror from the girl.

The cars separated and came screeching around the corner at the bottom of the hill with the Dodge in the rear.

In the pitch-blackness, their headlights illuminated the red reflectors on the taillights of the vehicle ahead. The girls in the rear seat of the Chevy screamed in fright when they saw the pickup truck. It was stopped beside the road with its hood up. The Chevy swerved to miss it.

John didn't see the truck until it was too late. The Chevy swerved out from in front of him leaving him no time to do anything other than jam on the brakes. He slammed head on squarely into the rear of the truck.

The Chevy veered into a ditch and rolled once down a shallow embankment.

Constable Hank Farr and his wife were sleeping peacefully when the phone rang around two in the morning.

The phone was on Hank's side of the bed. He came wide-awake as he knocked it off the nightstand in an attempt to pick up.

He swung his legs onto the floor as he frantically reached for the handset. Stella turned on the lamp as he answered.

It was officer Milan from the highway patrol. "Hank, there's been an accident. It's just outside of your jurisdiction but we need you to come."

"What?" Hank's voice elevated. "What happened?"

"Teenagers. Looks like they've been drinking. They're shaken up real bad. Looks like two of them are in serious condition. It was a rollover and a straight on collision into a parked truck. The ambulance is on its way."

"Oh, damn!" Hank exclaimed. "Anyone local? Who was driving?"

"That's why we called you." Milan said. "We know you like to be up to date on these things. The driver fled the scene; he's a local; one of yours. I'll fill you in when you get here. I've also called the Sheriff's department in on this. Looks like we may have a manhunt."

"Oh, damn." Hank murmured.

Officer Milan gave him directions.

"I'll be right there."

He told Stella not to worry and quickly got dressed. He rushed to his car and turned on the overheads and siren as he sped down the road and across the bridge.

Arriving on the scene of an accident is perhaps one of the most dreaded experiences for a local policeman. The chances were good that he would know those involved. Milan had said that several of the kids were locals.

Several other cars were already at the scene. The darkness was illuminated from the headlights and the blinking overheads of a highway patrol car and two sheriff's vehicles. Hank pulled over and left his headlights on as he approached the scene.

He nearly tripped and fell in the soft shoulder of the roadway as he sidestepped to stay clear of the ambulance. Someone shouted his name.

Patrolman Milan had been the first to arrive on the scene. The wreck had occurred in front of several homes, and someone had immediately called the highway patrol. He was now standing in the midst of a small crowd that had gathered. He waved for Hank to join them.

Several of the teenagers had been taken inside one of the houses. They sat around a kitchen table. They were trembling, knowing that they were all in a world of trouble. Most were only shaken up and had already called their parents.

"The wrecked Dodge belongs to Art Decotos." Patrolman Milan said. "His son John was driving. Looks like he panicked and fled the scene."

"Damn." Hank murmured. "This is serious."

Milan lowered his voice as he added, "His brother, Billy, is the one being loaded in the ambulance now."

"I can't tell you how many times I've pulled those two over." Hank said. "Speeding. Reckless driving. Possession of alcohol. You name it. Have you called the parents?"

"We tried to call his house, a couple times, but no one's answering the phone."

"Damn!" Hank exclaimed. "Will that boy ever learn? He's probably just scared. We can poke around here some, but I'm sure he'll show up at his house." He shook his head and added, "Young John is in some serious trouble this time. Did you know that he lost his license nearly a month ago? The result of one too many speeding tickets."

"I figured as much." Milan replied.

About then, a tow truck arrived on the scene. While the deputies and patrolman Milan focused on clearing up the mess, Hank began his search for young John.

The Decotos lived in a trailer about a mile from the scene of the wreck and he figured that John was probably already at home. He drove slowly on the way there, shining his spotlight out the window, hoping to see the boy walking in the darkness.

There were no lights on at the Decotos'. He left his car running as he pounded on the front door. When there was no answer, he left a note wedged inside the storm door.

As he drove back down the hill, he thought he saw movement in the abandoned shack that sat on the right hand side of the street. It had once been home to the Stone family.

He pulled into the drive. The car's lights lit up the dilapidated building in an eerie glow. He sat there and shined his spotlight through the broken panes of glass.

As his light shined beneath the sagging front porch, his thoughts wandered back to the day when he and Mr. Brooks had found young Kevin. It had been over four years ago, but seemed like only yesterday.

His mood instantly became angry as he recalled his initial shock at finding the nine-year-old boy nearly frozen to death beneath the porch. His small body had been covered in blood. They initially believed that they had found a corpse.

With these thoughts on his mind, he reached for the five-cell flashlight on the seat and got out. As he stepped up to the door, he forced a grim smile. It was still splintered and broken from when he had kicked it in that day so long ago. Someone had patched it from the inside with a board.

As he stepped inside, shining his light around, he sensed that someone was there.

"John! Is that you?" He spoke the words softly. "John, it's going to be okay."

He heard the sounds of the back door opening and closing fast and rushed to the rear of the house. He stood on the back step and once again called out as he shined his flashlight into the trees and brush of the back yard.

"John! This is constable Farr. It's going to be okay. John? Just calm down and come back here."

There was no answer.

Hank walked back to his car and radioed for assistance from the sheriff. A deputy sheriff arrived a few minutes later.

"I think John may be hurt." Hank said. "I found fresh blood inside. I heard someone duck out the back. He can't have gone far." Then he asked, "How are the others?"

"Looks like they'll be okay." The deputy answered. "They think Billy may have a few broken ribs and the girl has a concussion. Her face went right through the windshield. She won't be so pretty after this."

"Damn," Hank murmured. "How about the others? "

"Most of 'em have scrapes and abrasions, but it could have been a lot worse."

"How about the other driver?"

"Not a scratch on him."

"Well, Let's be careful." Hank said. "John's scared and may try something stupid."

"No doubt, after what's happened already." The deputy said. "He's man grown. This is serious."

A second sheriff's car arrived. They split up and started a sweep of the area.

The clouds had broken up and now the light of a half moon illuminated the early morning. As they started around the side of the house to begin their search, Hank's mind once again flashed back to another tragic scene.

He stood for a moment, looking at the trashed area where Rick Orin's trailer had sat. Tall weeds and bushes were growing randomly around the blackened, twisted, metal frame.

What had once been the front steps still remained almost as if waiting for another trailer to be moved into place. In the pale moonlight, the charred hand railing appeared to be shiny black.

He remembered feeling no compassion at all for Rick Orin when he died in that fire. There were few people who came to mind in the same despicable light as that man.

Rick Orin had beaten young Kevin nearly to death. Then he had allowed him to lie dying beneath the porch while the other children were sleeping. Rick had been Kevin's uncle. It never should have happened like that.

Hank shuddered at the coldness of the whole episode. He believed it to be some kind of miracle that the dog lying beside the boy that cold winter night, had kept him from freezing to death.

He recalled the three fires, all within the same family, and all within a few weeks of each other. First the grandmother's place had burned. That was a true shame. It had been a real nice house.

Then Rick Orin had died when his trailer burned. Everyone attributed that one to his being drunk and smoking in bed. A few days later, during his funeral services, the Decotos house had been gutted by fire.

Art and Zella Decotos were aunt and uncle to Kevin. Their boys, John and Billy were his cousins. Hank could never comprehend the open hostility and hatred that they had displayed towards young Kevin. He felt a shiver go all the way up and down his spine as he thought about some of the problems he had been called in on over the years.

The Decotos now lived in a new trailer house that sat where their old house had been. It was still his opinion that there was no way that all three fires could have been a coincidence.

His thoughts were interrupted when someone shouted, "He's over here!"

Hank hurried in the direction of the voice. He stumbled along on the narrow path behind the house.

John had taken refuge in a rusted out old panel wagon that sat abandoned a short distance behind the house. The deputy was trying to coax him out as Hank approached.

He shined his light inside and smiled grimly. John's shirtfront was soaked in blood. Apparently he had broken his nose against the steering wheel in the accident. He was curled up in the back, crying and shaking uncontrollably.

"I can't get him to come out." The deputy said. He sounded irritated. "It's been a long night." He raised his voice. "John, Damn it. Get out here. Now!"

Hank cut in. "John. We can do this the easy way or the hard way."

"I'm coming out." John sobbed.

Hank sat his flashlight down and helped young John out through the creaky back doors. He steadied him as he cried and wailed pitifully.

"John. Didn't I tell you that it's going to be okay?" Hank asked in a soothing tone. "Settle down. We need to see how badly you're hurt."

The deputy wiped a rag that he had picked up from inside the panel wagon several times across the side windows to get it damp. He passed it to Hank and held his flashlight steady as Hank gently wiped the blood away from John's face.

"You'll be fine." Hank told the frightened boy.

"It looks like his nose is broke." The deputy said.

"I'm sorry, Hank." John sobbed.

"Quit being a baby!" The deputy snarled, "You damn near got a car load of kids killed tonight."

"I'm sorry."

"Easy." Hank said. "We'll worry about all that later. It could have been a lot worse. Right?"

"Dad's going to kill me!" John sobbed.

"Serves you right if he does." The deputy said. "But he will have to wait in line. Hold out your hands." He placed John in handcuffs.

"Now. Quit your sniveling and let's go." the deputy said. "It's been a long night."

John offered no reply as they slowly started their way back to where the police cars were still parked with their headlights on. The second deputy had returned to the cars and stood waiting for them.

They escorted John to the deputy's car. Hank said good night and watched silently as they loaded John in the back and headed to the clinic in East.

It was nearly daylight. Hank realized that he had left his flashlight in the back of the old panel wagon and carefully made his way back along the trail.

The flashlight was still shining softly. It was nearly concealed beneath an old mattress that had been skewed sideways when they had helped John get out.

As he reached for it, he noticed an old envelope tucked beneath a corner of the tattered mattress. What caught his eye was the return address on the letter. It was standing out in the center of the beam of light. It was from his friend, Gene Richards.

He picked it up. It was addressed to Master Kevin Stone, in care of Henry Silva at a rural address in Exter.

Curiosity got the better of him as he took out a tattered single sheet of paper. It was typewritten.

He gasped and sat down abruptly. He said it aloud.

"Oh my God!" The full impact of what it meant hit him right between the eyes as his flashlight illuminated the date on the correspondence.

"Oh my God!"

There could be no doubt now that young Kevin had been in the area during the time of the fires. This was proof.

Once again his mind flashed to the scene of finding the boy half dead in the dirt beneath the porch. Clear as day he heard Mr. Brooks as he said, "Hank, I think he's dead!"

His mind was spinning as he remembered several of the times when he and Sheriff Benning had exchanged phone calls about problems with the Stone family. Young Kevin had clocked more time in the hospital than anyone he could remember.

Several times had been due to beatings he had received from his uncle Rick and his cousins, John and Billy Decotos. He was certain that they were the ones. He never had believed the story about Kevin being struck by a blue roadster.

Then there was that awful incident at the evangelical church. Now he was certain that young Kevin had been involved in that. It was so sickening that he didn't want to think about it.

It was the day after the funeral services for the Stone baby. He felt lightheaded as he tried to remember if it had been a boy or a girl. The child had died a day after birth. His wife had told him that she thought Kevin had gone into convulsions when they dragged him from the church services.

He had been called to the church by the preacher early the next morning. He had found Kevin a short distance away. He had been sitting beside the road, in a ditch, in the pouring rain.

"Those poor kids." He murmured as he put two and two together. He shivered involuntarily.

He could feel that his face had lost all color. He recalled the awful mess that someone had made in the church with a dead sheep. Kevin had only been nine years old at the time and too young to be a suspect. In the end, they had attributed the whole incident as being some kind of satanic prank, more than likely pulled off by teenagers.

"He was too small to carry it inside the church all in one piece." His mind was in a spin. "That's why he hacked it up."

He felt as if he was going to be sick as he figured it out. "It was supposed to be a sacrifice." He turned his eyes to the heavens as he spoke aloud again. "A sacrifice! Oh my God. He wanted to bring the baby back."

He was talking to himself when his thoughts returned to the death of Rick Orin.

"He was only ten years old then." His voice broke. He was talking to the heavens as he gazed skyward as if in search of an answer. "Ten years old. It was him! It was him that sent his uncle straight to hell."

He looked at the date on the paper in his hand. "Oh sweet Jesus." He sat on the rear bumper of the panel wagon with tears streaming down both cheeks as he thought of what to do.

He realized that it could just as easily have been him who had killed the boy's uncle. When he had found out that Rick Orin wasn't going to be charged for the actions against young Kevin, he had gone after the bastard himself.

It had been a long time ago but it seemed like only yesterday. He had kicked in the door seeking revenge for what had happened to young Kevin. Had Rick been there alone, who knows what would have happened.

He knew that he would have beaten Rick Orin and Kevin's dad to death if he hadn't gotten a grip on his anger. He had been blinded by rage, unstoppable as he beat the living daylights out of both of them. The courts had been sympathetic to him and that incident had only cost him a fifty-dollar fine.

"Oh sweet Jesus. That boy's no worse a vigilante than I am." He murmured.

The sun was peeking through the treetops when he decided what to do. He was trembling as he slowly reached inside his shirt pocket for a match.

He watched, almost in awe, as the envelope and its contents slowly curled up as the flames caught on. He smiled grimly as the charred remnants settled in a wisp of smoke on the damp ground. He finished the job with the heel of his boot as he stood up to leave.

He walked past the charred ruins of what was once Rick Orin's old trailer house. He shuddered as he recalled helping the coroner pull the grotesque remains of Rick Orin from the rubble.

He paused for a moment as he said under his breath, "Burn in hell. You sinning son of a bitch."

It was about a half hour after daylight when he got home. Stella was in the kitchen, brewing up a pot of coffee. He brought her up to date on last night's accident and the capture of young John Decotos.

He hugged her and asked if she would cook bacon and eggs for breakfast.

Chapter Twenty-Two

Conscious Decisions

<u>June 1965</u>

It was around midnight when Kevin slowly eased the back door open and started silently on his mission. He quietly made his way around the house and started running down the road.

It was a clear night with a quarter moon. He alternated walking and jogging until he covered the mile to a neighbor's house. He quietly borrowed a bicycle that was leaning against the detached garage and started peddling to town.

You call this a set of wheels?

Just wait.

He made his first stop at the local sporting goods store. It was around two in the morning when he smashed the glass in the rear door and let himself in. He had already cased the joint and knew where to find everything he wanted.

He left with a duffel bag stuffed with two fishing poles and lots of tackle. The store also sold snacks in a display on the counter. He cleaned it out. He thought briefly about leaving an IOU with an x for a signature. This thought caused him to laugh as he hurried outside.

It was awkward peddling the bike with a duffel bag slung over his shoulder. He didn't have far to go. He stopped at the used car lot that was across the alley behind the police station. Thus far he hadn't met a single car.

A really nice fifty-seven Chevy sat alone on a corner of the lot. There was a large for sale sign in its window. He was familiar with the wiring. It took him less than two minutes to shimmy open a wing window and start it up.

He opened the passenger's side door and loaded the bike in. His laughter was nearly out of control as he put the car in gear and drove off.

It was nearly four in the morning when he peddled the stolen bike back to its rightful owner. He had left the car stashed out of sight on an old woods road about a mile back. He had everything figured out.

I'll bet that jerk wishes he gave us a job.

Damn straight.

Let's work for the Sloans again.

Why not?

He left the house around ten every morning and kept up his charade of walking to work. He was sure to be home before dark everyday. It didn't bother him that he wasn't earning any money; he had a plan.

He kept the borrowed car parked deep in the woods behind their farm. It was only a mile walk through the woods along an old logging road to where he kept it stashed behind an abandoned cabin that was falling down from neglect.

A short distance in the opposite direction was a large gravel pit. It had been abandoned for years and the road leading to it opened up on another paved road. It was off the beaten path and ideal for him. The Sloan farm was about a quarter mile from the turn off to the gravel pit.

As he had expected, no one ever checked with the Sloan family to verify that he was working there. He seldom talked about it, and often used his 'extra pay' to buy clothes and toys for his younger siblings.

His nighttime escapades had risen to a new level. On more than one occasion he had resorted to shopping using his midnight credit. This included new clothes for school and anything he could quickly stuff into a sack. One night he drove clear to Dexter to check out the cash register in a fast food restaurant.

This second summer of his charade was going quite well. His routine seldom changed. He had figured on doing some serious fishing with his recently acquired tackle, and he did. He loved to fish and had already given away enough fish to total strangers to feed an army.

He had a hard time making up an explanation for being at Sebec Lake when he was supposed to be working, when he came home with a black eye and bruises. He and Mitch Nelson had nearly beaten the snot out of each other.

The fight was one that they would long remember. They had met at Sebec Lake. Kevin was fishing from the boat dock in front of a cabin when Mitch saw him and ordered him to hell off their property. Kevin recognized Mitch from school and wasn't about to take any crap from him.

He knew that Mitch had the right to ask him to get off the dock, but not from the shore. He moved his position a few feet away and stood casting his line from a large flat rock.

"I told you to get to hell off our property!" Mitch was shouting from the small porch of the cabin. "We don't want your kind here."

"Screw you. Loudmouth." Kevin retorted. "I laugh at pantywaist tough guys like you."

Kevin's mocking laughter caused Mitch to lose his temper. He stormed over and stood eye to eye with Kevin.

Kevin didn't hesitate. He nailed him with all his might. It was a straight punch from the shoulder to Mitch's mid section. It knocked Mitch backwards into the water.

"I don't take no more crap from jerks like you!" He shouted. "You don't own the damn lake and I'll fish right here anytime I want to."

Mitch got up gasping for air and charged at him. He tackled him off the rock. He was about Kevin's size and had been in more than his share of scraps.

Kevin was knocked off balance. Mitch gripped his shirt collar and dragged him to shore.

He lunged at Mitch and broke free of the grip on his collar. They both fell down on the rocky shore, cursing and throwing punches at each other.

He heard someone shouting. It was Mitch's father, Clarence, yelling at them from the porch. Mitch turned his head to shout something to his father. Kevin nailed him in the jaw. He followed it up with a tackle.

They were throwing punches, cursing and swearing at each other, when Clarence Nelson started laughing. He was a tall lean man with a pleasant laugh. He sat in a folding chair on the small porch area of the camp and put his feet up on the railing.

He sipped on a cup of coffee, lit a cigarette, and watched the show.

"I guess if you peckerwoods want to knock each other's teeth out, it's okay with me." He hollered.

Kevin gave him a surprised look. This gave Mitch an opportunity to jump and kick him in the chest with both feet. He went down with the wind knocked out of him.

"That should keep you down, you panty waist son of a bitch!" Mitch yelled.

"It'll take more than a pussy like you to keep me down!" Kevin said. He started laughing. He didn't know why, but Clarence's not caring attitude had spread to him. He realized that he had nothing against Mitch.

It turned out to be a near even match. First one boy would knock the other down and then fall over from exhaustion. Then it was the other one's turn.

Clarence's good-hearted laughter finally got their attention. They had wrestled back into the water; both were sitting in the shallows gasping for breath. Kevin started laughing along with Clarence. Soon Mitch joined in.

"If either of you have any teeth left," Clarence said with a smile, "Why don't you come up on the porch and finish bleeding while I cook up those fish."

That sounded like a good idea to Kevin. He looked at Mitch. "Truce?"

"Yeah," Mitch mumbled, "Truce."

Kevin reached out his hand and helped Mitch up. He checked back over his shoulder to make sure that Mitch was honoring their truce as he bent to pick up his catch.

Clarence visited and joked with them as he cooked up the fish. It turned out to be a good day. There was something about Clarence that Kevin really liked. About an hour before dark, he offered Kevin a ride home.

"I'm all set there, Mr. Nelson. I just need to go a few camps up and catch a ride."

"Okay." Clarence said. He shook Kevin's hand. "It's been a real adventure meeting you. I hope you hammerheads can get along after today." They both assured him that they could.

Kevin tried to come up with an excuse for Mitch not to accompany him on his short walk to where the car was stashed. He nervously anticipated what story to make up.

"Man, I can't believe we had to start out the day fighting." Mitch said. He rubbed his jaw. "This hurts like hell. What'd you have to hit so hard for?"

Kevin smiled and rubbed his eye. He knew it was black and blue. "You think that's something," he said. "At least you don't have to go home and try to make up some bull crap story."

"Yeah I do!" Mitch exclaimed. "Mom hasn't seen me yet. I don't know what Dad's going to say to her."

Mitch grinned as he added. "He always covers for me. When she hears his version, she's bound to like you."

"Huh?"

"She's always lowering the hammer on me for being a bully. So is Dad. I beat the crap out of Gary all the time. He's my big brother. Mom's favorite. If she thinks it was you who straightened me out, you'll never have to worry about her."

"Why in the hell do you always start fights?"

"I don't know. Something to do."

Kevin blurted out the truth about his borrowed set of wheels as they walked up to the car.

Mitch recognized the car the minute he saw it. "I'll be dipped in crap!" He exclaimed. "Clear to my eyebrows!"

"Yeah." Kevin replied. "It is sort of an oh crap situation."

Mitch took on a serious tone as he added, "We had better make damn sure that Dad never finds out about this!" He started laughing. "I mean never!"

"My lips are sealed." Kevin said.

Mitch was admiring the car when he told Kevin. "Don't worry. I hate that jerk you borrowed it from. What are you going to do with it once school starts? You can't give it back."

"Hell, I don't know." Kevin said. "Haven't given it much thought. This winter I just plan to keep it stashed at an old camp behind the house." He started laughing. "Maybe we should drive it off a cliff or something."

Nearly every day after that, it was Kevin and Mitch. They were always raising some kind of hell.

It was okay with Mitch's dad for them to use the camp anytime. He owned several old camps and cabins, and the boys were welcome to come and go as they pleased. They were expected to stay out of trouble. Clarence thought that his oldest son, Gary, was giving them rides.

Mitch was unquestionably a bold one. He claimed to have brass balls and attempted to prove it everyday. Kevin had never met anyone so brazen.

It was only a few days before school started when they decided what to do with the car. They already had a replacement vehicle, a borrowed four-door Ford sedan.

This one was only a year old. It had looked so appealing parked in front of a church over in Dexter. The keys had been left in the switch. Mitch took this to be a divine sign from above and was praising the Lord at the top of his voice as he roared off leaving rubber marks for about fifty feet on the paved road.

It was late afternoon. The hot August sun was shining brightly as the two ruffians prepared to dispose of Kevin's first car.

"Are you ready, Kevin?"

"Ready, Mitch. Start your engine!"

"This is as good a cliff as any!"

The heavy rock on the gas pedal assured that the engine was screaming at full throttle. Mitch was laughing with glee as he reached in through the window and put the Chevy in gear.

"Time to trade this son of a bitch in!" He exclaimed.

He was nearly knocked off his feet as the car came to life and lurched forward. They watched it pick up speed as it neared the edge of the gravel pit.

Kevin sat on the hood of their new set of wheels and chugged a beer as the Chevy went over the edge. It was easily a thirty-foot drop.

They had hoped that the car would have burst into flames when it hit the bottom, but what to hell. It was still fun. As time went by, that gravel pit would be home to at least a half dozen borrowed vehicles.

A few months later, a hunter discovered the wreckage. The local newspaper picked up on the story. The paper showed a picture of the pile of cars on the front page.

Their real cause for concern was that it was in the county's jurisdiction. If the sheriff's department ever found out that they were responsible, they would be sent away for a long time. Of that much they were certain.

They had nearly been caught and had already determined to lay low for a while. It had been such a close call that both had sworn never to pull that crap again.

After the hunter made the discovery, Sheriff Bradley was the laughing stock of the area. It was his patrol car that sat totaled at the top of the heap.

Mitch was especially nervous. He was the one who had heisted the Sheriff's car. Although Mitch had no need to be involved in these late night adventures, he reveled in participating. He had a larcenous streak through and through.

The night they swore off grand theft auto was one they would never forget. They had checked out a clothing store in town and had all the school clothes they wanted already laid out in a pile on a counter. They had everything sorted and placed for a quick pick up just as the place was about to close.

It was all too easy when they stopped in to pick up their purchases. As he had at the sporting goods store, Kevin opened the place up around two in the morning.

His heart was beating a mile a minute when Mitch smashed open the cash register with a fire ax that had been hanging on the rear wall. They helped themselves to fistfuls of cash. It should have been a routine excursion, but Mitch just had to be a smart ass. On the way out the back door, he reached up and pulled the fire alarm.

"Oh crap!" Kevin exclaimed. His heart was racing as the fire alarm bell started ringing. He ran to the car parked across the back alley. On this night it was a sixty-one Dodge Dart.

They had lifted it from an unsuspecting fisherman by a stream over in Dexter. It wasn't so much that they had wanted the car, but the guy had left the keys in the switch along with a six-pack of beer and his lunch on the back seat.

Kevin jumped in and waited anxiously for Mitch to open the other door. He floored it and sped off. They had only gone a few blocks when the right front tire blew.

"Oh crap!" Mitch exclaimed. "That wasn't too smart, was it?" He nervously looked back through the rear window.

"Are you crazy?" He shouted as Kevin pulled over. "We've got to get to hell out of here!"

He was nearly panicked as Kevin calmly put the car in reverse and backed into a parking space beside a liquor store. He shut the car off. The sounds of fire engines and police sirens were getting close.

"If you want to get caught for sure," Kevin said, "Just try and outrun those police two ways."

He laughed at Mitch's scared expression. He motioned towards the liquor store. "Hell, Mitch. Just look where we are."

He paused and they both ducked down as a police vehicle came screeching around a corner. The car sped past them. Kevin added, "See. Hide in plain sight. Besides, didn't you say we were running low on beer?"

With the cops busy in other places, Mitch made a quick shopping trip for beer while Kevin changed the tire. As he was accustomed to doing, he simply smashed the glass out of the rear door and helped himself.

Kevin was finished changing the tire when Mitch hurried back to the car. He was nearly staggering under a heavy load.

"Don't tell me I got no class!" Mitch said as he placed a couple cases of beer on the back seat. "Check this out!" He placed more beer in the front seat. "I got us an ice cold six-pack!"

He passed Kevin a beer and a handful of beef jerky that he had heisted off the counter and added. "No, I didn't forget. I checked. It ain't my fault the cheap son of a bitch didn't have any money in the till!"

Kevin opened his beer and spun the tires as they roared off. He kept to the back streets on the way out of town, making his way to the road that led back to camp.

They were driving fast and laughing uproariously when they met the Sheriff's car on a back road.

Their laughter was cut short when they saw the patrol car pull a u-turn behind them and turn on the overheads. They had about a quarter mile lead. Kevin floored it. As they dipped out of sight for a moment, he jammed on the brakes and shouted for Mitch to get to hell out.

"No need for both of us to go down! I'll floor it again when the son of a bitch gets out to check me."

Mitch bailed off into the brush along side the road as Kevin coasted the car to a stop. He was shaking with excitement as Sheriff Bradley pulled up behind him.

'Let the son of a bitch get right beside the car.' He thought.

He watched in his mirror as the Sheriff got out and started approaching his car. The sheriff had left his car door open. Kevin gasped for breath as he saw a shadowy figure run around the back of the patrol car and get in the drivers seat.

He floored it as Mitch closed the door and put the cop car in gear. Sheriff Bradley had to leap into the ditch to keep from being run over as his own car sped past him. He pulled his service revolver, but never got to use it as he slipped and sat down abruptly in the mud.

He was cursing in frustration as he scrambled back onto the road. He hadn't been able to get even a glimpse of either driver. His patrol car still appeared to be in hot pursuit as the two vehicles disappeared around a bend in the road.

Kevin changed his plans of driving back to camp as he raced past the Sloan farm. He turned onto the muddy road to the abandoned gravel pit. Mitch was close behind. He wished that Mitch would turn the overheads off, and found out a few minutes later that he didn't know where the turn off switch was.

Even though they were both scared crapless, they started laughing hysterically.

"That was too damn close!" Kevin exclaimed.

"No crap!"

"I thought for sure it was curtains this time."

"You should have seen the look on his face in the headlights!" Mitch exclaimed. "I wouldn't be surprised to find out that he crapped his pants!"

It was around five in the morning and nearly full daylight. The sheriff's car and the Dodge were lined up side by side as if to race down the incline.

They put both cars in neutral. Kevin glanced at Mitch who was seated in the sheriff's car. He raised his beer bottle and clinked it hard against the window ledge.

"Here's a toast to that low down, cheap ass lawman!" He shouted. "I hope that sorry son of a bitch gets blisters on both feet walking on his way back to town!"

"Here, here!" Mitch exclaimed. They drank a toast. Mitch flicked on the switch to the overhead lights and bailed out. They watched the cars slowly pick up speed coasting down the incline to the pits edge.

They vowed never again as they watched the cars join the collection of junk at the bottom of the gravel pit.

They stashed their loot a short distance away and started the walk back to Mitch's camp. They both solemnly swore off any more midnight raids.

Kevin never did figure out why Mitch was so eager to join in and participate in these escapades. He came from a good family.

His Mom was also really nice and Kevin liked her a lot. When they were around her, they went out of their way to act properly.

Kevin once again rode the bus back and forth to school. Mitch rode a different bus and often Kevin would ride home with Mitch and get a ride back to his house from Mitch's older brother.

Dad and Irene were pleased that Kevin was hanging out with Mitch. They were certain every night that Kevin had a place to stay when he wasn't at home and believed that he was staying out of trouble.

They had no television at Kevin's house. Whenever he was at Mitch's, he always sat and watched the nightly news with Clarence. He was infatuated with the nightly reports about the war in Vietnam.

Clarence thought this type of interest to be very mature on Kevin's part. They got along well together, and often talked almost as if they were father and son.

It turned out to be a pretty good year. Kevin now had several other friends and was fitting in the same as anyone else. He was slowly learning how to control his temper and knew when to watch his language.

As time went by, the nightmares were getting further and further apart.

At school, most of the teachers acted no differently towards him than any of the others. There was no more ridicule over his clothes, or his speech. As he got to know them, there were several teachers that he actually respected.

Kevin felt proud every time he heard that their team had won a basketball game.

Chapter Twenty-Three

Night Vision

The gentle breeze blowing off the lake had cooled off another hot summer day. It was well after midnight and he had just finished checking his catfish lines. He had already caught a really nice one. Clarence was sure to be pleased with that.

He had promised Clarence fresh catfish for breakfast. He smiled knowing that Clarence would act as cook when he stopped by in the morning. He was confident that he would have several more on his line during the night.

Kevin was bunking on the screened in porch of one of Clarence's lakeside camps. He had the place to himself. This small cabin was a considerable distance from the main camp and was the one that he and Mitch used when the adults were around.

He drifted off to sleep to the sounds of a hoot owl calling eerily in the darkness.

He could sense that he was dreaming. A feeling of dread settled in the pit of his stomach. His body jerked as he opened his eyes with a start. He tried to remember where he was.

He was lying flat on his back. The sky above was alive with swirling colors. Bright reds, orange and blue hues of light were dancing off enormous fluffy white clouds.

It appeared as if the most magnificent rainbow of all time had come to life and was playfully dashing across the heavens. The clear blue of the surrounding sky caused him to watch the light show with a feeling of awe.

A voice whispered.

Wake up.

He sat up slowly. His eyes were wide as he looked across an endless expanse of clear blue water. The light reflecting off the white sand was brilliant. He shaded his eyes with his hand.

"This place is beautiful." He breathed.

He turned slowly, taking in the splendor of a magical land. The lush forest behind him was alive with color. The bright green of the trees blended with the soft hue of the skyline.

"This is so beautiful." He murmured.

This isn't what I meant. Wake up.

Leave me alone.

He was surprised to notice that he was dressed in a nice short sleeve shirt. It was blue. His favorite color.

He was wearing a pair of khaki shorts. He smiled, realizing that this was the same outfit that he had seen someone wearing in a store catalog.

Wake up.

He ignored the voice and slowly started walking in the soft white sand. A gentle breeze caused the leaves in the trees to rustle softly. As it spoke again, it dawned on him that the voice had never spoken to him in his dreams before. He was determined not to respond.

Wake up.

He was enjoying his walk along the beach. He could smell the salt air from the warm breeze that was coming in off the ocean. The colors were dancing on the distant horizon with boundless energy. He smiled.

Wake to hell up. Now!

Go away.

It was a lovely day. He sat down and whiled away the time. A relaxing mood came over him as he sat there enjoying the feeling of the sand between his toes. Next, he walked slowly towards the ocean. He waded knee deep and marveled at the beautiful light show in the sky all around.

He was hoping to see the guardians again. This was the kind of dream in which he expected them to appear. It was a picture perfect world of peace and serenity.

A rustling noise in the forest caused him to turn around abruptly. He sensed that something was there. He stood watching in anticipation.

Wake up. Damn it!

I can't.

You've got to!

I can't.

You're not supposed to see.

See what?

Wake up.

The rustling sounds were getting louder. His instincts told him that he needed to get out of sight. He sought concealment behind a thick bush at the forest's edge. He waited in expectation, as the sounds got closer.

His eyes opened wide at the sight of the soldiers. They were walking silently in single file. They were carrying their rifles at the ready position as their eyes searched everywhere. The rustle of the branches as they passed through the thick underbrush was surprisingly loud.

He sensed a movement from over his shoulder. He looked back. To his surprise, the ocean was gone. Where the sandy beach had been was a large open area of cultivated marshland. There were several people standing ankle deep in the water that covered the fields.

There was something unusual about them. Their dress was different. Their clothes appeared to be made out of silk. Several were very young.

They were all wearing wide brim pointy straw hats. He knew he had seen them before. He had seen this exact picture, only in black and white. He was nearly overcome with frustration as he tried to remember where.

The soldiers stopped a few feet from him. He knew that he was in plain sight and slowly stood up. He waved at them.

They paid no attention to him as they continued along the edge of the thick forest.

Why can't they see me?

You're not here.

He reached out to touch the first man. His eyes went wide in awe as his hand passed right through him. This caused him to pause for a moment. His heart started racing.

He recognized one of the soldiers. He was sure of it but couldn't recall his name.

"Do I know you?" He asked.

The man ignored him and continued walking slowly.

"Hey! Do I know you?"

Then it dawned on him.

They really can't see me!

You've got to wake up!

Who are they?

You're not supposed to be here.

Tell me.

For a few moments there was only silence. Everything around him remained still as though frozen in time. The soldiers filed past him. He stood in awe as he reached out and passed his hand through each of them.

The earth started shaking. Kevin spun around at the sounds of explosions and rapid gunfire. He was alone. He hurried in the direction that the soldiers had disappeared.

Stop!

He ignored the voice and ran crashing through the thick underbrush. He felt his new shirt tear as the forest came alive with a determination to stop him. He was gasping for air when he came to another clearing.

Small clouds of red and green smoke were rising in the soft breeze. He could smell it. The sun was sinking low through the treetops.

He was still gasping for breath. The soldier he thought he should recognize was crouched beside a tree trunk. He was firing his rifle and screaming something over his shoulder. The left pant leg of his uniform was soaked with blood.

In the distance he could hear a helicopter approaching. He could feel the percussions of the rotor blades as it neared.

Get out of here.

To where?

His heart was racing as he viewed the scene from above. Somehow his view was elevated high above the forest. He could look down and see everything. He was panicked, gasping for breath as the scene unfolded.

Swarms of soldiers were approaching fast from nearly every direction. It was hill country and he could see through the thick forest as they came.

They were crouched low with their rifles at the ready. They slowly closed the distance to the clearing.

Are those the bad guys?

Yes!

They'll be here soon.

You've got to wake up!

They're coming.

It's supposed to be.

Our guys are trapped!
It's supposed to be.
Is there any way out?

The chopper was close. He could feel the sounds of the rotor as it neared. He was back as before, on the ground. He turned to look back. The young soldier was still firing his rifle. Blood was spurting from his leg. His nose was bleeding.

Kevin walked slowly across the clearing towards him. His eyes were wide in disbelief as he took in the scene.

"I know this man." He said softly.

His eyes were wide as he turned around slowly to see what was happening. There were soldiers everywhere. Some were motionless on the ground.

A soldier, darker than any man he had ever seen, dropped to his knees in front of him. He reached towards him. He clutched Kevin's shirt and pulled him down to his knees.

They were inches apart. The man's chest was stained bright red. His voice was clear as day as he chokingly whispered, "You've got to get out of here, Boy."

"Who are you?" Kevin screeched. He could hear the panic in his own voice.

"Now! Boy!" Bright red air bubbles sprayed from his mouth as he strained and coughed.

Kevin gasped and pulled away. As he stood up, the man's hand passed right through him. He caught the familiar scent of fresh blood. He stood looking down at the front of his shirt. It was stained with blood where the man had grasped him.

Into the sun. It's the only way out.
What?
Down that draw.
For Gods sake, tell someone!
Wake up first.
Tell someone!
You're not supposed to be here!

He could tell that there was lots of shouting and commotion going on around him, but sound and reality had changed. His mind was clouded with vivid images of anger and fear. Desperation. It was everywhere.

In slow motion, another soldier was approaching the first. He also looked familiar.

"Hey!" Kevin shouted. The man didn't notice him. "Do I know you?"

Once again he was ignored.

"You've got to go that way!" Kevin screamed at him as he pointed to the narrow opening in the trees.

"Look at me!" His voice was screeching. "Head into the sun! Through there!"

His voice slowed as he desperately whispered. "I know you." The colors all around blended into a shade of dark blue.

He sobbed, "Look at me!"

Sound stopped. The background changed.

Kevin felt the beating of his heart. The sound of his heart beating was audible as it slowed. He caught his breath as everything around them changed.

The two soldiers remained as before, except now they were in a freshly mowed pasture. The serene change of background startled Kevin. The sounds of his heart beating once again grew louder and faster.

The first soldier was kneeling, still firing his rifle. He was aiming at an old paint can that had been placed over the top of a fence post.

His leg was still bleeding. His expression was twisted in pain. The tears streaming down his cheeks cut trails of color through the grime on his face.

The second soldier was standing beside him with one hand on his shoulder. He was whispering something in his ear. Another man was standing behind them. He couldn't see who it was, only the blue color of his pant leg.

In the background he could see a bench beside a small stream. It made no sense.

He knew these men. He was sure of it. The scene faded in a swirl of color. He was nearly overcome with rage as he tried to recall their names.

The voices in his mind reached a level of panic.

Who are these people?

Snap out of it!

Another voice echoed in the back of his mind. It was a woman's voice. Even here, it was a soft soothing voice.

"Kevin."

Kevin recognized the voice.

"It's you! I know it's you!" He screamed.

"Kevin. Wake up."

"You've got to tell them!"

A desperate three-way conversation raged back and forth in his mind. He felt as if he was going to explode.

You've got to get him out of here!

You've got to wake up.

There's no time left.

I know these people!

Do something!

You can't let him die in his dream!

His heart will stop!

What?

You'll be dead, now!

It can't happen now!

What?

It has to happen then!

Where are we?

Wake to hell up!

He spun around, flailing his arms like one struggling to ward off unseen assailants. He was back in the clearing. The soldiers, the smoke, the explosions and the bullets were all moving in slow motion. The chopper was floating nearer, closing the distance ever so slowly.

The first soldier looked right at him. His voice was filled with pain and desperation. He shouted his name.

"Kevin!"

"You can see me!"

The soldier's eyes went wide in surprise. As he reached for Kevin, he slumped over.

"Kevin?"

"It's me. It's me. Just hang on!"

The soldier was prone on his side with his right arm outstretched. He was still firing his rifle. The shells were ejecting in slow motion. A hail of bullets shredded bark off the tree where he had been kneeling moments before. Shards of bark stung Kevin's face as they exploded from the tree.

Kevin's voice was screeching. "Go into the sun. Now! It's the only way out!"

"I'm tired, Kevin." The young soldier's eyes rolled back in his head.

He gasped for breath as the second soldier ran to them.

Kevin felt a force drawing him backwards. His tattered shirt was whipping angrily against his body. He struggled to resist.

The second soldier had taken his place and was kneeling by the first.

Kevin watched the stock of his rifle explode in slow motion. It was torn from his grip and spun slowly through the air. The first soldier was limp on the ground.

He was shouting in desperation as he watched the second soldier pick up the wounded man's rifle and start dragging him across the clearing.

The voices in his mind were screaming.

He saw me!

There's no more time. Wake up.

Oh God. He changed it.

He knows me!

It's too late.

He called me by name!

They were both supposed to die.

Tell them the way out.

Here! Now!

Tell them!

I cant! Damn it!

Then tell her to do it.

Bullets were flying everywhere. In slow motion they cut through the air, leaving transparent trails of vapor. The sound was slowed as they disrupted the rainbow of colors that still danced in the clear sky.

A man was racing towards him. His head suddenly exploded in a mess of blood and gore. What was left of him tumbled over several times on the ground and remained still.

The chopper landed.

A soldier with a Red Cross armband helped to load the wounded man into the chopper. They placed him beside the dark man. Someone had placed a mass of white bandages over his chest. They were soaked through with fresh blood. His eyes were staring blankly.

Desperate men loaded several others on board. Kevin watched in awe as a brilliant red cloud appeared on a soldier's back as he lifted another to the hands extended from within the chopper. The man spun around. Someone inside the chopper grabbed onto his collar.

The chopper lifted off.

Kevin could see the young soldiers face as clear as day. He nearly called out his name.

The young man was struggling to stay conscious. The man with the Red Cross armband was trying to tie a bandage around his leg. Spent shell casings from the machine gun mounted at the door's edge were falling slowly all around him.

The man who had dragged him to the chopper turned to face death with the others. Kevin looked in his eyes.

He awoke with a start.

Chapter Twenty-Four

Back to Work

Central Maine, summer 1966

The forest was momentarily silent as the sounds of the chainsaw stopped. The creaking and splintering sounds of a tree were heard as the tall fir started to lean slowly.

With a final snap, the slow motion stopped and the large conifer came crashing down to land with an earth quaking thud as it came to rest on the forest floor.

Kevin started his saw and quickly began cutting off the limbs. This was a large tree, and he made his first cut at eight feet. His second was made twelve feet further on. The remainder of the tree was soon one long log.

This was the third day this week that he had been falling timber. As soon as Rory and Bill showed up with the horse, his job would change to that of hauling the logs out to a central location. Rory would more than likely be the one to cut them into four foot long pieces and pile them.

Most of the local loggers, including Bill Riley, now used heavy machinery to haul out the logs. In rough marshy areas like this, a skidder or even a small lag tractor could easily get stuck in the soft ground. In a situation like this, there was no substitute for a good workhorse.

Bill had another horse named Trigger. There was something about that name that appealed to him. This one was also a buckskin with a long white mane. Unlike the old Trigger, this big brute had a bobtail and a mean streak that showed through and through. Bill had cautioned him sternly the first time they unloaded Trigger from the back of his pulp truck.

"I know you've got tons of experience doing this." Bill said. "But I've got to warn you. This one can be mean!"

Kevin didn't doubt it as he eyed Trigger.

"I've probably worked around worse horses than this, Bill. But I'll tell you for sure, I will be careful!"

"If that son of a bitch gives you any trouble we'll figure a way to get in here with the skidder and send that son of a bitch to the glue factory."

"Shouldn't have to go that far, Bill. Me and Rory will straighten him right out!"

"I hope so."

"Hell, don't even think about the glue factory. If the son of a bitch gets out of hand, let's sink a pickeroon between his eyes and have a big barbeque!"

Bill laughed and allowed that to be one hell of an idea.

Kevin and Rory had once again hired on with Bill Riley. They were looking forward to about a month of easy cutting. There were lots of tall trees in this marshy area and most of the area was easily assessable.

Kevin had tried to get Mitch to hire on with him, but Mitch claimed that he was allergic to hard work. He had taken a job in town pumping gas for a local service station.

The new camp was a thirty-foot long beat up old trailer house that Bill provided. It was dark green, and about as ramshackle as a trailer could get and still be livable by their standards. They had sealed the leaks in the metal roof, and all things considered, it was quite comfortable.

Bill had provided a pair of large propane bottles for the gas stove. This made cooking a lot easier. Without electricity, they once again resorted to using a bubbling cold-water spring in which to keep their beer and perishables.

The trailer was backed into the trees off a barely passable logging road that Rory and Bill had cut into this location. It was only a quarter mile from the railroad tracks.

Those same railroad tracks cut through the forest and were only a short distance from Kevin's house. Walking the tracks made it only a mile one-way to work. It was about five miles to the camp by road.

Kevin welcomed any chance to get away from the crowded farmhouse where he lived with his family. As the months wore on, it was harder than ever for him to make the adjustment of living there.

Dad now worked at a sawmill much closer to home and spent a greater amount of time with the family. Kevin helped him a lot on different projects and from time to time they got along quite well.

Artie and little Matthew were dad's constant shadows. Irene did what she could to insure that they were all raised properly. This included a steady dose of church services and a constant monitoring of school activities and report cards.

Kevin went out of his way to help with the younger ones when he could. In spite of himself and his sometimes-bitter attitude, he was starting to grow close to his new family.

K'leen had graduated high school in June, and was now engaged to be married. Her fiancé was a couple years older than her and they seemed to be a good match. Everyone in the family liked Ronnie, including Kevin.

It was his pent up hatred and bitterness towards the world in general that kept him from getting attached to anyone. As time went by, it would take a family of his own and an act of war to remove that continual chip from his shoulder.

Due to all the trouble and mishaps that he had been involved in, his dad made him walk to work every morning. They were actually glad to have him back working in the woods with Rory. They never did approve of his working on the Sloan farm.

He was usually making his way along the railroad tracks before sunup. As usual, he was expected to be home before dark, but that lasted for only a short time. As long as there was no more trouble, he would be allowed to work with Rory and come and go pretty much as he pleased.

Rory hadn't changed much. He still scratched out a living as best he could. In the cold winter months, he worked short-term jobs in the area where he could be inside. He was an excellent mechanic, but steady employment was forever eluding him.

Maybe it was because of his carefree callous attitude. He went through life half tanked, and generally didn't take things very seriously. Maybe it was because he had a problem showing up to work on time.

Whatever the reasons, Kevin was already learning what not to do. It would take awhile, but eventually he would determine not to end up in the same boat as his mentor.

The days of hell raising with Rory were far from over. He

still had that same huge shotgun, and as before there were no closed seasons. They were forced to use a lot more caution in using it at their new location.

They had thought for sure that they were busted when a game warden stopped in to ask them if they knew anything about the report he had received. It seemed that someone had heard shots around midnight and suspected them of poaching deer under the headlights of a car.

They assured him that it wasn't them and that they hadn't heard any late night gunshots. As the warden drove off, Kevin teased Rory about being so afraid over the whole deal.

"Hell, Rory. That son of a bitch has you so scared that you even act guilty when you ain't."

"What to hell do you mean? We shot three deer the other night. Of course I'm guilty."

"What's the deal? We gave the two big ones away, right? What's the harm in that? Those people needed the meat a lot worse than that asshole needs to write a ticket."

"Yes. That's true. But it's them tickets that cost. I sure as hell don't want to end up in jail."

"Just don't you turn chicken manure on me!" Kevin laughed and added, "You're sounding more and more like a law abiding citizen every day."

"Hell, Kevin. Sometimes I just get nervous."

"You have been acting like some kind of panty waist lately. Don't you think?"

"What I think is why don't you shut to hell up and go fetch us a couple beers."

Kevin started down the path towards the spring. He winced, and then shrugged, as he stepped in a fresh horse apple. He called over his shoulder.

"Just don't let me hear that you're thinking about going by the rules! Pretty soon you'll be voting and all that crap. That's the last thing I need to hear."

"Screw you!" Rory shouted.

From a distance he heard Kevin shout, "Next thing after voting, comes religion."

He laughed as Kevin's retort could barely be heard due to the distance between them. Kevin was still shouting to him as he reached into the spring and got the cold beers. He knew that Rory was shaking with laughter at each exchange.

"After religion, comes hell!" He shouted. He emphasized the word 'hell' extra loud.

"You hear me? You deaf prick. Hell!"

He laughed as Rory shouted his reply.

"I'll get religion the day after you do, you unholy prick. Then we can both sign up to vote."

Kevin raced back with an armload of beer. He stepped in the same pile of fresh horse manure as he vaulted over an empty fifty-gallon drum. He took the steps up to the trailer two at a time. He said in a normal tone.

"I vote not to vote; you law abiding prick."

They drank a toast to law abiding pricks and enjoyed a good meal of fried venison. Rory allowed that they needed to pick up some flour so Kevin could make biscuits. He admonished Kevin for not wiping his feet.

"Sometimes I think you were raised in a damn barn." He mumbled. They drank another beer and then Rory drove Kevin back to his house. They picked up a change of clothes, said goodnight to everyone, and drove back to camp.

Kevin was saving to buy a car. He got his drivers license back in January when Mrs. Riley had let him use her car to take his road test. That had been very kind of her.

He had his eye on a two door, 1959 Chevy Impala. It was sitting behind a garage in Milo. The owner wanted two hundred dollars for it. Kevin had been with Rory when he had stopped to look at it. Rory said that unless someone already had the parts, he figured the car to be worth maybe fifty dollars.

The exterior was nearly perfect. It was shiny black with a white roof and lots of chrome. It also had a new windshield. The interior was immaculate and everything worked. The tires were in poor shape, but the real problem was that the owner's son had ruined the engine and transmission.

Kevin had everything planned from the start. The thought of actually buying a car appealed to him. He already knew where to get a new short block as well as tires and a new transmission.

He knew of a 1962 Chevy Impala that had the same parts that he needed to fix this one. He was already planning on getting a really good deal.

He hadn't heard from anyone from the state in over a year

and hoped that it would remain that way. He had developed a real contempt for those people.

His attitude towards the local lawmen was less than respectful. He looked upon them with open contempt. In his mind it was they who had sold him out. Even when he found out that it wasn't them, it made little difference.

He believed that they should have known ahead of time what was going to happen. He knew this to be true and often referred to constable Hollis as 'Sheriff Andy' and deputy Hawkins from the sheriff's department as 'Barney Fife.' His nickname for Sheriff Bradley was quite profane.

Bill Riley was still as nice as pie to Kevin and helped him to finally realize that he hadn't been sold out after all. It had been a mix-up in the paper work that got him sent away.

It had been a mix-up that was traced all the way back to that Satterfield jerk. Two or three more people were fired and brought to trial over that whole deal.

Kevin felt as though he should apologize to Bill for the awful things he had said to him before realizing the truth. He did his best to make up for those hard feelings by doing whatever he could to help Bill in his logging business.

The steady routine and a somewhat shaky sense of security helped him adjust to a rather normal life. The memories were slowly fading and the voices in the back of his mind had been silent for over a year.

In mid July he was offered another job through the local high school. It was a federally funded training program. Mitch had told him about it and it sounded like a good opportunity. Kevin jumped at the chance to hire on. The job started the first week in August and he needed to have wheels by then.

As it turned out, Kevin needed only a hundred and fifty dollars to buy that Impala. Rory borrowed Bill's pickup truck to tow the car back for Kevin.

He thought that Kevin was quite unwise to buy something that needed so much work and minced no words in telling him so. He figured what to hell; it was Kevin's money.

The car's engine would start, but it obviously needed a new short block. The transmission had a grinding noise and the reverse gear was shot. Kevin laughed and assured him that he knew what he was doing.

Mr. Mathis had accepted an offer to teach at the new high school in Dover. He liked his new job and didn't particularly miss the school system back in Milo. That job had served as a stepping-stone in his chosen career path.

The last week in July, his 1962 Chevy Impala came up missing. Since he had only liability insurance, he was forced to share driving his wife's car and made plans to buy another before school started.

A week later he received a call from the police. His car had been found broken down beside the road in Dexter. His wife drove him to the impound yard and waited as he checked it out.

Mr. Mathis was surprised to find that other than two of the tires being flat, there were no signs of physical damage. The rear floor was littered with dozens of empty beer bottles. The police officer told him that he thought some teenagers might have just taken it for a joyride.

It took him about an hour to get the tires fixed at a gas station across the street. When he started it up, it nearly caused a panic for both he and his wife as clouds of black and blue smoke poured out of the exhaust pipe. When he attempted to back it up he discovered that the reverse gear was shot.

A couple teenagers had been driving by and stopped to offer their assistance. They helped to push it backwards onto the street while his wife steered.

These young Samaritans were laughing at him as he put the car in gear and started his drive back to Dover. His wife had to keep a safe distance behind to see through the billowing smoke screen coming out of the tail pipe.

It had taken a little convincing on Kevin's part to get Rory to help out in exchanging engine blocks and transmissions in his new car. He had helped Rory many times before in doing the same.

"Quit being such a chicken crap!" Kevin said. "It's no different than the time we borrowed those tires for your old piece of junk!"

"Yeah," Rory said, "But at least that one was sitting abandoned. I know damn well you stole this one! This is some serious trouble if we get caught!"

"All the more reasons to hurry this along so we can get it

back to its rightful owner!" Kevin laughed, "Hell, Rory, it's not the first car I've borrowed."

They had both cars parked deep in the woods near the logging camp. They started on Saturday morning. By Sunday afternoon, the switch over had been made and Kevin was pumping air into the tires that they had exchanged.

The last thing he did was exchange the battery. He made sure that all the non-returnable beer bottles and cans were on the floor behind the front seat of the borrowed car.

They waited until nearly midnight before setting out to return the car. Rory followed in his old clunker about a half-mile back to be out of the smoke screen. The car burned nearly four quarts of oil and the engine was hot by the time Kevin figured that he had driven far enough.

He left the car across the county line in Dexter. It still had nearly a quarter tank of gas. Before he jumped in with Rory, he took a minute to pour a little chainsaw mix in the car's tank.

He opened a beer for Rory and one for himself.

"Rory, you've been acting as nervous as a whore in church this whole time." Kevin said. "If you knew this prick you'd be happier than crap over this deal!"

Rory started laughing. "I'll quit being nervous in a few more miles." He clinked bottles with Kevin and added, "Here's a toast to that cheap prick, whoever he is."

They both laughed and enjoyed the ride back.

Chapter Twenty-Five

Misadventures

Kevin really liked his new job working in the federal training program. He was naturally talented in working with his hands and a large part of the summer job was working as a carpenter's helper. He caught on quickly.

Kevin really liked his new boss. Leroy Stage was known as one of the best all round carpenters in the area. When he complemented Kevin, shortly after they started working together, he had a friend for life.

"You've got the makings of a good carpenter." Leroy told him. Then he jokingly added, "As long as I can keep your mind on work and off women, you'll go far!"

Kevin smiled and listened to everything that Leroy said. Leroy was always teasing him. He didn't mind at all.

The dynamics of his life were about to change. He now owned a nice car and there were several girls who also worked in the program.

High school was going quite well for him. He was now in his junior year and it looked as if he was going to make it. His homeroom teacher was one of the best influences in his life.

Mr. Chad was his biology and science teacher. He was a fair man, and an excellent teacher. He treated everyone the same and Kevin always did well in his classes.

Over the years, Mr. Chad probably chewed Kevin out more than all the other teachers combined. It was his way of administering discipline fairly, and his never holding a grudge, that earned Kevin's respect.

Mr. Chad's oldest son, Jason, was also in the same homeroom and they shared several classes together. Although Jason was respected as one of the smartest and nicest boys in school, he had taken a liking to Kevin. There were countless times, when if not for Jason, Kevin would have quit and walked away.

Several of the other teachers didn't share Mr. Chad's point of view. They knew Kevin to be a troublemaker and an overall bad influence. He smoked cigarettes and had a foul mouth. They knew of his lack of respect for the local law and game enforcement officials.

The fact that Kevin was a good worker in the federally funded training program was about the only redeeming quality that they could see. About the only thing they could say nice about him was that he was never disruptive or disrespectful in their classes.

As he had in the past, he often found himself laughing aloud, late at night. Each time he filled his gas can he wondered if several of the teachers ever realized what awful gas mileage their cars were getting.

His grades were mostly average. It was his quiet smile and easygoing personality that led several of the teachers to believe that he did have possibilities.

It's a good thing they weren't with him after school.

Once school started, Kevin's summer job changed to one of helping the janitors, as needed, in the various school buildings. It was a good job and kept him out of trouble during the week. The pay was okay, but now he was on his own and had additional living expenses.

He had moved out towards the end of summer. The farmhouse was way too crowded and his temper often came to the surface. He was fighting with Irene or one of the others all the time. Dad never made much of a deal over the whole thing when Kevin decided to move out. He didn't get along that well with his namesake either.

There were many nights when Kevin stayed in different camps on the south side of Sebec Lake. He was familiar with the area and often stayed two or three nights at the same location.

Other than using a little of the camps firewood, he seldom left any trace that he had been there. Sometimes he would use one of Clarence's old camps. Occasionally, he would stop in and bunk with Rory.

Kevin had a couple of friends that he got along well with nearly all the time. Both came from good families and he stayed with both families from time to time.

Lewis Cross was about the best influence he could have had for a friend. They were in the same grade and did a lot of hunting and fishing together.

He and Kevin had more than their share of adventures and close calls. Like Kevin, he didn't mind skipping school on occasion to go fishing or hunting. Unlike Kevin, Lewis never did develop the callous attitude necessary to partake in some of the more daring nighttime escapades.

Lewis came from a nice family and was polite and well respected. He was talented in music and got good grades in school. Like the Nelson's, the Cross family displayed hearts of gold to Kevin. Lewis's father and mother were among the most respected people in Kevin's life.

Although Kevin was considered to be a bad influence by most who knew him, Mitch Nelson had also turned out to be a real hellion. Mitch's dad let him drive his old ford pickup back and forth to school. He was allowed five dollars a week for gas. In return, Mitch was expected to do the chores at home and keep his act together.

Clarence Nelson had a lot of respect for young Kevin. He had known Irene's family for years, and knew all there was to know about their wayward son.

He had been there the time that Kevin and his son Mitch had gotten into a knock down, drag out fistfight. The boys were about evenly matched and he stood back and let them slug it out.

The fight turned out to be a tie. They were both exhausted and bloody when they realized that neither could prevail over the other. Clarence had sat back and watched. As a result, Kevin and Mitch became inseparable friends.

Clarence really liked Kevin. He would turn out to be the closest thing to a father figure that Kevin would ever allow. Due to his sorted past, he never had warmed up to his own father.

His name was Dad; that was about the extent of it.

<u>November 1966</u>

The two hunters walked softly down the narrow woods road. They tried to walk quietly on the carpet of dried leaves. It was deer season. They had spooked some deer a few minutes earlier and were confident of success.

Mitch carried his dad's lever action thirty-two Winchester

special. He had the look of a killer on his lean face as he trudged on slowly. The red plaid coat he had borrowed from his dad looked a lot like a large blanket on his small frame.

Kevin had borrowed Clarence's bolt-action twenty-two rifle. He wore a bright orange vest over his brown work coat. His jaw was set as his eyes continually searched the thick underbrush. His finger was on the trigger. He was ready for anything.

It was still early, probably around nine thirty in the morning. They slowly made their way down to the banks of a small stream. The wheel ruts of the woods road disappeared briefly underwater, and then continued on the other side of the stream. They figured that the deer had already crossed.

As he walked slowly down the slope towards the stream, Kevin saw a huge cow moose standing right in the middle. He wasn't thinking when he raised that small caliber rifle and fired. His shot struck the moose behind its ear.

"What to hell are you doing?" Mitch's voice was panicked as Kevin's shot broke the silence. The moose lay twitching, half floating in the shallow stream. "They send people to jail for this crap!" He stood watching with an expression of astonishment as Kevin quickly approached his kill.

He started laughing as Kevin walked up to the moose and placed the barrel of his rifle in its ear and fired again.

"Hell." Mitch shouted, "Let's make damn sure!"

Kevin jumped back as Mitch emptied the lever action rifle into the carcass as fast as he could.

"I've always wanted to do that!" He exclaimed.

Kevin slit the moose's throat with his large hunting knife. He looked up at Mitch who was reloading and said, "Hell, Mitch, I don't know what got into me! I just wasn't thinking. I mean, the moose was here, I was here, I had a gun."

He paused as Mitch finished reloading. "You ain't going to kill it again, are you?"

They both laughed as Mitch fired another round into the dead animals head. "Hell, no." He said.

The moose was too heavy for them to drag it onto the stream bank. They quickly gutted it right there. Mitch gasped as he noted that the stream was running red with the fresh blood.

"I hope to hell there's no one down stream." He said. "If there is, we're in some deep crap!"

"Damn," Kevin murmured. "Let's get to hell out of here

and hope no one finds it while were gone. We need to figure what to do."

Mitch was starting to get scared over the whole deal. "If we've got any ass left after the game warden gets done with us, it's going to belong to Dad!"

"No crap." Kevin said softly. The gravity of the situation was starting to settle on him as well. "The first thing we need to do is get it to hell out of the water."

Mitch walked quickly behind Kevin as he made his way through the woods. They decided not to move Kevin's car. It was parked about a mile back up the woods road, blocking it from anyone else driving down there.

After going about a mile, they crossed the railroad tracks. As he had hoped, Rory was still working in that area, and the camp was still there.

There was no one around. Kevin led Mitch inside and they borrowed a couple pairs of dry socks from Rory's pile of dirty laundry. Then they went outside and got Trigger out of the hovel.

"Be very careful around this son of a bitch!" Kevin cautioned. "He's mean. Old Bill is talking about sending him to the glue factory."

"He's one big son of a bitch. That's for sure." Mitch said. "This ain't the same Trigger you used to work with, is it?"

"No." Kevin answered. "That son of a bitch is in the happy grazing field in the sky."

Kevin quickly put the harness on Trigger and they both rode him bare back to the stream.

They hooked onto the moose and Trigger easily dragged it to high ground. This had been the hard part. They were both scared crapless the entire time.

"You take my car," Kevin said as he passed Mitch his keys, "And go get your pickup. Then drive around to the camp and pick me up. We'll come back here and load this son of a bitch on back and hang it up at your place."

This sounded like a good enough plan to Mitch. Kevin took a few minutes to cut out a large portion of moose steak to take back for Rory.

It wasn't long before he had Trigger back in the hovel. He was riding on the way out with Mitch when they met Rory heading into the camp.

Mitch rolled down his window. Kevin leaned across the

seat to tell Rory, "Sorry we're in such a hurry! Your dinner is stashed in the bucket in the spring." He smiled at Rory's questioning expression. "We'll stop back and help you cook it up in a couple hours."

Mitch quickly drove back to the scene of the crime. They quartered up the moose with a long handled ax and an old handsaw that they had borrowed from Rory. Then they loaded it onto the back of the truck.

They both agreed that it was a shame to leave the large ribbed portion of the carcass there. They reasoned that the coyotes and foxes would be grateful.

Neither thought to cover their prize on the drive back to Mitch's place. Later they agreed that it was a miracle that no one had noticed their cargo.

Mitch opened the doors to the equipment shed behind the house and directed Kevin in backing the pickup inside. They tied rope to each piece and then to the overhead joist. Kevin drove out from under and they closed the doors.

Rory was really mad over the whole deal when he found out that it was moose meat. He called Kevin everything but smart as he ranted and raved.

"They send people to jail longer for killing a moose than they do a person!" He said angrily.

"Panty waist!" Kevin said in a mocking tone.

"Panty waist!" Mitch chimed.

"You'll think panty waist if that son of a bitch driving the green pickup shows up!" Rory retorted.

After about his third beer Rory started to relax. Following an excellent dinner of fried moose and Kevin's biscuits, everything was back to normal.

"When are you going to teach me to make biscuits like that?" Rory asked.

"Never."

"Cheap prick!"

"Hell, Rory, it's a secret family recipe. And you sure as hell ain't related to me!"

"Wouldn't admit it if I was!"

"I'd commit suicide if you was!"

Rory had a small mongrel dog that he took with him everywhere. The dog's name was Tramp. He had showed up at the camp, half starved and begging for food when Rory found him. He had taken Tramp in and now had a constant companion.

Mitch and Kevin were about ready to leave, around ten at night, when Tramp started barking. Rory shined a flashlight out the door and saw Tramp with his front feet high against a tall pine tree. He was barking incessantly.

"I'll bet that son of bitch treed a coon!" Rory exclaimed. "Quick, Kevin, grab another flashlight and get me the shotgun!"

Kevin handed Rory the shotgun. They were all half buzzed and no one thought it a bad idea to be firing the shotgun that late at night.

Rory shined the light into the tree. "It's a damned porcupine!" He exclaimed. "I sure as hell don't want Tramp getting a face full of quills!" He chambered a round, "I'll show that sorry son of a bitch!" He raised the huge shotgun and fired. His first shot missed.

The hapless porcupine scurried around to the other side of the tree high above as chunks of pinecones and tufts of pine needles showered down to the ground. "I'll get you this time, you son of a bitch!" Rory growled.

Mitch and Kevin were both cracking up over Rory's excitement. They were laughing hysterically as Rory got a short length of board to stand against the tree. "I won't miss your prickly ass this time, you son of a bitch!" Rory mumbled.

Rory put one foot on the board enabling him to stand higher and wrap an arm around the lowest branch. He was precariously balanced as he shined his flashlight again and aimed the shotgun straight up.

"Try this you son of a bitch!" His mumbled voice caused Kevin and Mitch to laugh uncontrollably. The flare of the shotgun lit up the night as he fired another round.

This time his shot blew the porcupine out of the tree. The downside was that Rory was still balanced on the board, gripping onto a lower limb, when it fell straight down.

"Crap!" He yelled. He lost his grip on the shotgun as he threw up his arms and attempted to get out of the way.

"Oh man!" Mitch said. "You sons of bitches are crazier than me."

He helped Kevin pick up Rory. He had fallen flat on his back in his effort to dodge the prickly bomb from above.

"It's a damn good thing you ain't sober!" Kevin said

between fits of laughter, "If you were, you'd a broke every bone in your body!"

Rory unsteadily brushed himself off. "Throw that son of a bitch on the back of your pickup so Tramp doesn't get at him" He said. "You can pitch him later." He was laughing once again as Kevin did as instructed and handed him another beer.

Rory was passed out on the couch when Kevin made sure that the shotgun was reloaded and stood back in its place in the corner. He and Mitch were quiet as they extinguished the kerosene lamp and cautiously made their way outside.

On the way back to Mitch's camp, they made a brief courtesy stop at the local police station. The city now had a police force of three full time, and several part time officers.

As usual, whichever officer was supposed to be on night duty was nowhere to be seen. They weren't overly worried about getting caught as they paid their respects.

The next morning, Chief of Police Ralph Hollis could only stand there and shake his head in dismay. A dead porcupine was discovered tied securely to the overheads on one of his shiny new police cruisers.

He hoped that this wouldn't make the newspapers. He was certain that someone was going out of his way to make him the laughing stock of the town.

It wasn't the first time something like this had happened. Ralph lived for the day when he could put the cuffs on the lowly son of a bitch responsible.

It was a good thing that Clarence owned several old camps in the Sebec Lake area. They never had to go back to the house until they had a chance to sober up. It was certain that if Mitch's mom ever got wind of what they were up to, it would have been curtains for the both of them.

The ass chewing they had received from Rory wasn't anything compared to the one they received from Clarence when he discovered that moose hanging in his tool shed.

Chapter Twenty-Six

Winter Wonderland

December 1966

Winter set in early that year. By mid December the lakes were all frozen solid. There wasn't much of a snow cover and this meant easy access to all the lakes in the area.

Mitch was one who especially liked to go ice fishing. He was looking forward to Christmas break. His dad had given permission for him to have several friends stay over at one of his camps for a weeklong ice fishing vacation.

His plans were changed when his relatives decided to visit. He didn't like the idea, but had no choice but to go along.

Two of his cousins, Phillip and Caleb were going to be there for sure. This meant that his older brother would be along and would undoubtedly be in charge.

Mitch wasn't too excited over the arrangements. His aunt and uncle would be visiting for a few days and had insisted that the cousins spend some time together.

He was somewhat relieved when his older brother, Gary, stated that he would be glad to check up on them, but he didn't want to go fishing or stay at the camp overnight.

His cousin Phil was his age and Caleb was a year younger. He was sure that having those two wimps around would ruin their vacation. He had also invited Lewis Cross and his partner in crime, Kevin Stone.

He had argued about it earlier with his dad.

"They're a couple of wimps, Dad. You know Phillip doesn't like me."

"Quit griping." Clarence said sternly. "They're your cousins, and they'll be here for three or four days. Get used to it and make the best of it."

"Phillip's a rat Dad. You said so yourself." Mitch said.

Clarence grinned. Mitch had made a point. Phillip had been a tattletale since he was old enough to talk.

"Just don't do anything to get tattled on." He said.

"It's not just that Dad. He and Caleb are really sissified. There's no running water at camp. They'll complain about that. No central heat. They'll complain about that. Do you think either of them will help with firewood?"

Clarence laughed again and said, "Maybe that's why uncle Lenny wants them to spend some time here."

Mitch realized that this was getting him nowhere. He smiled back at his dad and said. "I guess you're right. I'll take care of them." He frowned. "I just hope Lewis and Kevin can get along with them."

"I think Kevin can get along with just about anyone." Clarence said. "Lewis will be fine."

Mitch smiled. "Okay, Dad."

Mitch was anxious to try out Kevin's new fishing style. He knew that Kevin and Lewis had both skipped school just before Christmas break. They had bragged about catching over a dozen fish. He didn't doubt their claim, and was excited to go ice fishing with them.

His aunt and uncle and the two cousins arrived the day after Christmas. Since they planned on their boys staying at the camp, they had brought tons of groceries. Mitch thought that part of the deal was great.

Mitch told them that he was anxious to get fishing and they headed for the camp right after lunch. When they got there, Mitch threw the switch to turn on the electricity. Then, they built a fire in the heater stove and put the groceries away. He intended to waste no time getting out on the lake.

His cousins were in no hurry. Caleb pointed out that it was going to be dark in an hour or so and he thought it best to wait until the next day.

"When are your friends supposed to get here?" Phil asked. "Shouldn't we wait for them?"

"Hell no! There's no telling when they'll show up."

"Maybe we should wait."

"They'll get here sooner or later." Mitch answered. "Let's go have some fun."

Cousin Phil was a freckled faced boy with a short haircut. He really didn't like his cousin Mitch, nor did Caleb.

Their parents had insisted that they spend part of Christmas break with him. Like Mitch, he was also a junior at his high school. He was an honor student and had little in common with his cousin.

His younger brother, Caleb, was already taller than him. He was a gangly type and also had a GI haircut. He was also an honor student.

"It's cold." Phil whined as he stooped to look out a window at the frozen lake.

"We got a heater in the truck." Mitch said.

"And look, the wind is blowing a hundred miles an hour." Caleb added.

"You didn't come here just to be a pussy? Did you?" Mitch asked.

"The chill factor has got to be way below zero." Phil's whining was starting to irritate Mitch.

He looked at Caleb, "How about you?" He asked. "Are you going to be a pussy too?"

They both reluctantly agreed to go. They were city boys and neither was thrilled at being stuck there for vacation. They agreed that spinning around on the lake would beat sitting around at the camp.

"No TV?" Caleb asked.

"Nope." Mitch answered. "We get one station out here. Dad took the small television back to the house."

"This sucks." Phil muttered.

"What?" Mitch asked.

"Nothing." Phil said.

"You guys get bundled up." Mitch said. "We can't treat this like a regular ride. We'll be spinning around way out on the lake." He knew that neither boy was taking him seriously. He smiled and added, "I'll get the fishing gear ready."

Mitch threw their gear on the back of the truck. He was smiling from ear to ear as his cousins got in the cab of the truck. Neither was wearing winter clothing.

He realized that too much of Kevin Stone had rubbed off on him. He thought this when he came up with a plan to get rid of these two sissified pussies.

Kevin and Lewis arrived just before dark. The camp was empty. The fire in the stove was about out. Lewis put some kindling wood in the stove and opened the damper to get some heat circulating.

"Suppose they're out on the lake?" Lewis asked.

"Yeah." Kevin said. "As soon as you get that fire going we'll go looking for them."

"Maybe we should wait." Lewis said.

"Do you know either of his cousins?" Kevin asked.

"Yep. They're a couple of pussys. That's certain. Tell you one thing. That wimp, Phil, will rat us out over anything." He started laughing.

"What's so funny?" Kevin asked.

"Mitch called me this morning. He said that if the place was empty when we got here, to just wait. Said something about de pussifing the camp."

Kevin started laughing too. "If anyone can de pussify a place, Mitch can!"

They stashed the cases of beer and a couple bottles of hard liquor behind the wood box and covered everything with a top layer of firewood.

Kevin got out a deck of cards and turned on the radio. They played a few hands and drank some hot chocolate laced with their own brand of mineral spirits.

It was pitch dark outside when Lewis checked his watch. It was nearly seven o'clock. He thought he heard someone outside. They put on their coats and stepped outside to listen. In the distance they thought they could hear the voices of someone coming across the lake.

A pickup truck was approaching on the camp road. Clarence and his brother drove up. They went back inside to greet them as they approached the camp. Clarence came inside carrying a large sack of groceries.

"How are you hammerheads doing?" Clarence asked in a jovial tone.

"Fine Mr. Nelson, how are you?"

Clarence introduced his brother. "Boys, this is my brother, Lenny." He smiled and introduced them as they shook hands. "Lenny, this young man is Lewis Cross."

"Pleased to meet you." Lewis said.

"And this young man is Kevin Stone."

"Pleased to meet you, Sir." Kevin said.

As they exchanged pleasantries, Kevin thought that it was hard to picture Clarence and Lenny as being brothers. Clarence was tall and thin. Lenny came about to his shoulder and was nearly as wide as he was tall.

He was a striking contrast to his brother. Clarence was wearing a heavy brown work coat; Lenny was dressed in a bright yellow ski parka.

"Where are the boys?" Lenny asked.

"We don't know, Sir." Kevin said. "We just got here a little while ago, and we're waiting for them. We thought it was them coming when you drove up."

They were all quiet as voices could be heard outside, coming from the lake.

Clarence took a flashlight from the counter and shined it out the door towards the dock.

In the dim light, they could see three figures slowly approaching.

"Is that you Mitch?" Clarence yelled.

"Yeah, Dad. We've got trouble!"

Lenny rushed out to meet the boys. In the dim light cast from the back porch light of the camp and Clarence's flashlight, they appeared as ghostly shadows. They approached walking huddled together. Lenny nearly slipped and fell on the ice as he walked out to meet them.

"What do you mean, trouble?" Lenny asked. "Are you all right?"

Clarence had walked to the lakes edge, and stood waiting. Kevin waited on the porch steps, watching quietly and grinning from ear to ear.

"The truck stalled!" Mitch said. "Clear over on the other side of Black Island. These guys are only wearing their wind breakers and we've got to get somewhere warm!"

"Quick!" Lenny exclaimed, "Let's get you guys inside." He was nearly panicked as he placed his arm around Caleb. Both of his sons were nearly frozen to death.

When they got inside, Lenny nearly threw a fit. His sons got a severe scolding as he examined them. It was obvious that they both had frostbite on their ears and more than likely on their hands and feet.

"How could you boys be so stupid?" He exclaimed. Neither Phil nor Caleb were wearing mittens or gloves. "Your mom's going to have a cow over this!"

"What were you boys thinking?" Clarence asked. He noticed that both were wearing blue jeans and sneakers. Neither was wearing a hat. They were shivering uncontrollably.

Mitch was no worse for the wear. His wool pants, heavy winter coat and long underwear had served him well. He was wearing two pairs of wool socks inside his heavy winter boots.

"I tried to tell them to dress warm!" He exclaimed. "I told them that we would be getting in and out of the truck."

"Not your fault." Lenny said. "Their warm clothes are right here." The boys had left their heavy ski parkers heaped with their other belongings on one of the beds.

"We just want to go home." Caleb said. His whining made him sound as pathetic as Phil.

"I guess that would be best." Clarence said. He looked at Mitch. "Will you guys be okay?"

"Sure, Dad."

"We'll help round up their stuff." Lewis offered.

"What about the truck?" Clarence asked.

"The truck's fine." Mitch said.

Kevin had to turn and face the window to keep his smile from showing as Mitch continued.

"It stalled and wouldn't start again. I think the gas line filter may be plugged. It just turned over and over until the battery wore down. It's just sitting out there. In the morning we can go out with Kevin's car and either jump start it or tow it in."

"Okay, Son." Clarence put his hand on Mitch's shoulder. "You did the right thing. If you guys had tried to stay with the truck, you probably would have frozen to death. We wouldn't have known where to look for you."

Kevin added. "If you want, Mr. Nelson, we can go check on the truck tonight. I'm sure my car will start."

"What ever you guys want." Clarence said. "Just be careful and stay out of trouble."

Mitch, Lewis, and Kevin all walked outside. They carefully loaded Phil and Caleb's overnight bags onto the back of the truck. They waited as Phil and Caleb crammed into the cab of the pickup between the two adults.

"Sorry it didn't work out." Mitch said to Phil.

Phil was shivering as he said. "You probably did save our lives Mitch. I'm glad you talked us out of staying with the truck."

"Think nothing of it, Phil. You guys are family."

Kevin tried not to gag.

They waved good-bye to the truck and stood watching silently as it got to the stop sign at the end of the camp road. Kevin and Lewis burst out laughing as Mitch murmured,

"Camp de pussification complete."

It was nearly midnight when the boys decided to venture out and get Mitch's truck.

"The battery should be fine." Mitch exclaimed. "I only had to crank it a few times to be convincing."

Lewis was shaking with laughter. His face looked as if someone had painted it red as he proposed a toast to Mitch.

"Let's have a drink to this cheapest of cheap pricks!" He clinked beer bottles. "Mitch! You truly are a prick. You really do take the cake."

"Here, here!" Mitch retorted. "That kind of flattery will get you nowhere."

"Here's a final toast to the true master of de pussification!" Kevin said. As they drank to that, Kevin passed them each another bottle. "For the road."

"I call shotgun!" Lewis exclaimed as they raced for Kevin's car.

The frozen ground and lack of snow made it easy to drive the Impala onto the ice. The lake was a smooth, frozen playground that stretched for miles. Kevin slowly accelerated until they were going about sixty miles an hour.

"Watch this you pussys!" He exclaimed as he jerked the wheel and floored it.

"Yee haw!" Mitch yelled from the back. "This is one wild ass ride! Count how many cookies. Let's see if you can beat my record."

The car spun around and around and around and around. They lost count of how many cookies as Kevin and Mitch shouted and laughed with glee.

Mitch noticed that Lewis was being awfully quiet in the front seat.

"Oh crap!!" Mitch shouted. "He's had his limit, now he's going to puke!"

"Roll down your window! Roll down your window!" Kevin yelled. "Lewis, for craps sake, you've got to open your damn window!"

"Stop this damn thing!" Mitch yelled.

"Yeah, sure!" Kevin answered.

Lewis got his window down just in time. Kevin and Mitch both laughed hysterically as Lewis got his head and shoulders outside the window and started throwing up. The car continued to go around and around.

"Oh Crap!" Kevin exclaimed. "I hope none of that freezes onto the side of the car!"

Lewis was still throwing up, choking and gagging with his head and shoulders out the window, as the car made its final spin and slowly came to a stop.

"Are you okay?" Kevin asked as he turned on the dome light. Lewis was looking pale.

"Screw you." Lewis gasped. He wiped his mouth with his coat sleeve. "Do I look like I'm okay?"

Mitch and Kevin continued drinking and laughing as they finished the drive to where Mitch's truck sat abandoned on the far side of the lake.

"You guys really walked all the way back to camp from here?" Kevin asked in disbelief. "Hell, it's got to be at least a couple of miles."

Lewis was nearly over his bout with his upset stomach as he added. "I told you. This prick is the cheapest of cheap when it comes to being a prick!"

"We'll just see about that!" Mitch exclaimed. Lewis got out and held the door for Mitch.

"Just watch this!" Mitch opened the door of his truck. He smiled as it started right up. "Guess you're right!" He exclaimed over the sounds of the engine. "I am a prick! I even talked those dumb sons a bitches into cutting the first hole in the ice!"

Lewis rode with his head back and his eyes closed on the drive back to camp. When they got there, he hurried inside and went right to bed.

Each night the sounds of loud rock and roll music and gunshots could be heard clear across the lake. They mostly had the lake to themselves and no one ever said anything about it.

The stop sign at the end of the camp road was getting more ventilated each day. It was usually around one or two in the morning when they performed their final nighttime ritual of blasting the hell out of it.

They blazed away with a twenty-two rifle and a twenty-gauge shotgun. They generally used up a couple dozens rounds of ammo each, before staggering back inside and going to bed.

By the end of the third day, the old galvanized washtub on the camp's porch was nearly full of white perch, bass, and pickerel. Lenny stopped by just after dark with his boys to say goodbye. Mitch proudly filled a paper sack with fish for them to take home.

Clarence and Gary showed up at about the same time.

"I've never seen better luck!" Clarence exclaimed. "What are you using for bait?"

"Live bait." Kevin answered. He brought in a bucket of live minnows from the porch to show everyone.

"That's what we always use too." Clarence said, "But we've never caught this many fish."

"We're just naturally lucky." Kevin said. "Plus there are three of us."

"Where are you fishing at?" Lenny asked.

"Over by the outlet."

"Be careful over there." Clarence cautioned. "Anytime there's running water, there's bound to be thin ice."

He didn't notice that both Mitch and Lewis had to leave the room to hide their laughter.

Clarence and Gary stayed for supper. They had brought more groceries with them and it was a good visit.

They nearly panicked when Gary mentioned that he might stay overnight and go fishing with them tomorrow.

"That's great!" Mitch exclaimed. "We are tired of cutting the holes in the ice. It'll be your turn!"

"Yeah." Lewis cut in. "That ice chisel gets harder and harder to use. It would be great if you would come along."

"We generally get on the ice about daybreak." Kevin chimed. "Don't worry, we'll get you up."

"The ice is only a foot or two thick." Mitch added. "Don't you pussy out on us!"

The idea of having to do the work didn't appeal to Gary. He decided to go home after all. He helped his dad load the rest of the fish on the truck to take back and put in the freezer. Once again the three partners in crime waited outside, watching the taillights of the pickup as it stopped at the end of the camp road.

"I've got a name for this." Kevin said.

"What?"

"Well. We did work together to get rid of that pussy. I guess we'll have to call it 'team de pussification.'"

They were laughing uproariously as Lewis said, "Here, here. Let's get back inside and drink to that."

It was sometime around noontime the next day when they finally got up.

"I can't believe that pussy thought we would be up before sunrise." Kevin said.

"What?" Lewis said. "Who?"

"Gary."

"Yeah. Hell, what time is it?"

"Think we can limit out again today?" Mitch asked. "Come on you pricks. It's almost daylight."

"Let's get something to eat first." Kevin said.

Lewis looked at his watch. It was almost twelve thirty. The sun was blinding as it reflected off the thin layer of fresh snow outside. "Yeah." He agreed as he squinted his eyes. "It'll be daylight soon. We need to get going."

Kevin cooked up a quick breakfast of bacon and eggs. They laughed and joked over how easy it had been to get rid of Gary. They finished off a pot of coffee.

"It's going to be cold out there today." Mitch said. "Better make up two thermos's."

"We're going to have to make another whiskey run after today." Kevin said. He slowly poured the last of the booze in with the coffee in the two thermos bottles.

"How's our beer holding out?" Mitch asked.

"Plenty for me." Lewis answered, "But you and Kevin are going to be up crap creek after tonight!"

Mitch went outside to start the truck. They drank their first beer of the day while it was warming up. Around two in the afternoon they were ready to go fishing.

Mitch was driving. As always, he tried to outdo himself in counting how many cookies he could spin across the expanse of ice at sixty miles an hour.

Somehow they got safely to their favorite fishing spot. It took only a few minutes to break through the thin layer of ice that had frozen over the hole during the night. The hole had been cut about thirty or forty feet from the open water of the lakes outlet.

Kevin got the long handled net out of the truck bed. He walked about a hundred yards away to take up his position. He stood ready on the shore next to the open water a few yards down stream. The gentle currents of the flowing water would do most of the work. He shouted to Mitch.

"Hey! Let's remember to gut these sons a bitches before they freeze today. Did you bring the knife?"

"Got it right here!" Mitch yelled back.

Lewis had the extension cord ready. Mitch hooked the wires of the electric fence charger to the positive and negative post connections on the trucks battery.

"Let the electrocution begin!" He exclaimed.

"What are we waiting for?" Lewis asked.

"Fishermen! Prepare to bait your hooks!" Mitch shouted.

"Hook baited, Sir!" Lewis exclaimed as he lowered the other end of the extension cord into the water.

Mitch was grinning from ear to ear as he started the truck. "Live bait! Coming up!" He shouted.

"Zap it!" Kevin yelled.

"It is zapped!" Lewis answered as he turned on the powerful charger.

It took a couple minutes before the first stunned fish floated out from under the ice. It wriggled slightly as it drifted downstream in the open current of the lakes outlet.

"Fish ahoy!" Kevin shouted. He easily dipped it out of the water. It was a really nice white perch. He carefully deposited it on the shore.

"Hey Mitch!" He shouted.

"Yeah!"

"This is one stunning experience."

"Damn straight!" Lewis said. He looked at Mitch. "I told you. Kevin really knows how to fish!"

They only fished for about an hour. Lewis was taking a turn at netting when it became obvious to them that he had reached his limit.

"How much coffee has he had?" Kevin asked.

"Hell, that light weight panty waist is going to get sick again!" Mitch exclaimed.

From the netting position down stream Lewis could hear them. He yelled, "Who are you calling a panty waist?"

"If I had a mirror I'd show you!" Mitch yelled back.

They had netted over a dozen fish when Lewis got his feet wet and decided to call it a day. He was looking pale as he staggered back to the truck.

While Kevin and Mitch were putting up the gear, Lewis sat on the tailgate of the truck. He was trying to put on a pair of dry socks when he started throwing up.

"That's disgusting, Lewis." Kevin said. "You've got to learn how to handle your liquor."

"Got a cigarette?" Lewis gasped.

"You sure you want one?" Mitch asked. "Man, I've got to tell you, you look like crap."

Kevin lit a cigarette and handed it to Lewis. "Here's a smoke." Lewis was momentarily too busy to take it.

"I feel like crap!" Lewis chokingly exclaimed. He heaved again. He took the cigarette from Kevin and took a drag. "Too bad." He heaved again. "That was a good breakfast."

"Damn." Kevin said. "This is making me sick."

"Are you guys ready for a beer?" Mitch asked.

"I'll wait." Kevin answered.

"Screw you!" Lewis gasped.

They had a good laugh over it and agreed that when the ice melted come spring, the fish were bound to enjoy all that second hand bacon and eggs.

When it was decided that vacation was over, Kevin released the live minnows into the lake.

Chapter Twenty-Seven

Good Times

Summer 1967

Nadine Miller was basking in the early morning sun on the sandy beach in front of their summer camp. They owned a nice cabin on the east shore of Sebago Lake, about a half-mile from the general store in Raymond.

Brett had taken his namesake with him to the store to pick up a few things for this afternoon's barbeque. They were expecting a full house, and she enjoyed this short break.

She had told him, "Don't you be spoiling that boy anymore than he already is. Grandpa will be here soon, and that's supposed to be his job."

"Don't worry." Brett replied, "We're only going to pick up a few essentials."

"Just be sure that essentials don't include too much candy!" It was hard to sound scolding to either of them as Brett stood with their son astride his shoulders.

Raising their three-year-old son was her life. She thought she might be pregnant again, but hadn't told Brett. She was waiting until she was sure.

Brett was an excellent husband and father. She never told him, but she had known that he was the man for her that first day they met formerly in his office. It was his easy smile and no nonsense approach to life that she liked the most. Although she was constantly accusing him of spoiling little Brett, it was something that drew them ever closer.

Ruth and Roy were due to arrive around noontime with their two children. She could hardly wait. Marilyn was a very well behaved teenager and they had a lot of fun together. They were all proud of her many awards for sports at her high school.

Nadine laughed as she thought of what a contrast Marilyn was to her six-year-old brother. Even if he was her only nephew, she knew that he would always be her favorite.

She smiled and thought, 'What a little hellion.' That boy was a never-ending source of energy, and mischief. He was always into something. It was the cute way he always grinned and stuck out his lower lip that kept him out of trouble. She laughed aloud thinking that her little Brett was following in his cousin's footsteps.

The last time they had visited, he had accidentally put her cat to bed in their mailbox. He had been playing house with poor Taffy and she had somehow come up missing.

Brett had assured her not to worry, Taffy would return like she always did. It had been three in the morning when she awoke to Taffy's pitiful yowling coming from outside.

She had searched everywhere. Finally, dressed in her robe and slippers, she had stood by the mailbox calling for her. When Taffy yowled right next to her from inside that mailbox, she had nearly jumped out of her skin.

She anxiously looked over the tops of her sunglasses and picked up her wristwatch from the towel beside her to check the time. As soon as Brett and his shadow got back, she would get up and start making preparations.

"Hey gorgeous, you're going to turn into a lobster if you don't get out of the sun!" Brett said. "We're back." Then he added, "Here he comes!"

Nadine smiled and rolled over in time to catch little Brett as he tried to run past her to the water.

"Hey little guy!" She blew a raspberry on his tummy. "You don't go anywhere without a kiss!"

Her parents showed up a few minutes later. They fussed over little Brett and asked him if he had missed them.

"I missed you this much Grandpa!" Little Brett couldn't contain his excitement as he spread his arms wide apart.

"As soon as your cousin gets here, us men are all going for a boat ride!" Grandpa exclaimed. "Me, and your dad, and Uncle Roy, are going to teach you guys how to fish! What do you think about that?"

Little Brett thought that to be a terrific idea. For the next few minutes he enjoyed being the center of attention. It wasn't long before the others arrived.

"I hope you're ready for your wild one Grandpa!" Nadine said. "Here he comes."

"Quick!" Grandma exclaimed, "Someone hide the cat!"

They laughed and gathered around the car to welcome Roy, Ruth, Marylyn, and little Kevin Green.

****

At another lake, four teenage boys were also having a great day. They were spending the weekend at a camp that Clarence Nelson owned. It was on the rocky shore of a small and nearly unknown, mostly deserted lake. They decided that it was time to go fishing.

Clarence had already been by to check up on them. Now that they didn't have to worry about him, it was time to fish. Mitch and Kevin had just made a beer run and the rest of the day was theirs to while away as they saw fit.

Lewis was with them as was Mitch's older brother, Gary. They borrowed a boat from the camp next door and started loading it with their gear.

"Checklist!" Kevin said. "Who brought what?" He asked each of them the same question.

"Mitch?"

"Beer!"

"Check. Lewis?"

"Beer!"

"Check. Gary?" Gary was the oldest and by far the one with the most common sense.

"Food! Potato chips, two loaves of bread, mustard, lunch meat. Beer!"

"It's a good thing you pricks have me around to remember the important things!" Kevin said.

He passed more items to those already in the boat. "Here are the fishing poles." He passed the poles to Lewis. "Here's the bait." He handed over a can of worms and added, "Can't forget this." Kevin carefully handed them another sack. "Beer."

"What to hell are we waiting for?" Mitch was laughing as he shouted. "Shove this boat off and jump in. Them fish are thirsty!"

"Wait! Wait!" Lewis exclaimed, "We forgot the damn shotgun!"

"Like hell we did, Pilgrim." Mitch said in his best John Wayne voice. "It's under the seat, along with plenty of shells."

"What to hell do you guys need a shotgun for to go fishing?" Gary asked. This was the first time he had been along and he was yet to be enlightened as to the rules.

"You'll see!" Kevin exclaimed as he pushed the boat off and jumped in the bow.

To them it was another typical afternoon. Gary started the ten horse outboard and guided them across the lake to fish off the point at Black Island.

They had their usual bet going as to who would get sick first. Generally it was Lewis. After about his fourth beer, he usually had to throw up and lie down for a while.

Gary had graduated high school the year before. He had received his draft notice about a month ago. He wanted to spend a little time with Mitch before going off to Navy boot camp. They were discussing his choice of service.

"What a pussy!" Kevin said. "There's a real damn war going on, and you join the Navy?"

"I'd rather be a live pussy than a dead hero!" Gary retorted, "Besides, the girls really go for those sailor uniforms!"

"A real pussy in search of real pussy!" Lewis cut in. "I'll drink to that!"

"Seriously, Gary," Kevin said, "I'm proud as hell of you! I hear that those Navy boys develop immunity to penicillin. You know, catching the clap as often as they do!"

"Yee ha!" Mitch cut in. "Speaking of dead soldiers, toss me another beer!" He pitched his empty bottle overboard.

"Wait Mitch!" Lewis shouted. "You know the rules. You've got to bury that one first!"

Mitch picked up the shotgun, a single barrel twenty gauge and chambered a round.

He used his John Wayne voice to explain the rules to Gary. "Sailor. You know how pissed Dad always gets when he sees a can or bottle floating in the lake."

Gary was nearly beside himself with laughter as Mitch continued. "Well, Sailor, here's how we bury them." He raised the shotgun and blasted the floating bottle. Then he remained standing with his hand over his heart as he added, "Rest in peace."

"You guys are some crazy sons of bitches!" Gary laughed.

"When we're too drunk to sink em, it's time to quit fishing." Lewis said as he pitched his first empty.

They talked about the war and some of their older friends they knew that had been killed in action. Mitch agreed with Gary's philosophy and decided that if he ever got a draft notice, his first choice would be to join the Navy or Coast Guard. Kevin and Lewis thought the Army or perhaps the Marines would be the proper way to go.

"How in hell are you going to get even with those slant eyed sons a bitches if you're out whoring in the Navy?" Lewis exclaimed, "Hell, I hear Earl joined the Marines. I'll bet he shoots a bunch of those yeller skinned bastards."

"Crap," Mitch said, "Earl is so full of it. You ever seen him shoot? He couldn't hit the broad side of a barn."

"They teach 'em that crap." Lewis said.

"Yeah." Kevin said. "Even those Navy pussys have to learn to shoot. Right Gary?"

Gary finished his first beer and allowed that Kevin was right. "Most basic training is the same." He said.

They laughed and had a great time. They were catching fish and burying the dead soldiers with the shotgun.

They talked about the war. Gary and Mitch mostly made light of it. Kevin and Lewis were taking the whole subject a lot more seriously.

"How'd that all start anyway?" Lewis asked.

"We're trying to stop the spread of communism." Gary answered. "That's what it's all about."

"Yeah, right!" Mitch exclaimed. "We all know that it's so those rich assholes can sell more helicopters."

They were all laughing and talking at once.

"You guys are so full of it." Kevin said.

"Oh yeah. Why?"

"I don't feel so good."

"Political sons a bitches."

"Why what?"

"Gimme another beer."

"It was all over a dollar bet."

"I don't feel so good."

"Wouldn't surprise me."

"Come on you prick. Why are we there?"

Kevin thought of just the right answer as a big fish got on his line. "So pricks like you can ask," he said as he stood up. "Quick! Someone get the net ready."

It was starting to get dark. They had eaten most of the food and drank nearly all the beer. They had caught nearly a dozen white perch. Lewis was looking pale as Kevin struggled to reel in.

He had a really nice pickerel on his line. It looked to be nearly two feet long and was putting up an awesome fight.

"Reel that son of a bitch!"

"Yee Haw!"

"Look, his poles bent double."

"I don't feel so good."

"Oh damn it!"

"Get the net ready!"

He would have landed it for sure if Mitch hadn't blasted 'the slant eyed son of a bitch' as it neared the boat.

It was a good thing they ran out of ammo before they ran out of beer. On the way back to the camp Lewis nearly tipped the boat over as he puked his guts out over the side.

****

Their days and nights of hell raising and adventure didn't slow down until well into their senior year of high school. It was nothing short of miraculous that they got away with some of the things they did.

They gave new meaning to the name 'Thunder Road' as they referred to the gravel road that led out to Sebec Lake. Mitch was an awesome driver and could make the run quicker than anyone. He was the prime suspect anytime the sheriff's office received a complaint about reckless driving on that stretch of road. Clarence was forever chewing him out because if it.

It was pitch dark. Mitch was driving about seventy miles an hour with his headlights on high beam. He had vowed to straighten out the curves on Thunder Road, and was in the process of doing it. They were in his dad's new Oldsmobile. It was a beautiful car with a powerful eight-cylinder engine and an automatic transmission.

"Come on you son of a bitch!" Kevin yelled. "Swerve over. I haven't missed yet."

Lewis was in the back seat, shouting encouragement. "Come on, you pricks!"

The curve sign was coming up fast. The bright yellow reflected in the headlights. Kevin had his head and shoulders out the window. He drew back and let the beer bottle fly.

"You did it!" Lewis shouted as the bottle struck the sign and smashed into a million pieces.

"You're damn right!" Kevin exclaimed. "Have I ever missed? Hey, Mitch! You race driver, want to be, son of a bitch! Have I ever missed?"

"Hell no!" Mitch said. "Have I ever missed a curve?"

Lewis yelled from the back seat and Kevin held on for dear life as the car screamed around the corner. The rear end fishtailed a little as Mitch floored it.

"Let's see how fast we can hit the stop sign!" Lewis exclaimed.

"Okay, you sorry sack of crap." Mitch said. "You watch the speedometer. I've got my hands full driving!"

Lewis passed Kevin his empty beer bottle as the car approached the stop sign. Mitch barreled through it with the engine floored.

Kevin pitched the bottle. Smash! "Another perfect hit!" He yelled. All four wheels left the pavement as the speeding car jumped over the intersection.

"Forty! No! Forty-two miles an hour! Not bad Mitch!"

They slowed down as they approached the camp. "Okay you guys. Don't forget your manners." Mitch cautioned them.

He pulled over long enough for them to chuck the remaining empties off into the ditch. "If Mom or Dad ever suspect, we'll never get to gas this thing up again."

"Here." Kevin said as he reached into his shirt pocket. "Better have some gum."

Kevin and Mitch had both sworn off grand theft auto and grand larceny. For the most part, it was a time of nearly harmless fun and adventure. For the most part.

There were those times when they nearly drove the local lawmen nuts. Kevin often commented about it, usually late at night when they staggered safely back to the refuge of one of Clarence's old camps. One of his favorite sayings was, "There will be gnashing of teeth and rendering of garments when those sorry sons of bitches find out about this!"

The winter of '66 and nearly all of '67 turned out to be some kind of record breaker for the local newspaper reports on vandalism and general hell raising. It seemed as though no rural mailbox in the county was safe after dark.

The sheriff had stopped counting the complaints. These innocent metal boxes met their fate at the mercy of a heavy hammer and more often than not, a charge of buckshot from a twenty-gauge shotgun.

Mitch had taken to buying the newspaper every week. He always made Kevin cough up a quarter to buy this weeks issue. It became a short-lived tradition.

"Gimme a quarter! Come on you cheap prick. I want to see what we did last week!"

They were sitting in the back booth of the drug store sipping on milkshakes and going over the local news the first week in August, when two teenage girls walked in.

Mitch greeted them with his usual wolf whistle. The girls ignored him and sat in the booth furthest from them.

"The brunette, who is she?" Kevin asked.

"Hell, no sense telling you." Mitch said. "She's a Carter, and too damned good for the likes of you!" He grinned and whispered, "She wouldn't let you sniff where she last pissed!"

Kevin slugged him in the arm. "Pervert!"

"Hell, I'll just introduce you right now!"

As he started to get up, Kevin grabbed his sleeve and pulled him back into the booth.

"I just want to know who she is," he whispered, "I don't want her to throw rocks at me!"

"Chicken!" Mitch replied.

They continued going over the newspaper, talking and laughing quietly. Both thought it hilarious that chief Hollis had raised an awful stink in a letter to the editor several months ago.

He had admonished those 'individuals of low character' who had sadistically tied dead animals and a live chicken to the overheads on one of his police cars. That time it had been a road kill raccoon, and an illegally shot duck.

They had determined to find a way to outdo themselves, and in this weeks issue they had.

"Look here!" Kevin exclaimed. He read the title of a front-page article. "Police suspect juveniles in another elaborate prank." He laughed along with Mitch as he read the first line. "At least a half dozen cats and two dogs were freed from a police cruiser by a local locksmith."

They were cracking up trying to get through the entire article. The lady behind the counter kept looking over and smiling at their having such a good time.

"What do you mean a half dozen?" Mitch whispered, "I counted more than that!"

"No crap." Kevin whispered, "We got four from your place and at least three from Rory's mom. Boy was she upset when those cats came up missing!" They both laughed remembering the night they had pulled it off. "Lewis donated two of his barn cats plus there was that one we found."

Mitch cracked up again as he asked, "Do you think that potato farmer will ever leave dogs on the back of his pickup again?"

The article went on to say that the door locks had been injected with some kind of glue and had to be replaced. The total damage to the police cruiser was estimated to be in excess of two hundred dollars.

Whoever wrote the article went on to state that the locksmith had thought the whole thing to be quite humorous. He eventually had to smash out a wing window to reach inside for the door handle. They quoted him as saying that 'Those animals were real anxious,' and that he stepped 'Way back' when he finally got a door open.

"Chief Hollis has gotta be crapping rocks!" Mitch said. "I wish we could have been there to see his face!"

Kevin was nearly in hysterics as he said. "Can you imagine all those cats and dogs trying to get out of that car at the same time?"

"The locksmith did say that he stepped way back!"

"Here, kitty, kitty." Kevin said with a laugh. "Freeze you pussy! You're under arrest."

"Woof, woof, here boy!" Mitch mimicked. "Come on, nice doggie, into the pussy wagon."

Kevin heard the two girls laughing as they got up to leave. He particularly liked the way the brunette looked in her short skirt. "I've gotta get her name." He said softly.

Mitch twisted around to look over his shoulder. "Her name is Sarah."

Kevin slugged him in the arm again. "Why couldn't you have just said that in the first place?"

"Cause I didn't want you to drop your straw just to get a look under her skirt."

They laughed again and finished their shakes.

As Kevin and Mitch went out the door, the lady behind the counter smiled and laughed quietly as she heard them saying, "Here kitty, kitty."

"Woof, woof."

Life in general took a more serious twist Kevin's senior year of high school. He was growing up, maturing at about the same rate as anyone else his age.

Before he turned eighteen, he had already attended the funerals of two students who had preceded him through high school. One he had known well.

Like so many others in his graduating class of '68, he thought the war in Vietnam to be a real disaster.

Those rampaging days and nights of midnight credit for gas and miscellaneous supplies were nearly over. Those endless incidents of hell raising, spinning wheels and fast driving were about to end.

It all came to an abrupt halt when Kevin met Sarah.

Chapter Twenty-Eight

Countdown

May 4th, 1970

Joan was relaxing on the front porch, waiting for Adam and Henry to get back from town. It was a warm day and she was enjoying a cup of tea and taking in the sights and sounds of spring.

Shep was lying blissfully at her feet with his head resting on his crossed paws. Occasionally he would stir as he too enjoyed a lazy afternoon.

The winter snows had melted and the April showers had brought about the change she had been waiting for. Springtime was her favorite time of year. The creek was flowing at full capacity and she knew that soon Henry and Adam would once again get the fishing fever.

The cherry blossoms were nearly gone from the trees and now it was time for the apple trees to come into full bloom. The pink petals from the apple tree in the front yard were collecting on the ground as a gentle breeze swirled around them.

Their farm hadn't changed much over the years. Henry and Adam were constantly working on some remodeling project or other. Last year they had repainted the outside and put new shingles on the roof. They had done a lot of work on the old barn to keep it in good condition. They still had several Holsteins. Adam was active in the local 4-H club and had won several ribbons with his projects.

The old chicken coop still looked the same. They had stopped raising poultry several years ago, and now it served as a small storage shed. They had talked for a while about tearing it down, but decided to keep it as it was.

They had a couple new neighbors across the road. One had moved a really nice mobile home in on a five-acre tract just down the hill from them. The lot directly across now had a new house with an attached garage. Both neighbors were folks that they had known for years, and both families had several children.

The county planned on paving the road soon. The area was growing, changing rapidly as jobs were created in the nearby towns. Work had been completed on the new high school just last year, and Adam's class would be the first to graduate from it.

She smiled as she noticed one of the barn cats crouched low under a shrub by the walk leading up to the porch. His tail was twitching as he fixed his gaze on the birds that were perched on the lowest limb of a small maple tree.

Shep sat quietly at her side, staring at the cat. He had learned years ago that he couldn't catch the cat, but still he was awaiting an opportunity to chase after it.

The cat began slowly stalking towards the birds, several of which were on the lawn. Shep growled and leaped off the porch after him. The cat took off like greased lightning in the direction of the barn.

Joan was laughing at the familiar scene. She called, "Shep! You leave that poor cat alone."

Shep returned and once again took his station at her side. His ears perked up as he heard the sounds of a car. He raced to the end of the driveway and sat waiting. A moment later, a car appeared. It was Henry and Adam.

She noticed that Adam was driving in more of a rush than usual. Her eyes went wide in surprise as he slewed around the corner and sped down the drive. The car skidded to a stop. Henry and Adam both got out in a hurry.

"Mom!" Adam called, "Quick, we need to turn the TV on!" As they rushed past her and into the living room, Henry said, "You won't believe what just happened."

Adam had the TV turned on and the channel set for the news just as the news report came on.

"What's so important?" She asked.

A moment later, she sat in amazement as the report of the shootings at Kent State University aired. Several students had been shot to death and nearly a dozen had been wounded.

Her voice was strained as she said, "My God. What on earth have they done?"

Henry placed a hand on her shoulder and said, "This is bizarre. It started out as just another protest until something went wrong." She could sense the anger in his voice as he added. "It's all because of that damn war. That cursed damn war."

"Will it ever end?" Joan said softly.

Adam turned to them. He had tears in his eyes as he said, "How could this happen?"

Henry shook his head. "I don't know Son."

Adam said, "That's our National Guard that did the shooting." His tone was one of disbelief.

They tuned in again, to the eleven o'clock edition of the news, as the report was updated. It was a somber time for them. Henry and Joan had openly supported the war effort for years. This changed everything.

It was that day that Henry and Joan both came to the realization that we were involved in a war that could not be won. Without public support, there was no hope of victory.

For the next few nights, the incident at Kent State dominated the news. Just about everyone they talked to agreed that there was no need of it happening. Those were our kids who had died. Americans.

The horrors of war had come home to roost.

The high school band presented its final concert of the year a few days after the news story first broke. Adam was first chair with his trumpet, and played 'taps' in memory of the four students who had been gunned down.

A few weeks later it was time for Adam's graduation. Adam's two aunts, Beth and Jan and Jan's husband, Uncle Tommy, came to cheer for their favorite nephew.

Joan had tears in her eyes as the seniors slowly walked down the center of the gymnasium. Henry stood watching solemnly as they slowly took their seats.

His look to Joan confirmed that he too was remembering those long ago graduation ceremonies. Those times when they had watched their first two sons doing the same.

Adam's girlfriend, Joyce Barker, and her mom and dad were sitting in the row of seats in front of them. Joan had given her camera to Joyce to take pictures for them. She turned around after each flash of the camera and smiled at Joan.

Henry's older sister, Beth, was seated between them. She was nearly eighty years old and was enjoying the event. She commented when they were introduced that she loved Joyce's shoulder length blonde hair.

The first time Joyce turned to smile at them, Beth said to Joan, "She sure is a pretty girl. Smart too. Remind me to tell Adam to hang onto that one!"

Joan smiled and nodded agreement. She whispered back, "We've already told him that. Dozens of times."

Joyce had overheard them. It was easy to tell that she was blushing. She had fair skin and natural blonde hair.

"No need to blush dear." Beth said. "It's true."

"Thank you." She whispered to Beth.

Henry smiled when Beth said, "You and Joan have certainly done a great job raising that boy. He even looks just like you, Henry. Doesn't he Joan?"

"Shhh. It's starting."

The guest speaker gave a touching speech. He spoke about the bright future in store for this first class to graduate from the new high school.

As soon as the graduation exercises were over, it was time for pictures. They used up nearly two rolls of film taking pictures of Adam and his friends. Beth laughed as she insisted that they take several snapshots of Adam and Joyce kissing.

Adam was a handsome boy with dark hair. Joyce was a couple inches shorter. She had a bright smile and everyone agreed that they made a cute couple.

The war effort now was in its dying stages. Everyone was fed up. Each night the news reported how many American soldiers had been killed. Each night the nation watched as one, wondering when it was ever going to end.

As the days and weeks wore on, Joan came to the realization that Adam was now eligible for the draft. She was determined to find a way to keep him out of the mix. They had already lost two sons in a faraway war.

Joan knew that she could never stand that kind of heartbreak again. She had two American flags folded into triangles to remind her.

It seemed like only yesterday.

August 1970

Joan and Henry Silva were very proud of Adam. He was an excellent musician and had won several scholarships to the

University of Maine.

He was already enrolled at the main campus in Orono for the fall semester. He wasn't certain what his major would be, and had signed up to take general college courses his first year.

Sending him off to college was an exciting time for Henry and Joan. They knew they were going to miss him at home, but this was a dream come true for them.

They would have plenty of time and chances to drive to Orono and visit with him. Henry had retired nearly four years ago. They had sold their business, and were enjoying a comfortable retirement.

On his eighteenth birthday, they surprised him with a nice car. Adam had been saving for one, but they insisted that he keep his money in the bank to help with his college expenses. They knew that eventually he and Joyce would be getting married, and encouraged him to save for that.

Adam had received his draft notice within a month of his birthday. Henry and Joan breathed a sigh of relief when he was awarded a college deferment.

It was in mid August when Adam came down with the mumps. It was unusual for someone his age to catch such an illness, and he was sick for nearly a month. They really had no choice but to delay his going to college until the following year.

The draft board didn't agree at all.

There was nothing they could do about the draft notice. Henry did what he could to try to get Adam another college deferment. When it looked like that wasn't going to work, he and Adam went together to meet with the Army recruiters.

They were advised that if Adam would enlist for four years and be inducted as regular army, his chances of choosing his occupation and duty station would be greatly enhanced.

Adam decided to quit fighting it. He was determined to serve his country with pride. He wanted to do as Henry and his sons had, all those years ago.

They had discussed all of the options. They talked about him joining another branch of the service and even taking an extended trip to Canada. He decided that the quickest way to get it over was to serve out the two-year active duty draft notice.

Henry and Joan had no idea that Adam had chosen to sign up for airborne training and the infantry.

They had a going away dinner for Adam the last week in September. Aunt Beth's health had failed and now she was in a nursing home. Although she couldn't come, she wrote Adam a nice letter saying that her prayers would be with him. Joan's brother Tom, and his wife Jan were there. Over the years, Uncle Tommy and Jan had become a very important part of his life.

It was just the two of them, sitting on an old bench by the stream at the lower end of the property. Adam enjoyed these few times when he and his uncle Tommy could talk undisturbed.

"This old bench is holding together pretty good after all these years." Tom said.

"Remember when Dad and Kevin and me built it?" Adam asked. "That was a long time ago."

"Yes." Tom replied.

"Remember that year? Everyone of us got a deer."

"What are the chances of you getting sent to Vietnam?" Uncle Tommy asked.

Adam knew this subject was bound to come up. He still wanted to talk about anything but that.

"Sometimes, Joyce and I come down here and just sit."

"It is a nice place to find peace and quiet. Well?"

"Pretty good."

"Can't you sign up for someplace else?"

"I've already put in for Germany." Adam said.

"What are the chances?" Uncle Tommy asked.

Adam grinned. "About the same as building a snowman right out in front of the house in July."

"You could always enlist for four years in the Navy."

"I just want to get it over with. Joyce and I have plans. Don't worry. If I get sent to Nam, I'll keep my head down."

"It's not always that simple."

"What was it like in Korea?"

"Not much different from where you're going. Colder."

"What's that mean?"

"I still think the Navy would be safer."

Adam's quiet answer surprised him. "Don't you remember, Uncle Tommy? Henry's first son was in the Navy."

"I remember. Young Henry was a chip off the old block. He looked just like his dad. You remind everyone of him."

"How about Andrew?" Adam asked. "Did you know him

well?"

"Yes. He was a hellion. Looked and acted just like his mother. Joan nearly died when the telegram came. He was the first you know. Young Henry died a week or so later."

"I wish I could have known them." Adam said.

"Your Aunt Jan and I were here when the military people drove in with that second telegram." Tom said. "We were all sitting on the porch. Joan was still crying over Andrew."

"Damn." Adam murmured.

"The look on her face when that car stopped." Tom choked as he recalled the moment. "I could hear her heart break."

"Damn."

"Loosing their two sons nearly killed your mom and dad." Tom said softly. "If they lose you, I'm afraid it will."

Tom couldn't help but shudder. He placed his hand on Adam's shoulder. "This won't be easy on your mom. You know that. Or your dad. Promise me you'll write to them often and that you will be extra careful."

"I promise."

From the back porch of the house, Henry called to them that company had arrived.

Joyce ran across the pasture to meet them on their way back to the house. Her parents were already inside. They could hear the loud voices and laughter. The Barkers and the Silvas had been friends for many years.

She greeted Adam with her usual kiss.

"Hi Uncle Tommy." She said. Her cheerful smile caused Tom to perk up. "What have you guys been up to?"

"Oh, just man talk." Tom leaned over to embrace her. "It's good to see you."

They waited for a minute before following Tom into the house. As the door closed behind him, Joyce asked.

"Has he been crying?"

Adam didn't answer as they walked arm and arm inside.

Adam and Joyce had been going steady since Joyce had started high school. They were inseparable. Anyone who knew them couldn't think of either without thinking of both. Joyce was a year behind him in school. They planned on going to the same college when he got back and talked often of marriage.

The going away party was a good time for everyone. Several couples from the church and several of Adam's friends came to say goodbye and show their support.

Joan prayed for Adam every night before she went to sleep and every morning when she awoke. She prayed that he wouldn't be serving in a combat role. She prayed every day for someone to watch over him.

She often sat in the over stuffed chair in the evenings and reminisced as she looked at their collection of photographs.

Adam's senior picture from high school and the one from his eighth grade graduation stood in golden frames on either side of her favorite one.

She smiled every time she looked at the picture of her, Henry, Adam, and Kevin. Sometimes she would sit quietly, hugging the picture close to her. She often cried quietly as she wished that Kevin were still there to take care of Adam.

Joan thought Adam was going to be a company clerk, or something that seemed relatively safe. She had been off balance since he received his draft notice. The weeks and months of worrying were starting to take its toll on her.

The time passed quickly. He was very good about writing to them and she looked forward to his letters. He was constantly reassuring her that he was going to be fine.

In less than five months, Adam was finished with his training. The first week in February he came home for a one-week leave prior to being shipped out.

Henry figured it out the minute he saw him. He was wearing silver wings and an infantry badge on his uniform.

He did a good job of hiding the truth from Joan. She didn't find out. Not until the military car pulled slowly into their driveway July 4th 1971.

END PART SEVEN
'Before Then'
'Throwaway Child' (Book Two) 'White Knights'

Epilogue

- One -

In mid June 1971, four American GI's were reported missing in action in the area a few kilometers north of the Pleiku airstrip. It had been a routine patrol in what was considered to be friendly territory. An American soldier died and a Lieutenant was left for dead at the ambush site.

The bodies of five Vietnamese soldiers, including an officer and one KC scout were also recovered from the scene. The four soldiers that survived the initial firefight were taken prisoner. Two of them were severely wounded.

It was a blunder that never should have happened. The dead Vietnamese were all allied soldiers from the South Vietnamese government. None of the captors spoke English and the American soldiers had no choice but to believe that they were captured by some real bad sons of bitches.

This was only one incident out of possibly hundreds that never got the press it deserved. Perhaps it was a political move on behalf of the military to keep it out of the headlines. Incidents like this were sure to undermine what little public support remained to continue with the war effort.

What makes this story different was one soldier who did everything by the book. His name was Stone. He was in the right.

He had an attitude.

<u>Kon Tum Province, Republic of South Vietnam, July 1971</u>

The first time I saw Kevin Stone, he was standing in front of a mirror that had been placed at the end of the short entrance to the military command bunker.

He had been escorted there by a couple of lifer pricks in MP uniforms. One kept a firm grip on his arm as they stood on either side of him. The Corporal was armed with a standard M-16 Rifle, the Lieutenant with a side arm. I could see them both in the mirror. They had faces that could have been cut from stone.

The mirror had been placed there for soldiers to be able to check their uniforms and make adjustments, if needed, prior to standing before the commanding officer. This is where his armed escort had paused, waiting to be admitted into the inner office.

Sunlight poured in through two small openings high in the sand bagged corridor that served as windows. Particles of dust, and smoke from the Corporal's cigarette, were swirling in the columns of bright light.

Stone was standing directly in the sun's rays. The way the light shone in, one would swear he was directly under a pair of spotlights. The two guards appeared to be in the shadows, like ominous figures outlined in blackness.

For the most part, the days and details of my tour in Vietnam run together in memory. There were few days that stand out as vivid as this one. This day in particular, is still as clear in my mind as if it were only last week or even yesterday.

At that time, I was right in the eye of a crap storm. I had no way of knowing just how well I was to get to know this man standing accused as the Colonel angrily put it, "Of every imaginable crime in the military code book, plus a page!"

Colonel Bowman was kind of a jerk anyway. It was predictable that Stone would be hung out to dry. Hell, those bastards needed a scapegoat. Someone had to be held accountable for the screw up.

There were no military lawyers, no press, nothing that would explain the presence of all the Field Grade Officers who had preceded them into the inner office. Whatever was going on was definitely hush hush, and intended to be kept quiet.

I stood watching him in the mirror. I decided first of all that he was one handsome son of a bitch. I must admit it was hard for me to be objective. He couldn't have been much over 20 or 21 years old. He had the posture of a proud man, a man much older than his years.

He stood with shoulders back, chin up, and had the air of someone important for reasons other than why we came to be here in chains.

What struck me as strange was his startled expression as we made eye contact. Every time I moved, he moved. It was as if the mimicking son of a bitch was looking out a window, or through a doorway. You would have thought that he was looking at someone else, rather than at his own reflection.

First, his gaze focused on the new uniform, clean and pressed. His name, Stone, appeared to be written backwards on the nametag. An expression of recognition of the name and uniform briefly showed in his eyes.

As though looking at a picture, he noted the Airborne Patch on one shoulder, the Army Emblem on the other, and his rank, Sergeant, on each collar.

It was as if he was trying to recognize someone whom he hadn't seen in a long time. Our face was bruised. We each had one eye swelled halfway shut and a large purple and blue swelling on opposite cheeks. He had tuned out all that was going on around him. His focus was on my reflection.

It was subtle at first, but waiting there with guards on either side of him, he suddenly did recognize me. I would have waved and said hello, but that would have been too obvious. This could be defined as the very moment that he became aware of the reality and seriousness of our situation.

The temperature in the room seemed to drop a few degrees. I shivered involuntarily as a wave of cold air swept over the entire scene causing chills to go up and down my spine.

In the suppressing heat and humidity of this land far from home, the wave of cold air was real. I could scarcely control the wave of nausea that came over me. It was quite confusing.

Oh crap!

Is that really you?

One of the guards spoke softly. It took sheer will power to look away. I gazed straight ahead. I knew he was doing the same.

What the hell is going on here?

- Two -

Lt. Jackson was used to a hot humid climate. He was from southern Mississippi. He had two years of college behind him when he decided to join the Army, and planned on finishing a four-year degree when he got out.

When he enlisted he had been assured of going to Officers Candidate School. If he made it through that, he was guaranteed to receive an officer's commission. He had made the grade, the Army kept its word, and he was now a First Lieutenant.

It wasn't that he was particularly gung ho, or overly patriotic. He was a good soldier and believed that he had done the right thing in enlisting. His father had served in the Army in Korea, and two of his Uncles had served in the Navy. He wanted to be the first from his family, and to the best of his knowledge, the first black man from his small hometown to serve as a commissioned officer.

Lt. Jackson was a big man, over six foot three and well conditioned. Even though he had a pleasant smile, he was all business and a man to respect.

Since being stationed in Vietnam, he had dealt with all types of problems. He thought that he had seen just about everything, until now.

At the military police academy, they had been trained and disciplined to enforce the law. Their mission was one of keeping law and order within the ranks. He enjoyed his work and had volunteered for duty in Vietnam. This was his first tour of duty, and he was considering one more. It certainly looked as if Captain bars were in store for him if he did.

He had escorted all sorts of low life types, deserters, thieves, rapists, cons and murderers to this same bunker. He had had almost no compassion for any of them.

Although there was the occasional time when a soldier may have done something while drunk, or under undue circumstance, as a rule he generally paid little attention to the circumstances surrounding his prisoners. His only concern was his duty to escort them to various military installations.

In his mind, this assignment was different; this was absolute fubar. This was one of the few times he felt as though he was doing his job reluctantly.

He knew little of what was going on, or what was going to happen with this prisoner, but was hoping that the rumors circulating were true. If not, he thought, it's time to go home after this tour and they could shove those Captain bars.

He knew that Sergeant Stone had no recognition of him, but their paths had crossed stateside during airborne training. He felt bad for this poor son of a bitch. If the Army decided to make him a scapegoat, he would more than likely face a firing squad.

He knew that whatever was about to happen in the inner office would determine Stones fate. As he stood silently beside him, waiting to be admitted in to see the Brass, he couldn't help but feel proud.

"Let's go Sarge," the Lieutenant said in a quiet voice. Stone slowly looked up at him as though it required extra energy to turn his focus away from the mirror. The Corporal, who had a firm grip on his arm, stomped out his cigarette and began escorting him into the inner office.

The small room was crowded. Colonel Bowman sat at a table that served as a desk. On his right was a Major from I Corps, on his left stood a Major from the South Vietnamese Army and an Aide. The Division Commander, General Brathem, and his Aide were sitting off to one side, and ended a quiet conversation as Stone was escorted in.

A Colonel from the MP's, and an Army Lt. Colonel from the JAG's Office in Saigon were also seated and waiting quietly. Behind them stood Stones commanding officer, Captain Curten, and two noncoms. The small room was packed and had an air of seriousness equal to that of a funeral parlor.

Behind them all, peeking out over the tops of the sand bag wall and looking nervously about, was a very curious cat. No one moved as the Sergeant stopped before the table, except the cat. His gaze was fixed as his tail twitched from side to side. It was as if he too was affected by the somber mood that cast a pall over the room. It seemed that he too was looking only at the Sergeant.

"Sgt. Stone." Colonel Bowman spoke in a loud voice that virtually shattered the silence. "It seems that even though you are back among us, you just can't seem to shake those damn chains."

Stone stood expressionless before him, almost as if he wasn't paying attention.

In a more subdued tone, the Colonel said, "I think we can remove the hand cuffs Lieutenant."

The Colonel glanced to his left at the South Vietnamese Major and then over his shoulder at General Brathem who gave him an affirmative nod. He then turned his attention back to the paper that the Lieutenant had handed him.

As Lt. Jackson removed the handcuffs and placed them in his pocket, the cat climbed down from his vantage point. He slowly made his way across the room and began rubbing himself against the leg of the table.

The Colonel signed a form that the Lieutenant had given him and passed it back, "You and the Corporal are dismissed."

"Thank you Sir." The Lieutenant, sounding relieved, saluted and did a quick about face. With the Corporal following close behind, they left the room.

Before the door could close behind them the cat darted out through the opening and scampered down the corridor. He didn't want to be in that room either.

Corporal Stilling and Lieutenant Jackson walked outside into the sunlight. They both had the appearance of hard-core professionals, and indeed they were.

Stilling also had a callused attitude towards the prisoners they were assigned to transport. They worked well together and had developed a strong friendship over these past few months. Although Stilling had to look up at Jackson, he was still a big man.

"What do you think is going to happen?" Corporal Stilling asked. "Think they'll let him go?"

Lieutenant Jackson held his reply until they were seated in their Jeep. "Could be we'll know real soon, how about if we wait right here for a while."

"Fine by me Sir." Corporal Stilling settled himself behind the wheel as he continued; "You said you remembered him from back in the world?"

"Yeah," Jackson answered. "I'm sure he doesn't remember me, but I saw him get the crap kicked out of him at jump school." He smiled as he recalled the scene. "Not that he actually got beat, but fact is, I sure thought he was. Never saw anyone get up and turn it around like that."

"What do you mean?"

Jackson grinned; he decided to tell the whole story. He

liked Corporal Stilling. They had been working escort duty for so long now; that unless they were in a situation where they had to act the roles expected of their rank, they were more like partners.

"Well, let's put it this way, he got knocked down twice, the second time we all thought it was over."

"Is that why you've been so nice to him since we picked him up from those gooks? You've been acting different since we first started guarding him at the hospital." Stilling had made a point; Jackson began.

"It was more or less a racial thing. It started with two black soldiers, a couple 'brothers.' They were giving some little white guy crap. None of Stones business, but for one reason or other, he decided to jump in." Jackson chuckled. "There were a bunch of us that saw it, in fact, I had to go before the top sergeant to explain why I hadn't broke it up."

"What do you mean, you had to go before an NCO?" Stilling asked, "Didn't you outrank him?"

"Sure, at that time I was a Second Lieutenant, fresh out of OCS. We had just finished jump school. Man, did these silver wings shine then!" He glanced down at the embroidered wings on his uniform. "The top sergeant was in charge, make no mistake about it. What got my dick in the pencil sharpener was for one, I was the only commissioned officer present, and two, they figured I should have broken up the first fight."

Stilling interrupted with, "Why didn't you?"

"Didn't have time. Those two jerks were giving crap like you wouldn't believe to that little white dude." He grinned again as he continued. "He was a cocky little bastard and wasn't about to take it from them. Both got after him at the same time, and all at once one of them had the little guy down flat on his back."

"He was sitting on the guy's chest, pinning his arms to the ground with his weight. It should have been over then, but this little white guy was a mouthy bastard, just didn't know when to shut up! He made some reference to this guys mother and Aunt Jemima." Jackson laughed again.

"Then, as he had the guy pinned down, the big son of a bitch started slapping his face from side to side like this." Jackson made a back and forth motion with his hand, "He was really knocking the piss out of this guy."

"That's when I stepped in. Someone recognized me as an officer and yelled 'Attention.' Before I could get more than four of five feet away, Stone flew into that guy, and man; I mean flew!" He made another motion with his hand, "Just like a damned OD green superman, right through the air. You should have seen him tackle that son of a bitch!"

"What did you do then?" Stilling asked.

"There wasn't much I could do. Everyone formed a circle and hell, I could barely see in, let alone be heard."

"So how'd they kick the crap out of him?" Stilling asked.

"Well, the first guy was out of it! I mean out of it. He was one comatose GI. They had to break out the smelling salts for him. It was the other one, that son of a bitch was bigger than I am, and I'm six three."

"He picked Stone up like a big rag doll and threw; I mean threw him to the ground. A couple of the others grabbed him and tried to pull him back. Before they could, he landed a kick to the stomach that knocked what wind Stone had left right out of him."

"No crap!" Stilling was amazed. "Usually those fights are broke up before they go that far. What happened next?"

"Well, Stone got up, real quick like, and lit into him! The others had let him go, so he could fight I guess, and wham! Before he knew it, he was knocked on his ass again!"

"This time, the others grabbed on him, so he couldn't get hurt any more, but I'll be damned if he didn't break loose."

"That big bastard was fuming, he charged at Stone and then I seen a move I've never seen before."

"Don't crap me sir! What happened?" Stilling exclaimed.

"The big guy charged him. Just as they were about to make contact, Stone dropped to the ground. He tripped over him and fell face down."

"It was all over in about two seconds. As he rolled over to get up, Stone jumped and landed both feet in his sternum, right here," Jackson placed his fist on the Corporal's chest. "That dumb son of a bitch started puking all over himself."

"You can bet your ass that fight was over!" He laughed again, "Poor Stone was about done in. I finally did get to step in and raise some hell. Got everyone to attention, and Stone, well he walked right by me and left the area."

"You should have seen his face. Hell, he didn't see me; he didn't see anyone. I doubt he'd ever recognize me from that day. Maybe I'll bring up the subject to him if I get a chance."

"How'd the top sergeant find out he was involved if he left

the area? Stilling asked, "And how'd you get in trouble?"

"No real trouble. The top sergeant appreciated a good fight. I think he was just acting that way. Mostly he didn't want word to get up to Battalion."

"He came down hard on those two brothers once he got the full story, but it was them two that turned Stone in. They thought they could get him in trouble, but no one got in any real trouble over it."

Stilling changed the subject. "Do you think he did it Sir?"

"Depends on what you mean by 'it.'"

"Did he really do all that killing?"

"No way to know."

"If he did, holy crap, they gotta do something!" Stilling was talking almost as if to himself. "No one could have done that crap, not like they say."

"He did get all his men out." Jackson said.

Stilling sounded frustrated as he asked, "What is it they call it when civilians get in the way like that?"

"Collateral damage." Jackson said softly. "It's called collateral damage."

"No crap Sir."

"Well, it's certain, there's enough brass in there to decide one way or the other. At least they let me take the cuffs off him."

Stilling still sounded disgusted. "Remember when we escorted him to HQ at camp Red Bluff? He could barely walk; remember?"

Jackson nodded in agreement. "It did seem strange to take one man by chopper all that way to a damn fire base. What do you suppose General Brathem was doing there? It's not like him to be that close to the action."

"I did try to find out more from Stone at the stockade." Stilling said. "He wouldn't say much about it; kept asking me about his men."

Lieutenant Jackson looked skyward as if in search of an answer as Stilling added, "Did you know he hasn't seen or heard from any of them since the gooks busted 'em? I told him they were all okay, and he liked hearing that."

"Here comes the General's driver." Jackson nodded his head in the direction of a jeep that was pulling over across the compound from the command bunker. "It won't be long now."

Several more military vehicles entered the compound.

"Looks like a damned convoy." Stilling murmured. He looked at the Lieutenant. "Should we move?"

"Hell, Corporal," Jackson said. "We're military police. We'll wait right here."

Now it was Jackson's turn to sound frustrated. "His commanding officer is in there, maybe he'll help."

"Sir, what if they turn him back over to the gooks?"

"Let's try not to think about it."

"Crap," Stilling said, "I hope them rumors we heard this morning are true."

"Yeah," Jackson replied, "Me too."

General Brathem and his aide were the first to leave the command bunker. The jeep made a u turn from across the compound and stopped to pick them up.

Several soldiers were passing by. The General returned their salutes and got in the back seat. The jeep drove out of sight in the direction of the airstrip.

Jackson looked at his watch. It had been no more than fifteen minutes.

- Three -

Adam had surprised Joyce with a diamond engagement ring the same day he arrived home. He only had a week until he shipped out to Vietnam, and he wanted to make the most of it.

Henry and Joan were pleased. Joyce had become a part of the family over these past few years. It was an announcement that they had been expecting.

Her family threw an engagement party Adam's last night home. They lived in a large two-story house in town. The wrap around deck was crowded all afternoon until late in the evening. It was another real nice time for everyone.

No one had much to say on the drive to the Bangor airport. Joyce sat close to Adam in the back seat. His plane took off around eight in the morning. They stood arm and arm as they watched it disappear from sight.

Henry and Joan were in no hurry to get home. Neither was looking forward to returning to an empty house.

Joyce agreed with Joan that they should do some shopping. There were several new shopping centers, and Henry said that he would like to check them out as well.

Joyce had a bubbly personality, and soon they were enjoying a good day. Joyce was trying to talk Joan into buying a new dress and matching pair of shoes.

"You never buy anything for yourself." Joyce said. "Isn't that right Henry?"

"That's true." Henry said.

"See, anytime a husband approves, I say go for it!" Joyce's cheerfulness was starting to rub off onto Joan. Soon she was smiling and having a good time as Joyce helped her try on more dresses and matching outfits.

Henry tagged along and was a good sport over the whole shopping thing. He was smiling and joking with Joyce as she insisted that he try on the most ugly green plaid sport coat he had ever seen.

They enjoyed a quiet lunch at a new fast food restaurant and decided to take in a matinee at one of the down town movie places. The movie theater could just as well have shown a blank screen. They each sat there with their thoughts on anything but what was playing.

On the drive home, Henry tried to shake his blue mood. He had a foreboding feeling. One look at Joan and he knew that she was experiencing the same thing.

Joyce did her best to comfort Joan and tried to convince her that Adam was going to be all right. Despite her best efforts, by the time they dropped Joyce off at her house and said their goodbyes, Henry was in tears too.

They got their first letter from Adam two weeks after he arrived in Saigon. He wrote that he was being assigned to an airborne unit located somewhere in the central highlands. He promised that he would try to write at least once a week.

The Guardians.

They were watching Joan from their place of solitude as she cried softly. She was sitting in her favorite chair clutching a picture to her chest.

Angels voice was soft as she said, "Now can you see? There are more reasons than we can ever know."

Marla felt sad watching Joan. She was wishing she could physically embrace and comfort her.

It wasn't that long ago that they had watched another scene. Another young soldier. This one was saying goodbye to his family at an airport.

Angel smiled sadly as she watched him kiss his baby and give his wife a final embrace. Her smile faded as she watched him turn and walk away.

He didn't look back.

July 4 1971

Joan was sitting on the front porch, enjoying a nice summer day. She was writing another letter to Adam. She had just written about the severe thunderstorm that had blown through two days before, and that the power had just come back on.

She was looking forward to a good day. Joyce and her parents were going to be stopping by later in the afternoon. They planned on having a barbeque and then they were all going to the fireworks together.

They hadn't heard from Adam in nearly a month. Everyday she walked expectantly to the mailbox, hoping to get another letter.

The leaves were rustling in the gentle summer breeze. Shep was sitting patiently beside her. His ears stood up as he sensed that a car was approaching. He stood on the edge of the porch, prancing excitedly in place, as a military car slowly turned into the driveway.

"Henry!" Joan's voice broke as the car came to a stop.

In her rush to stand up, she bumped against the table. The glass of iced tea on the small table tipped over. For a moment it seemed as if time had slowed. The glass took a long time to land on the floor of the porch. There was no sound as it slowly tipped over, spilling the contents.

"Henry!"

Henry quickly walked outside. He stood quietly with his arm around her shoulders. His face was ashen as his eyes took in the scene. The terror in her voice had spread to him. It was a scene that they had both been dreading.

"Henry!"

"I'm here."

She could feel that her knees were about to buckle. If not for Henry steadying her, she would have had to sit back down. Neither dared to breathe as the passengers' door opened.

They recognized the Army Chaplain who got out of the front seat. They had met him several times at the funeral services of young soldiers. The Chaplain smiled at them and turned to help someone get out of the back seat.

Joan stood with her hands clutched to her chest not daring to breathe.

Her heart leapt for joy as Adam slowly got out and leaned on the crutch that the Chaplain handed him. His smile was such that Henry and Joan remained frozen in place, not daring to believe what they were seeing. Shep sat silently beside them.

Neither dared to move as Adam slowly made his way to the porch. For the next few minutes there were only tears of joy as they embraced.

They were both hugging him and crying at the same time. Adam broke the silence as he tearfully whispered, "Mom, Dad, Kevin said to say hello."

Standing As One

Courageous deeds, sacrifice, lost and fallen men
Credit them, for they are one
Now, as they were then
As time goes by it cannot change
To them we owe it all
In memory we hold them close
Those who stood so tall

Wives and children left behind, grieving mothers cry
Yes they are one with those who fell
And always wonder why
An empty place at the table, a void that still remains
A smiling boy secure at home, and almost never sad
Bring back the memories of those who cried
He looks just like his dad

Make clear to those who did return, those torn and shattered men
Who stood as one and cheated death
How proud you are of them
Peace and calm seem near at hand, though the price was high
Undo the torment, the guilt and blame
Let them know they have respect
They have no cause for shame

They fought and died to keep this land, exactly as it was
As one this land must not forget
Their brave and noble cause
Throughout the land proudly show, the great red white and blue
Remember them with open hearts, and all will see your pride
Remember them, is all they ask
Of you, for whom they died

About the Author

Name: Frederick H. Savage
Date of birth: January 2nd, 1950
Place of birth: Millinocket, Maine
Military Service: US Army - Airborne Infantry
Rank: Sergeant: Served proudly in Vietnam

Fred Savage lives in central Wyoming with his wife and children. He is a small business owner and teaches part time at a community college.

e-mail - fredsavageauthor@hotmail.com

Footnote: The final book in this trilogy is entitled: 'Standing As One.' Release date to be determined.